Cheating and Lies

MARK BASFORD

CHAPTER 1

From his new office Marcus gazed out at the panoramic Peak District skyline. Seeing the millstone grit outcrop known as Carl Wark, he wondered what factors might have persuaded an Iron Age tribe to use it as a hill fort in preference to its higher neighbour, Higger Tor. With no water source close by he assumed it could only have served as a temporary stronghold. His strategic analysis was interrupted by the telephone indicating an internal call. To create the impression of being hard at work he answered it with a snappy, 'DCI Priestley.'

Superintendent Yelland responded, 'It's Richie. I've an interesting case for you: a woman in her seventies, found dead at home in suspicious circumstances. It's a Mrs Sylvia Batter. And no, she wasn't battered.'

'So how did she die?'

'We don't know yet, but something's not right.'

'Well, what makes it suspicious?'

'The playing card crammed into her mouth.'

'Which one was it?'

'Only you would ever ask a question like that. You'd better get over there and see for yourself.'

Priestley drove to the bungalow and parked behind a row of liveried vehicles. DS Neil "Witty" Whittington saw him arrive and brought two full sets of forensic clothing. They donned the white hooded scene suits, shoe covers and face masks. After a quick blow into each purple latex glove, they squeezed their fingers into the ends and overlapped their suits' elasticated cuffs.

As they signed in with the crime scene manager, he delivered his trademark gallows humour, ending with 'The dead body is in the living room.'

Priestley grimaced at the final pun before heading inside to examine the crime scene. Though focused on the task in hand, his observations were coloured by the CSM's plays on words. He observed how the corpulent corpus was slumped sideways in the red brocaded armchair by the gas fire, and the excess flesh around her neck had doubled and redoubled under downward pressure from her heavy head.

Examining the antimacassar closely, he thought the patch of pink powder was consistent with the victim having pressed her face against the cloth as though shying away from something.

Her green merino wool twin-set had eight buttons of a creamy hue that clashed with the white translucent pearls hanging loosely about her throat. Under the plain black skirt that reached below her knees were rumpled grey woollen stockings. On her feet were black patent leather shoes with a silver buckle. Spotting a pair of frayed carpet slippers discreetly positioned to the wall side of her chair, he guessed she had chosen not to wear them because she was expecting a visitor. Turning to Witty, he asked, 'Do you have the playing card?'

Witty fetched the clear-sided evidence bag and held it up for him to see through.

After peering for a moment at the Queen of Clubs, Priestley asked to see the other side. He gave a fleeting glance at the patterned red back with its white border, before stating confidently, 'Waddington's Number One Superior Quality Linen Finish.'

As Witty's face was largely hidden behind his mask,

he showed how impressed he was by striking a pose of wide-eyed wonder. 'I suppose you once made a study of playing cards, Holmes.'

Priestley enunciated, 'Do you mean you never read my monograph on the subject, Watson?' He accepted a rumble of appreciation before pointing to the open box of cards on a nearby table, off which he had just read the description. 'You'd better bag that up and have it checked for prints. It looks brand new, so it may have been bought especially for the occasion; we should try to find out where from. I'd guess it was opened here, judging by the sharp edges to the paper security seals.'

Witty took the box with its incomplete set of cards and carefully deposited it into a separate evidence bag.

Priestley, looking around the room in the hope of gaining some insight into the deceased's background, drew several inferences from four shiny silver-framed photographs. The deceased had married in her twenties. Her husband had at least reached sixty. A daughter, or perhaps a niece, had graduated from a university. Their son's wife had displayed her visibly Chinese origins by choosing to wear traditional red on her wedding day. Grandchildren were conspicuous by their absence.

The picture window provided an unobstructed view of the tree-lined street, except where the full-length net curtains had bunched vertically to obscure several strips of the scenery; their white nylon had developed a grey patina, indicating they had not been washed for months. A thick film of dust dulled the television top, and there were grimy edges to the six prints of English cathedrals arrayed horizontally on the wall opposite the fireplace. He inferred there would be no cleaner to interview.

Leaning up against the back of the sofa was a folded

square wooden table with an inlaid green baize top, a type he recognised as popular for playing card games.

In one corner of the room was a slim, clear-fronted chestnut display cabinet standing on ball-and-claw feet. Peering through the dusty glass, he found three equally-spaced shelves. A tarnished silver trophy sat in splendid isolation on the top sector. Six Lladró figurines huddled together directly below.

On the lowest level was assorted bric-à-brac that had been arranged into three sets. In the centre was a circular purple pincushion that swelled proud within a four-inch diameter mahogany base, pierced by a dozen two-inch arrows with gemstone finials. Three silver thimbles bearing similar bas-relief geometric patterns formed a tight equilateral triangle to its left. A Ronson art deco shagreen petrol lighter occupied the right side. Next to it was a silver-gilt cigarette case of an earlier vintage. Noticing some of the gold had rubbed away, he imagined decades of desperate owners scrabbling at it for their nicotine fix.

Confident that any self-respecting thief would steal such readily saleable pieces as the two smoking items, he assumed this was not a case of aggravated burglary that had escalated to murder. Considering the placing of the playing card in the victim's mouth, he concluded the motivation was almost certainly personal.

After scanning the floor, walls and ceiling, Priestley walked over to Witty. 'Once it's been dusted for prints, I'd like you to research that trophy. It shouldn't be too difficult; there are names engraved around the band at the base, and there's something on the front face about a bridge competition. Let me know what you find.'

Following a brief chat with various colleagues, he

headed back to the station.

The afternoon was almost over when Priestley heard Witty's familiar knock at his open door. 'Come on in, Neil. What do you have for me?'

'I phoned the bridge club. They told me Mrs Batter was a regular, and she got to keep that trophy when she won it for the third time, nearly twenty years ago. They bought a much nicer one to replace it, apparently.'

'Have you made a list of all the past winners?'

'Ask me that again in five minutes.'

'Is the club open now? We need to ask the members what they knew about her.'

'The afternoon session will have already finished. They reopen at seven, for play to start at seven thirty.'

'All right. So, what's your plan?'

'I'll go to the club for seven to find out as much as I can about the deceased and see if anyone can suggest a motive, before I hand over to DI Baker from Northern Command in the morning. You do know her reputation for being a right bitch, don't you? Are you sure *you* can't handle the investigation?'

'I'm really pulled out at the moment. The most I can do is take a supervisory rôle, unless I have a word with the Super; maybe he'll be willing to take back some of his workload he's so generously given to me!'

'Right. By the way, this may not matter, but I don't know the first thing about bridge.'

'Really? It's a good game; I used to play it a lot when I had the time. What card games do you know?'

'Pontoon, whist, rummy, beggar-my-neighbour.'

'Not poker?'

'The nearest I ever came was three-card brag.'

'You haven't mentioned playing *happy families*.

How's Lily doing? Remind me, when's the baby due?'

'We've another six months to go, yet. So, is bridge your favourite card game?'

Priestley smirked. 'No, it's strip poker.'

Witty grinned. 'I should have guessed.'

'In the army, me and the lads played poker whenever we had a spare five minutes, and I remember one time this really fit young woman asked to join in, so we told her it was *strip* poker. She said she'd be right back, and we all thought that's the last we'd see of her; but she proved us wrong, just a few minutes later. The only problem was, she'd put on so many rings and bangles, she hadn't removed a stitch before we had to pack in. It was so unfair; I hate that sort of cheating.'

Seeing Priestley trying his best to look disgruntled, Witty laughed good-humouredly. 'It serves you right, boss; strip poker is definitely sexist.'

Priestley grimaced. 'Well, it certainly isn't PC.'

'You'll have to watch what you say when Ms Baker comes over; she's severe with a capital S. We could do with a quick breakthrough so she can sod off back.'

Priestley frowned at him. 'Don't be unkind, Neil; it takes all sorts. But I'm thinking it might be best if *I* go to the bridge club this evening and see if I can join in; chatting to people over cards may be more effective than official questioning, and I might get a lucky break. You take the evening off and look after Lily.'

'Thank you, sir.'

As Witty was not in the habit of addressing him as "sir" when just the two of them were together, he took it as a sign of facetiousness. 'Now bugger off; I'm busy.' Witty grinned at him before leaving the office.

Priestley immediately telephoned DC Lin Plummer.

'It's me. Are you familiar with bridge, the card game?'

'I've played a bit, but not much.'

'I'll be going to the local club this evening for seven o'clock. Do you want to be my partner?'

'Sure! But I'll play bridge with you as well.'

He laughed. 'I'll pick you up at a quarter to seven.'

'Don't you want to come earlier?'

Her emphasis indicated she was inviting him over for sex, but he thought it would be impossible to be discreet at that time of day. It was a couple of years since she had seduced him, and now he had come to accept their relationship as a parallel life. He often wondered when she would lose interest in him, an older man, knowing he was happily married and would never leave his wife; but for now she seemed as determined as ever to maintain their affair. With a hint of regret, he responded, 'I can't. Just remind yourself of the rules.'

She recalled the first rule of their relationship, that they must always keep it hidden from Helen. 'I know, I know: it's too risky.'

'I was meaning the rules of bridge.'

'Oh, yes. I'll do a bit of research at home. Quarter to seven, then. You're sure?'

'I'm certain.'

He logged on to the computer, but struggled to focus on his work as he thought about his dangerous liaison. Rather than wasting time staring at the screen in the forlorn hope of inspiration, he tidied up his inbox and processed the simplest of his e-mails.

When he returned home he found Helen busy in the kitchen. 'Hello, love. I'm going out playing bridge this evening. I'll be setting off at half six.'

She stared at him. 'What's brought this on?'

'An old woman who played regularly at the bridge club has been murdered, so I'm going there to see what I can sniff out about her by chatting to other players.'

'Who's going to be your partner?'

He tried to sound nonchalant. 'Lin Plummer.'

She frowned severely. 'You're forever taking up that girl's evenings; you need to give her more time off, so she can have a social life and get herself a boyfriend.'

'But she's always first to volunteer for everything. Besides, she seems happy enough, living on her own.' He quickly steered the conversation back to bridge. 'Do you know if I've an old scorecard hanging around? I could do with reminding myself of all the conventions I used to use; I wouldn't want to look like a novice.'

'I binned them all, ages ago, like you asked me to when you stopped playing.'

'Well, I still have my books; I'll glance through them and it will all come flooding back... I hope.'

In one of them he found a used scorecard that had been left as a bookmark. After reminding himself of the once-familiar bids and conventions that were recorded on it, he slipped it into his jacket pocket and went in search of their children, eight-year-old Edwin and six-year-old Alice. They were playing ludo on the floor in Edwin's bedroom. When Alice moved her final counter for a narrow victory, he asked them, 'Would you like to play cards, now?'

Edwin responded, 'What game?'

Marcus thought for a moment. 'Knock-out whist?'

Alice jumped up. 'Yes, knock-out whist.'

They went to the kitchen and played at the table while Helen prepared food nearby.

Marcus was surprised to find they would all be

dining together, as the children normally ate first. Helen explained, 'If you're going out at half six, there isn't time to make the salmon soufflé. You do like spaghetti and meatballs, don't you?'

He expressed far more enthusiasm than he felt. 'Oh, yes, definitely. That will be great.' He turned to Alice. 'I know a song about spaghetti and meatballs; shall I teach it to you? Would you like that?'

She clapped her hands and laughed. 'Yes; sing it!'

He performed a parody of *On Top of Old Smoky*, initially cupping a hand to his ear in the style attributed to folksingers. When he added in some hand signals, he diligently avoided any vulgar variants or references to cigarettes. As he ended the first verse with the words '…when somebody sneezed,' he looked at Edwin as a cue for him to make a contribution.

Edwin delivered a powerful 'Aaaah-tchoo'.

Helen complained, 'That's enough of that; I don't want your snotties all over the place.'

Edwin responded gleefully, 'Ah! Naughty! You said "snotties"! Snotties, snotties, snotties!'

Marcus intervened. 'Yes, your mother was being polite, otherwise she'd have said "your slimy bogies"!'

Alice gasped in mock-shock before having a fit of the giggles.

When Helen was ready to dish out the food, Marcus tidied away the cards.

Edwin began experimenting with sucking up single strands of spaghetti.

Helen sighed, 'It's like feeding time at the zoo.'

Edwin inquired with overtly insincere innocence, 'Which animals eat spaghetti?'

CHAPTER 2

Approaching the entrance to the parking under Lin's block of flats, Marcus pointed and pressed the spare electronic zapper she had given him. The full height metal gates eased open quietly; he had recently oiled a screeching part to stop it announcing his visits to all and sundry. As usual he parked in her space, her own car being in a borrowed bay; the arrangement was to avoid his vehicle being reported for occupying someone else's reserved place, as that could prove embarrassing. He took the stairs rather than the lift, to minimise the likelihood of his meeting anyone.

Knowing he was almost invariably punctual, she had watched the road until she had spotted his Volvo. With precise timing she opened her door and looked down the corridor. He appeared at the top of the stairs. She silently acknowledged him before drawing back inside.

He entered her flat and closed the door behind him. To confirm the sole purpose of his visit, he asked, 'Have you been brushing up on your bridge? Are you all ready to knock 'em dead?'

Her big blue eyes stretched wide. 'I said I know how to play; I didn't say I'm any good at it.'

'I'm sure you're just being modest. We'll work out a system at the club; nothing too complicated.'

'Seriously, don't expect too much from me.'

'All right. Let's get off.' She grabbed her coat.

In the car, he speculated about the murder victim. 'It's interesting that the card in the woman's mouth was the Queen of Clubs. It may relate to her bridge playing, or perhaps some other card game; but there again, it might be symbolic of something else entirely. Was she in some sense a Queen of Clubs? Why choose clubs rather than diamonds, hearts or spades? It's the lowest suit for bidding, but a club has other meanings. She wasn't struck with a club. At her age she didn't look like a nightclub sort, but who knows what she was like when she was younger. We know she was a member of the bridge club, but there are lots of types of clubs she may have belonged to. She could have clubbed together with other people for a particular purpose. She could have been top dog, I mean top bitch, a queen of her set. I assume we'd have been told pretty sharpish if "she" was actually a "he", so I think we can discount that particular type of queen. What do you think, Lin?'

'I think you may be overthinking it. What if it was simply the first card that came to hand?'

'Hmm, there is that possibility. The Five of Spades would have been far less interesting. Do you think my way of speculating is just a load of nonsense?'

She put on a visibly false expression of confidence. 'No, sir; I believe everything that comes from your lips is a pearl of wisdom.'

Defensively, he replied, 'Thinking around a subject can sometimes lead to useful insights.' He laughed. 'But other times, it's just one blind alley after another.'

He parked in a cul-de-sac near to the club. The place was open, with no one checking for strangers. Hearing a hum of voices through a door to the left, he led the way into the bar. A middle-aged man in a bow tie was dispensing drinks. Marcus asked him, 'Is there someone we can see about playing this evening? We're new.'

Before the barman could answer, an old gentleman rose to his feet. 'I'm Graham Flint, the club chairman. Just follow me though to my office and I'll take down your details. You can play three times as guests before deciding if you wish to apply to become members.'

In the room with the door closed Priestley decided the man should be trusted with the true purpose of their visit. He showed him his warrant card. 'I'm Detective Chief Inspector Priestley, but do call me Marcus. And this is Detective Plummer; Lin, to her friends.'

Flint assessed him coolly. 'And you're here about the murder of Mrs Sylvia Batter. Correct?'

Priestley raised an eyebrow. 'Correct.'

Flint remained poker-faced. 'Don't look surprised; we bridge players are good at assessing probabilities. The likelihood of you being here for any other purpose seems comparatively low. So, what can I do for you?'

'First of all I'd like some background information on the deceased; and then I'd like for us to stay and play, if that's all right by you.'

'So you can wheedle more information out of the members.'

'Sometimes it's useful to hear what people say about someone when they don't know who we are. Do you have a problem with that? Or do you feel it would be unethical not to tell everyone?'

'Unless the law has changed considerably since I retired as a solicitor, I'm sure there'd be implications for any evidence you uncovered by that route.'

'You're quite right, Mr Flint; but I'm really only looking for background information at this stage.'

'Please call me Graham. So long as you understand the limitations of your proposal, I have no objection to facilitating your exploratory conversations. I'm as keen as the next man to find out what happened to that old battle-axe.'

Priestley smiled. 'I'm sure there must be plenty of meaning behind your description. You may not wish to speak ill of the dead, but would you care to elaborate?'

Flint nodded. 'It's actually the best time to speak up; the dead can't sue you for libel or slander. I was never sure whether her local success came from being a good player or from knowing so many ways of cheating; she was certainly an expert in the latter, but no one would stand up to her, so she got away with it for decades. You could argue, if I was any sort of a chairman, I'd have dealt with her myself years ago; but in the end, life's too short for that type of hassle.'

Priestley gave him a hard stare. 'Unless, of course, you did deal with her, Graham.'

Flint stared back. 'You're not serious.'

Priestley smiled. 'No, not really. Is there anyone you would say particularly disliked her?'

'I could just hand you the membership list.'

'Well, is there anyone who might have felt strongly enough to do something about it?'

'Not really. Many of the younger players were smart enough to beat her anyway, and the ones of her age are mostly old and frail. Take Mrs Liversedge for example: she's despised her for years, but now she's very weak. I'm sorry to say the old dear is terminally ill. No, I think you'll just have to find out for yourself. But you will be subtle, won't you; I don't want anyone getting upset about you asking questions.'

'Subtlety is our middle name, Graham.'

'Very well, then. You'll both need to sign the guest

book, and I'll make sure the tournament director settles you in a suitable place; there are people with mobility problems, so they get the non-moving positions. I'm assuming you know how it all works?'

'Duplicate? Yes.' He turned to Lin. 'We deal the cards in the first round, and then they're passed along in boards so that everyone gets to play the same hands. After each hand we agree the result and record it on the traveller; that's a slip of paper that stays with the board. I'll handle the scoring for our side. At the end of the evening, each hand's set of results are compared for north-south and east-west. A pair gets two points for every opponent they beat, and one for every opponent they draw with.'

Flint nodded approvingly. 'Very succinct. What sort of level are you, Marcus?'

'I only made it to County Master before I became too busy with other things.'

'Nevertheless, that's a decent enough standard.' He turned to Plummer. 'And what about you, Miss?'

She smiled at him. 'Call me Lin. And I have to tell you, I haven't a clue what standard I am, which I guess speaks volumes.'

Flint smiled back. 'Well, I'm sure your partner will help you out as much as he can. Just remember not to give away information unfairly, and to keep your face as unrevealing as possible when you're bidding. Due to our recent change in membership we're probably one of the most ethical clubs in the country, now. If you fill in your score card properly before you start, and stick to what's written there, everything will be fine.'

In the bar, Marcus bought a G&T for Lin and a half of bitter for himself. They sat at a table, where he reeled off his preferred bids and conventions and wrote them on his score card, Lin copying the entries onto her own. 'Basic system: Acol. Opening one no-trump, twelve to fourteen; vulnerable, fifteen to seventeen; fourth bidder, twelve to fourteen.'

She asked, 'Twelve to fourteen whats?'

He laughed. 'Very funny, Lin.' She frowned. 'You do know how to calculate your high card point count, don't you? Four for an ace, three for a king, two for a queen, one for a jack. Maybe a half for a ten, if your higher cards in that suit suggest it can be developed into a trick. Perhaps another point for any more than four in a suit you intend to become trumps. Are you saying you use a different system, such as Quick Tricks?' Seeing her still frowning, he proposed, 'Let's keep it simple. Just count your points for aces to jacks.'

She forced a wavering smile. 'Yes, of course, aces to jacks, four points down to one point.'

'Except singleton kings, doubleton queens...'

She slugged back the G&T. 'I'll have another; I think I'm going to need it.'

The barman had been listening in; he brought over the G&T without being asked. She looked up at him. 'Thank you. And keep 'em coming.'

Marcus specified the remaining sections of the card. 'Opening two-bids: strong. Opening three-bids: weak. One no-trump overcall, fifteen to seventeen points. Jump overcalls: six or seven playing tricks. Defence to one no-trump: natural. Defence to pre-empts, over threes: DXCC-X. Over twos: treat them as ones. Slam conventions: Blackwood, with Gerber over no-trumps. Leads: Mud against a suit; ace from ace, king, bit; TON against no-trumps. Signals: Held. Discards: Held. Other conventions: Stayman two clubs, Baron three clubs, Sputnik doubles to two spades.' He noticed she had stopped writing. 'Am I going too fast for you?'

She shook her head. 'I haven't a clue what you're on about. What do they all mean?'

'Well, DXCC-X means diamonds over clubs, double diamonds, clubs over hearts and spades, and... Maybe we should drop that one. Mud is middle, up, down. TON is top of nothing. Held is high encouraging, low discouraging. But I've had a better idea; let's start again from the beginning.'

He fetched another two blank scorecards. After the no-trump ranges, he wrote, 'We bid what's in our hand and we throw away what we don't want to keep.'

She looked him in the eye. 'This is going to be a complete disaster. You do know that, don't you?'

He smiled confidently. 'It'll be fine, Lin. If you've a good hand, bid up; if you've a poor hand, say nothing. How does that sound?'

She sighed. 'I only hope I don't get any good hands; then I can just keep passing.'

When the tournament director had seated them east-west in the larger upstairs room, Marcus introduced himself and Lin to the north-south opponents. 'Good evening. This is Lin and I'm Marcus. We're a scratch pairing, so don't take advantage of us, will you.'

Mr McLarty introduced himself and his equally elderly wife. 'We're Jim and Dora. And you can expect no mercy from us, or anyone else here tonight; but at least we'll try not to make you feel bad about it!'

Jim dealt the first hand. After four passes, all except Lin placed their cards face-up on the table. Marcus smiled at her. 'Let's see what's in your hand, then. You must have fifteen points; why didn't you bid?'

She held her cards forward somewhat sheepishly. 'Sorry, I miscounted. Can we re-deal it?'

Jim spoke quietly to Marcus. 'We're not supposed to re-deal passed hands, but it'll be better than missing a board and having to wait for everyone else to move at the end of the round.'

Marcus directed Lin to reshuffle the pack and place it in front of him for cutting. Jim quickly re-dealt.

Lin picked up her cards and sorted them into suits. She read the vulnerability status off the empty board that had been placed in the well at the centre of the table. When everyone appeared to be ready to proceed, Jim silently tapped the "Pass" option from the symbols displayed around the well. Lin calculated she should bid one no-trump. Unfamiliar with silent bidders, she hesitantly tapped her pencil against the "1" followed by the "NT". After a pass from Dora, Marcus made a bid of three no-trumps, having no wish to explore other options despite the strength of his hand. Lin played the contract, making an overtrick. Dora commented to her, 'I think many pairs might be in six, going one off, so it could be a good score for you.'

Lin smiled gratefully at her.

The next two boards proved uneventful, largely due to Lin happily receiving hands with few points. As they packed away the cards and the score sheet, Marcus asked Dora, 'Did you know Mrs Batter? Did you hear what happened to her?'

Dora grimaced. 'Yes, isn't it dreadful. She was such a, um, nice woman. Who'd have wanted her dead? It's getting like you're not even safe in your own home.'

Priestley nodded. 'I suppose someone must have had

a grudge, or something.'

Dora shook her head. 'It must have been some drug addict looking for money.'

Their conversation was curtailed by the tournament director calling out, 'Move for the next round, please.'

Throughout the evening Lin relied on a stream of G&T to make the occasion more bearable.

They played the final round against another elderly married couple, Derek and Edith Bottomley. After the three boards, they had several minutes to wait until the last table was finished. Derek excused himself. Marcus did likewise, hoping to elicit from him in the sanctity of the men's room an honest opinion of Sylvia Batter.

Lin remained seated and turned to Edith. 'I'm sorry about messing up the bidding on that last hand. What did you call it? An insufficient bid?'

Edith touched her arm. 'Don't worry about it, love; we've all done it. I can remember the first time I played with my husband; I kept getting confused about the bidding. When he went to the loo, I said to the others, "That's the first time all evening I've had any idea what he held in his hand!"' Lin, taken unawares, laughed loudly, receiving a few shushes in return. Edith smiled at her. 'Haven't you heard that one before?'

Lin smiled back. 'No; it's a good one.'

Edith commented, 'I suppose your boyfriend wants you to learn to play bridge; it was the same with us.'

Lin blushed. 'He's not my boyfriend.'

Edith leaned closer to her. 'I'd never have guessed. Is it too early to say he is, officially?'

Lin glanced down for a moment, before looking her in the eye. 'He's married.'

Edith held her gaze 'So, you're playing with fire.'

Lin blinked hard. 'No, you don't understand; he's my boss.' The conversation halted as Derek returned.

Marcus followed immediately after, having had no opportunity to discuss the deceased. Receiving a glare from Edith as he took his seat, he asked, 'Hello; have I missed something?'

Edith wagged a finger at him. 'I don't know what you think you're doing with this nice girl, you being a married man, and all.'

Marcus turned to Lin. 'What's been going on?'

She shook her head. 'It's just a misunderstanding. I told Edith you're my boss and that you're married.'

'And did you say what we're doing here?'

'No sir.' Lin blushed, realising she had revealed too much; she blamed the alcohol.

Derek and Edith looked first at her and then at him. He explained in a low voice, 'We're police officers, investigating the death of Mrs Sylvia Batter. I thought we might find some background information about her from her friends, if we just came along for a game.'

Edith responded quickly, 'Well, if you're looking for any friends of hers, I don't think you came to the right place; we all hated the cow.'

Marcus nodded. 'Yes, I'm certainly starting to think she wasn't the most popular person around. But do you know of anyone who hated her enough to kill her?'

Edith replied, 'Lucy Liversedge certainly hated her enough, but she's on her last legs at the hospice; she went in a week ago. It's cancer, you know.'

The official scorer collected the travellers from their boards and the elderly couple took their leave.

Fewer than half the players waited for their overall positions to be calculated and announced. Marcus and

Lin hung around in the hope of starting conversations with people they had not yet met, but everyone seemed focused on discussing hands they had found especially interesting. Lin was relieved to discover they had only finished fourth from bottom.

The remaining players began to disperse, so Marcus walked with Lin back to his car. She complained, 'After what you've just put me through, how are you going to make it up to me?'

He opened the passenger door for her. 'I didn't like to say so before, but you've had far too much to drink.'

She held her response until he was in the driver's seat. 'You'd better take me home and put me to bed.' He made no reply as he drove them back. She closed her eyes and drifted off to sleep.

He parked in her bay. After watching her slumbering innocently, he climbed out and walked around to the passenger side. Quietly easing open her door, he half-whispered, 'Come on, Lin; you need to wake up.'

She dragged her eyelids apart and peered out from behind the slits. 'That was hell! You owe me, big time.'

He helped her to the lift, while she held onto him without caring who noticed. As they stepped out of it, a dark-haired woman in her mid-twenties was about to enter the adjacent apartment. She gave Marcus a broad smile. 'So, you're Lin's mysterious lover, are you?'

Lin shook herself more awake. 'This gen'l'man is jus' helping me home. I had a bit too much to drink.'

The woman smiled even more brightly. 'Yes, of course he is, Lin. Pull the other leg; it has bells on.' She unlocked her door and disappeared inside.

Lin searched her handbag for her keys, increasingly concerned they had gone missing. Marcus took the bag from her and quickly found them hiding in plain sight. He opened the door and walked her to the settee. She pulled him down to her. 'You'll have to stay; I'm in no fit state to be left alone. It wasn't the alcohol; it was when the cold air hit me. I was fine until then.'

He prised off her gripping fingers from his right arm. 'Now that your neighbour has seen me, there's no way I can stay tonight; you must know that. I'll just make you some black coffee and then I'll be on my way.'

She tried to look alert when he brought her a mug of strong coffee, but only wished to sleep. Finding it was cool enough to drink straight away, she gulped it down, before holding out the empty mug to him. 'Look, I've finished it all, so now you can go home to your wife.'

Detecting reproach in her voice for the first time, he masked his concern. Once he was sure she was well enough to take care of herself, he headed off. In the corridor, he paused to call out 'Goodnight, Miss,' before closing the door as noisily as the mechanism would allow. He hoped the next-door neighbour was listening to his deliberately heavy footsteps as they retreated down the corridor.

CHAPTER 3

Stepping out of his car at Midshaw police station, DCI Priestley was greeted by the morning sun as it found an opening in the stratocumulus clouds; it seemed to him a good omen. Before he had reached the steps he was accosted by DS Whittington. 'She's here. Queen Bitch. DI Penny Baker. She's already been bossing us about.'

As he immediately revised his opinion, the deceitful yellow orb hid itself. 'I'm sure she can't be all that bad. She's probably just trying to assert her authority and to make a powerful, positive initial impression.'

'Try telling Lin that.'

Marcus felt a surge of protective concern. 'Why? What's happened?'

'You know how Lin always looks bright and gay in the morning; well, this morning she didn't look quite so bright or quite so gay. DI Baker saw her and gave her a grilling. Lin said she'd been working undercover on the investigation with you last night. Baker wanted to see the report, but Lin hadn't written one, so she demanded she write one straight away. Lin said she would first have to refer the matter to you as the senior officer. Baker's now waiting outside your office.'

Priestley sighed. 'Thanks for the warning. I'll go and put her straight on a few things.'

'While you're at it, can you get her to cut us some slack? She's issued a complete blanket ban on anybody doing anything without her prior approval. I was going to work through the list of people on that trophy, just a bit of general background, but she's already decided it's too much in the past to be relevant. She told me it's a complete waste of time and I need to focus on the here and now.'

'All right. I've already had a quiet word with the Super and he's authorised me to become as involved as I think necessary. He said he'd explain it to her boss.'

Priestley headed for his office. As he approached within a few strides of the door, a woman stepped out and blocked his path. 'Good morning, sir. DI Baker. I need to discuss the Batter case with you straight away, so I can get things moving.'

The severe haircut and determined stiffness of her slight frame convinced him his usual charm would be lost on her, so he suppressed his naturally welcoming smile. 'I'll see you in a quarter of an hour.'

'But sir, I can't move without your authority; I've been given my orders.'

'Give me a minute, then.' She continued to block his way. He skirted around her and went into his office, closing the door firmly behind him. Through the narrow vertical glass panel adjacent to the jamb he saw her standing motionless, watching him. After a few minutes of asserting his right to keep her waiting, he signalled her to enter.

She marched swiftly up to his desk. 'I'm sure this is only a formality, sir, but my boss insisted you give your approval to how I run things.'

He indicated a guest seat. 'What should I call you?'

As she perched on the edge of the chair, she gave a puzzled stare. 'DI Baker, sir. I did introduce myself.'

'Do you have a first name?'

'Yes sir. Of course, sir.'

After waiting for a few seconds, he guessed she had obstinately taken him literally. 'And it is…?'

She frowned. 'It's Penelope, sir.'

'And is that what people call you?'

'No sir, people call me Penny.'

'Then shall I call you Penny?'

'I'm not sure I'm entirely comfortable with that level of familiarity from a senior officer, sir.'

'Well, if we're to work together effectively, don't you think we need a certain degree of familiarity?'

'I'm not anticipating working with you, sir; I only want your approval for me to get on with organising the investigation my way.'

'You seem to be suggesting you know exactly how to proceed.'

'I do, sir; everything will be done by the book.'

'But "the book", if I can call it that, only defines the procedures. How do you go about interpreting them and deciding what direction the investigation should take?' He read her deliberate look of incomprehension. 'How do you establish the MLE?'

She chanted her mantra. 'The chosen main line of enquiry at any point in time should always be that which is the likeliest to achieve a positive outcome.'

He shook his head slowly. 'Your response appears to be informative, but your words taken together are a tautology; they don't actually mean anything, Penny.' He wondered if her audible wince stemmed from his reply, or from his using her first name. 'Do you ever go with gut instinct to decide on the MLE?'

She retorted instantly, 'No sir. I consider how much evidence points in a particular direction and make that the way to proceed with the investigation.'

He gave her a moment to reflect. 'Do you not feel there's ever a need to interpret the evidence? Do you see a difference between quantity and quality?'

'That would imply a level of subjectivity, sir.'

'So what you're telling me is that you don't employ human insights. In that case, you could be replaced by a computer.' He saw her face muscles tighten. 'Do you have an opinion of my interpretation?'

'Do I have your permission to speak my mind, sir?'

'Certainly, go right ahead.'

'I was warned you're a free-thinker, a radical; but it's solid police-work that solves cases. That's why I want you to let me get on without interference.'

He looked her in the eye. 'And yet my free-thinking approach, looking for different ways of examining the evidence, has often produced good results. How do you explain that, Penny?'

'I can't without more information. Will you give me an example of your thinking outside the box, sir?'

He opened his desk drawer and took out a pack of playing cards. 'I bought these yesterday, the same type as were at the crime scene.' He broke the paper seal, removed the pack and shuffled through to extract the four queens. 'The card that was found in the victim's mouth was the Queen of Clubs. What significance do you think there might be behind that choice?'

'The card represents the victim, sir?'

'That's a good start, but why not one of the other queens?'

She snapped, 'Does it matter?'

He responded calmly, 'Maybe it does and maybe it doesn't, but sometimes it can help our understanding if we use our imagination.' He handed her the four cards.

'How do they differ?'

She gave them a cursory glance. 'Four suits, two red, two black, diamonds hearts spades clubs.'

'Anything beyond that?'

'No, nothing.' She passed the cards back.

Though he knew she was looking contemptuously at him, he persevered. 'What can you tell me about the individual characters of the queens?'

'They're playing cards; they don't have characters.' She almost spat out the words.

He selected the Queen of Hearts and held it up. 'This one's the oldest, rather plain and a little world-weary. She knows her aging husband has a fondness for young women, but she turns a blind eye to his philandering.' Next, he displayed the Queen of Spades. 'The youngest of them all, convinced she'll forever be the centre of attention. Her massive ego blinds her to the reality that her attractiveness will diminish over time.' He held up the Queen of Diamonds. 'She's the second-youngest, famed throughout the land for her baby-face prettiness. It's starting to fade, but she's a nice girl, and her looks will hold up the longest; after that, her sweet nature will keep her subjects loyal.' Finally, he waved the Queen of Clubs at her. 'This one's the second-eldest. She's still desperately trying to hold onto her youthfulness. Look closely at her face.' He handed over the card. 'She's done so much whoring, her come-to-bed eyes have started to look old and wrinkled before their time. From a certain angle you can see the sneer that's always hiding behind her mask, ready to surface at a moment's notice to dismiss a politician as just another worthless commoner.' He held out his hand. 'I'll keep it face-up at the top of the pack, so it's always the first card I see when I take them out.' He returned the pack to the box before asking, 'Have you ever played bridge, Penny?'

She shook her head. 'No, sir.'

'The deceased was a bridge player.' He shrugged his shoulders. 'It may turn out to be irrelevant, but I went with DC Plummer to the club where she was a regular, to obtain some background info. I'll write a short report to say she wasn't popular with the other members.'

'I spoke to DC Plummer earlier, sir, and I didn't like her attitude. She refused to write a report about your visit to the bridge club without referring to you first.'

Priestley weighed his words carefully. 'Hearing you have already formed a negative opinion of one of my best team members makes me wonder whether you are competent to play a leading rôle in this inquiry. Taking into account other feedback I've received, I have severe misgivings about your suitability, so I'll be keeping a close eye on you. Don't do anything beyond normal evidence collection without my specific authority. If you intend to take any action, you must obtain my prior permission. Is that clear?'

Her words burst out angrily. 'I can't work like that!'

He waited, having expected more from her, but she had dried up. 'And yet, isn't that the same instruction you gave to Sergeant Whittington this morning?' He stayed silent until she gave in and responded.

'Yes, sir; but I'm senior to him.'

'And I'm senior to you, so by that same argument you must accept my instruction to you is equally valid. Or have you perhaps changed your mind about it being a sensible way of working?'

Eventually, she nodded. 'I was only trying to assert my authority, sir.'

'And yet, the reality is, you've already upset the smooth running of my team. Your regular colleagues from Derby have started arriving, and I don't know how they feel about your manner of dealing with them, but you'll afford my people the consideration and respect that is their due. Is that clear?'

'Yes sir.'

'If I need a sergeant I'll call on Neil, and if I need a DC I'll use Lin, seeing as you already appear to have started off on the wrong foot with both of them. First thing every morning I shall expect you to give me a detailed progress report along with your plan for the day. Subject to my approval, you'll be free to take the investigation forward on a day-by-day basis. Do I have your full acceptance of this plan of action?'

'Yes sir.'

Though he heard the angry snap in her voice, he felt confident she would follow his instructions, convinced she believed hierarchy trumped common sense. In the hope that she might unbend a little, he finally offered, 'When in Rome, if you know the expression. I've been addressed as "sir" more times by you in the last ten minutes than I have by everyone else in the previous ten days. When we're having meetings together I'd like you to drop the "sir" and simply call me Marcus; or is that something else you wouldn't be comfortable with?'

Having honed her skill at taking offence from every little thing she perceived as Politically Incorrect, she considered escalating the matter, but decided this was one away-game she was bound to lose. Attempting to sound relaxed, she replied, 'I'm fine with it, Marcus.'

He smiled at her as though he had not heard the residual brittleness in her voice. 'Good. Now let's you and me work like we're in a football team with two attackers. You can do what you're good at: following procedures. Kick off with collecting evidence on the usual suspects and local low-life, check any CCTV including buses, interview local residents, and so forth. I'll scout around and see if I can pick up any other leads, and I'll pursue the bridge connection as well. How does that sound to you, honestly?'

'Honestly? I think you may be wasting your time. But so long as I can do my stuff, I'm happy enough.'

He thought she looked not even remotely happy, but played along. 'Good; I'm glad we've cleared the air.'

She departed and immediately found an empty room to telephone her boss in Derby. 'Ma'am, I've just had a meeting with DCI Priestley. Did you know he's off his head? He's completely certifiable. He looked at the four queens in a pack of playing cards and then gave me a description of their personalities and history. What am I supposed to do with someone like that?' She heard an untypical giggle at the other end of the line.

'I know Marcus very well and I know his record. Rather than complaining yet again about everyone, just for once, this time, assume there's more to police work than following the rules. You never know, you might even learn something from him.'

Baker remained unconvinced, but gave the answer she believed she ought. 'I certainly hope to benefit from the opportunity of working with a successful DCI.'

'Excellent. So, do you think you'll be able to get on well with him? Despite thinking he's certifiable?'

'Yes, I hope so, ma'am. He's quite friendly; he calls me Penny and I get to call him Marcus.'

She giggled again. 'Well, don't get too friendly with

him; he's a married man.' She terminated the call.

Baker wondered why her boss seemed so cheery this morning. Lacking evidence to support any theory, she dismissed it from her mind as she entered the major incident room that had been allocated for the Batter inquiry. Looking around at her colleagues who were settling in, she told herself she could now commence the proper investigation with some real police work.

Mid-morning, Priestley phoned Witty. 'Neil, come and see me, will you? And bring that spreadsheet you made of all the names on the bridge trophy.'

Witty knocked at the open door as he entered. 'I've listed them all by year. S. Batter and L. Liversedge had both won twice before the deceased made it three wins. Do you really think there could be a motive lurking behind this? Is L. Liversedge someone to investigate?'

'Lucy Liversedge has been in St Luke's hospice for a week, so she isn't a suspect. All the same, if she's well enough to talk, she may be able to give us some insight into the deceased. Give them a call, will you? Let's go along and see her as soon as we can, before it's too late.'

Witty drove them to the island of serenity within the evergreen woodland. Melanie on reception asked them if they would like "elevenses" before visiting Lucy. They both had coffee and chocolate cake while Melanie offered a prognosis on the visitee. Afterwards, Marcus made a donation, cramming a ten pound note down the plastic jaws of the blue collecting box's lid.

Melanie delivered them to Lucy's warm, airy room, which looked out over pine trees to the sunlit green hills beyond. A painfully thin old lady lay propped up by pillows in the white-sheeted bed, her eyes closed.

The young man sitting holding her hand accepted their introductions with no more than a glance at the warrant cards. Lucy opened her eyes and licked her cracked lips as though preparing to speak; they all waited silently in respectful anticipation. 'This is my boy, Aden.'

Marcus tried to find a smile that conveyed sympathy as well as appreciation for her making the effort to talk, but the attempt died all too quickly. 'Do you feel well enough for a little chat, Mrs Liversedge?'

She in turn managed a more confident smile. 'It's Miss Liversedge. Lucy. Sit yourself down.'

Aden took the initiative and unstacked two plastic seats, which he placed at the other side of the bed to his own. He explained, 'Mum is actually my great-aunt, my mother's mother's sister. When my parents died, she adopted me. I was just three, so she's been my mum for as long as I can remember.'

Priestley gratefully acknowledged his explanation, before turning to Lucy. 'I have some sad news about someone you played bridge with. Mrs Sylvia Batter has died suddenly.' Despite her condition he was sure he saw a twinkle in her eye.

'Aden mentioned it, but he doesn't know any details. Can you tell me all about it? I always wanted to outlive her, though I didn't expect it to happen, what with my illness. I'll close my eyes for a bit, but I'll be listening to every word you say.'

Priestley decided not to hold back the information regarding the playing card, believing this visit may prove to be his one opportunity for discovering any special significance known only to Lucy. 'We're still investigating exactly what led to her death, but there was something intriguing about how she was found.

The killer put a playing card in her mouth, the Queen of Clubs.'

Lucy opened her eyes. 'I'm sure it's a coincidence, but it was the Queen of Clubs that cost me a bridge trophy, oh, twenty years ago. Aden knows the story.' She closed her eyes again.

He looked over the bed at Aden. 'Would you mind explaining? I play bridge myself, so you can give me as much detail as you like.'

Aden half-closed his eyes for a moment as though trying to recover a distant memory. 'Mrs Batter was in three spades, which Mum had doubled. At trick twelve there were no spades left, the Ace of Clubs had gone, and Mrs Batter had to lead a low club from table. The contract was going to go one off, because Mum had the King and Jack of Clubs sitting over Mrs Batter's Queen and Seven. Mrs Batter started huffing and puffing, and spent ages fiddling with her cards as though trying to decide which one to play. Then she revealed her cards just enough to show Mum she was putting down the Queen, so Mum took hold of her King and put it down straight after. Only, Mrs Batter had switched her cards at the last moment and had actually played the Seven, which meant she had the Queen left to take the last trick. The scores for that hand made all the difference, and that's how Mrs Batter won the trophy. It should have been Mum's trophy, by rights. She never forgave her for that, did you Mum?'

Lucy opened her eyes. 'I know I don't have long to live, but I feel much more at peace now that I know I've beaten her in the end. Not that I condone murder, of course.' She closed her eyes. 'I need to sleep now.'

Priestley invited Aden to step outside. He observed

him closely as he prepared to broach the subject of an alibi. 'This is obviously a very difficult time for you.'

Aden sighed deeply. 'She kept telling me she wasn't too bad, but I knew better. Melanie, who brought you in earlier, kept me in the picture. That's why I flew back from the States last night to make sure I got here in time. I'm the only family she has.' His eyes took on a glassy appearance. He rubbed them to clear the excess moisture, and forced a smile. 'Catching the red-eye gives me a good excuse for looking like this.'

Priestley nodded deeply in sympathy. 'I'm sorry to be meeting you under such unhappy circumstances. Your presence here must be a great comfort to her.'

They took their leave. In the car, Witty observed, 'He could have been a suspect if it wasn't for his being in America.'

Priestley had had a similar thought. 'We need to be certain. Check all incoming and outgoing flights under his name to make sure he really was out of the country.'

In the afternoon, Priestley received the interim postmortem report on Sylvia Batter. Though toxicology would take weeks to provide a comprehensive analysis of any drugs in her system, initial indications were that she had died from sodium cyanide poisoning.

Later, Witty knocked on Priestley's open door and started to speak as he crossed the floor. 'I've checked flights for Aden Liversedge.'

Marcus looked up. 'And?'

'It's just like he said, so he couldn't have done it.'

'Oh, well; and he would have made quite a decent suspect, what with his obvious emotional attachment to his adoptive mum. I suppose we'd better check what's been turned up by good old-fashioned police work:

ANPR, CCTV, DNA, GPS, mobile phones…'

Neil laughed. 'That's not what most people would call "old-fashioned".'

In the MIR, Priestley looked at the timeline on the whiteboard and called out to Baker, 'Do you have any suspects yet, Penny?'

She strode over. 'We're still sifting through the evidence, Marcus. Have you come up with something?'

He grimaced. 'I thought I might have, but it turned out the guy was in the US.' He waited to see if her interest was piqued.

She looked away. 'Oh, well.'

He tried again. 'It was to do with that bridge trophy.' When it became evident she would not be asking him for details, he offered them unbidden. 'Another woman would have won it if the deceased hadn't employed sharp practice; what most people would call cheating. But the lady in question is terminally ill in a hospice, and her son, her only relative, was abroad. I suppose he could have organised a hit…'

She laughed loudly, believing he was joking. 'You do have a vivid imagination, Marcus. Not like me; I always stick with the facts.' He performed a hurt look, as though offended by the insinuation. She read it as genuine, so applied a little balm. 'I expect people find you very amusing to work with, though.'

He offered a weak smile. 'A bit of fun sometimes oils the wheels. I'll leave you to it, but do let me know if something crops up that might be worth a closer look.'

As he turned and headed away, she was surprised to discover she was still smiling.

CHAPTER 4

Baker glared sharply at Witty as she crossed Priestley's office, then threw herself into the vacant chair and stared intensely at Priestley. 'I thought these morning meetings might be just the two of us, Marcus.'

He held a smile until her gaze softened. 'It will save me time later if Neil learns how the case is progressing without my having to brief him.'

'He could join the eight thirty briefing with the rest of my team, Marcus.'

'That's an excellent idea; he could do that as well, so he can relay any thoughts I may have had.'

'But it seems a bit of a waste of his time to attend both meetings, Marcus.'

Having invited her to address him as "Marcus" rather than "sir", he was hoping the overuse would soon diminish as the novelty wore off. He turned to Witty, and with an almost imperceptible nod and a sideways glance, encouraged him to direct his reply to Baker. 'Do you think you might benefit from attending both meetings, Neil?'

Witty turned and smiled at Baker. 'I'm sure it would be a big help to me to see how you operate, Penny; how you pitch your briefings to match your audience.' The grin from the visible side of Priestley's mouth told him his response had been exactly what he was wanting.

Believing smiling must be the norm at this station, Baker attempted to manufacture one of her own. 'In that case, Marcus, I'll proceed, if I may.' She looked down at her briefing sheet. 'There are no CCTV or ANPR cameras near the crime scene; it's a residential area. We're going to expand the radius until we have both, and then we'll produce a list of all the vehicles in the vicinity based on ingress and egress times relevant to the estimated TOD. Door-to-door enquiries have so far revealed no suspicious activity.'

When Priestley realised that that was the full extent of the briefing, he rubbed his chin. 'Anything useful from the house? Fingerprints, perhaps?'

'There were lots of fingerprints found in the room. Manual comparison with records has already begun, but there have been no matches so far.'

'Were any used packs of playing cards found?'

'Yes, there were two.'

'One with red backs, one with blue, by any chance?'

'Yes, as a matter of fact. Is that significant?'

'It's normal to have two different-coloured packs for playing bridge; one's made while the other one's dealt.'

'Made?'

'Shuffled ready for cutting and dealing. When you went to the crime scene yesterday you no doubt noticed the bridge table. Fingerprints on the playing cards could help us identify past visitors. Have they been checked?' Her spontaneous glance to one side told him the answer was a negative.

'I'll make sure they are.'

'Good. You said none of the neighbours had noticed any suspicious activity; did any of them see anything at all in the vicinity around TOD?'

'I'll get back to you on that.'

Witty took the momentary silence as an opportunity to speak. 'I expect you'll be delivering a fuller analysis at the team meeting, so I'll pick up the information there and report it back to Marcus as appropriate, if that meets with your approval, Penny.'

Her face initially indicated the idea was not to her liking, but she was trying hard to avoid being negative. 'Thank you, Neil; that will save me some time.'

Marcus checked his watch. 'Speaking of which, I'd better not keep you any longer; you've obviously plenty to do, today.'

She stood up quickly. 'Yes s… Marcus.' She turned to Witty. 'I'll see you at the team briefing.'

After she had left, Priestley motioned Witty to close the door, before asking him, 'What do you think, Neil? Is the investigation moving forward?'

He thought for a few moments. 'If the evidence just isn't there, it can be difficult to make any real progress. I suppose there's nothing for it but good old-fashioned police-work.' He smirked. 'That's knocking on doors, checking out likely lads, et cetera.'

'Indeed. What about the modus operandi?'

'Death by cyanide is almost unheard of around here. I could look for similar crimes nationally if you think it's relevant? So far we've only found evidence of the victim having lived locally, so it would be surprising if she'd made enemies outside the area.'

'Even so, it's worth researching. Raise it at the team meeting. If Penny tries to turn it down, you can say we discussed it and I'd like it progressing; but otherwise, you can claim the credit for the idea yourself. All right, that'll do for now.'

'Do you have any other lines of inquiry in mind?'

'I only have one, but you're unqualified to help me with it.' He noticed how Witty was unable to hide his disappointment. 'I need a bridge partner, and you don't play. I'm going back to the club this evening.'

'Are you taking Lin again?'

'No, I don't think she'd be too keen. Berry used to play, so I'll try him first; otherwise, I'll have to cast the net wider. Maybe the Chief Constable would like a game; I know he occasionally plays rubber bridge with his wife and friends. He mentioned it once when we were discussing how detectives need to avoid attaching significance to random events during an investigation. He used his wife's irrational bidding as an example.'

Witty grimaced. 'You'd really invite the Chief for a game of cards? You're not serious, are you?'

'Well, probably not.'

When Witty had left the office, Priestley telephoned DS Beresford. 'Hello, Tony. How are things?'

'Things are great. So, what do you need me for?'

'Straight to the point; I think that must be Susan's influence. Does she allow you out in the evenings?'

'Of course she does… if I promise to behave.'

'Are you free this evening?'

'We've nothing planned. What's it about?'

'I need a partner to play bridge with.'

'Social or competitive? Any gambling?'

'No gambling; just the local bridge club. How good a player were you?'

'I think it's fair to say I held my own against top notch players when I was misspending my youth.'

'I really don't think that counts as misspending, Tony; at least, not when I compare it with *my* youth. I'll pick you up from home at twenty to seven and we'll thrash out a system. I played with Lin two nights ago and we weren't exactly a success, so I'd like to put on a better showing this time.'

In the evening, Marcus parked outside Tony's house. Susan opened the door and proprietorially led him to her husband, who was standing in the kitchen, drying the dishes. She asked Marcus, 'What time will you be bringing him back?'

He gazed at the ceiling as though giving the question some thought. 'I expect the bridge club will be closing around eleven, and then we'll pursue our enquiries at that recently opened gentleman's club, so I expect it could be some time after two.'

Susan's jaw dropped, but she eventually managed to get it working again. 'You're not taking him there! You could corrupt him with that sort of thing.'

Tony, certain Marcus was just winding her up, took a moment to consider whether short-term amusement was worth long-term pain. He frowned. 'You shouldn't say things like that, boss.'

Marcus tried for hurt innocence. 'Like what?'

He gave way. 'Getting my hopes up when you don't mean it; you know I've never been there, before.'

Susan wagged her finger at her husband. 'You're not going there, ever, and that's an end to it.'

Marcus nodded at Susan. 'I'll have to go on my own, then.' He held her gaze, and then grinned.

She stared back at him. 'Weren't you being serious?'

He broadened his smile. 'Sorry, Susan; I don't know what gets into me, sometimes. I'll have him back by half eleven at the latest.'

Tutting loudly in lieu of laughter at being fooled, she made a performance of storming out of the kitchen.

Marcus sat at the table and pulled out the scorecard that had previously been used as a bookmark. 'These were my usual bids and conventions, but we can try others if you prefer.'

Tony scanned down the list. 'I'm fine with these; best not to overcomplicate things.'

At the bridge club, Marcus led the way to the bar, where he ordered a pint for Tony and a half for himself.

Edith called over to him, 'Hello, Marcus. What have you done with that nice girl you were with?'

He spun around to see her toasting him with a brandy and orange. 'I swapped her for a better player.' They joined her and her husband at a small, round table. 'This is Tony. Tony, meet Edith and Derek.'

After they were seated, Edith leaned over to Marcus and whispered in his ear, 'Are you hot on the trail? Is that why you're here tonight? My money's on Graham Flint; the worm finally turned, and all that.'

He whispered back, 'You could be right, Edith. It was maybe a way of celebrating his eightieth birthday.'

She giggled like a schoolgirl, enjoying the moment of intimacy with the handsome police officer.

Derek frowned at her. 'What's all that about?' He added as an aside to Marcus, 'As if I didn't know,' before laughing to confirm the question was rhetorical.

Marcus quietly explained to Tony, 'Lin let the cat out of the bag, so I had to put them in the picture.' He added for their amusement, 'You give them a grilling while I have a quick word with the barman.'

At the bar, he surreptitiously displayed his warrant card. 'Hello, Niall; I'm mixing business with pleasure this evening.' He hoped the implication of enjoying being at the bridge club might improve his chances of receiving a comprehensive reply. 'Do you remember I bought a pack of cards a couple of nights ago? I was wondering if anyone else had bought a pack, recently.'

Niall remained as unruffled as his neat red bowtie. 'Members only ever buy packs in pairs, one red, one blue. If they've organised something bigger than just a single table at home, they might buy four, six, eight, or whatever, but they never buy new ones like you did. We sell our used ones at a big discount, you see, the moment they start to look the least bit marked. Apart from yourself, I really couldn't tell you the last time anyone bought a brand new pack.'

Marcus nodded. 'Thanks, Niall; you'd be surprised how much that helps me.'

When Marcus returned to his seat, Derek leaned forward and glanced around, as though a conspirator checking for eavesdroppers. 'Is Niall in the frame?'

Edith shook her head at him. 'I heard Sylvia died in the afternoon, so Niall's alibi would be rock solid. He'd have opened the bar at noon for the usual crowd.'

Marcus joined the leaning heads. 'How do you know when she died, Edith?'

She flicked a thumb toward a table in the corner of the room. 'Dora told me.'

He tried to avoid looking desperately interested. 'And how did she know?'

'She phoned her at midday to see if she'd like to go to the afternoon session; the two often played together.'

'And what did she say?'

'She said no because she was expecting a visitor.' Suddenly, her eyes sprang wide open. 'You're going to have to give Dora a grilling, aren't you. Well, fancy that: I've just helped the police with their enquiries.'

Marcus looked steadily at her and then at Derek. 'You won't spill a word of this, will you.' The couple shook their heads in confirmation.

As though reacting to a prearranged silent signal, the bar suddenly began to empty. The four stood up and headed for the stairs. Marcus directed Tony to stop and sign the guest book, where he intimated they should aim to join Dora after the first round, so as not to be too obvious about wishing to speak to her.

Noting the number of the table where Jim and Dora were sitting north-south, they claimed the east-west position at the table that was numbered two lower, as the movement card indicated this would bring them to Dora's table after the first move. When everyone was seated, the director changed the movement because of the increased number of tables in play. They finally joined Dora and Jim for the penultimate round.

Dora was Declarer for the first two boards. Despite slow, careful play, both contracts went down heavily. She was the Dealer for the final board and began the auction with a pass. Marcus was keen to be Declarer as he wished to complete the hand as quickly as possible to give him time for a quiet chat with her. He hastily drove the auction forward and finally signed off with a small slam in no-trumps, requiring him to lose no more than one trick. Dora nonchalantly indicated "Double". He assumed she must be holding the Ace of Clubs together with the missing king that had been revealed by the conventional bidding.

Jim placed a card face-down and issued the standard invitation of 'Any questions?' On receiving no response he turned over his Two of Spades.

Tony placed his cards face-up, separated into suits that descended in ordered columns. Marcus compared the fit with his own cards. Not only were the Ace and

King of Clubs held by the opponents, but so were all four queens, along with the Jack of Hearts. He knew he had seriously overbid his hand, but hoped there might still be a winning play. With no long suit, he realised he would have to take the first twelve tricks with four each in diamonds, hearts and spades.

The double now indicated Dora held seven points in clubs. His holding of Ace, King, Ten, Nine of Hearts meant he would have to play her for the Queen and Jack, giving her ten points. Yet, sitting south, she had begun the auction with a pass. If she held a further queen, she would have had enough points to make an opening bid, unless she had discounted a bare queen or queen doubleton, as they would be less likely to take a trick than one supported by at least two lower cards in the same suit. He would therefore play Jim for the other three queens.

Reading Jim's lead as showing four to an honour in his strongest suit, Marcus was confident he held the Queen of Spades and predicted he also had the Ten. Counting the four spades on table and the three in hand, he was certain Dora must hold a doubleton.

He decided he should take the first trick on table so he could test the hearts at trick two before Dora could indicate her top clubs; that way, if Jim held either heart honour, he might only go one down. He played the Eight from table, satisfied he could maintain the tempo even if Dora overtook it and he had to use his Ace.

Dora, noting he had not followed the simple maxim "second player plays low", flashed a sideways glance at him as she prepared to peter with her Six and Four.

At trick two he led the Two of Hearts from table. Dora played her Four. He successfully finessed the Ten, indicating she held the Queen and Jack.

He knew the probability of the six missing diamonds being distributed four-two was almost fifty-fifty, and that an even split was over one-in-three. With the lack of an opening bid by south, he therefore anticipated Jim held the Queen of Diamonds with at least one other. He led the Ten, intending to let it ride if Jim played low, before realising he should first have played the Ace to drop a singleton Queen in Dora's hand; though the probability was low, he knew he should have made the play, and hoped Tony had not spotted his faux pas.

Following the principle of covering an honour with an honour, Jim played the Queen of Diamonds, which was driven into Dummy's tenace. After taking the trick on table with the King, Marcus led the remaining heart. Dora failed to split her honours, enabling him to finesse the Nine; without a third heart to lead from table, he knew she could have defeated the contract by playing the Queen or Jack.

He played the remaining tricks without hesitation, maintaining a steady rhythm to avoid any suggestion of placing undue pressure on the opponents.

Dora appeared reluctant to discard her King of Clubs at trick twelve, but put on a brave face as she took the final trick with the Ace.

Jim entered the agreed score on the paper traveller, before looking sympathetically at Dora. 'It would have been a bottom anyway, even if you hadn't doubled.'

Marcus smiled apologetically. 'Sorry; I overbid my hand and was ever so fortunate to find all the court cards were just where I needed them to be.'

She peered at him. 'Who are you, really?'

Assuming he had been rumbled, he took out his

warrant card. 'I'm Detective Chief Inspector Priestley.' He saw the shock register on her face. 'I thought you must have guessed I'm a police officer.'

She shook her head. 'I only meant "who are you" as a bridge player. That play was brilliant, but you didn't do so well the last time you were here. I was thinking you must be a hustler; you even have a look of Paul Newman. Except that was pool, wasn't it.'

Jim leaned over. 'You're burbling, love.'

She stared at Marcus. 'If I put two and two together, will I make four? Sylvia Batter gets murdered, and then a top bridge player starts coming to the club, only he just happens to be a senior police officer.'

He nodded. 'You're half-right, Dora. I'm looking for background information on Mrs Batter, but you're far too kind when you describe me as a top player; I was just lucky with that last hand.'

She shook her head again. 'There was no luck in it. So, what do you want to know? I probably knew her as well as anyone. We used to play, afternoons, when Jim was at his allotment. I even spoke to her on the phone the day she died. It was just after twelve. She said she couldn't come out because someone was coming to interview her for a magazine article. She said she'd tell me all about it later, but of course she never did.'

'Was it a brief conversation you had on the phone, or did she mention anything else?'

'It was very brief. She didn't tell me what magazine it was or anything about the interviewer, or even what the interview was to do with.'

'Hmm. Would you say you were *close* friends?'

'I'm not sure I'd even describe us as friends, really. It's probably nearer the mark to say we were close acquaintances because we had an interest in common. So, will the police want to interview me?'

He smiled. 'I'll come and see you personally if we have any questions, but it may not be necessary.'

The tournament director called for the move. Despite Dora and Jim having been thrashed on all three boards, they nevertheless followed protocol by thanking their opponents.

Marcus and Tony were due to sit out the final round, there having been an odd number of pairs playing that evening. With no reason to remain, beyond receiving confirmation of just how well they had performed, they excused themselves and left the club.

In the car, Marcus glanced at Tony. 'You've nearly an hour before your mum wants you home. Shall we go to that strip club? You said you wanted to.'

Tony sighed. 'You seem determined to get me into trouble. We're happily married, just like you and Helen, and I want to keep it that way. Anyway, I know you don't mean it; you'd be in even worse trouble if Helen found out you'd been misbehaving.'

Marcus felt his sense of fun deflating as he reflected on the difference between the two couples. Tony and Susan were happily married with no one else in their lives, whereas he and Helen were only happily married because she was unaware of his relationship with Lin. He sincerely hoped that his belovèd wife would never discover his affair; yet he had no intention of ending it, believing himself merely a passive bystander, unable to influence the course of events.

CHAPTER 5

Baker drove in early for the eight a.m. meeting. She had persuaded herself her only reason for wishing to see Priestley alone was that Witty would not be present to witness her report on the lack of progress. Finding them already deep in conversation, she knocked at the open door as she tried to hide her disappointment.

Priestley stood and called out, 'Come on in, Penny; you're bright and early. Neil was just filling me in on some office gossip. You kick off, and then I'll tell you about my latest visit to the bridge club. I partnered Tony Beresford, by the way; do you know him? He spent some time in Derby, last year.'

She turned her chair to face Priestley more directly, minimising Witty's view of her. 'Yes, I remember him, Marcus. He's the computer guy, isn't he?'

'I suppose you could call him that.'

Awkwardly, she asked, 'Shall I start, now?'

'Sure. You were going to let me know via Neil about strangers seen in the vicinity, but you must have been side-tracked because you haven't updated him yet. Start off with that, if you will.'

'I was holding off until I had something positive to report on that front, but I'm sorry to say there haven't been any suspicious sightings.'

'Well, tell me about the unsuspicious ones, then.'

'A neighbour, working in his garden, recalled seeing an old woman in a bobble hat, carrying a shopping bag. She was walking in the direction of the vic.'s house in the early afternoon. He didn't know whether she was calling in or just passing by, as he didn't see her again. We're trying to trace her in case she saw the perp.'

'She could even *be* the perpetrator, of course.'

'Oh, yes, of course, in theory. But she hardly fits the profile of a killer, does she.'

'I doubt we've anywhere near enough background information to be talking about profiles at this stage, Penny; we're really still at the speculation stage. Was the gardener able to give us a good description?'

'Not of the woman, but an excellent one of the hat.'

Marcus laughed. Penny smiled at him, recognising he had thought she was aiming to be amusing.

Realising her intense smile was showing no sign of fading, he adopted a thoughtful expression to break the moment. 'What about phone activity?'

'There was a call from a pay-as-you-go at eleven forty-two, and then one from a local landline at twelve o-four. There was nothing further until the emergency services were alerted by a neighbour at two thirty-nine.'

'Have you tried tracing the mobile?'

'Yes, but it's turned off.'

'Who's the landline registered to?'

'James McLarty. We'll contact him this morning.'

'There's no need. It was his wife, Dora, who made the call; I spoke to her yesterday. It narrows down the TOD, because Mrs Batter was still alive at that time. She mentioned to Dora that she was being interviewed for a magazine, but that was all she said, so we don't know which one, or anything about the interviewer. The victim had always lived locally, which suggests it wouldn't be one with a national reach, except possibly if it related to bridge. You should make the search for the journalist a high priority. Of course, if it wasn't one, it may well have been the perpetrator.' Baker sat in stunned silence. Marcus gave her a smile. 'Are you all right? You look like you've just seen a ghost.'

Impressed, she gazed at him. 'How did you come by all this information, sir? I mean, Marcus?'

'Oh, just from chatting with people at the bridge club. I've already put a note on file, but you obviously came too early to read it. A case of the early bird misses the worm.' She stared at him blankly. 'You being the bird, and the file note being the worm.' She wondered if there was any significance to him calling her a "bird". Though she knew she could have objected to the term, she found she was far too pleased to consider doing so.

Witty suspected his boss was being too charming, yet again, so decided to break the spell. 'He's always using figures of speech; you have to get used to it.'

Wondering if that were true, Priestley made a mental note to monitor himself. 'Was the woman's shopping bag at all distinctive? Could it give us some clue as to where she'd been?'

Baker made a written note. 'I'll make sure we check that out, Marcus. Is there anything else I should know about your visit to the bridge club?'

'Yes, I made a small slam in no-trumps, doubled, with only twenty-four points. Ah, but you don't play bridge, so that wouldn't mean anything to you.'

Feeling marginalised, she responded quickly, 'I'd be willing to learn, if you'd teach me. I mean, if you think it's important for the investigation.'

Taken aback, he held his smile for far too long, as he wondered how to react. 'I doubt whether it's essential for you to know anything about the game, really; but if you're interested, we could maybe find some spare time for me to give you a crash course.'

When the meeting was over, Witty stayed behind and closed the door. 'What are you trying to do, boss? I'm sure she thinks you're giving her the come-on.'

Priestley felt shocked, and showed it. 'I don't know what you're on about. If you mean learning bridge, I'm sure she won't mention it again; she was just wanting to show how keen she is.'

Witty shook his head. 'You mark my words, she'll be all dressed up for you, tomorrow.'

Priestley laughed. 'Come off it, Neil; you must know her reputation.'

Witty shrugged. 'She may be a ball-breaker, but I'd put a tenner on it she'll be making an effort to look her best for you in the morning.'

Unconvinced, Priestley slapped his hand down hard on the desk. 'Done!'

Witty grimaced as he withdrew his wallet. 'I didn't think you'd actually take me up on that. You're right, of course; she isn't the type. Shall I pay you now?'

Priestley pointed an accusing finger at him. 'That'll teach you to gamble! Save your money 'til tomorrow. Right now, I'd like you to research Aden Liversedge. If he normally spends time in the US, then it's reasonable for him to have been there when the murder took place. But if not, it would certainly be a way of establishing a cast-iron alibi.'

'You don't think his motive's a bit flimsy, do you?'

'It's all a matter of perception. If he thought it was the only thing he could do for his mum before she dies, it could take on great significance for him. But I do agree it's rather weak, as motives go. Maybe Penny will find a likelier suspect.'

'OK. Once I've checked out his background, should I just go and have a quiet word with him, or should I make it a formal interview, maybe with both of us?'

'I'm working on a strategy paper, so I really can't spare much time for this case at the moment. Let me know what you find out about him and then we can decide how best to take it forward.'

In the late afternoon, Witty gave Priestley his report. 'Aden Liversedge works for a small outfit in Sheffield.' He read from his notes. 'I spoke to a lady who reeled off some spiel about implementing tailored solutions to real-world problems that enable senior management to interact efficiently with logistical support operatives, functioning in a controlled fulfilment environment. When I asked her to tell me again, only this time in English, she said it's stock control.'

'And what does Liversedge do?'

'He's described as an IT consultant in the UK, but a software engineer when he's in the US.'

'Does he go over there regularly?'

'The vanilla system, whatever that is, is developed in the States, and he has to visit once every few months to check on future plans. They're large conferences, so he has no choice about the dates. In addition, maybe once or twice a year, he gets to attend a convention, which is basically a jolly with some sales pitches thrown in. They're big events that are organised well in advance, so again there's no choice about when to go to them. And occasionally he puts in an ad hoc request to visit a company that represents an income-positive symbiotic scope-extension opportunity.'

'Which means?'

'The two companies are both developing solutions to the same problem, so it makes sense for them to put their heads together and decide how best to do it. They also have to agree who is going to do what, which can mean one company does it all, or they may divvy up the work. In the end, both companies benefit by sharing rights to the software.'

'Did you find out exactly when Liversedge was over there, this last time?'

'Yes. He travelled out on the Friday afternoon and arrived back in the UK on the Tuesday morning.'

'It sounds like he was having a weekend jolly rather than a business trip. Was it a convention?'

'No, it was a speculative symbiotic scope-extension opportunity investigation.'

'Has it proved to be an income-generating one?'

'Not yet, but the inter-company executive bonding may yield a positive outcome in the fullness of time.'

'And what exactly does that all mean?'

'He went to see two mates who he thought might be able to put some business their way, but it was a no go; so he just hung with them and chilled.'

'Like a poacher's hare that's dangling from a hook, maturing in a cellar?'

'Like a bloke taking his mates out on the piss and getting a traffic violation. The company accountant has told him he has to pay it himself, as it isn't classed as a valid business expense.'

'What do you make of it all?'

'If I were of a suspicious nature, I'd probably say he took himself out of the country and made sure there was some official record of where he was, to be certain his alibi was watertight. But then, I'm not that type.'

'Whereas I am, of course. Get him in for interview.'

Witty left the office and called Liversedge on the mobile phone number his employer had provided. 'Am I speaking to Aden Liversedge?'

'Yes, that's me.'

'This is Detective Sergeant Whittington; you may recall we met briefly at St Luke's.'

'Yes, I remember. I won't be going there again; my Mum's gone, now.'

'I'm sorry for your loss.'

'Thank you. In the end it was a release.'

'I'd like to talk to you about her. When would it be convenient for you to come to the station?'

'I'm taking a week off work until after the funeral, so I suppose I could come over anytime.'

'Would tomorrow morning be possible? Say, ten o'clock?'

'Yes, all right.'

'Ask for Neil Whittington. I look forward to seeing you again, Mr Liversedge. Marcus Priestley will also be present; you met him at the hospice as well.'

'Yes. See you tomorrow, then.'

Witty reported the conversation to Priestley, adding, 'He didn't ask why we wanted to see him about his mother. Perhaps it's because he's not thinking straight, what with being upset at losing her. Or maybe it's because he was expecting to be contacted.'

'We'll find out soon enough. Don't be surprised, but I'm going to bowl him a googly. I'm going to come at it from the angle that his mother hated Sylvia Batter and was the only person we know of to have a motive for wanting her dead. If he thinks her reputation might be sullied by an investigation, he may let something slip.

But I'm not expecting him to admit to anything, so I'm not even going to ask him if he was behind the murder. I'm playing the long game.'

'He'll think we're not very smart if we don't ask if he was involved.'

'That may well match his expectations of the police in general.'

'So, you're to play dumb; it won't be easy for you.'

'Not dumb; that means being incapable of speaking. You're to be the silent one while I'm playing at being intellectually challenged.'

'I think you've just proved my point, boss.'

'I'll have to watch myself. Is Penny still around? Let her know I want to put her in the picture, and then you can push off home.'

Witty informed Baker and then had a chat with her.

Five minutes later she knocked at Priestley's open door. 'You wanted to see me, Marcus?'

'Yes, come in.'

She gestured with her thumb. 'Should I close it?'

He sensed a hint of anxiety. 'As you like.' She left the door open. 'I'm just letting you know that I'm interviewing Aden Liversedge tomorrow morning. It's a long-shot, but his mother was the only person I've discovered with any sort of a motive. Have any other possible motives come to light?'

She stared blankly. 'No, Marcus.'

He thought she seemed distracted. 'Is there anything troubling you at the moment, Penny? You can tell me, if there is.'

She hesitated. 'I know some places have dress-down Friday's, but I've never heard of any that have dress-up Fridays. I don't know what to wear.'

He guessed Witty was behind the lie. 'We don't have dress-down or dress-up Fridays, or any other day of the week for that matter. I think maybe someone's having a bit of a joke with you.'

'So you don't want me to dress up, tomorrow?'

'If you wish to, go right ahead. I'd certainly have no objection to seeing you in glad-rags, but it's entirely up to you. Everyone else will be dressed as normal of course, so you may feel more comfortable as you are right now.' It occurred to him she may interpret his words as suggesting she looked dowdy in her black shirt, black jumper, black trousers, black boots. 'Which is very nice, by the way; very, um, functional.'

She blushed as she looked away. When she turned back, her expression had hardened. 'I wish to make a formal complaint against DS Whittington. He set me up to look like a fool.'

Priestley realised he had to defuse the situation. 'I'm sure there wasn't any malice behind it, Penny.'

'Then what was behind it? Hmm?'

'I think it was just a silly bet he and I made. I guess he thought he could win a tenner by getting you to come dressed up.'

She frowned. 'You're betting on how I dress?'

'I picked up on something he said, so I thought I'd teach him a lesson not to speculate on your appearance, or any colleague's for that matter.' Seeing her holding her frown, he added, 'I was defending your honour.'

She blushed again. 'So, let me get this straight, then. If I come dressed up tomorrow, you pay him a tenner. And if I don't, he pays you.'

'That's exactly right. But obviously, all bets are off, now that you know about it.'

'I want him to pay for what he tried to do to me.'

Attempting to lighten the situation, he laughingly responded, 'We could split the winnings, a fiver each.'

Her expression softened. 'Let's make it a fiver each, plus you give me a lesson in the basics of bridge. I want to understand why you think someone could commit a murder for the sake of a card game.'

'It would take hours just to cover the basics.'

'Then we'd best get started.'

'Right now?'

'Unless you want me to put in that complaint.'

He took out the new pack of cards. 'I can only give you an hour at the most, today, but it may be enough for what you might wish to know.' She closed the door.

Ten minutes later Witty peered in again through the glass panel. Seeing their heads were still bowed over the desk as they examined columns of playing cards, he gave a timid knock. Marcus called out, 'Come in.'

He opened the door but stayed beyond the threshold. 'I was hoping to have a quick word with Penny before I go. Something I wanted to clarify before morning.'

Penny and Marcus exchanged knowing glances. She responded, 'See me at my desk in two minutes.' As he slinked away, she spoke bitterly through clenched teeth. 'I'm going to make him pay more than just a tenner.'

She kept him waiting for five minutes. Finding him with his head hanging, she asked, deliberately lightly, 'You wanted to speak to me, Neil?'

He grimaced. 'Yes, Penny. I'm sorry; I lied to you. There's no such thing as dress-up Friday. I wanted you to come dressed up so I'd win a bet with Marcus.'

She asked calmly, 'How much was the bet?'

He replied hesitantly, 'A tenner.'

'Up it to fifty and I'll split the winnings.'

He stared at her. 'You're not serious?'

'Either that, or I put in a complaint against you.' He trudged away, his head hanging low.

Priestley heard Witty give a simple double knock and recognised his reluctance to enter. 'Spit it out, Neil; what's your problem?'

'That bet we had: what would you say if I said I'd like to increase it to fifty?'

He shook his head. 'I'd say DI Baker is a shrewd operator when she wants to be. You can tell her I won't go above twenty.'

A few minutes later, Baker entered Priestley's office and closed the door behind her. 'Only twenty?'

'It's enough.'

'All right. But when he hands over the money in the morning, I want you to give me half straight away, so he knows he's been played.'

'I have to say, I'm uncomfortable with the idea of taking his money; he has a pregnant wife to support.'

'It's a small price to pay.'

'Well, I'll be returning him my tenner.'

'Fine; I'll do the same, later. Now, let's get back to the cards. What do I bid if I've four hearts and fours spades of equal strength?'

'Show your hearts first, which gives your partner the chance to respond in spades without going up a level.'

'Right, then; I'll bid one heart.' She found herself smiling at the expression.

CHAPTER 6

Baker arrived just on time for the eight a.m. meeting, wearing a burgundy cotton dress with a bright flower-and-butterfly design. Priestley looked her up and down; though her pale pink lipstick was a poor match for her clothes, it seemed highly suitable for her skin colour. He realised she was holding her breath, waiting for him to speak. 'Well, Penny, you have scrubbed up nicely. But I don't get it; this means I've lost the bet.'

She wagged her finger at him. 'It takes two to make a bet. May this be a lesson to you, not to treat women as sex objects by gambling on how they're dressed.'

Priestley extracted two ten pound notes from his wallet and handed them to Witty, who immediately gave one back before placing the other on the desk in front of Baker, accompanied by an apology. 'I'm truly sorry, Penny; it was just meant to be a bit of fun.'

Baker accepted his words with a curt nod, before turning to Priestley. 'And here's yours; I can't keep it.'

Priestley tucked the two notes back into his wallet. 'Neil and I used to go to the pub after work most Fridays. Let's resurrect that tradition with all three of us today. Half past five and I'm buying.'

Baker shook her head. 'I can't do that; it's not me.'

Witty felt he should add his support. 'Yes, do come, Penny. And I'll be buying, as well.'

Priestley added, 'Out-of-hours bonding is a valuable team-building concept, so you ought to attend as part of your continuing professional development.'

Baker gave a playful smile. 'Well, if you put it like that, sir, how can I refuse?'

The business of the meeting was covered quickly, as the substantial effort put in by the team of detectives allocated to the case had yet to reap any reward.

Aden Liversedge arrived for his interview twenty minutes early. Witty checked the room was available; Priestley informed him they should start without delay. After reintroductions, Priestley began, 'Thank you for coming in today, Mr Liversedge, and I'm sorry for your loss.' He paused. 'When we last spoke, you mentioned a hand of cards that your mother had played against Mrs Sylvia Batter. I'm sure you'll be surprised to hear this, but it turns out that the police investigation has only found one motive for anyone wishing to kill her, and it's a rather slim one. That underhand play meant your mother didn't get the trophy she deserved; so, as it's the only motive we can find, we're working on the basis that she must have organised a contract killer.'

Liversedge stifled a laugh. 'You can't be serious. For one thing, my mum wouldn't have hurt a fly. And for another, even if she had wanted to get rid of Mrs Batter, she wouldn't have known where to begin, arranging for a hit man.'

Priestley had nodded in agreement throughout. 'I can't disagree with you, sir, but we have procedures to follow. If it's the only motive we can find, we have to operate on the basis that it is indeed the underlying reason. This means we'll have to publicise it, so that anyone with any information might come forward.'

'You mean like when someone makes unfounded sexual abuse allegations, and then you drag their name through the mud, even if they're completely innocent?

Haven't you people learned your lesson, yet? Well, at least mum won't be around to have to put up with all this nonsense.'

'True, but others who were close to her may suffer. Friends could end up believing she was responsible, even if she wasn't; people do often think there's no smoke without fire.'

'At least there's only me left from her family, and I would never believe that of her.'

'No, of course not... but other people might.'

'Who cares what stupid people think. But it isn't right that the police can just slander someone and get away with it.'

'Actually, if anything, it would be libel, because it would be in all the newspapers. The only way it could be stopped is if we found another suspect, but we just don't have anyone. If we could find out who carried out the killing, we'd then try to connect them to whoever paid them to do the job. It wouldn't be easy, though, if it was a professional; they hardly ever talk.'

Liversedge immediately asked, 'Do you not have any sort of description of the killer?'

Priestley shook his head. 'We are pursuing one line of inquiry, but I'm not optimistic. No, the best chance we'd normally have of a breakthrough is when the person who arranges a hit finds they've bitten off more than they can chew. The killer can be guaranteed to keep coming back to them to demand more money; then, when they've emptied their bank accounts, they kill them, so they can't squeal.' He thought a flicker of concern may have crossed Liversedge's face.

'Well, mum's dead now, so they couldn't pursue her even if they wanted to. Not that she had anything to do with it, of course.'

'You have to hope she hadn't, because you'd be next in line. If they can't get money off the person who put out the contract, they simply turn to the next-of-kin, which in this case is you. It's totally standard practice.' Priestley observed how Liversedge had pressed his lips tightly together. 'So, my advice to you is, if at any time some bad guy makes contact, you should come and see us immediately. Otherwise, you might find yourself wearing a concrete overcoat.'

Liversedge could barely conceal his contempt. 'But, as it had nothing to do with my mum, there isn't some bad guy looking for me.'

Priestley stood to terminate the interview; with no real evidence, he had achieved as much as he could. Now, if Liversedge had had anything to do with the killing, he may not sleep quite so easy in his bed.

Witty escorted Liversedge to reception and then met up with Priestley in his office. As he walked toward his usual chair by Priestley's desk, he gave him a puzzled stare. 'Squeal? Concrete overcoat? Isn't it overshoes, anyway? What was that all about?'

'Concrete galoshes might have been a neat touch, but too late now. I was living down to his expectations, so he wouldn't think I had the imagination to play him.'

'Do you think you may have got to him?'

Priestley sighed. 'I think there were some signs, but nowhere near enough for me to be confident. Anyway, that's as much as I can do on this case for now, so I'm getting back to my other work. I'll see you at half five.'

At five twenty Witty popped his head around the door of Priestley's office. 'Sorry, Marcus; I have to go home. Lily's suffering from morning sickness.'

Priestley immediately realised the consequences for himself. 'But it's the afternoon!'

'All right, it's afternoon sickness, but I still need to go home and look after her.'

'Can't someone else take care of her for a bit? What about her sister, Violet?'

Witty grinned. 'If I didn't know you better, I'd say you're displaying cowardice in the face of the enemy. Except, Penny isn't quite the enemy she was.'

'Well, if you're dipping out, you need to find me some more takers; tell them it's free beer. I'm not going on my own with her all dressed up; people might talk.'

At half past five, Penny knocked at Marcus's open door. 'Are you ready, then?'

He stood up and grabbed his coat. 'Just hang on a minute; there might be some more coming.'

Almost immediately, Lin rushed to the door and called over to him, 'I heard you're offering free beer.'

Penny, standing at her elbow in the doorway, spoke loudly enough for Marcus to hear. 'I'm starting to wonder if you have an alcohol problem, DC Plummer.'

Lin flushed scarlet. Marcus stepped in to rescue her. 'I'm sure she only drinks in the line of duty, or to be sociable.' He switched his gaze to Lin. 'We're off duty now, so you can call us Marcus and Penny.'

In the pub, Penny would only accept a half of a guest beer, as she would have to drive home later. Lin chose a different brew, and Marcus a third. Penny determinedly shut Lin out of the conversation. As Marcus looked at the three halves, he knew this was turning into the most awkward Friday wind-down he had ever experienced.

When Lin and Penny began fencing, he tuned out and quickly drank two-thirds of his beer, hoping they would finish theirs before the conversation turned too bitchy. He decided to call time when he heard Lin say, 'Your hair really suits you; did you cut it yourself?'

He drained his glass. 'Sorry, I have to go back; I forgot about some work I need to do before I leave. I'll put money behind the bar if you two ladies would like to let your hair down.' He glanced involuntarily at Penny's short crop. 'We must do this again sometime.'

Penny drained her glass. 'I forgot something as well; I'll walk back with you.'

Lin gulped her beer as quickly as she could manage. 'I'll get off home, then.' Marcus encouraged Penny to lead the way out, while he followed ahead of Lin so he could pass a silent apology to her. When he turned, she jabbed a finger toward him and then pointed at herself. He read her lips as she accompanied the conventional signal for a phone conversation with the word 'Now!'

He went to his office, intending to outstay Penny in the MIR. Lin called his mobile. He answered, 'Yes?'

'Yes nothing! I feel completely humiliated! Come and see me on your way home.' She terminated the call.

At six fifteen, Marcus decided he had had enough. Penny intercepted him as he walked to the main exit. 'I'm finished as well. Shall we go back to the pub?'

He looked at his watch with considered deliberation. 'It would have to be a quick one.'

Back in the pub, Penny asked Marcus to recommend a beer. He picked the one with the lowest alcohol level, and had the same. After they had taken their first sips, she held up her glass as though admiring the beer's colour or shine. 'Very nice. I should have asked you to choose last time; the other was a bit bitter.'

He thought the latest selection was a little bland,

lacking bite, and guessed she was trying her best to be agreeable. 'It's very pleasant.' On impulse, triggered by remembering the awkward incident that had led to them being there in the first place, he added, 'To match the company.' As he watched her face glow, he suspected he may have made a serious misjudgement.

She looked steadfastly at him. 'Do you mean that? Or are you always this nice to women?'

He quickly cast around for an escape route. 'Yes and yes. I'm sorry if I've embarrassed you.' The warmth of her smile warned him she may be misinterpreting, so he manoeuvred the conversation to her work. 'How would you say this first week has gone for you, Penny?'

She glanced around. 'Let's sit in the corner; I want to talk to you about something.'

Though he had no idea what she wished to discuss, he nevertheless felt uncomfortable. She settled into the padded bench seat behind a circular wooden table. He positioned a hard stool directly across from her. 'This is nice. So, what is it you'd like to chat about?'

She took a swig of beer and then carefully placed the glass at the exact centre of the nearest mat. 'When I came here I thought it was going to be my big chance to make a name for myself. It's my first time leading a murder investigation, which is why I didn't want you too closely involved as my supervisor. I know I was out of order. I owe you an apology.'

He felt relieved she was not there to complain. 'Think nothing of it; I knew you were just being keen.'

She gazed at him. 'Thank you, sir. Marcus. I now know I do need your guidance. HOLMES is up-to-date, and I've done everything by the book, but in the end this investigation is going nowhere. It's been nothing but negatives so far; searching local dustbins, checking fingerprints, interviewing local residents. That is, all except for the sighting of the old woman carrying a shopping bag. I checked, like you said I should, and it turned out to be a jute one from Waitrose. I know your reputation for seeing things that others don't, though I can't pretend to understand how you get your insights; but my boss reckons you're the best thing since sliced bread, and has told me I should ask you to give me as much direction as possible.'

He checked to see if she felt committed to the idea. 'What do *you* think, though? Do you wish me to give you direction? Doing things by the book, it would have to be recorded, so it would tend to take the shine off a successful outcome for you, further down the line.'

She continued to gaze at him. 'Unless something moves, there won't be a successful outcome. So, yes, I do want you to give me direction.'

He focused on his glass of beer in contemplation. When he turned back to her, she was still gazing at him. 'I'm happy to share my thoughts with you, but they don't amount to much. If the old woman wasn't really an old woman, he or she becomes the prime suspect. But let's assume it was an old woman. You've found no evidence of a car being parked nearby, so she probably didn't drive there. If someone dropped her off, you'd have to wonder why they didn't take her all the way to her destination. So let's imagine she came by bus. You need to look at all routes in the vicinity. Don't restrict yourself to those that pass close to a Waitrose; she may not have been out shopping. For each route, and bearing in mind the direction she was seen walking, calculate which houses would be closer to the stop she would have alighted at, compared to the next stop. People generally get off at the nearest stop to their destination, though they might get off at a more distant one if it enables them to avoid having to walk uphill. Once you have your full set of properties, ask at every one of them if they saw the old woman, or if they had any visitors within an hour either side of the time she might have been passing by. That could generate a mass of movement data; if so, put in a formal request for Berry, I mean Tony Beresford, to process it.'

'He's a specialist in that sort of thing, is he?'

'He's a very smart guy; if he isn't already an expert, he will be by the time he's finished.'

'Right. Well, thank you, Marcus; that's really helped me to scope the house-to-house more clearly.'

'Hang on; we're not done yet. There's the possibility the woman set off from home. Interview the man who saw her; see if he had any impression of how quickly and easily she was walking. If she was just hobbling along, you'd have to think, not very far. But if she was striding out, obviously the potential distance increases.'

'That could include a lot more properties.'

'Indeed it could. You just have to keep expanding the search parameters until you reach the appropriate confidence level; again, ask Tony for guidance. He'll no doubt talk about standard deviations, but pin him down and get him to define the actual properties that should be included in the first, second and third waves. If nothing turns up, we'd have to make a judgement call together on what level of search to stop at.'

'Well, that gives me something to go on, as far as the old woman is concerned. What about your bridge angle? Do you think you're getting anywhere with it?'

He instinctively prepared to pick up his glass to give him time to think about his response. Seeing his beer had somehow disappeared, he thought of evaporation as the cause, before recognising his mind was in danger of shooting off at a tangent. 'I still have a feeling it may be connected, but there's nothing we can do to progress it, short of putting the son under surveillance.'

'Should we do that, then?'

'I think we'd just be wasting resources, even if he was involved. We could spend months watching him without discovering anything, if the killing was a one-off. Everyone knows of high-profile investigations that have squandered millions on wild-goose chases, but in our case there's no family-driven media pressure that would distort sound policing judgement. Besides, what exactly would we be looking for?'

Her head bowed dispiritedly. 'So there's no point.'

He bent low at an angle to catch her eye. 'Chin up, Penny! You can always put in a request for electronic surveillance. We have his work mobile number. Unless he uses that for everything, he'll also have a personal mobile. Then there's e-mail traffic we can intercept, unless he's using a strong encryption protocol. It may pay dividends eventually, if he really is involved.' As she looked up at him, he saw her smile spread quickly from her mouth to her eyes until it encompassed her entire face. He thought it could have been a danger signal, had it not been emanating from someone with her man-hating reputation.

She responded enthusiastically, 'I'll go back to the office and see about it right now.'

'Right now? Don't you have a home to go to?' He saw her intense frown and guessed she was concerned he would think she was all work and no play.

She answered hesitantly, 'I live in a one-bedroom flat. It's quiet, great soundproofing. My bedroom has a really nice view. I could show you, if you feel like coming back with me.'

He felt a sinking feeling as he realised she may not be quite the ice maiden he had been led to believe. 'Maybe another time, Penny. I have to be going home now; my wife and children will be expecting me.' He automatically re-drained his glass as he stood up.

Back at the car park she gave him a brief goodbye and headed into the station.

As he climbed into his car, he reflected on how he had been anticipating some awkwardness with her at the pub, but knew it was nothing like the type he had experienced. He decided her invitation had probably been intended innocently, and yet he felt pleased with himself for having displayed his determination to keep to the straight and narrow of happy family life.

Remembering he would need to appease Lin before returning home, he acknowledged he may be imperfect when measured against British standards, but argued he should be assessed in accordance with French attitudes; having just the one mistress would then be classed as positively conventional.

CHAPTER 7

Over several weeks DI Baker pursued the unrewarding task of eliminating everyone who appeared on the radar for any reason. Simply living within walking distance of the crime scene was enough to warrant a background check. At five thirty on the fifth Friday she wandered into Priestley's office and flopped down into a chair. 'Take me to the pub, Marcus.'

Their working relationship had softened, yet he was still surprised to hear the familiar way she made her plea. 'Good idea; I'll round up a few more.'

She looked him in the eye. 'No, don't. Make it just the two of us. I won't bite you.'

He heard the concern underlying his light laugh. 'Sure. Or would you rather have a chat here?'

She closed the door. 'The investigation has ground to a halt. If it winds down now, I'll have failed. What am I supposed to do?'

'You're already doing it, Penny: you've recognised the lack of viable lines of inquiry. We need to release resources for reallocation; there's no point in having a large team of detectives scratching around looking for something to do. Obviously we won't close the file; it'll just be put on the shelf waiting for a cold case review, sometime in the distant future.'

'And I'll have failed my first murder case.'

He suspected her principal feeling was akin to the dispassionate professional disappointment associated with accepting defeat at solving a puzzle, rather than the torment of failing to obtain justice for a victim. Perhaps hers was a more balanced view than his own, where the anguish that accompanied the thought of a criminal evading retribution had often pressed him to push the boundaries of PACE. As he reflected on how she was handling the situation, his thoughts moved tangentially to the various methods people employed for coping with disappointment. He felt embarrassed as he imagined the two of them taking intimate comfort together for their shared failure, and hurriedly brought his mind back to the principal subject of their meeting.

She had watched and waited for a response, trying to read his mind. 'Tell me what you're thinking, Marcus.'

The more he told himself he mustn't blush, the more he found himself reddening. 'The stats tell us we have to be prepared to fail sometimes. This just happens to be your first, but it's very unlikely to be your last.'

'How did you feel about your first failure?'

'Well, of course I didn't like it. A toe-rag with ears like Mr Spock wasn't picked out in an identity parade, because his solicitor was allowed to make them all wear hats pulled right down. The law can be so stupid.'

'And he got away with murder?'

'No, it was just a minor offence. And we picked him up again within a week, so he didn't escape justice for long.'

'But what about when it's a murder case?'

'I haven't had a failure, yet; touch wood.'

'What about other major offences?' She interpreted his glance at the floor. 'Are you saying you've never failed?'

'Well, this is my case as much as it's yours, so I'd have to say it counts as my first failure, just like you;

but it's the luck of the draw. Anyone can take on a case they can't solve; you've simply started with one.'

She stared at him. 'Doesn't it bother you that you're losing your perfect record for solving major crimes?'

He shrugged. 'What the law sees as a minor offence can be a life-changing event for a victim, so it's fairly arbitrary to define major and minor crimes the way we do. And of course I've had plenty of failures on what we class as minor crime.'

'But no major crime; how interesting. Have you ever done anything outside the rules to engineer a result?'

'Are you asking me if I've ever rigged evidence?'

'Well, have you?'

'I'm shocked you would even ask me that question.'

'So how come you've a perfect record?'

He shook his head. 'We really shouldn't be having this conversation.'

'Are you saying you always abide by the Police and Criminal Evidence Act? Do you believe it's perfect and we should never try to get around the rules?'

'We need to stay within the rules, even if we believe they're badly flawed.'

'So you uphold the law even if you don't believe it's correct. I hope you don't mind, Marcus, but I did some research on you and found a whiff of suspicion you didn't even believe in the Geneva Convention in your army days.'

'I refer you to my earlier answer, to use a legalistic phrase. The Geneva Convention is badly flawed, but I still believe we should try our best to uphold it. At least, unless we're certain we won't ever be found out, and we're sure we'll never feel an overwhelming need to reveal the details to anyone.'

She searched his eyes for any underlying meaning, until she realised how long she had been gazing at him. 'Don't tell me what you've done in the past; I'm sure you wouldn't want to trust anyone with your secrets, and I certainly wouldn't want to be burdened by them. So, just tell me what's wrong with the Convention.'

He pressed himself back into his chair, trying to appear relaxed. 'According to the Geneva Convention, it isn't permissible to kill enemy combatants once they are captured. But if you're standing over a boy who is so badly wounded he has absolutely no chance of living more than a few minutes, and those minutes will be spent in the most excruciating pain as he looks at his bowels spilling out of him, how can anyone with an ounce of humanity not put the boy out of his misery? But to do so is to go against the Geneva Convention. I say "boy", but the same would apply to any human being. And yet, if it were an animal suffering such pain, any right-minded person would see it as their duty to terminate such a terrible, hopeless existence.'

'There must be a reason for the Convention saying you can't kill people even under those circumstances.'

'Must there? How often do we hear on the news that something is against international law? Who are the people that come up with these laws?'

'Well, lawyers, I assume; and maybe politicians.'

'And lawyers and politicians are, of course, the most trustworthy and honourable people around! The reality is that there are different perspectives on what should, and what should not, constitute international law, and many of the people involved in framing the law have their own personal agendas.'

'Well, I only know about our own laws, those of the

United Kingdom. So, what's wrong with PACE, then?'

'Imagine you're investigating a current abduction, and a bloke you're interviewing suddenly admits he murdered a different woman in the past. You take him to the countryside, where he leads you to where the body was buried. Then you ask him if he knows about the recent abductee. At that point you're hoping she's still alive, so you just want him to tell you what he knows. You press him on it, out there in the open, and he tells you he killed her and buried her body nearby, and even takes you to the exact spot. Don't go thinking you did well and your career will benefit; you're more likely to find yourself dismissed for failing to question him back at the station under caution.' He knew she was willing him to continue, but he decided to call a halt for fear of undermining her belief in PACE.

She broke the silence. 'Hypothetically, how would you go about breaking this case, if you didn't mind bending the rules a bit?'

He took her opening word at face value. 'If it had nothing to do with Aden Liversedge, I'd say there's no point in looking at bending the rules. But if he knows something about it, then there might be a way to make him react. We haven't publicised the theory that the murder may have been carried out by an old woman, to avoid spurious sightings swamping the investigation. If we brought him in and told him about it, we could see his reaction. Even if he failed to react to the revelation, we could still take it a step further. We'd get a woman to telephone him, though we'd have to cancel the phone tap first so it wasn't recorded; voice print recognition can still work even if they use a muffling device.'

'If he knew the murderer, presumably he'd know her

voice, and would just expect her to call him without distorting the sound. So, wouldn't that stop any other woman from fooling him that they did it?'

'You're right; that's why the call wouldn't be from the murderess, but only from someone with knowledge of the murder. If a man was connected to the killing, it might be expected that he would have committed the murder himself. Such an attitude may technically be sexist, but let's hope women don't strive for equality in that area of behaviour. So, if a woman committed the offence, it would be far more credible for another woman to make the call, on the assumption that no man was involved.'

She gave a wry smile. 'It isn't often I agree with any form of sexism, but I guess I have to concede that one.'

He nodded. 'If the hypothetical woman on the phone were to demand money with menaces, he may then ask for our protection. That might indicate his innocence, but not necessarily. If he failed to react, a hypothetical police officer could harass him, perhaps by stalking him or damaging his car. If the intimidation were ratcheted up, the pressure may reach a critical point where he snaps and does something that provides an insight into his involvement. Depending on his behaviour, the officer could then use the new evidence and charge the suspect with the offence. But here's the problem: if that evidence wasn't obtained according to PACE, it would be inadmissible in court.'

Though she recognised he was about to continue, she interrupted him excitedly. 'But we could use what we then know to restart the inquiry, and even push him to confess, staying within the rules from then onwards.'

He responded calmly, 'Don't forget we're speaking

hypothetically, Penny.' Seeing she was holding a smile, he continued with a frown. 'And even a confession isn't enough without supporting forensic evidence, which is something we're lacking.'

'If there was a payment involved, maybe we… maybe the hypothetical officers could trace the money. Once the connection is made to the perpetrator, they could then begin the search for an evidential trail. It isn't as though anyone can buy sodium cyanide powder over the counter, which is what we think the killer used in a puffer spray. So we could end up not only finding the contract killer but also any conspirators. First, we need to apply pressure on Liversedge. Do you intend to interview him yourself?'

He stared at her. 'Penny, this is entirely hypothetical. But having said that, the first step of pressuring him into revealing information regarding the identity of the killer, that *would* be within the rules, so I'll go ahead and call him in for interview. If he reacts immediately, we may be able to make progress. Otherwise, we're left hoping for a lucky break.'

She stood up. 'Let's the two of us interview him on Monday; that's something for me to look forward to, this weekend.'

He guessed her days were quite empty away from work, but recognised the dangers of asking a single woman about her private life. Nevertheless, he thought he should do something to break the monotony of her existence. 'Now let's go to the pub, shall we?'

Her response was immediate and emphatic. 'Yes. And don't you still owe me? You can take me for a bite to eat, as well. I was thinking fish and chips.'

In the pub, she scanned the pumps and noticed one

that was decorated with a golden jar. 'What about this?'

'It's very good; very mellifluous.'

'You mean it *sounds* nice?'

'I mean it's made with honey and has a good flow.' As she laughed freely, he was pleased she appreciated his linguistic humour.

She tapped the counter. 'I'll have a pint.'

'It's high alcohol; you're driving, aren't you?'

'You can give me a lift to the chip shop, can't you?'

'Are you serious about fish and chips?'

'Yes, and I want to eat them out of a newspaper.'

Priestley chose a half of the same beer. He thought she seemed almost a different person as she chatted about her childhood in Nottingham.

She continued blithely, 'I was brought up in Basford. Everyone from Nottingham pronounces it Base-f'd, but not everyone knows it's because the Normans spoke with a lisp. I was told there was a woman called Ann Beresford who transferred ownership of a large plot of land, and the person doing the conveyancing must have misheard, which is why they misspelled her surname. So that's how the name Basford came into existence.'

He smiled as he recalled something from his own childhood. 'I can remember when I first heard about Normans lisping. When I was a boy I watched a film, *Ivanhoe*, which was loosely based on Sir Walter Scott's novel. The eponymous hero is in the lists at Ashby, and his father says something like, "No lisping Norman will unseat my son." I read the book after that, but I don't recall it mentioning lisping.'

'Is that Ashby-de-la-Zouch?'

'The very same. Each knight jousted for the honour of the lady who had tied her favour to his lance.'

She leaned in closely, despite there being no one within hearing distance. 'I can imagine you as a knight in shining armour. I'd be delighted to give your lance my favour.'

He drew his head away and responded normally, to suggest he would not allow himself to be drawn into an intimate and suggestive conversation. 'Shall we go for those fish and chips, now?'

As she climbed into the passenger seat of his car, she leaned over and checked the petrol gauge. 'Nearly full.'

'I wouldn't like to be in a car chase and find I'm low on gas.' He knew his attempt at a Bronx accent had been a complete failure, and yet she had laughed as though it were the funniest thing she had ever heard. 'So, where's the chip shop.'

'Head for Nottingham and I'll give you directions.'

'Are you serious?'

'Yes, it's near my home. They're ever so good.'

Knowing he had been played, he put the car into gear and set off in silence.

She opened the CD rack. 'You're into opera, then.'

'I cannot deny it; guilty as charged.' He knew he was hearing more laughter from her today than he had heard in the whole of the previous month.

'May I?' Hearing his "uh-huh", she slid in a CD of Puccini tenor arias. 'Do you normally sing along?'

'No, I don't; well, not very often.'

'Because it would put you off your driving?'

'Because they all go too high for me.'

As the incipit sombre notes of a clarinet began the first track, *E lucevan le stelle*, Priestley's chest swelled in anticipation, though he knew he would remain silent on this occasion. She saw how his jaw had set itself.

The CD was still playing as they approached their destination. She stopped it at the end of a track and ejected it. 'We're nearly at my flat. I need to stop off for a few minutes anyway, so come inside and sing some for me.' She placed the disc in its case.

'No, I can't. Really I can't.'

Taking the refusal as limited to singing rather than coming into her flat, she instructed him exactly where to park, before stepping out of the car and leading the way, CD in hand. He reluctantly followed her, steeling himself for the awkwardness he now believed was inevitable.

Within the converted nineteenth century villa, at the top of two flights of stairs, she opened her door and stepped inside. He stayed at the entrance, waiting there as though she really would be only a moment. After turning on the heating, she inserted the CD into her stereo, before pausing it. 'Come inside. I'd really like to hear you sing that first track.'

'You wouldn't say that if you heard how I murder it. Just play it while you're getting yourself ready for the chip shop. And don't overdress; I'm fairly certain they won't be expecting formal wear.' She giggled freely.

While he listened to the CD, she used the bathroom and then went to her bedroom. By the time she stepped out, the subsequent track was about to finish. Seeing she was now wearing the dress that had lost him his bet, he commented, 'Must be a posh chip shop.'

She responded hesitantly, 'We could try somewhere else, now I'm more presentable. There's an Indian place just a short walk from here.'

He studied his watch. 'We could do that some other time, maybe, but I have to be getting back soon.' He saw her bitter disappointment burn through her faltering smile. 'But I've time for fish and chips in a newspaper.'

They walked to the chip shop that advertised itself well in advance with an unmistakable smell. As she prattled on about the surrounding area, he thought she seemed excited or nervous. An obese man scooped their food into Styrofoam trays, placed newspapers under them and left them open for eating in the streets.

Marcus wolfed down his food, estimating he would have just enough time to finish before they reached her apartment building. She still had plenty of hers left as they approached the door. To avoid being impolite, he followed her inside and up the stairs. She nodded at the stereo. 'Put the CD on. I'll finish this in the kitchen.'

He held up his hands. 'I'd better give them a wash, first.' She pointed him toward the bathroom, though he already knew the way. By the time he returned, she was sitting on the settee with the stereo already playing. He suspected she had binned the remainder of her food. 'If you'd like to listen to the whole CD, I could leave it with you over the weekend. But how are you intending to get to work? Your car's still at the station.'

'I can get a lift in on Monday, no problem; and I've no plans for this weekend that need a car. But I wanted to talk to you about the case. Couldn't you stay a bit?'

He checked his watch. 'Sorry, I have to be going. If I'd known you wanted to discuss work away from the office, we could have talked while I drove, instead of listening to the music.'

'That's my fault; I was the one who put the CD on. I'll come back with you so we can talk on the way.'

In the car, she placed the CD back inside the rack. 'I've heard you're a really good singer. I would like to hear you, sometime. Maybe the next time you're at my flat you can give me a performance. And you wouldn't need to worry about neighbours hearing us. I mean *you*. The soundproofing is really good; the only noise that gets through is stiletto heels on the stairs.'

He sighed. 'I wish I were even half as good as you seem to think I am. Anyway, what was it you wanted to talk to me about?'

She screwed up her face as though debating with herself. 'Let's put it off until I have something more definite to say. Come to my flat again next week, after hours, so we can have a confidential discussion. And I'll make sure I show you the view from my bedroom this time; I hope you'll be impressed with it.'

'Is it important it's outside normal hours?'

'It is; otherwise people might get suspicious.'

'Does it really have to be away from the station?'

'Trust me, Marcus, we need to be away from prying eyes and ears.' To terminate the discussion, she took out the Puccini CD again and slid it into the machine.

The music was still playing when they reached the car park. She touched the pause button. 'I know what you want from me, and I'm very willing to do it. I'm sure you'll be satisfied.' She climbed out of the car.

He set off with a brief wave. As he drove away, he wondered why she had been so ambiguous. If she was offering sex, he hoped she would keep it vague, as that would avoid the awkwardness of his openly declining.

CHAPTER 8

Baker and Witty arrived together at Priestley's office for the early Monday morning meeting. After the usual preliminaries, Priestley informed Witty, 'Penny and I will be interviewing Aden Liversedge as soon as he's available. We'll be acting as though he isn't a suspect. I'll let him in on the sighting of the old woman. We'll see how he reacts when we…'

Baker interrupted him. 'Actually, Marcus, I'd rather observe him on the monitor while you and Neil do the interviewing.'

Knowing her keenness for being involved, Priestley felt surprised. He wondered if it stemmed from his declining to spend time with her at home last Friday. 'Are you certain, Penny? I'm sure we could perform well together.' He thought her smile seemed genuine, suggesting she had not developed a sudden aversion for working closely with him.

'You and Neil have met him before, so he may not be on his guard as much with the two of you. Besides, it could be useful in the future if he can't recognise me, depending on how things progress.'

Priestley accepted the first argument, though thought the second a little puzzling. Nevertheless, he preferred the idea of interviewing with Witty, who had always instinctively known when to speak and when to remain silent. 'All right. Neil, give him a call after this meeting and get him in as soon as possible, so he doesn't have time to think about why we wish to see him.'

Priestley turned to Baker. 'Do you have a plan for winding down the investigation? Unless something happens with Liversedge that moves us forward, there's not much more to be worked on.'

She picked up a binder. 'I checked for flavour of the month with the College of Policing. I was thinking I could send people on training courses while they're awaiting redeployment. There are national standards being implemented on the use of Stop and Search, but that's more for frontline officers. I enquired about late cancellations on any other sessions at local colleges. South Yorkshire are running a two-day Public Order training course, starting tomorrow; there are three spare places, so I'll see if any of the team could usefully attend. Other than that, everyone's up for grabs. We could do with another murder, really.'

Priestley grinned at her. 'Your words are capable of misinterpretation, DI Baker.'

She put on a show of reflecting, holding an index finger to her chin. 'I see what you mean.'

Priestley considered how much she had mellowed since their first meeting; even her hair now looked less severe, having not been cut for over a month. 'I'll leave the wind-down in your capable hands.' Baker took the hint and left.

Priestley explained to Witty how he intended to start the interview, and then invited him to suggest what possible reactions Liversedge might have. They talked through various scenarios until both felt fully prepared.

Witty attended the nine o'clock team meeting and heard several dispirited detectives give their progress reports. Straight after, he called Liversedge and asked him to come at once to the station. He heard a note of concern in his voice as he responded, 'Why do you want to see me straight away? What's it about? Can't you tell me over the phone?'

Witty kept to the plan. 'There's something important I'm not permitted to disclose to you over the telephone. Can you get over here straight away under you own steam, or should I send a police car to pick you up?'

'I'll drive straight over.'

Witty went to Priestley's office to inform him in person. 'I think Liversedge may be panicking. Let's hope he doesn't crash his car on the way.'

Priestley sighed. 'Yes, otherwise we'll be blamed for causing the accident; like when some boy racer wraps a stolen car around a lamp-post because he heard a siren.'

'If he sticks to the speed limits he should be here a bit after ten. Shall I wait for him in reception, to whisk him through without time to settle?'

'Yes, good idea.'

At nine fifty-six Priestley took Witty's call and went to the interview room. He opened the outward-swinging door and found the two silently facing each other across the screwed-down metal table. As he sat next to Witty, he began in an apologetic tone, 'Mr Liversedge, I know you previously stated you couldn't believe your mother had anything to do with the murder of Mrs Batter, but the evidence is starting to mount against her.'

Liversedge shook his head dismissively. 'What type of evidence? Only circumstantial, I'll bet.'

Priestley assumed he had picked up the term from television or films without fully understanding it, so felt no compulsion to answer directly. 'I'm going to have to reveal some information to you that we have obtained in the pursuance of our enquiries, but I must insist on you keeping it to yourself. Do I have your agreement?'

Liversedge nodded. 'Sure.' Priestley stared at him, waiting for him to repeat his acceptance. 'I promise.' Priestley smiled inwardly at his earnestness.

'The only suspect for the actual killing is a woman of a similar age to your mother, seen proceeding in a south-easterly direction on foot in the vicinity of the deceased's dwelling, holding a *non-see-through* bag, the contents of which are currently unknown to the police.' Priestley had raised his eyebrows to suggest deep significance behind the bag being non-transparent. 'We are conducting the investigation on the basis that the killer was a close friend of your mother, or was in some way in thrall to her.'

Liversedge jerked his head. 'You what?'

Witty offered, helpfully, 'Perhaps the woman owed her money, or maybe she was being blackmailed. Was your mother a loan-shark? Or did she ever suddenly come into large sums of money?'

Liversedge pushed his chair back and stood up. 'This is bullshit! My mother didn't do murder, money-lending or blackmail. You people are off your trolleys.'

'I know this must come as a huge shock to you, sir. Could I get you a glass of water?'

Liversedge released a deep sigh. 'I've never heard such stupidity.'

Priestley spoke soothingly, hoping to have the same anger-generating effect that beat officers achieve by demanding someone should calm themselves when they are already calm. 'Please sit down, sir; I hope it won't be necessary to restrain you.'

Liversedge looked incredulously at Priestley, but nevertheless returned to his seat. 'I'm sat down, but I don't know what for. This is a complete waste of time.'

'You may think that, sir, but who knows where it might lead. My reason for wishing to speak to you is that we would like you to help us with our enquiries. You may be the only person who knows the elderly ladies who were friends of your mother, aside from those at the bridge club where she used to play. If the killer were simply a friend, it could have been someone she had known for a long time, perhaps all the way back to her schooldays. I would like you to cast your mind back to all the ladies she ever met, that you're aware of, and provide us with a list. We will then work through *your* list and eliminate them from *our* list of possible suspects. If all goes according to plan, only one name should remain.'

Liversedge looked at Priestley as though he were some sort of idiot. 'Fine, I'll do that. But I know for a fact you're looking in the wrong place.'

Priestley avoided reacting to the response, knowing it may simply have been a loose expression, but hoping otherwise. He stood and offered a handshake. 'Believe me, sir, I do understand how distressing this must be for you, but we have to go where the trail leads us. I'll ask you to provide the information in due course to Sergeant Whittington. Once you have presented your initial list, do please feel free to add to it at any time, if you remember anyone else. Thank you for your help.'

After escorting Liversedge back to reception, Witty headed for Priestley's office, where he found him and Baker already seated. 'Have I missed anything?'

Priestley responded, 'No, we were waiting for you, so we can share our first thoughts.' He turned to Baker. 'What were your impressions of the interview? Did you spot anything we didn't seem to have noticed?'

She kept her face expressionless, though inwardly pleased to have been given the opportunity to be the first to claim observations, knowing that the others may have had the same thoughts. 'He seemed sincere when saying his mother was nothing like you had suggested, which of course he will have been. When you wound him up, he could have become very angry, but instead he still had himself under control. Pushing the chair back and standing up was really quite a mild reaction. So, either he doesn't *do* angry, or he was making sure he didn't let anything slip inadvertently. I'd say he's still a suspect, based on what I've just seen.'

Priestley nodded in agreement. 'Thank you, Penny; that was very helpful. And you, Neil?'

'I agree with Penny. I would just add, though, that he stated he knew for a *fact* that his mother wasn't involved. Facts and logic are supposed to go together, aren't they? And he works in computers. So maybe, for him, a fact really is a fact. That would imply he knows something about who's actually behind the murder.'

Priestley held in check the smile he would have given for what he believed to be the key observation, so that Baker would not feel disappointed with her own testimony. 'He may have meant it literally, or it could simply have been a loose figure of speech. But we're all in agreement: he's still a person of interest.'

Knowing she had missed a trick, Baker rushed in with another observation. 'He came to see us quickly enough, didn't he? That could mean he's keen to know what we're doing because he's involved.'

Priestley nodded. 'And what *are* we doing, Penny?'

She smiled at him. 'Leave it to me.' As she began to

stand, she realised it was not her place to terminate the discussion.

Priestley stood up, confirming the meeting was over. 'Keep me informed of developments.' After they had left, he gazed out of the window. The sun shining its light down the Hope Valley gave him hope there would be light at the end of the tunnel.

In the late afternoon, Baker knocked at Priestley's door. Having been sitting at his computer for hours in a fixed position, he stood to relieve his stiff joints. 'Come in, Penny; how's it going?'

Interpreting his rising as an acknowledgement of her womanhood, she felt a warm glow of pleasure. 'That after-hours meeting I asked for, we should have it now.'

'You need to give me a clue as to what it's about.'

She went to the door and checked outside before closing it. 'I bent the rules a bit, but I'd rather not talk about in the office. I want to go somewhere we can't be overheard.'

Wishing to avoid another invitation to her home, he grabbed his coat off the stand in the corner. 'Let's take a stroll down the valley.'

As they sauntered along a path, sporadic ramblers forced her to remain silent. Finally, she accepted they were all too distant to overhear. 'I phoned Liversedge.'

'To see if he's compiled a list, yet?'

'No; to put the frighteners on him.'

He stopped and touched her on the shoulder so she also would halt. 'Tell me what you said. Exactly!'

She closed her eyes for a moment. 'I said, "I know all about the murder of Sylvia Batter, and I want paying to keep my trap shut." Or something like that.'

Shocked, he asked simply, 'And?'

'He said, "But that's not right." He didn't say, "I don't know what you're talking about." He didn't say, "It was nothing to do with me." He simply said, "That's not right." And then he put the phone down. What do you think of that?'

'I think you've done more than *bend* the rules.'

'Yes, but what do you think he meant?'

'I agree his response was rather strange, but it's also quite ambiguous, as was what you said.'

'I had to phrase it in a way that wouldn't be wrong if either he *or* his mother was behind it.'

'And you did that very well. But if you were hoping for a much clearer reaction, I think you might have had to take a punt on him being responsible, rather than his mother, and make a more specific threat.'

She grasped his arm. 'So, should I try again?'

'I really wouldn't like to say. Let's sleep on it.'

She gripped his arm tighter and widened her eyes. 'Good idea; let's do that.'

Eschewing the idea that she had just invited him to sleep with her, he turned to retrace his steps, forcing her to release her hold. More hikers were approaching, so he began a discourse on the geology of the area as though that were the reason for their presence.

When they entered the car park, Lin stepped out of the shadows and spoke to Priestley. 'Been enjoying the scenery? I was looking for you. I know it's getting late, but I need to discuss something with you, urgently.'

Baker snapped at her, 'Don't you ever address him as "sir"? We're not in the pub now, DC Plummer.'

He turned to Baker. 'I'd better deal with whatever this is; I'll see you tomorrow.'

She looked intently at him. 'I don't mind waiting

until you've finished with DC Plummer, *sir*.'

He had no wish to support her over the point she was making; he was more concerned about the extent to which he might have to support her earlier action. 'I wouldn't want you to be hanging around, Penny; you just get off. We'll talk some more, tomorrow.'

Through clenched teeth she gave Priestley a terse 'Bye.' Studiously ignoring Plummer, she reluctantly trudged off toward her car.

Lin went with Marcus to his office and closed the door behind them. 'You'll have to tell me what you were talking about. And why have you never taken me for a walk down the valley?'

He sighed heavily. 'I don't wish to keep secrets from you, Lin, but this is one you really don't want to know.'

She read the concern etched on his face. 'Oh, all right, I believe you. I'm going home now; you set off in ten minutes. All right?'

'Yes, sure. Being with you always makes me forget my troubles.'

'I hope there's more to us than that, Marcus.'

'Sorry, of course there is. And I will take you for a walk down the valley, sometime; it's one of the best views in the country, if you don't look at the cement works.'

CHAPTER 9

During the Tuesday morning meeting Priestley made no mention of the threatening phone call, to avoid Witty being drawn into the conspiracy or perhaps feeling obligated to report the incident, which would have led to an investigation by Professional Standards that could have ended Baker's career.

At the end of the meeting, Priestley expected Baker to request a one-to-one, but instead she hurried away without a backward glance.

After lunch, Priestley went looking for Baker to give her the opportunity to express any further thoughts she may have had regarding the appropriateness of making threatening phone calls. On learning she had left the office and turned off her mobile, he hoped she was not sitting sulking somewhere. Keeping the concern from his voice, he left her a simple message asking for her to phone him.

Shortly after four o'clock he took a call from Baker. 'Are you free to leave the office right now?'

'Yes, if necessary.'

'I need picking up, but don't tell anyone.' She gave directions to a point by a path on a quiet stretch of road flanked by woodland. 'Switch your satnav off, and your phones, before you come.' He left immediately.

As he approached the specified place, he scanned the area for any sign of her. Seeing no one, he parked up, intending to begin a search. Suddenly, a slight figure in blue jeans, trainers, a black hoodie and a baseball cap appeared from behind a tree. Recognising Baker as she limped toward the car, he reached over and opened the front passenger door.

She eased herself into the seat and implored him, 'Please take me home.' As she peeled off a pair of clean woollen gloves, latex ones were revealed underneath.

He looked her in the eye. 'How bad is your injury?'

She turned away. 'Not bad.'

'Do I need to take you to the hospital?'

'Don't you want to know what happened?'

'Of course, but do you need a doctor?'

'No, you'll have to take care of me.'

'Just what have you been up to?'

'I crashed a van.'

'Where? I didn't see one.'

'Outside Aden Liversedge's house.'

'That's a good mile away.'

'Yes; I walked. I tried not to show I was limping.'

He started the engine. 'Tell me all about it. Begin at the beginning.'

'I'll explain back at my flat; right now I just want to sit quietly. Put your Puccini on.'

He inserted the disk and set off. She kept her hood up and her cap on. He noticed she had closed her eyes.

They travelled without speaking, the singing playing quietly. As he was parking close to her flat, he thought she was sleeping.

She opened her eyes when he turned off the engine. 'I'm not tired. I don't know why I fell asleep.'

'It could be a reaction to stress. Do you need help getting out?'

'No, I'll be fine.'

On the stairs, she held onto him as she winced at

every alternate tread. Inside the flat, she carefully sat herself down on the settee and then pulled off her jeans. 'Come and take a look. How bad is it?'

One concern had been replaced by another when she started to remove her clothing, before he realised her only intention was to have her injury checked by him. Her slender legs had taut muscles and rather more hair than he had anticipated; he found himself comparing them with Helen's and Lin's, who both kept theirs silky smooth. 'I see you've picked up a good bruise.'

She took his hand and pressed it against her thigh. 'Just check there are no bones broken.'

He touched her where she had indicated, and then ran his hand up and down a few times with increasing pressure to test her pain level. 'I'm sure it's just your muscles that have taken a knock. Are you going to tell me what you've been getting up to?'

She patted the settee next to her, inviting him to sit. 'This morning I made another phone call to Liversedge. I told him I wanted fifty k. He said, "Or else?" So I said, "You'll find out if you don't pay up." Then he put the phone down on me again.'

He considered taking her to task, but she seemed so fragile and vulnerable as she sat quietly in her plain white knickers that he decided to remain silent.

She turned her head to face him directly. 'You know I've been assigning officers to tasks on a temporary basis; well, one of the things was vehicular theft. When a report came in of a stolen transit van being found, I picked up the job and allocated it to someone who isn't around today. Then I went out and bought a new set of clothes and got changed into them. After that, I drove to a residential road about half a mile from the van, and parked up. I walked to the van and found the door was already unlocked, as I expected; thieves don't normally lock up after themselves. Then, I hotwired it; there were none of the fancy electronic features you get on newer vehicles, so it was pretty easy. I drove to Liversedge's house and saw his car was parked on the road outside, so I crashed into it on purpose, though I didn't intend to use quite so much force. I wanted it to look realistic, only I overdid it. I was going to drive away after, but the side just crumpled up, so I had to get out and leg it.'

Though she had fallen silent, he was reluctant to fill the void. Finally, accepting she was waiting for him to speak, he asked, 'Why are you doing these things?'

She looked earnestly into his eyes and responded quietly, 'Because it's what you want me to do.'

He felt shocked by her words, and yet knew she meant them. 'What makes you think it's what *I* want?'

'You explained it all; don't you remember? I know you said we were speaking hypothetically, but it was obvious what you really meant.'

He shook his head. 'I meant what I said. We can't go threatening the public and crashing into cars; we're supposed to uphold the law, not go breaking it. You've imagined it was what in the army we called "implied tasking", but it wasn't.' He thought she was about to cry, but instead she twisted around and began to beat on his chest with the sides of her fists. The blows seemed so pitifully weak, he allowed her to burn herself out. When they had subsided, he gently restrained her by the wrists. 'You really should talk to me about such things and not go making assumptions.'

'So you were just setting me up, then. Is that how you've solved other cases? Huh? Get someone else to do the dirty work and then you take the credit?'

'No. Honestly, nothing like this has ever happened before.'

Ignoring his denial, she continued with increasing vehemence, 'That explains why you've been so nice to me; no one is nice to me without a reason.' Though he could only remember treating her normally, and even recalled being severe with her at the outset, he could see her sincerity blazing through. 'And I thought it was because you liked me; liked me a lot.' Her elfin face screwed up and she began to cry bitter tears. 'I really thought you fancied me. God, I'm stupid! Why would someone like you ever give someone like me a second glance. I should have known it would end like this.'

He tried to understand how their interactions could reasonably have led her to draw such conclusions, but knew instinctively that logic had little to do with her thought processes in the matter. Feeling guilty for his part in the drama, he released her wrists and drew her close to him. 'Of course I like you, Penny. Of course I fancy you, as much as I'm allowed, being a happily married man; but I really didn't think I'd let it show. And I certainly didn't intend you to go bravely risking life and limb to try and break this case.'

'So you do fancy me? I knew you did; I just knew it. Well, we're both consenting adults, so let's go and do something about it; I'm already half-undressed.'

As she scuttled off to the bedroom, he hardly felt like a consenting adult, but accepted it would shatter her confidence if he failed to join her.

He first went to the bathroom. When he washed his hands, he looked in the mirror and asked himself how this could have happened; in response, he shrugged his shoulders and shook his head. By the time he entered her bedroom, she was already between the sheets, wearing a shiny blue pyjama top that reflected the bedside light. He piled his clothes onto a chair, trying not to appear too careful. She edged back the duvet and the top sheet, revealing very little of herself. Still wearing his boxer shorts, he slipped in beside her. She guided his hand to the painful part of her injured leg. 'Be careful; it still hurts.' After a moment, she ran his hand up higher, forcing him to discover she had removed her knickers.

When he began to unfasten her pyjama buttons, she suddenly blocked him with a hand. Uncertain whether she was being genuinely reluctant, or modest, or merely coy, he asked, 'Is it all right to do this?'

She gazed at him anxiously. 'They're not very big.'

He slowly unfastened all five buttons and peeled back the material. 'They're just perfect.' He gave the nearer nipple a kiss and a suck to emphasise the point.

Encouraged by this, she removed her pyjama top. 'Now take off your shorts and make love to me.'

He winced inwardly. Having sex with Penny was one thing, but making love to her was something entirely different, something reserved only for his wife. And, of course, for Lin.

Though he understood Penny was doing her best to be sexually exciting and excited, he quickly realised she had had a severely limited education up to this point. By extending the foreplay he succeeded in giving her a little of the pleasure he guessed had been missing from her past experiences. As he eased her legs even wider, she suddenly stiffened. 'What about protection?'

He stopped immediately. 'You're not on the pill? I

don't carry condoms around with me; I'm not like that.'

She pushed him away to one side. 'I'll give you a blowjob.' He rolled onto his back and waited for her to make the next move. She stared deep into his eyes. 'What am I supposed to do?'

He smiled in amusement. 'Don't you know?'

She looked away. 'Yes, of course I do… in theory.' He propped himself up on one elbow and explained in more detail about fellatio.

After she had finished taking him into her mouth, she went to the bathroom and brushed her teeth. When she returned, she commented casually, 'I didn't expect it to taste salty. We'll do it the proper way, next time.'

As her matter-of-fact attitude had broken the feeling of intimacy, he felt able to raise another subject. 'We'd better fetch your car before someone notices it. Ideally, we should go under cover of darkness, but with these light evenings…'

'Sometime between nine and ten would be best. If it's later, we might be spotted by a patrol.'

'All right, but are you able to drive?'

'Yes, I'm fine. I didn't go back to the car because I thought I might be noticed collecting it, and someone could connect me to the crash because of my limp. We have a few hours to kill…'

'Not the best expression for people in our line of business.' He saw her smile briefly as she continued.

'…and it may not be very smart for you to be seen buying condoms locally, so I'll go out and get some. Just make yourself at home. I mean, stay in bed.'

'I need to let people know I won't be back 'til late.'

She dressed quickly, keeping her back to him the entire time; he thought it indicated a lack of confidence in her body. Without saying goodbye, she limped away.

He retrieved his phone and made his brief excuses before returning to bed, where he considered what other actions may be needed to cover up Penny's activities. He assumed she would have had the sense not to call Liversedge using a traceable mobile phone or landline, but how well had she masked her voice? Would he recognise it again? There was now no monitoring of Liversedge's phone, but he may have recorded the calls himself. If she were to make official contact with him, he may even record her voice again and arrange for a technological comparison. He concluded Liversedge must never be allowed to meet her.

The crashed van was a nest of vipers. According to Locard's Exchange Principle, Penny would have left some trace of her being there. Similarly, some trace of the van would have come away with her. Thankfully, she had survived without cuts, so there would be no blood to make life easy for their colleagues in forensics. He hoped she had neither coughed nor sneezed.

She had put on a new pair of gloves in anticipation of fingerprint and palm print matches being checked on IDENT1. The forensic investigators would be able to compare them against the samples on the Glove Mark database that Derbyshire Police had helped to create, but they would find a match only to commonly-used plain, woollen ones. DNA evidence would not have seeped into them from her hands and thence onto other surfaces, as she had worn latex gloves underneath.

Her footwear was of a popular type; a search of the Boot Outsole Print database would quickly identify it. Exact markings on the undersides would be unique. Scrubbing off some of each sole would be possible but problematic. Disposing of them, especially as they were new, could bring other difficulties. It was too late now for her to contaminate the crime scene by climbing into the van without overshoes when visiting in an official capacity. He concluded she must therefore keep them hidden, and only consider using them again in the distant future. She should buy another pair of exactly the same type and use those instead; then, if someone were to make the connection with her, they would find her trainers were not a match to prints found in the van.

Collecting her car would be a problem if someone had already linked it to the second theft of the van; but if the police knew about it, they would already have been hammering at her door. An enquiry about the inquiry into the second theft could lead to an officer making a connection, so it was better not to ask. The solution may be to drop her off somewhere near her car, and then she could walk to it and drive it away, unless there was evidence of surveillance, in which case she should report it as stolen, except it was too late for that because delayed reporting would suggest there was a cover-up going on. The only viable solution was to collect her car and deny any connection with the van.

As he continued to ruminate on how to keep her out of trouble, he heard her return to the flat.

She entered the bedroom and declared triumphantly, 'I've got some.'

He looked at the condom box she had dropped onto the bed next to him. 'I'm only staying a few hours.'

'They were cheaper by the dozen.'

'Thank God they didn't have a special offer on a gross; I'd be exhausted.'

She giggled. 'I'm sure we would have worked our

way through them all, eventually. And here's one more, to make a *baker*'s dozen.'

He laughed, trying to hide his concern that she was expecting much more than a one-night stand.

She quickly began removing her clothing as though keen not to miss a moment. When she was down to her bra and knickers, she turned her back to him. Certain it was due to a body image issue, he gave a firm yet gentle order. 'Turn around, Penny; I want to see you.' She put her thumbs into the top of her knickers. 'Do it the other way, bra first. And don't be in such a hurry; I'm enjoying this.' She unhooked her bra at the back and slowly slipped it off. 'They stand up very nicely.' She pushed down on her knickers. They caught on her thigh, so she gave them a nudge and they dropped to the floor. After allowing him a few moments to enjoy the view, she slipped into bed. Confident he genuinely appreciated her body, she felt entirely relaxed. When he finally penetrated her, it released all her inhibitions, as she discovered physical feelings so unlike anything she had ever felt before.

Afterwards, he fell asleep. She turned out the light and nestled up to him, certain she was deeply in love, yet fearful this would only be a short-term relationship because he was happily married, as he had so often said to her. Once the case was solved or closed, she would be moving onto the next investigation, which doubtless would be elsewhere. But perhaps he would still find time for her in the future.

His body-clock suddenly woke him. In the dim light, he reached over to his watch; it showed twenty to nine. He touched her gently on the cheek. 'Wake up, Penny.'

She took his hand. 'I love you, Marcus.'

That was not at all what he had wanted to hear. 'We have to go and get your car. And I need a shower; I smell of you, which is nice, but…'

'…your wife wouldn't approve. And you're happily married, so you don't need to mention it again. I do understand your situation. Maybe we can sleep together just a couple of times a week.'

He wondered how, despite his best efforts to remain faithful to his wife, he had found himself in such a situation as this… yet again. 'I'm getting up, now.'

She turned on the bedside light. 'You stay there; I'll go first and get a nice towel for you.'

When he had showered and dressed, he found she had laid the kitchen table and had microwaved two different meals-for-one, both of them involving pasta in sauce with no sign of meat. She pressed him to eat most of the food, while she picked at scraps like a sparrow.

They talked in circles about the case. It was well after nine when they left the flat. In his car, she insisted on playing the Puccini arias again. As they approached the area where she had parked, he turned off the music. 'Keep your eyes open; look out for surveillance.' He drew up thirty yards short of her car and watched as she tried to mask her limp. When she had driven away from him, he used a series of side roads to reverse direction, before heading home.

Helen saw how tired he looked. After checking he had eaten, she packed him straight off to bed. When she joined him shortly after, she found he was sleeping placidly, apparently without a care in the world.

CHAPTER 10

Priestley arrived early at the station hoping to find out about the van incident without showing too obvious an interest in it. His usual line into recent activity was Witty, but the father-to-be was ministering to his wife who was suffering the symptoms of her first pregnancy. He walked into the MIR and witnessed a hive of activity. DI Baker walked quickly across the room and intercepted him. 'Good morning, sir.'

He heard how she delivered the untypically formal greeting too loudly, and hoped no one else was paying such close attention. As he looked into her eyes, he saw her pupils dilating as she failed to mask her feelings for him. 'Good morning, Penny.' He knew anything more formal from him would have sounded false to anyone listening. 'How's the investigation going?'

'While I was pursuing another line of inquiry, there may have been a breakthrough.' Again, her voice was too strident. 'I'm still getting the details now, sir, but it seems someone deliberately crashed a stolen van into Aden Liversedge's car while it was parked outside his home. A witness saw the driver running away.'

'Do we have a description?'

'Yes. An elderly gentleman saw a juvenile wearing a black hoodie and blue jeans. He thinks he was probably no more than fourteen.' She was unable to keep the grin from seeping into the edges of her mouth.

Priestley sucked in his lips and pressed them tightly together to avoid her grin spreading to his own mouth.

'There are lots of lads who would fit that description. We might get lucky, but we shouldn't waste too many man-hours on trying to track him down. Let's approach the incident from the opposite side. I'll call Liversedge in again, to see if he can explain why it might have happened.' Just before he turned away he gave her a wink. Seeing her face light up like a Christmas tree, he realised he would have to be more careful in future.

Witty arrived just in time for the morning meeting. Baker waited until he had entered Priestley's office, to avoid any suggestion to her colleagues that she wished to be alone with Marcus. As she joined them, Witty was not so much complaining about Lily's morning sickness as celebrating it. 'I was listening to Ralph and Hughie; she certainly knows how to chuck.'

Priestley frowned at him. 'You might not look quite so pleased about it if you were the one throwing up. Apart from that, how is she progressing?'

'She's bearing up well. She reckons that the sickness phase should stop after sixteen weeks, so she'll soon be able to enjoy things more.'

Penny, who had never previously paid attention to Witty's pregnancy chat, asked him, 'How big is she?'

Neil demonstrated by placing his hands well in front of his stomach and then slowly drawing them back until the gap disappeared. 'We're not actually showing, yet.'

Marcus smiled at his inclusive pregnancy. 'Let me know when she feels up to having visitors; Helen's keen to see how she's doing.'

Witty smiled back. 'Will do.' He began to grin. 'You two missed all the action, yesterday. Someone crashed a van into Liversedge's car.'

Baker responded, 'I was pursuing a separate line of

inquiry on my own, but it proved to be a total waste of time. I've read the witness statement. Some thirteen- or fourteen-year-old boy, apparently, but not enough detail in the description to warrant allocating resources. Is there anything else of interest?'

Witty replied, 'A patrol car came along ten minutes later, after a member of the public had called it in. The officer asked Liversedge why he hadn't reported it himself, it being his car, and he said he was going to, but was still trying to decide if he was supposed to dial nine-nine-nine or one-zero-one. Not the best excuse I've ever heard.'

Priestley asked, 'Have you spoken to Liversedge?'

Witty nodded. 'I called him and asked if he had any idea who had done it. He said it must have been some woman who had claimed he was responsible for killing Sylvia Batter, and who had demanded fifty thousand quid to keep her quiet. I told him it was actually a lad in his early teens, according to an eye-witness report; he said the woman was probably his mother. He sounded quite shaken, considering he hadn't actually been in the car. I took the liberty of inviting him in for interview this morning to investigate his allegations further.'

'Good move, Neil.'

'Will you and Penny be doing this one?'

Priestley felt his neck muscles tighten as he avoided looking at Baker. 'Let's stick with the tried and trusted formula, shall we? You and me, together.'

Witty turned to Baker. 'You don't mind, Penny? I wouldn't want you thinking I'm treading on your toes.'

'It's fine, Neil; I'll watch on the monitor again.'

Liversedge arrived slightly early for his interview. Priestley began, 'I've been looking at the report of an

RTC involving a stolen van and your car; that's a road traffic collision.' He had used the redundant acronym to support his dumbing down. 'The driver of the vehicle was a boy, believed to be about fourteen years of age, and you have a theory he may be the son of a woman who has been demanding money from you. Would you like to tell us *why* you think this woman has asked you for hush-money?'

Liversedge rushed into an explanation. 'Maybe it's like you said, before: my mother had something to do with the killing of Mrs Batter, and now they want me to pay because I'm next-of-kin.'

'How exactly was the money demanded?'

'It was in a threatening phone call. "Pay the money, or else!" So I need protection, now.'

'Protection from an unknown person is very difficult to provide; the threat could have come from anyone. Well, at least, any woman.'

'Maybe the woman was just paid to make the phone calls, and there's really a man behind it.'

'So it could be anyone. We need to understand much more about where the threat originated if we're to have any chance of providing adequate protection, sir. But you said "phone calls", plural. How many calls have there been?'

'Two. I put my phone down on the first one before she had time to say very much. I killed the second one, as well.'

'You killed two people, Mr Liversedge?'

'I haven't killed anyone! I killed the phone call! Have you never heard anybody say that, before?'

'Keep calm, sir; otherwise we may have to restrain you. So, you terminated both calls abruptly. If you receive a third call, would you please allow them to continue speaking, so that we may learn more about their reason for believing you are directly or indirectly responsible for the death of Mrs Batter.'

'And what do I do while I'm waiting for another van to be driven at me?'

'Factually, sir, the van was driven at your car when you were not in it, so it wasn't actually being driven at *you*. But I wouldn't worry about it; they have already achieved their objective of making you aware of their willingness to back up threats with action. What they want from you now is your money. If and when they make further contact, let Sergeant Whittington know at once and we'll respond immediately.'

After Liversedge had left, Baker and Witty joined Priestley in his office. She began, 'What if the woman doesn't make contact again?'

Priestley responded, 'I'm sure she will, though not necessarily by phone. Now she's arranged for some lad to back up her threat, she's bound to take it forward.'

Witty observed, 'It's a pity we stopped monitoring his calls, otherwise we'd have had a voice recording. We'd better get it turned on again.'

Priestley nodded. 'Indeed; if there is another call, we need to make sure we're ready. Until then, I don't think there's much we can actually do, is there?'

Baker and Witty agreed with him. As they stood to leave, Baker asked for a one-to-one with Priestley. She closed the door behind Witty. 'We need to talk, offsite.'

'We do indeed. Another walk down the valley?'

'Another visit to my flat. I'm not sure how long it'll take us to thrash everything out. Let's go this afternoon. I'll set off at one; you leave at quarter past.'

'Will do. We need to plan exactly how we're going to handle the investigation from here on in.'

She grinned. 'There's something else I want you to investigate and handle, Marcus. Oh, and don't phone me to say you're outside; you never know whose calls are being monitored. Just ring my bell.'

On schedule, Priestley arrived at Baker's flat and pressed the top button. She activated the door release. As he approached the top of the stairs he saw her standing waiting. She beckoned him inside. Trying to sound businesslike, he began, 'Hi Penny. We need to talk about what might happen on the investigation.'

She grinned and pointed toward the bedroom. 'First things first.' Without checking that he was following, she headed off. He knew resistance was futile.

To hide any unwillingness he may have been feeling at that precise moment, he began to undress her. She responded in kind, until they had stripped each other down to their underwear. After discarding her bra, she pressed herself against him, before slipping off his shorts. As she eased them down, she bent to kiss him intimately, before standing again. He pulled off her knickers, performing an equivalent manoeuvre. Seeing the large purple bruise on her thigh, he bestowed a few kisses on it, before working his way in tiny steps all the way up to her lips. Recognising how excited she was becoming, he pulled back the sheets and lifted her onto the bed. Rather than applying the condom himself, he invited her to try her hand at it, after she admitted it was something else she had never done before.

Having found her keenly ready for intercourse, they achieved mutual satisfaction in a bare minimum time. He found the act to be in stark contrast to the previous day, when she had needed lengthy foreplay.

She lay by his side with an arm around his chest, clasping him as though he might be lost to her if she were to relax her hold.

He waited until enough time had elapsed for him to move onto other matters. 'The fun's over now, Penny; we need to have a discussion about you-know-what. Let's get up and work through our options.'

'Will we be making notes?'

'It's better not to put anything in writing, otherwise it might be used in evidence against us.'

'In that case, let's talk about it in bed.'

'But I won't be able to think straight, what with you lying there next to me, all naked and alluring.'

She giggled. 'If only you really meant that.' She hoped he really did mean it. 'I'll get up first.'

Once showered and dressed, they sat opposite each other at her small kitchen table. As she placed a mug of black coffee next to him, she smiled apologetically. 'I'll get something nicer in for next time, and some meat for the weekend. I'll drop being a vegetarian if that's what you want.'

Rather than debating visitation plans and foodstuffs, he put off the subject entirely. 'You really shouldn't be making any assumptions; it's far too early for that.'

'Yes, Marcus; of course. I shouldn't plan anything for us; I should just live for the here and now.'

He heard the apparent sincerity in her delivery, yet knew she was thinking the opposite. 'We need to focus on the case. Obviously you mustn't make any more phone calls; we need to make contact via an untraceable route. I suggest we use e-mail with a routing facility that hides the IP address.'

'I've heard of Guerrilla Mail; is that what we need?'

'No; they only provide disposable e-mail addresses, for people to avoid spam hitting their main accounts. Their aim isn't to give anonymity; outgoing mail has the originating IP address in the header, which can still be traced back to the computer that sent it. There are ways of using a shared IP address that would make us just one user in a thousand, but experts would be able to narrow down the search area, which isn't good enough for what we're doing. What we need is a more secure mechanism. It's a pity I can't ask our own people to set up an anonymous proxy server, but this has to stay just between the two of us.'

She opened her eyes wide to indicate she was paying close attention. 'I completely agree.'

'I could ask GCHQ to organise something. They still owe me a favour, but I don't believe this is the right occasion to call it in. Besides, it would involve letting outsiders know what we're doing.'

'So what can we do?'

'We can download the TOR browser that's used for accessing the Deep Web. It works on the principle of adding layers of encryption, which is why the method used to be called "Onion Routing". The FBI took down the TOR Mail option in 2013 because they'd linked it to child pornography, so we'll have to use a different e-mail facility. We'll also need a VPN that doesn't log IP addresses; maybe the free trial version of CyberGhost. And then we'll just lie through our teeth and open a Gmail account with false information, giving a pay-as-you-go number as the mobile contact.'

'What's one more little lie; I suppose our lives have become one big lie, now that we're lovers.'

'Don't think about it like that, Penny. The hardest way of keeping a secret is to tell yourself it's a secret that you have to keep. Instead, just put it into a separate part of your mind and set up a firewall.'

'Sounds painful.'

'I mean, compartmentalise it. Tell yourself we're only lovers while ever we're in this flat. Anywhere else, we're colleagues and nothing more.'

'I'm going to find it hard, Marcus.'

He chose not to react with a pun. 'It won't be easy for either of us; we'll need to focus on work. Speaking of which, here's how to cover our tracks when sending the e-mail. Download a VPN and TOR onto a computer that's been stripped back to factory settings, and then open a new e-mail account. Keep the machine for this one purpose only. Don't use a standard browser on it at any time; don't open TOR to full screen; and never use it over public Wi-Fi. Are you happy with that?'

'I might be, if I knew what you were talking about.'

'You're not a techie, then. Don't worry, I'll sort it. We want to message Liversedge but we only know his work e-mail, so we'll have to take a look at his social network footprint to decide how best to contact him.'

'Is there a reason why we can't use his work e-mail? It would certainly grab his attention.'

'His employer may be monitoring his activity; it's the norm, nowadays. Of course, if we actually wanted his employer to know, we could deliberately write to that account; but we do need to remind ourselves he's only a suspect, and not a confirmed criminal that we're targeting. Maybe we should send him a brief message that invites him to contact us by his own secure method. If he doesn't have anything suitable, I'm sure he could set something up; he is an IT guy, after all. We ought to stick with the idea that there's just a single woman behind the blackmail.'

Her well-honed PC antennae picked up a possible sexist interpretation. 'What do you mean, "*Just* a single woman"? I *am* a single woman, but there's no "*Just*" about *me*.' She laughed lightly, making fun of the Politically Correct woman she used to be.

He smiled at her. 'Get some paper, so we can work out exactly what we want to say. We can burn it when we're done.'

After numerous revisions, they had almost agreed the wording. "You got my message. Contact me when you're ready to discuss settlement, but don't leave it too long or the price will go up. Miss Take." He argued that it would be a mistake to employ such a clever sign-off. She insisted it would hint she had prior experience of blackmailing. He reluctantly yielded.

Recognising that there was little more they could do at that point, Penny asked Marcus to come to bed again. He smiled as he shook his head. 'We'll wear each other out if we don't give it a rest. Besides, I need to send that message, and I can't use your computer in case someone's clever enough to track it back to its source. Anyway, we should both go and show our faces at work, otherwise people might start to talk.'

'You'll need to leave here first, unless you'd like to have my spare keys?'

He read the manoeuvre. 'I'll go straightaway and do that computer set-up at home; it'll take quite a while. If you go just after me, you'll still arrive well before me.'

As he was about to step through the doorway, she thrust a bunch of keys into his jacket pocket. 'Have them anyway; they may come in handy sometime.'

Rather than arguing with her, he set off down the stairs. In the car, he took the keys out of his pocket and looked at the bright red fob; it was in the shape of a heart. He wondered if she had just bought it for him.

When he reached the station a couple of hours later, he went to the MIR and found that the original team of detectives had been halved. Baker explained, 'There were no other sightings of that boy who crashed the stolen van. We had a team meeting and agreed it may have had nothing to do with the case, so we should just park it for now. You know what joy-riders are like; most are them haven't a clue how to drive safely, so it may have been accidental.'

'It's certainly possible it was unrelated; just a case of wham, scram, thank you van.'

She found she had laughed too freely, so put on a severe face. 'I know where that expression comes from, and it's highly inappropriate for a work environment. It's sexist, sir.'

Priestley noticed a few officers exchanging smirks, and knew she had made a convincing job of recovering from being visibly amused. He stiffened his neck and responded sternly, 'Perhaps it is, DI Baker, but some day you'll come to realise a little bit of humour does no harm whatsoever. Come to my office and we'll discuss your leadership attitude.'

As they left, one detective remarked to another, 'I'll bet she's for it, now; she never knows when to keep her trap shut.'

With the door closed, Priestley informed Baker he had sent their simple message and had received an out-of-office response. He added, 'He did say he was taking time off work; I never thought about that.'

She shook her head. 'Me neither, but he may still be checking his inbox. Should we try another route, or do we just wait?'

'I'll keep monitoring the account at home. If there's nothing by morning, we'll discuss our next step first thing.'

'You could come over to my place this evening and we could wait together to see if anything happens. That way, we'd be ready to respond immediately.'

He held out his hands, palms facing upward to claim honesty. 'Sorry, but it isn't possible. I set up the VPN, TOR and G-mail over my home broadband using SSL technology to apply encryption security that's essential for masking the IP address. If I were to use the machine anywhere else it could trigger a metadata escape that would blow our cover.' Seeing her unwavering look of admiration, he felt confident she had not interpreted his glib technobabble as merely an excuse.

CHAPTER 11

Marcus checked for incoming e-mails once an hour throughout the evening. Helen questioned why he had resurrected an old laptop. Rather than make this another secret to be kept from her, he explained enough of the background to justify his setting up the computer.

She asked, 'Shouldn't that sort of thing be handled by your experts?'

He smiled winsomely. 'But I am an expert.'

She gave a single shake of the head. 'You only think you're an expert. Things move on so quickly in the IT world, you must be some distance behind the field.'

'Maybe a few steps.'

'Maybe a few giant leaps.'

'Well, I'm sure I know enough to handle this little problem. If I had to involve someone else, I wouldn't be able to keep things under the radar.'

'Haven't you let anyone in on your hunch?'

He thought for a moment. 'There's just one officer.'

'Who is he?' She scrutinised his face for a reaction. 'Or she?' Seeing a slight twitch at one eye, she sensed it was the latter. 'Not Lin, by any chance?'

Wishing to avoid any mention of Penny, he allowed Helen to believe her guess had been correct. 'That's something you're better off not knowing, just in case there's any fallout from my bit of off-roading. Lin's doing a great job, by the way; well above her pay grade. Maybe she should be promoted, but I'm reluctant to put her forward, myself. People might think I'm showing favouritism toward my little protégé.'

'That sounds rather condescending. You'll have to watch what you say outside these four walls; there are people just waiting to pounce on any type of expression that might be interpretable as sexist or ageist. I have to say, though, I'm rather surprised she hasn't already been fast-tracked. Once the police fully adopt an equal opportunities attitude, you could find she rockets up the system in next to no time. She could even end up being your boss. What would you think of being under her as you get older?'

Alert to the possibility that such a misinterpretable question was one of her traps, he held a straight face. 'Always assuming I survive long enough for that to be feasible.'

Her sense of concern went into overdrive. 'Are you mixed up in something dangerous? What makes you imagine you wouldn't survive?'

He smiled disarmingly. 'I was only meaning that I might be retired before she could make superintendent. I am almost fifteen years older than her, you know.'

Recognising how readily he had recalled their age gap, she stored her observation for later contemplation, before trying again. 'It isn't something you've ever thought about, then? Being under her?'

Remaining poker-faced, he shook his head. 'That's all far too hypothetical to have ever occurred to me.' At least he knew he could rely on Helen not to misinterpret the word "hypothetical".

In the morning, before breakfast, Marcus checked his new account's inbox; there were still just the three items. The first was a standard welcome message. The other two were spam, which he had found surprising, as he had not disclosed the account name to anyone.

After breakfast, he made another check and found one new e-mail. It read, "Meet me today at noon. Come alone. Meadowhall, ground floor, food court. Carry two recyclable jute bags, one Waitrose, one Sainsbury's." As there was no reference to the earlier e-mail, he could not guarantee the invitation had come from Liversedge. He read it through twice, certain there was a substantial amount to be gleaned about the writer. Grateful for having a psychologist on hand, he called Helen in to discuss it with him.

After studying it at length, she finally commented, 'Fascinating. What do you think of the instruction to bring two different bags?'

'If they had asked for a single item that anyone might carry, it would have been an unreliable way of identifying someone. Having to bring in two specific bags from different supermarkets greatly reduces the probability of someone else doing the same by chance. It indicates the writer possesses a highly logical mind, which fits the suspect's profile. If there's a different author behind it, I suppose it would be sexist to say it's more likely to be from a man than a woman.'

'It would indeed, though statistically it may be true. Any other observations about the bags?'

'They're environmentally friendly? In which case, I might have said it was more likely to be from a woman than a man, if I hadn't already said the opposite.'

'So, putting those two interpretations together?'

He recognised she had already formed an opinion and was now leading him to reach the same conclusion. 'A homosexual?'

'Possibly, but try again.'

'Someone androgynous? If they're a hermaphrodite, it would certainly cut down the list of suspects.'

'Think probabilities.'

'A man and a woman together!'

'Well done, Marcus; you got there in the end.'

Having long ago accepted he would always have to bow to her superior intellect, he could never find it in himself to be offended by her apparent condescension. 'So, it's probably a couple.'

She shook her head. 'I didn't say that. It might be two people working together who are not a couple as such; it isn't as though *you* can't work closely with a woman without having to have sex with her.' He felt his eyes bulge and hoped she had not been watching him too closely. 'It could be more than two people, or just one person; I'm only guessing. Like you often say to me, psychology isn't *real* science.'

'Nevertheless, it could mean there's little point in trying to profile the sender; if more than one person is involved, the number of combinations of profiles would make it impracticable to unpick the individuals.'

'True, which is why you should consider the profile of the composite organism.'

'Meaning?'

'For people working in concert, you should establish what their collective objective might be. Bank robbers aim to rob banks. Like-minded people may get together to kill for some perverse pleasure.'

'What's the technical term for people like that?'

'They're called "nutters", Marcus. Or "wackoes" in the US.'

'Thank you for that elaboration, Professor Priestley.'

'My pleasure.' They exchanged smiles.

'Anything else to be gleaned from the e-mail?'

'Are you asking me to speculate?' She accepted his nodded invitation. 'Either a single author shops at both Waitrose and Sainsbury's, or two contributors shop at one each. The latter is more likely; as a species we tend to be creatures of habit, so brand loyalty is a factor.'

'I suppose one person who may not shop at either supermarket could have Googled them both to find out if they sell jute bags.'

'They'd have to be quite savvy to think of doing something like that just to put you off the scent.'

'If we assume there *are* two people involved, could you have a shot at profiling them?'

'Sure. I never shop at Waitrose because I think too much of their food is overpriced for the same quality that I can get elsewhere; Sainsbury's is slightly cheaper, but the same argument applies to some extent. So, I'll start with the man. He shops at Waitrose and therefore pays over the odds, suggesting he's comfortably off. He reads the Guardian, passionately backed the "remain" campaign in the EU referendum, and would never admit to voting Tory. He may travel by jet plane for work, but not for holidays, because he's too concerned about carbon emissions; that's why he uses the ferry to go to France every summer. He often cycles to save petrol, even though it probably burns more fuel as a consequence of motorists having to dawdle behind him when it isn't safe to overtake.'

He knew she was having a bit of fun, but pretended to take her seriously. 'What about the other one?'

'She shops at Sainsbury's because that's where she's always shopped, and wouldn't dream of switching to a better value supermarket nearby. Though she claims to be a vegetarian if ever anyone asks, she has a freezer full of guilty secrets. When she was in her twenties she tried going braless, but soon stopped when she realised no one was looking.'

'What might the two of them have in common?'

'It could be almost anything. I can only discount the possibility that they're both grocers; notice correct use of the apostrophe.'

He tittered. 'Is there anything you really *can* say?'

'Yes: more than one person may have contributed to constructing the e-mail. I might be able to make some proper observations if you'd give me the full picture.'

'I'll hold back on that, if you don't mind. You've already been a big help by raising the possibility that there's more than one person behind the e-mail.'

'But why all the secrecy?'

'Because I wouldn't want to get you into any bother; you must realise I'm not exactly abiding by the rules.'

'Well, I would like to give you more help. You said nothing was stolen, but that might merely mean they fled in panic. Just tell me, was the victim wealthy?'

'No, not at all. In fact, she was an old woman living on a pension.'

'How very interesting. In that case, I would suggest you assume there are multiple actors, and focus on the common purpose aspect. Why would a group of people wish to orchestrate the murder of a poor, old woman?'

'Maybe I'll find out at noon.'

'You aren't going to the meeting on your own, are you? That would be far too dangerous.'

He knew he would have to let Penny take the risk, as they would be expecting to meet a woman. 'I won't be making the rendezvous myself; the contact has to be a female who is old enough to have a young teenage son. I'm going to have to find a volunteer.'

She responded emphatically, 'So, not Lin, for once.'

Uncertain how best to reply to her implied criticism, he silently focused on closing down the computer.

Baker and Witty were standing outside Priestley's office when he arrived at eight a.m. 'Sorry, but I need to postpone the meeting.' The two turned away. 'Not you, Penny; I have something to discuss with you.'

Witty walked off, thinking Baker was in trouble.

She followed Priestley into his office and closed the door. He began, 'There's been an e-mail.' He extracted a slip of paper from his wallet. 'It says: "Meet me today at noon. Come alone. Meadowhall, ground floor, food court. Carry two recyclable jute bags, one Waitrose, one Sainsbury's." The sender used a forward proxy server to block their details, so we can't guarantee it's actually from Liversedge. It could be dangerous to go there without protection, but it would be too obvious if you were to wear body armour. Are you up for it?'

'I'm sure I can rely on you to take good care of me, Marcus. We can handle this, no problem.'

He heard in her voice far more than a colleague's confidence in him. 'I'm not prepared to risk something happening to you.' Seeing her face light up, he assumed she had read more into his words than he had intended. 'If we go ahead, it has to be with full support, including firearms; don't forget, this is a murder case.'

'It's a very public place; I'm sure I'll be safe enough without armed officers if you're close by.'

'I'll have to stay well away in case it is Liversedge who turns up; we can't risk him recognising me. But we shouldn't assume it will be him. I talked to an eminent psychiatrist who doubles as a psychological profiler, and they concluded the note may have been constructed by more than one person.'

'You don't need to be shy with me, Marcus; just say you discussed it with your wife.'

He grinned. 'I discussed it with my wife, and she read signs of both a man and a woman behind it.'

'If there are only two of them, we can deploy the remaining team members; that should be sufficient.'

'She wasn't able to say if there are only two, and we need enough people who don't stand out like coppers.'

'I'm sure we have enough capable officers to cope. What should we include in the briefing?'

'The operation itself has to be entirely on the record, but we shouldn't reveal any more than we have to.'

'We certainly shouldn't mention my crashing a van.'

'Of course not; that's just between the two of us.'

'One of our little secrets.'

He smiled, though a little nervously. 'Indeed. We mustn't disclose the two phone calls you made, either. The same applies to the e-mail I sent, and what I think is almost certainly a reply to it; otherwise we'd have to justify having the concealed account.'

'That doesn't leave anything to explain why we're having the meeting in the first place. What can we do?'

'Let's say someone requested it.'

'How would they have made the request?'

'It can't have been by phone from a landline; even blocked numbers can easily be traced. We need to make the call ourselves from a pay-as-you-go.'

'I could phone you now, from the same one I used for making my blackmail threats to Liversedge; then we could say it was this call that requested the meeting.'

He thought about it for a little while. 'I foresee two problems with that. One, as they're expecting a woman, you have to be the one at the meeting, which means you should be the one to receive the call. And two, it needs to be made from close to Liversedge's house, so that the distances to the cell towers that relay the message indicate it could have come from him.'

'People are more likely to notice if *you* left the office, so *I* need to be the one to go and make the call.'

'You could be right about that, but how would you request a meeting with yourself? Would you ask for you by name, or would you give a description?'

'I could just ask for someone non-threatening, such as a lady.' She smiled at him and held it, hoping for a complimentary response.

'I suppose you could reasonably ask for the most senior woman on the case. Let's stick with that, and not go into the question of how much of a lady you are.'

Her smile flared more brightly, before burning out as she stood up. 'I'll leave my coat in the office and nip out the back way. Let's hope no one misses me.'

'When you phone me, don't call the landline in case that stupid conference mechanism triggers and someone overhears. Phone my official mobile, as it has to be a number someone might know from my business cards. Mobiles can be cloned, so muffle your voice in case someone's unofficially listening in. We have to hope there's no official recording going on, though I don't see why there would be. When you read out the note, remember to add in a bit about wanting a lady, so the call duration is just right if anyone checks the records.'

He closed the door behind her to discourage any casual visitors.

A quarter of an hour later, Superintendent Richie Yelland was walking by and noticed Priestley's door was shut, which he knew was unusual. He knocked and opened it a little way. 'Are you busy, Marcus? I was wondering what's been happening on the Batter case?'

'Greetings, Richie. I'll give you a full briefing later this morning, once I've cleared up a few things.'

'You could give me the gist right now, if you like.'

'I could give you the superfast version. Nothing's happening, so the team's winding down.'

'That certainly is brief. Perhaps I should ask Baker; she must have more time to spare than you.'

'I'd prefer to tell you myself, sir, if you can wait.'

He gave a chuckle. 'You really are under pressure, aren't you; I don't normally merit a "sir" from you.'

Priestley laughed loudly. 'Sorry, it was just a slip of the tongue.' His mobile rang. He grabbed it and peered at the display. It indicated an unknown number, but he nodded at it as though it were one he recognised. 'Excuse me, Richie, I'd better take this.' Yelland gave a brief wave, before closing the door and retreating down the corridor.

Marcus answered the phone, making his voice sound natural. 'DCI Priestley.'

Penny recited the script verbatim, before adding, 'Send the prettiest woman on the case.'

He responded, 'I know just the lady you want; her name's Penny.' He heard a delighted little laugh before she terminated the call.

CHAPTER 12

Knowing the team would be expecting a nine o'clock briefing, Priestley checked his watch repeatedly as the hour approached. By his calculation Baker should be back just in time. With only a minute to go she had still not appeared, so he left his office and headed for the MIR. As he entered unaccompanied, Witty spoke up. 'What have you done with her, then? Has she been naughty?' A few smirks were relayed around the room.

Priestley gave him a withering look. 'I have come here today, ahead of our esteemed colleague, in order to deliver a eulogy, not in praise of an individual, but of an entire team. My thanks are overdue, insofar as some of our officers have already been reallocated and are therefore not present to receive my few, humble words of gratitude. I shall nevertheless ensure the record reflects every individual's contribution, both singly and collectively, within our team environment.' Heads were still facing his way; he thought the implication of possible rewards was holding their interest.

'We have no doubt all felt the rush of excitement and the warm feeling of satisfaction as a difficult case suddenly finds a solid route through a muddy morass, and we achieve the long-hoped-for outcome, the arrest and conviction of the perpetrators of the crime which we have all been so diligently investigating.' Checking their faces, he knew he still had their close attention, and thought perhaps they were wondering if he had an announcement to make regarding a breakthrough.

'How much more, then, should we appreciate those who toil ceaselessly without receiving the rewards, both professional and personal, of the satisfaction associated with cracking a case. Up to this point in time, we have all put in the graft but not received the pay-off. And yet, with your continuing dedication, we may in due course reach the Promised Land.' Wondering what to say next, he found himself increasingly keen for Penny to enter the room. He hoped she had not been delayed by an RTC, especially one close to the suspect's house.

'As many of the mundane yet essential tasks have been completed, and any unhelpful findings consigned to the wastebasket of history, nevertheless we have built the solid foundations upon which we can go forward with confidence. I am sure I speak for us all today when I say we have bonded as a team; and yet that team is shrinking at every turn, leaving our own responsibilities spread more widely. But to those who remain, I say to you, we are enough. Do not wish for one more. Indeed, if anyone has not the stomach for the case, let them depart. And to those who stay, we few, we happy few, we band of brothers...' He scanned the room, smiling at the females. '...and sisters, you shall all be rewarded, if not on earth, then in heaven.'

The door opened and Baker entered. 'Ah, Penny, I was just offering a few words of thanks.'

She stared at him, uncertain about his speechifying. 'Yes, I heard you; I was outside the door, listening. Is something kicking off?'

'There has indeed been a development.' He shared his final words around the room. 'This meeting will reconvene shortly; don't leave the building.'

He pointed to Baker and Witty as he headed out.

'You two: my office.' Behind him, a hubbub broke out, revolving entirely around whether Priestley had been demonstrating what it takes to become a senior officer, or whether he had merely lost the plot.

He maintained a rapid pace to discourage any casual conversations. In his office, he motioned Witty to close the door. 'Earlier, I took a brief phone call. Someone asked for a meeting at Meadowhall with the senior female officer on this case, which of course is Penny. They stated she must come alone. It may just be a hoax, but we have so little else to go on, I'm minded to take it seriously. Penny, how do you feel about trailing out there on what may prove to be a wild goose chase?'

She responded without hesitation, 'I'm up for it.'

'Good. The meeting is requested for noon today in the food court.'

Priestley turned to Witty. 'Any thoughts, Neil?'

'Obviously we have to follow it up. The question is, should we go mob-handed.'

Priestley nodded. 'I believe we should deploy all available officers; at least, those who look like they can fit in. Shopping is more of a woman's thing.'

Witty rapidly sucked in air noisily. 'You can't say that nowadays, boss.'

Priestley put up a hand to discourage him from interrupting again. 'I just did. So, Penny, include all the females, but no windcheaters and tight jeans. Choose younger males you're confident will be able to blend in. Any older males are at your discretion, but make sure they aren't the sort to stand out as obvious detectives. Now, do you know Meadowhall?'

'Well enough.'

'Once you have the headcount, work out the specific

deployment. Get them over there early, so they can start looking the part with some shopping. I'll have a word with Lin Plummer; she can stay close to you.'

'I wouldn't want her to give the game away.'

'Trust me, you can rely on her to blend in; she's a great actress when she needs to be. I need to go and put Yelland in the picture, now.'

As they stood to leave, he turned to Witty. 'As a form of identification, the contact requires Penny to have two jute bags with her, one Sainsbury's and one Waitrose. Just to prove men can do shopping as well, it's your job to resource them. You mustn't be seen handing them over to her where someone might notice; they have to be in her possession in advance. I'll leave you to work out the logistics.'

By eleven thirty, Priestley and Witty were sitting with two Meadowhall security officers and monitoring a bank of screens. Six of the detectives were circulating as male-female couples, and four more females were walking around in pairs. Priestley exchanged amused glances with Witty, as they watched Lin narrowly avoiding bumping into people as she struggled on her own with masses of shopping bags.

At five minutes to twelve, Lin joined a food queue directly behind two teenage boys. When she nudged them both with her bags, they turned to see who was being annoying. Barely able to conceal their hormonal delight, they vied for which of them could be the more helpful with holding things for her. She suggested she give them money for her food, while she sat with her bags and waited for them to join her.

At midday, Penny walked into the food court and sat at an empty table close to Lin. She repeatedly looked around, to inform any observer that she was waiting for someone to join her. The two hessian bags remained close at hand and visible from a distance.

A few minutes later, Lin's two worshippers brought three burgers and chips, and then sat waiting for her to speak. She shared the conversation equally with them, talking about recent films and asking which ones they liked. Each one answered their questions factually. She enquired why they were not at school, and found they attended one in the private sector that had given them time off "to prep for exams". Knowing the intake was exclusively boys, she guessed it might be a factor in the overawed way they were interacting with her. She kept them spellbound for twenty minutes as Penny sat alone, silently playing with her smartphone. With the food long gone, Lin finally stood and thanked the boys for being so helpful. They offered to take her bags to her car, having assumed she must have one to cope with so much shopping. She accepted and set off for the distant exit that was nearest where she had parked.

Priestley saw her leave and decided to intercept her. He left Witty watching the monitors and hurried outside to Lin's car, before turning and walking toward the exit. Lin appeared with her helpers in train. He called out, 'There you are, darling. You *have* been busy! And who are these young men you've recruited to help you?'

When she introduced them they smiled awkwardly. One of them mumbled, 'We have to go, now.'

Marcus took the bags from them and thanked them for helping his wife. They smiled again before heading back inside. He asked her, 'What gave you that idea?'

She set off toward her car. 'Admit it; I didn't look anything like a surveillance operative.'

He held out a few bags. 'But now you don't look anything like a wife; carry some of your own stuff.' They loaded the shopping into the boot. 'I think we may have to accept it's going to be a no-show. You can't really extend this performance of yours, so you'd better go back to the station.'

She leaned in closely. 'And fill in an expenses form? I can claim for my shopping, can't I?'

He surreptitiously gave her a small double-pat on the bottom. 'You know the answer to that, but I'll fund you myself if you're nice to me.'

She giggled. 'I'm always nice to you.'

He knew the epicentre of the smile that appeared on his lips came from far deeper; Lin was always a willing partner when he played the unreconstructed male, one of those pleasures becoming increasingly marginalised due to the restrictive rules of modern society.

When Lin had left, he returned to the security room. Witty confirmed there had been no attempted contact. They watched together as Penny bought food. Priestley commented, 'She's right to do that, otherwise someone might start asking why she's sitting there.'

Baker ate her vegetarian sausage and mash. Priestley phoned her at five past one. 'Hi. I think we can assume they're not coming to see you there; maybe their plan was to intercept you as you leave. Wait five minutes and then head off to your car; the team will converge on you and watch over you while you go. If someone does make contact, don't take unnecessary risks, but only give the signal if you need an intervention.'

No one attempted to contact her, so she drove away. Priestley wound up the surveillance operation. Before leaving, he obtained copies of all the CCTV recordings for the two hours leading up to her departure. Perhaps, he reasoned, they had intended to meet up with her but something had spooked them, in which case they had probably been recorded at some point.

Back at the station, Priestley held a de-briefing. 'We had a no-show, but maybe we picked something up on CCTV. When you review the footage, don't just look out for Liversedge. We were hoping for contact with a man or a woman, or maybe a couple, but there's no way of knowing who they might be among the thousands of shoppers, so check for anyone behaving suspiciously. Let's see if we can achieve some sort of positive result out of today's excursion, so don't limit yourselves only to people who seemed interested in looking toward the food court. If you spot any retail theft, let's put it on record and pass it onto uniform.'

Priestley held a tête-à-tête with Baker in his office. He began, 'The two options are, we contact Liversedge again, or we wait for something else to happen.'

She responded, 'Whoever it was that requested the meeting must have had a reason, beyond wasting police time. Perhaps they'll get in touch again.'

He checked his watch. 'It's too late to do much more today. Let's wait and see if there's another e-mail by morning. If there isn't, we'll have to take another shot at Liversedge. What time can you come in tomorrow?'

'I can be early if you like. Half seven?'

'It's a date.'

She smiled. 'When will we be having a proper date?' Seeing his look of concern, she added, 'Don't worry; I understand. I'll pretend it's our first date, only I'll be early so you know I'm not standing you up.'

CHAPTER 13

The radio at Marcus's side of the bed burst into life ahead of the six o'clock pips. Helen picked up her mobile phone and waited for it to beep before turning off the alarm. She listened to the news headlines and then slipped out of bed, wondering how he had been able to persuade her to move to British Double Summer Time. His arguments regarding wasted daylight and the benefits recognised during the Second World War had been less persuasive than the bottle of chilled Prosecco Spumante, the box of chocolates and his chat-up line.

Marcus was delighted to catch a fleeting glimpse of her naked body in the light from the bathroom window, before she closed the connecting door. Yesterday he had sincerely declared his undying love for her, though he had to admit to himself that the wine and chocolates were also intended to persuade her to start today an hour earlier than usual. It was not only because he liked her to make breakfast; the day always felt better if they began it together.

Penny had lain awake long before her six o'clock alarm had given her permission to get up. She took a shower, then dressed as usual in dark trousers and top, and headed for the kitchen, where she turned on the radio. The broadcast of local news, sport and weather was of limited interest to her, but it was better than the oppressive silence she had had to endure throughout her adult life. For a moment she allowed herself to imagine the meeting was a date; after all, he had said it was.

Her breakfast, as usual, was toast and marmalade with black coffee, though today the juice was grapefruit instead of orange. Despite frequent time checks on the radio, she glanced repeatedly at her watch; this was not a day for being late. By twenty to seven she could wait no longer. As she walked down the stairs she heard no sounds from her neighbours, but then they were quiet at virtually all times of day.

She stepped out onto the pavement, where she heard someone exiting a van; at least she was not alone in being an early riser. As she turned to close the door behind her, she felt a sharp prick in her right buttock, and a hand grabbed her collar at the back of her neck. She tried to face the assailant, but a new hand had now taken hold of her left shoulder. She felt her legs buckle under her as she was frogmarched back indoors, the hands at her coat keeping her from falling.

Marcus checked his watch again: Penny was late for the early meeting. Perhaps she had forgotten to alter her alarm, or maybe she had been delayed by traffic. He hoped she was not sitting brooding somewhere, fretting about her feelings for him.

At twenty to eight he gave her a call, but received only a recorded message that indicated her phone had been switched off. Feeling slightly concerned about her, he checked to see if Witty was around. Nowadays Neil tended to arrive only just on time, and sometimes even slightly late, since Lily had started needing his frequent ministrations. Picking up a post-it note by Neil's desk, he scribbled him a timed message saying he was going to see Penny who had failed to arrive for a meeting.

In the car, Priestley switched on his voice-activated phone kit in case Penny wished to contact him. As the overwhelming evidence was that reaction times were worse than for drunk drivers, he disliked receiving calls while driving, and only ever made outgoing calls in dire emergencies. He felt annoyed with the law that limited police to taking action only if it appeared a driver was being distracted by use of their hands-free phone, as it was difficult to prove in court. Furthermore, the law provided no simple test regarding levels of usage, so someone could make sixty calls an hour with impunity.

When traffic conditions reduced his need to focus on driving, he began considering the various scenarios he might encounter at his destination. She was testing him to see if he would come to her. She had taken two hours off the clock instead of the alarm and was still sleeping peacefully. She had fallen off a ladder when changing a light bulb and was now lying on the floor, unable to move. She was stressed at the investigation's lack of progress and had ignored procedure by turning off her phone to shut everything out. Her frustration with the case had pushed her into despair and she had taken pills, either to end it all, or as a cry for help. She had been thinking about their affair and had realised it was destined to die almost before it had begun, so she had chosen to die with it, and was now hanging by the neck, still alive and hoping he would rush in and rescue her.

He parked immediately behind a white van close to her flat. To avoid pressing the bell button and giving her a rude awakening if she had merely overlaid, he took out her house keys and let himself in.

At the top of the stairs he knocked gently at her door. With no response, he opened it a little way and quietly called through the gap, 'Penny. Penny, it's me.' Receiving no reply, he pushed it wider and stepped inside. He looked into her bedroom; the unmade bed indicated she had probably slept there the night before. He tried the living room. As he saw her sitting slumped on a wooden chair dressed only in bra and knickers, her wrists tied to the arms with white bindings, he reacted immediately. Anticipating the presence of one or more intruders, he ran for an area of the room he could see was clear, but something struck his head from behind. Having suffered only a glancing blow, he turned with fists at the ready to connect with anyone behind him.

Two people were facing him, dressed in clean blue boiler suits and wearing white surgical masks. One was short and stocky with broad shoulders, and holding a solid wooden walking stick. The other was substantially taller. He knew he should take on the stronger target first, which he initially assumed would be the taller one. As he stepped forward, he realised it was a woman.

In his momentary hesitation, he lost the advantage of attack. The man caught Priestley's supporting ankle with the stick's crook, and yanked at it. As he toppled, he aimed a punch at the hidden face and connected with the nose. Army training had provided him with a wide skill set, with blows ranging from disabling through to killing, but his instincts told him some lesser techniques should be sufficient for opponents such as these. He scrambled to his feet and kneed the man in the groin, causing him to crumple to the ground.

As he saw the blood red stain spreading over the man's white mask, he felt something sharp pierce his right buttock. He lashed out with an arm and knocked away the hypodermic syringe. She brought her hands up to her face, as though fearing a broken nose more than any of the other injuries he could inflict. The drug was already beginning to take effect. He felt he could still manage to swing a fist at her, but his mind rather than his body held him back.

She sprinted for the door, overtaking the man who had hobbled there ahead of her. He gamely staggered after them, but knew they were getting away. Fighting to overcome the wave of blackness that was engulfing him, he dropped to his knees. Certain he was about to lose that particular battle, he slumped forward before slipping into unconsciousness.

Witty prepared to give his usual excuse for tardiness, but was surprised to find Priestley and Baker had not yet arrived. When he saw the post-it note Priestley had left him, he read it and put it aside. By half past nine he was becoming perturbed. He phoned Priestley, but the call went straight to voicemail. When he phoned Baker, a message stated her mobile had been switched off. He asked around; no one had heard from them.

Increasingly concerned, he explained the situation to Superintendent Yelland, who authorised him to run a GPS location check on Priestley's work mobile.

When Witty had established that Priestley's phone was now at Baker's property, he sat in a quiet corner and pondered on the possibilities. Almost certainly they were having an off-site meeting to discuss the case, though why that should be necessary was beyond him. He cast around for other realistic options but none sprang to mind. Having involved Yelland, he returned to explain the position.

Yelland asked, 'What do you think's happening?'

Witty replied, 'They're meeting to discuss the case?'

Yelland shrugged his shoulders. 'Or?' Witty wished he had thought harder, knowing he might be expected to offer alternative explanations. 'Any ideas?'

Witty panicked and relayed the first though that came into his head. 'They could be having sex, except we're talking about DCI Priestley and DI Baker.'

'And why not those two?'

'DCI Priestley is probably the second-most happily married man I know, after me. And DI Baker is, well, she's, erm, not really his type, shall we say.'

'I take your meaning. So, what should you do?'

'Go and see what's happening?'

'And if you can't gain entry?'

'Force the door, I suppose.'

'What would you do if you found them *in flagrante delicto*?'

'What should I do, sir?'

'Don't look so worried, Neil. I'm sure you're right: they're just having a meeting and forgot to keep people informed. Even so, you'd better go along and see, just in case something has happened. It could be carbon monoxide or food poisoning, God forbid. And if they *have* simply failed to report their whereabouts, tell them they're both due a bollocking. Oh, and take someone with you, just in case it's not what you're expecting.'

Witty recruited Plummer for the trip to Nottingham. As they approached the Basford area, Witty remarked, 'I'm sure this will be a wasted journey.'

Plummer looked less certain. 'What if something's happened to him; I mean them?'

'I'm sure they're not in any danger.' He gave a short laugh to reassure her. 'Yelland asked me what I'd do if I found them having sex.'

Plummer punched her right fist into the palm of her left hand. 'He'd certainly be in danger, then.' She saw his puzzled glance. 'If he's being unfaithful to Helen, he ought to be punished for it. You could hold him down while I hit him.' She saw him flash a smile, sure he had read no more into it than just a bit of humour.

As Witty reversed into a gap between two parked vehicles, Plummer noticed Priestley's car. 'That's his Volvo up the road, so he can't be far away.'

They walked to the entrance and scanned the column of bell buttons. The door suddenly opened from inside and a woman of about sixty blinked at them in surprise. 'Do you want somebody? If it's me, I'm just off out.'

Witty kept his warrant card in his pocket. 'We're just calling in on Penny; Penny Baker.'

The woman stepped to one side. 'She's at the top of the stairs, the first door you come to.'

They accepted her gestured invitation to enter, and heard her close the door as they climbed the stairs.

Witty knocked at Baker's door. It rattled, as it had not closed far enough to lock into place. Marcus, semi-conscious, heard the noise as though a distant warning from a far-off place. He forced himself to open his eyes. Penny was making a grunting sound as she looked at him, nodding her head vigorously. He crawled over to her chair and drew himself up on it, then pulled the gag down over her chin.

Penny croaked, 'There's someone at the door.' They heard the repeated knock.

Witty called out, 'Police! We're coming in.' He entered the living room two steps ahead of Plummer. Baker screamed at him, 'Look the other way! I'm not dressed!' He turned to Plummer, the shock still clearly registering on his face.

Plummer stared at Priestley. 'What the…'

Baker interrupted her. 'I've been drugged.'

Plummer responded, 'Not by him; I don't believe it.'

Priestley tried to rise from his knees, but was still fighting to overcome the drugs.

Baker snapped back, 'No, of course not by him; he's obviously been drugged as well. Untie me and then get SOCO over here.'

'And an ambulance?'

'That won't be necessary. I've been conscious for quite a while and I'm sure there are no lasting effects. We'll need blood tests, but first, get me unfastened so I can put something on.'

'Shouldn't you be checked for semen? Or at least given a clock check for evidence of any recent sexual activity? You know the procedure.'

She recalled having sex with Marcus. 'I do, and I'm not having anyone staring at my posterior fourchette.'

Plummer unfastened the bandages that bound her wrists and ankles to the carver. Baker watched Witty like a hawk, making sure he kept facing away from her. Once released, Baker exercised her joints to bring back some circulation and stave off the cramp. She allowed Plummer to help her to her bedroom, where she closed the door firmly, keeping Plummer out.

Priestley was showing more signs of consciousness, so Witty knelt on the floor next to him and asked, 'Are you all right, boss? Should we get you an ambulance?'

Priestley drew himself up onto the chair. Hearing Plummer requesting emergency assistance, he asked, 'How's Penny? Does she need one?'

Witty replied, 'She said she doesn't.'

'Then I don't either, but take us in for tests. And get SOCO in; I hit one of them and made his nose bleed.'

'Lin's already dealing with it. So, what happened?'

'I found Penny in her underwear, tied to this chair. She should be tested…'

'She says not to; she's certain nothing happened. Maybe she hadn't got dressed before she was drugged.'

Baker returned from her bedroom wearing a cotton dressing gown and hurried over to Priestley. 'Are you all right? What happened to you?'

He remained seated, still unsure whether he would be steady enough to stand. 'What happened to you is more the question.'

'I'd just gone out the front door and was checking it was closing properly, when two people grabbed me from behind. One of them jabbed me in the bum and then they forced me back inside. The next thing I knew, I was tied to this chair, with you lying on the floor.'

'You were never conscious while they were here?'

'No, not at all. So, what happened to you?'

'I…' he was just about to say "…let myself in," but realised that would lead his testimony in a direction he wished to keep not only from Neil, but especially from Lin. 'Erm, my head's still a bit foggy. I walked in; they hadn't closed the doors. When I saw you tied to the chair, I ran over to you. Someone whacked me on the back of the head from behind. I turned around and saw a short man and a tall woman. The man yanked my ankle with his walking stick. I just about managed to smack him in the face while I was falling. Then I got to my feet and kneed him in the balls, only the woman jabbed me with a hypodermic syringe. I knocked it out of her hand, but it had obviously done its job, because I felt myself losing consciousness as they ran out. The syringe should still be around here somewhere.'

Witty asked, 'Can you give me their descriptions?'

He thought for a moment. 'They were wearing white surgical masks. Neither of them wore glasses, but I still couldn't see enough of their faces to recognise them again. He was completely bald with a light scalp that hadn't weathered; I'd guess IC1 and in his fifties. She looked much younger, with short, dark hair. It's quite difficult to place her skin colour; maybe IC2 or IC4, darkish, somewhere between Mediterranean and Asian. They were wearing blue boiler suits that looked new, with pale yellow latex gloves and black boots. Judging by the man's movement, I'd say that walking stick wasn't just for show, so that may be our best clue. Oh, apart from any blood he dripped on the floor.'

'I'll get the investigation into gear right away.'

Baker interjected, 'I'll be the one leading it.'

Witty looked around at her. 'But you need to get yourself checked out, first.'

She nodded. 'Yes, but as soon as I'm back...'

They heard the sound of sirens rapidly approaching. Plummer went to the window and looked down. 'There are three squad cars coming. That was quick; when it's one of our own... I mean two of our own...'

Baker instructed Witty, 'Go downstairs and stop them from coming in to contaminate the crime scene. I'll be down with DCI Priestley in a minute, once I'm dressed. And don't ever tell anyone you've seen me in my underwear.'

He smiled at her. 'You've just been through all this, and that's what you're concerned about?'

She jabbed her finger at him. 'Yes, so don't forget. I mean, do forget.'

CHAPTER 14

By the time Priestley and Baker had had blood tests and returned to her flat, the CSIs were reaching the end of their forensic examination. As some of the solution was still present in the hypodermic syringe, they had sealed it into a two-piece polycarbonate tube and sent it for immediate laboratory testing; this was to minimise the risk that any active compounds in the liquid would have broken down into chemicals that can be by-products of various decay profiles, thereby making identification of the original substance less certain.

The SOCOs had collected samples from the blood trail that traversed the flat, the stairs and the pavement. They had interpreted the size and shape of the droplets, and concluded their directionality and dispersion were indicative of someone having only walked.

Baker explained to the senior CSI that she needed to collect some clothes and toiletries as she was uncertain where she would be staying that night. Anticipating an objection, Priestley added, 'They wore latex gloves, so you won't find anything on her clothing.'

Priestley watched Baker as she packed a few items into a small suitcase. 'Maybe you should take more than that. Whoever they are, they know where you live, so you might not be back for quite a while.'

She stopped her packing. 'Actually, it might make more sense not to move out. If they do come back, we could make sure we're ready for them.'

He shook his head. 'You've had enough danger for

one day, Penny.'

Her own shake of the head was more vigorous to reflect her determination. 'It's the best way.'

He gave an almost imperceptible final shake. 'We'll discuss this back at the station.'

She removed the items from the case, indicating she would brook no contrary argument.

Priestley accepted Witty's reasoning that he should avoid driving until certain he was entirely recovered. Baker emphasised she had been injected earlier and so had had more time to clear the drug from her system. Priestley attempted to persuade her to accept a lift. She parried his arguments, insisting she had no ill effects.

Priestley returned to the station with Plummer and Witty. Gloria on reception signalled to him to stay. 'Oh, you silly sausage, why on earth did you let them stick that horrible needle into you?'

Marcus grinned. 'It was just a jab in the bum; it's only like going to the doctor's. Shall I show it to you?' Plummer playfully punched him on the arm.

Gloria remained troubled. 'It's no laughing matter. And little Penny, as well; I don't know. Was it the same needle? Sharing needles is very dangerous.'

'Good question, Gloria. I'll make certain we're both thoroughly checked out.'

'Well, make sure you are, and don't ever go letting anyone do anything like that to you again.'

He smiled. 'I'll do my best not to.'

On his desk, a prominently positioned handwritten note from Chief Superintendent Barbara Watts invited him to go and see her immediately. He went to her office and knocked at the door. She bellowed, "Enter."

'You wanted to see me, ma'am.'

She motioned him to sit. Before he had reached the hard chair, she yelled 'Stop! Do you need something softer to sit on?'

He hesitated. 'It wasn't much, ma'am; I only had a little prick…'

She stifled a smile. 'Don't lie to me.'

'I could show you if you insist, ma'am.'

She laughed in her stern way. 'I'll just take your word for it. Now, how are you feeling?'

'I'm completely recovered.'

'Well, if you're certain, you can come to a senior leadership team meeting in the boardroom at one o'clock. There'll be a buffet lunch. Now, go and find somewhere comfortable to lie down if you need to.'

Back at his desk he checked Helen's schedule. At half past twelve he gave her a call. 'Hello, sweetheart.'

'Hello, love; are you wanting something? I'm too busy for sweet-talking.'

'I just thought I'd let you know that I'm perfectly safe and well.'

She immediately pushed aside her papers, knowing something had happened to him. 'Why should I think you wouldn't be?'

'No reason; not unless you'd heard something from someone.'

'Tell me all about it, love.'

'A detective was grabbed outside her home by two people wearing surgical masks. They injected her with something to knock her out, and then tied her up in her flat. When she was late for a meeting, I phoned her and discovered her mobile had been turned off, so I drove to where she lives in Nottingham, to investigate. I looked in at her door and saw she was unconscious, tied with bandages to a chair, so I gallantly, nay, heroically, charged in to rescue her. Unfortunately, they injected me too, but I courageously fought back and put them to flight. Then I passed out for a while, until the cavalry arrived.'

Despite having prefaced his statement by stating he was now well, she felt her heart racing. Concerned that together they would generate a negative emotional feedback loop if she were to reveal her anxiousness, she forced her voice to sound calm. 'So, what you're saying is, you blindly blundered into a dangerous situation where someone was able to inject you with something that knocked you out, but now you're feeling fine. What was the drug they used? Or was it a cocktail?'

'I don't know, yet. There was still some of the stuff in the syringe, so I should find out sooner than if I were having to wait for my tox screen results to come back.'

'Hmm, it sounds like you're over it, anyway. What about the woman? Has she recovered?'

'She says she has. So, all's well that ends well.'

Helen had a whole string of questions to put to him, but decided to wait until she could see him at home. 'I'm glad you're all right. Was there anything else?'

'Yes, I'd like your expert opinion on something. The assailants, a white man in his fifties, and a younger woman, maybe Mediterranean, maybe Asian, stripped her down to her bra and panties and then tied her up; but she's absolutely certain she wasn't interfered with. Why would they take her clothes off her if there wasn't any sexual motive? Of course, they may have just been waiting for her to regain consciousness.'

Helen considered the question for several seconds. 'It sounds as though they were intending to interrogate her. They may have believed that if she came round to find she'd been stripped down to her underwear, she could have felt even more vulnerable and would be likely to break sooner.'

He pondered for a few moments. 'In that case, why didn't they strip her entirely?'

She responded immediately, 'It would leave them no way of taking that particular threat any further.'

'It all sounds rather deep to me. Why wouldn't they use the normal route of escalating violence?'

'You must ask them, once they're in custody. But it doesn't sound like they're run-of-the-mill bad guys.'

'As I said, one guy and one gal, which in itself is unusual, even before taking into account the atypical age-and-ethnicity combination. And did I mention he had a walking stick? He looked like he needed it to get around. It's almost as though two people with nothing in common had come together for a joint enterprise.'

'Do you know which investigation it might relate to? If you understand what the case involves, it might give you an insight into the reason behind the incident.'

'It must be linked to the murder of the bridge player. Thanks, Helen; you're quite useful, sometimes.'

'We'll talk about it later in more depth, if you like. You are coming home at a reasonable hour, aren't you? Not intending to burn the midnight oil?'

'I might even be back early. Getting up at six has a downside: I'll be wanting to go to bed by ten.'

She softened her voice. 'Let's make it half nine.'

He knew she had made an offer he couldn't refuse. 'Baby doll nightie?'

'Whatever turns you on. And what shall I wear?'

He laughed. '*Très amusant. À toute à l'heure.*'

As he waited for the scheduled one o'clock lunch, his stomach informed him of the main downside to getting up at six in the morning. He went along to the meeting a little early, in the hope of getting a head start on the sandwiches. Baker had been watching out for him, not wishing to enter unaccompanied. Seeing her hurrying to join him, he stopped and waited. 'How are you feeling now, Penny? Any after-effects?'

'None whatsoever. And yourself?'

'I'm fine. And you're not upset?'

'Women have always been more resilient than men; didn't you know that?'

'I can't say I did.'

They pushed open the boardroom doors in unison. Priestley glanced around and saw the great and the good assembled. Superintendent Richie Yelland gave him a nod, as did Chief Super Babs Watt. Deputy Chief Constable Dotty Forbes-Smythe caught him looking in her direction and gave him a discrete wave. Assistant Chief Constable Archie Cameron held a stiff pose.

Chief Constable Charles Coker headed for Priestley with hand outstretched, and began brightly, 'Do you know why we're all here, Marcus?'

Having not the slightest notion, he dredged up an oft-used witticism. 'Free lunch, if there is such a thing?'

Coker made a monumental effort to find it hilarious. The others dutifully accepted it was ever so amusing. 'Very good, Marcus; very funny. We are here both to reprimand you off the record, and to congratulate you on the record. Your devil-may-care attitude led you to rush in and rescue DI Baker...' He smiled at her. '...without waiting for backup, hence the reprimand.' He paused for effect. 'You took on two masked villains who were armed with a hypodermic needle and a club, and vanquished them single-handedly. We are minded to put your name forward for a bravery commendation.'

Priestley felt genuinely shocked that his blundering might be rewarded. 'But sir, it was a middle-aged man who needed a walking-stick to get about, and a woman who had no idea how to fight.'

Coker shook his head. 'You are too modest, Marcus. Did you know that's who they were when you went barrelling in?'

'No, but…'

'Then no buts.' He spoke a little quieter. 'Look, this force needs some good publicity, and you make an ideal poster-boy.'

'I do appreciate the honour you wish to bestow on me, sir, but I really believe it would be in the force's best interests to wait until we have the two in custody. You never know, there might be something about them that would undermine the credibility of the honour.'

'I can see how that makes sense, in which case we need to get the case solved as quickly as possible. Once we've had a bit of nosh we'll discuss how to take this forward in a positive direction.'

The canteen kitchen provided two food options for meetings. One was the basic variety with sandwiches of sliced meat, cheese and egg, plus coffee and bottled water. The other, currently laid out on the pier tables, had a wider variety of sandwiches, garnished with cress and other salad. In addition there were cherry tomatoes, scotch eggs, mini-pork pies, quiches, vol-au-vents, and oatcake crackers with smoked salmon and soft cheese. Priestley stood with Baker so that he could wolf down as much food as possible without needing to converse with his superiors.

After several chicken and sweetcorn sandwiches and two pieces of quiche, he was biting into his second pork pie as Coker took his seat at the head of the table, a sign that they should stop collecting food and sit to eat what they already had on their plates. He grabbed two scotch eggs and three sandwiches, along with a mushroom vol-au-vent. Baker followed him with her prawn and tuna sandwiches and vegetarian quiche, and then went back for two black coffees.

Coker delayed commencing the meeting proper until Priestley's mountain of food had diminished to no more than a hillock. After checking that everyone was now focused on him, he began with a few opening remarks. 'As you know, I rarely become involved in operational matters, but it seems to me the investigation of the abduction of DI Baker brings a political imperative that dictates I should take a personal interest in ensuring the matter is treated with the utmost urgency and afforded the highest priority. We should identify the resources necessary to ensure this case is resolved in the shortest possible time, and make them freely available, subject only to the most essential overriding factors.'

ACC Cameron was the first to respond. 'I'm sure everyone present here today buys into your vision for this investigation, Charles. Resourcing will not be an issue; I shall make sure of that, personally.'

Coker replied, 'Thank you for your support, Archie.'

Next, it was the turn of DCC Forbes-Smythe. 'If any deficiency is discovered in our resource profile, I shall take the opportunity of filling that gap personally, at any level, be it ever so humble.'

Coker accepted her gracious offer. Those of lower

rank inwardly told themselves they must ensure no such opportunity ever arose.

Chief Superintendent Watt responded to her, 'Those of us closer to the sharp end will put our resourcing requirements together, and then we shall be pleased to invite you to fill any hole we may discover.'

Superintendent Yelland added, 'Not that we should necessarily anticipate any resourcing deficiency at this stage. We're awash with detectives needing reallocating from the Batter case, except I'm not as yet prepared to discount the possibility that this latest incident isn't in some way connected to it. What's your view of this, Marcus? Do you believe they may be linked?'

Priestley swallowed his last mouthful of food and quickly washed it down with coffee, giving him time to consider how he might respond in the tone that the meeting appeared to demand. 'As DI Baker has been entirely focused on the Batter case for several weeks, it would seem a not unreasonable supposition that the two are tightly bound. However, if that proves in the fullness of time to be a correct hypothesis, then we must accept that resourcing is not necessarily the key difficulty to be addressed. In reality, we have found so little that we can...' He located a stray morsel in his mouth and swallowed it. '...get our teeth into, we may find we are over-resourced and underintelligenced.'

Coker frowned at him. 'Then what do you propose we do about it?'

'I'm optimistic that the evidence coming out of the attempted abduction incident will provide insights that will enable the investigation to move ahead rapidly.'

'And when do you expect to have those insights?'

'I anticipate the forensics will be collated over the

weekend, subject to our colleagues' best endeavours. This will enable us to put together a clearer view of the way forward.'

'I see.' Scanning the room for anyone obviously wishing to comment, he finally noticed the most junior attendee. 'Do you have something you wish to add, DI Baker... Penny?'

She felt her chest tightening as she held her breath. 'Yes, sir.'

'Then do share it with us.'

'They may try again.'

'And you wish to be given a place of safety.'

'No, sir. I want to stay at my place and wait for them to come back again.'

'Well, that's very commendable; very brave.'

Unsure how to continue, under the table Baker put her hand on Priestley's leg and shook it a few times. He turned and saw her urgent eye movements in Coker's direction. 'What DI Baker may have in mind is that we allocate sufficient resources to mount a twenty-four times seven surveillance operation on her, so that we are ready to react if and when there is a second attempt to abduct her.'

Coker responded, 'What do you think of that idea?'

Priestley nodded as though in support. 'In theory, it has something going for it. However, on a practical basis, I fear we could expend considerable resources over an extended period of time without ever reaping any reward for our operation. If it *is* tied to the Batter case, then the one thing we know is that we are unable to force the pace of progress. Without an insight into the reason behind the abduction, we would struggle to anticipate future events and to predict their timing.'

'Well, where is that insight going to come from? You're an ideas man, aren't you? Do you not have any sort of theory about what's been happening?'

Priestley pursed his lips and half-closed his eyes, as though thinking on the subject for the first time. 'I can't rate my thoughts any higher than mere speculation, but I'll share them if you wish.'

'I appreciate your caveat, Marcus. Go ahead.'

'Probabilistically, I would say that the Batter case and the abduction are directly linked. Some part of our Batter investigation must have come close enough to one or other of the conspirators to cause them to be concerned we know more than we actually do. In order to find out how much we *do* know, they abducted DI Baker with the intention of interrogating her. Having rendered her unconscious with a drug, they then had to wait around until she recovered, so they could put their questions to her. The act of tying her to a chair in a partially undressed state was no doubt intended to increase her feeling of vulnerability, thereby improving their chance that she would crack under pressure. A corollary is that the method differs sufficiently from the standard violent techniques generally employed by hardened criminals as to suggest that these people are playing by a different set of rules. Even the age-gender-ethnicity pairing itself indicates there has been a joining of forces by people who would not normally associate, which in turn implies there is an unusual reason for their actions. I would say, finding what caused them to come together is the key to the whole conundrum. In essence, to reach the heart of the matter, we need to profile the combination of people, as opposed to any one individual, and so discover their common purpose.'

The others remained appreciatively silent, waiting for Coker's response. Finally, he replied, 'That was a brilliant piece of analysis, Marcus. But where do we go from here? Just how are we going to get that insight?'

'This weekend, DI Baker could be kept under round-the-clock surveillance in case there's a second attempt. If nothing comes of it, we should examine the latest forensics on Monday and reappraise the situation.'

Watt interjected, 'Surveillance ops have been known to scare off the bad guys; it isn't easy keeping an eye on someone without being spotted. We should bring in the technical bods with their bags of tricks so that we can maintain electronic monitoring.'

Baker immediately responded to her, 'May I make a suggestion, ma'am?' Receiving a nod of permission, she continued, 'If DCI Priestley were personally to provide twenty-four hour close cover, no one would think there was any surveillance in operation.'

Coker clapped his hands almost silently. 'Thinking outside the box; I like it. You don't mind covering her this weekend, do you, Marcus? While you're waiting for forensics to turn up trumps?'

Knowing he had no real choice in the matter, he gave a half-hearted smile. 'Well, I have to admit it's certainly a pragmatic solution.'

CHAPTER 15

Mid-afternoon, Priestley knocked at Watt's office door. She bellowed 'Enter!' He opened it and stepped inside. Before he could speak, she shook her head at him. 'No, you can't change your mind. I know you were backed into a corner, but it would look bad all round if you were to alter the plan after the boss has given his approval.' Having already reached the same conclusion, it had not been his intention to withdraw the offer of close protection for Baker. Seeing a possible advantage in appearing reluctant, he turned around and began to saunter slowly toward the door, theatrically dragging his feet. She called out, 'Come back; let's talk about it.'

He accepted her gestured invitation to sit. 'A man's gotta do what a man's gotta do.'

She gave a snort of amusement. 'Are you worried you'll need to put a lock on your bedroom door?'

'It's much worse than that, ma'am: there is no door. I mean, there's only the one bedroom.'

She held a grim smile. 'I'm sure you've nothing to fear from that quarter.'

'All the same, I'd better fetch my chastity boxers from home.' He waited until she had recovered from her burst of laughter. 'I have a plan. It's likely she was trailed from Meadowhall back to the station, and then again to her home in Nottingham. When she leaves today, we can have her under surveillance. If she picks up a tail, we'll arrest them.'

'That's an excellent idea; we could position people in advance all along her route home.'

'If we focused on the usual route to Nottingham, they could predict where she's going, and that might enable them to make a tail more distant and harder to spot. I was thinking we might like to try a route to somewhere else; then, they may believe she's changing location as her own place is compromised.'

'But she'd end up in the wrong place.'

'Only temporarily. My plan is for the two of us to travel together in her car over a monitored route. Once we're certain we don't have a tail, either because there never was one or because they've been picked up, we'll go to my home; I need to collect a few things, anyway. Then we'll head for her flat, which is the only place they'd know of that she might be staying. If they're watching it, they may try and break in. But if nothing happens, she can go out on her own to give them a chance to try and grab her; except, of course, she'll be under surveillance by other officers.'

'You've obviously thought this through thoroughly. Let me know if something happens over the weekend… apart from you having to fight her off; just keep that between yourselves.' She snorted at her risqué humour.

Laughing in appreciation, he realised how different their one-to-one interactions were, compared with those when other officers were present and no one would risk being non-PC.

He went to the MIR and invited Baker to come with him for a meeting.

She closed his office door behind them. Anxiously, she asked, 'You're not backing out, are you?'

He gave her a reassuring smile. 'No, it's still on. We're going to start off by driving over a route where lookouts are watching for anyone tailing us. If it's all clear, we'll then go to my home for me to pick up some things, and then we'll head for your place.'

She frowned, despite him appearing to be relaxed. 'But that would mean meeting your wife, wouldn't it?'

'You don't mind, do you?'

'No, I don't mind, but I thought you might.'

He kept to himself his reasons for wishing Helen to meet her. 'Just act as normal; you're simply a colleague who was abducted and now needs close protection.'

Priestley and Baker set off at four thirty, with Witty following at a substantial distance. Three detectives in unmarked cars were already in position.

Baker completed the route with no sign of anyone attempting to follow them. Priestley instructed Witty to ensure all the in-car video recordings were retained for possible future examination. If later some vehicle were to come to their attention in connection with the case, they would take a closer look at those videos to check if it had been following them without their noticing.

They headed for the Priestley home. Penny silently contemplated the awkwardness she was about to suffer. Marcus had no such misgivings.

Penny parked on the driveway by the wall. Helen opened the outer door and then disappeared inside. As Marcus accompanied Penny to the door, he commented, 'You'll like Helen; she's ever so nice.' She put on a fixed smile as she followed him in.

Marcus led Penny to the kitchen and introduced the women with a considered formality. 'Helen, this is DI Baker. Penny, meet my wife, Professor Priestley.'

Helen held out a hand, which Penny shook briefly. 'Ignore Marcus, Penny. I'm Helen to everyone; well, almost everyone. I understand you were grabbed off the street; how do you feel about that, now?'

Penny shrugged. 'These things happen in our walk of life.'

'It took place this morning, didn't it? So you haven't slept on it, yet. You might find you're disturbed in the night as your subconscious replays some variant of the events. If you are, just let Marcus know; he understands about such things.'

'That's very thoughtful of you. I'll be sure to go and find him in the other room if I'm especially troubled.'

Marcus assumed Helen would have picked up on the way Penny had pointedly referred to "the other room", which had sounded over-elaborate to his ear.

Helen indicated the oven that was humming away. 'I've made a vegetarian lasagne for you, and a beef one for Marcus. The children will be joining us, and once they've made their choice, I'll have whatever's left.'

Penny glanced at Marcus before looking at Helen. 'That's ever so kind of you. I never wanted to put you to any trouble; we could have eaten back at my place.'

Helen smiled. 'It's no trouble at all; it's a pleasure to have a guest with us. I will just apologise in advance for our son, though; he does sometimes become a little overexcited about things, so this may not be the most civilised of meals you've ever had.'

Marcus took Penny to the living room while Helen stayed in the kitchen. Edwin and Alice appeared at the doorway. Marcus called out, 'Come in, you two. This is my colleague, Penny.' He turned to her. 'These are my lovely children, Edwin and Alice.'

Edwin responded, 'Hello, Penny. Where are you going with my father, this weekend? He was supposed to take us to the park.'

Marcus interjected before Penny could respond. 'It isn't Penny's fault that we have to go away. Some bad people may be looking for her, so I'm going to be her bodyguard. We can't tell you where; it's on a "need to know" basis, as they say in films.'

Edwin replied, 'That makes it sound very exciting.'

Penny smiled at him. 'It's the sort of excitement I could happily do without, though.'

Alice looked worried as she whispered to her father, 'Is Penny in a lot of danger?'

Marcus smiled at her. 'She isn't now; not with me to look after her.'

The children headed out, starting their whispered conversation before the door had closed behind them.

While they waited for the food to cook, Marcus and Penny deliberately discussed nothing but the case.

When Helen invited them into the dining room, Marcus indicated where Penny should sit, and then chose the seat to her left, to the right of Helen's place. As the children entered, they realised one of them would need to sit next to the guest. Edwin claimed the place by his mother, leaving Alice on Penny's right.

Helen brought in the two lasagnes and returned to the kitchen. Marcus asked Penny to serve the children, as the vessels would be too hot for them to handle. Alice chose the beef option; Edwin asked for the same. Marcus quipped to Penny, 'If you're playing mother, you might as well give me the rest.' When she had emptied the remainder onto Marcus's plate, he invited her to serve herself from the vegetarian dish. As she hesitated, Helen returned with the salad and insisted she serve herself next.

Marcus assumed the children were reluctant to talk because they had a guest, until Alice suddenly asked Penny, 'Has anyone ever shot at you?'

She smiled at her. 'No, things like that don't happen in this country. Well, not very often.'

Alice looked relieved. 'I wouldn't want anyone to shoot at you and hit my daddy... or you.'

Edwin whispered loudly to Alice, 'Dad was shot at, lots of times, in the army.'

Marcus interrupted them. 'Let's have no more talk about shooting.'

Edwin responded, 'But you're Penny's bodyguard. Does that mean someone wants to shoot her?'

Marcus replied, 'No one wants to shoot Penny. They just want to get hold of her and make her answer some questions, which is why I'll be there to stop them. It's really nothing to worry about.' He turned to Helen. 'Now, what's for pud? Did I see tiramisu?'

When Marcus went to pack a case, he found Helen had already completed the task, leaving it open on the bed for him to check that it had everything he needed. He closed it and brought it downstairs.

Helen corralled the children into the hallway for goodbye kisses. Penny edged her way into the porch and slipped outside. The children bounced up the stairs as Helen gave Marcus a kiss on the lips. She whispered, 'Thank you for putting my mind at rest.'

In the car, Marcus gave directions for an alternative route to Basford. Penny put on the CD that was already in the slot. 'If you can't sing high enough for Puccini's tenor arias, what about this?' Before the first six notes of the introduction had played, he knew this was *Trees*. The crackle and hiss left little doubt he would soon hear the inimitable voice of Paul Robeson.

When the track ended, she pressed the pause button and asked, 'Is that more within your range?'

He looked at her facial profile, her eyes fixed on the road ahead. 'How come you have this in your car?'

She flashed a glance. 'I got it this afternoon when I popped out for some shopping. Do you like it?'

'Mmm. It has a transcendental beauty.'

'You could sing it if you want to.'

'I can't, it's too deep, literally and metaphorically.'

'I'll try and find something for a baritone next time. Is there anything in particular you'd like?'

He pondered at length before replying, softly, 'You really mustn't keep buying things for me.'

They were now on a quiet stretch of road, so she risked giving him a longer glance. 'You didn't need to take me for tea with your family.'

He responded automatically, 'It was no trouble at all. Helen can cook for five as easily as for four.'

She replied immediately, 'That isn't what I meant. I understood exactly what you were doing. Your wife is beautiful and intelligent and kind, and your children are lovely, and you don't want anything ever to get in the way of that. I get it; I really do. I know I'm not much to look at, and that you'd never choose me over Helen, but that's not what I'm wanting from you.'

He heard too much despair in her voice to sit idly by. 'How people look on the outside is entirely superficial; I hope I'm better than that, to think beauty is all about someone's external appearance. But anyway, even if looks were all that mattered, I'd still find you attractive;

you have such a pretty face.'

She allowed a smile to linger. 'I knew you fancied me from the moment we first met. That's why you took the trouble to put me straight, because you thought I was worth the effort. No one else has ever bothered.' Travelling at sixty miles per hour, he decided this was not the moment to suggest her logic was entirely spurious. 'I felt something special when you started telling me off. It was love at first sight.'

With no recollection of gaining any such impression at the time, he decided this was a clear case of historical revisionism. 'A *coup de foudre*; I didn't realise. If you'd told me at the time, I would have explained my situation, and then you'd have changed your mind before the idea could take root.'

'I'm sure I wouldn't have changed my mind. You're my heart's desire, though I know I'm not really yours; only, just for a few days, couldn't you pretend I am?'

He hoped their time together would be less awkward if he agreed to inhabit her world of make-believe for the weekend. 'Just like in that film, even though I'm your bodyguard, it doesn't mean we can't be lovers.' When she turned to deliver him a heartfelt smile, he looked away at the traffic. 'Only, keep your eyes on the road.'

CHAPTER 16

Marcus touched her still-boyish hair. He wondered if she intended to develop a longer style, or whether she would revert to her short crop when summer took hold. He reflected on her rapid development into this sensual woman; every trace of the viraginous image she had first sought to portray had been discarded like layers of clothing, and now she was all affectionate, sensitive and feminine.

Despite the stillness of his body, something broke her satisfied sleep; perhaps it was that very lack of movement. She pressed his shoulder to encourage him onto his back, before easing her light frame onto him. Resting her head on his chest and shoulder, she reached up and gently stroked his hair.

Though he knew she was still in her fairy-tale world, he was already slipping back into reality. He tenderly ran his hands down her back, slowing to explore the ribs that were prominent under her smooth skin. When he reached her tight buttocks he squeezed them gently, before turning onto his side so as to displace her. 'We'd better get up.'

She stretched an arm around his chest and pressed herself against him. 'I want to stay in bed all day.'

He ran his fingers over her head, feeling her hair spring back like meadow grass touched by the wind. 'Have you forgotten we've some work to do?'

'I've forgotten the whole world.'

An hour later, he knew she was still basking in the

afterglow of their latest love-making, but felt he must disturb her languid state. 'It's all been arranged for ten o'clock. What if our colleagues come knocking at the door to check if we're all right?'

'Well, I'd have to put some clothes on, for a start. You're the only man who's allowed to see me naked.'

He gave her arm a tiny shake as though to draw her attention to something. 'I thought I heard someone on the stairs. It could be our lot coming up to break down the door.'

'Only if Nottingham police wear stilettoes; it's the one sound that carries.'

He laughed. 'All right, Penny; maybe I didn't hear anything. But we still need to get up.'

She reluctantly released her hold of him and edged out of bed. 'If I must, I must.'

By the time he exited the bathroom, she had loaded the kitchen table with several types of fresh fruit, a new box of cornflakes, a full bag of an expensive brand of muesli, two sealed jars of coffee of different types, half a loaf of sliced wholemeal bread, a jar of marmalade and a small tub of olive oil margarine. She brought the coffee jars to him in the bedroom as he dressed. 'Which would you prefer?'

Though he had no particular preference, he knew an answer of 'Either,' would sound to her disappointingly unappreciative. He studied the labels and chose one at random. 'This'll be nice.'

When he entered the kitchen, he saw the spread and felt certain it was entirely for his benefit. 'That does look good; do you normally eat this well at weekends?' He had thought of adding, 'I should come here more often,' but stopped himself in time.

She looked anxiously at him. 'It's what you like, isn't it? If there's something else you'd prefer, I can get it in for next time.'

He held a smile, despite the sinking feeling that their visitation expectations were at considerable variance. 'It's just perfect, Penny.'

She looked relieved. 'Call me Pen.'

'Why? Is that what your close friends call you?'

'No, I've never been called Pen by anyone. That's why I want you to; you'll be the first and only.'

They were standing close enough for him to take one small step to reach her. He kissed her on the top of the head. 'You are funny, Pen. Do you think it makes you stronger? The pen is mightier than the sword?'

She laughed. 'You're the funny one.'

After breakfast, Priestley made a call to check with the surveillance team. 'I'll be leaving at nine fifty-five and DI Baker at ten zero-five. Are we all set?'

'All officers are in position.'

Priestley left the flat on time and went downstairs, where he let himself out and headed for his car. After a quick look back, he climbed in and drove away.

Ten minutes later, Baker stepped onto the pavement and glanced around, trying to appear anxious as though wary of a repeat abduction attempt. She hurried to her car and drove to the nearest supermarket, where she rushed up and down the aisles, choosing meat dishes at random. Though the shop was as busy as usual for a Saturday morning, there were enough attended tills for her not to suffer much delay. By eleven o'clock, her colleagues had watched her all the way back home.

Meanwhile, Priestley had driven to Old Basford and was now taking a walk in Vernon Park to kill time, the working assumption being there was less chance of a second abduction attempt while ever he were with her.

A little after eleven o'clock the surveillance team leader phoned Priestley. He stated disappointedly, 'The operation has concluded without incident.'

Priestley responded, 'The chick is back in the nest?' Hearing no reply, he tried again to obtain confirmation. 'The subject is back at the flat?'

'Delta Indigo has returned safely.'

'In that case, you can stand down. Thank you for your help. It was a bit of a long shot, but it might have worked.'

He left the park and headed for his Volvo, passing a bearded man wearing a crash-helmet and standing by a mud-spattered, high-powered Kawasaki. The man bent down to examine the front forks. As Priestley fished in his pocket for his car keys, he heard a squeal of tyres. Looking at the road, he saw two balaclava-wearing, broad-shouldered men jump from the back of a van and run toward him. When he saw the motorcyclist stand up and rush in his direction, he assumed the man was not intending to even the odds.

With three attackers, he went for the nearest first, the motorcyclist, hoping to disable him so that it would leave only two against one. With the head protected and the neck difficult to access past the full-face helmet, he punched him in the solar plexus. The leathers provided the man substantial protection against the blow, but not enough to cushion it entirely. The biker stopped dead in his tracks, allowing Priestley the time to connect with a knee to the groin followed by a full-blooded kick to the same area. The desperate groan as he fell to his knees left Priestley in no doubt he had scored a direct hit.

The first of the two men from the van reached the pavement directly ahead, as the second circled around to approach from behind. Priestley read the manoeuvre and ran away from the opponent at his front, to close in on his rear attacker, who held a metal bar in his hand. He knew the opponent's weapon gave him a substantial advantage, but rather than simply trying to grab it, he veered off at the last moment and threw his body low to the ground to kick at his legs. The man dropped the bar as he put out his hands to stop himself from falling. Priestley snatched it up and swung it at his back, hard enough to crack a rib.

Having seen his numerical advantage dissipate so quickly, the third assailant approached more cautiously. Priestley saw he was wielding a wooden baseball bat, an inferior weapon to his own solid metal bar. When he swung the bar at the man's arm, he raised his bat in a defensive blocking motion. Hearing only one cracking sound, that of the bat splintering, he knew his attacker had reduced the bar's momentum sufficiently to stave off a shattered humerus, though may still have suffered a hairline fracture.

As Priestley prepared to inflict further damage to his third opponent, he felt a blow to the back of the head that felled him. Holding onto his metal bar, he scraped his knuckles as he struck the ground. Stunned, he tried to scramble back to his feet.

He saw the motorcyclist gingerly climbing onto the Kawasaki; after a brief cough of the starter motor he heard a rising whine as it accelerated away. The two injured attackers were helping each other into the back of the van, as a third man climbed into the driver's seat; he assumed he was the one who had struck him on the head and knocked him down.

Thinking an immediate report might enable fellow officers to apprehend the attackers, he pulled out his phone as they drove away. When he called it in, he had to explain he had neither registration, as their rear plates had been covered with mud; he hoped that alone would make them stand out sufficiently to be spotted easily.

While he waited for his colleagues, he examined the crime scene as he stood guard over the baseball bat that lay on the floor. A few minutes later he heard a siren heralding their arrival. The liveried vehicle scorched up to him, its lights flashing. A second police car reached them shortly after, with a similar fanfare. Following a brief explanation of the incident, it was agreed Priestley should not be driving; they would take his Volvo back to the local police station and whisk him off to hospital for a check-up.

As Priestley was being driven away, his phone rang; it was an exasperated sergeant. 'I have a problem, sir. I phoned DI Baker and told her about the attack on you, and I said we now need to provide protection to both of you. When I suggested we should post someone inside her property, she said, and I quote, "That will only happen over your dead body." She meant my dead body, if you see what I mean, sir.'

Priestley smiled inwardly, understanding the reason. 'She's clearly very determined not to let anyone force her out of her castle, so to speak. Let me talk to her and I'll call you back.' He instructed his driver to take him to the flat rather than the hospital, convincing him the injury was too slight to warrant medical attention.

As they approached Baker's flat, Priestley asked the officer to let him out a short distance away, so as not to draw attention to the place. The driver did as requested, parking up and watching him every step of the way.

Rather than letting himself in with his keys, he rang the bell so as not to appear too much at home to any watcher. Baker released the door lock, but also came rushing down to greet him. She insisted he walk up the stairs ahead of her, so she could catch him if he fell. Touched by her concern, he decided not to point out he was about twice her weight and she would simply be flattened.

Once inside, she examined his head and concluded the swelling was only minor. Then, as though he were a child, she kissed the lump to make it better.

He raised the subject of protection and relayed the phone conversation he had had in the car.

She responded, 'There's no way I'm letting anyone in here. You just fought off four attackers on your own, so what good would one more officer do? To make a difference we'd need a whole squad.'

He frowned. 'You're exaggerating: I only fought off two of them. I was about to sort out the third when a fourth one took me down from behind. If we're given protection, it will be round the clock; we do have to sleep sometime.'

'And just where do you think you'd be sleeping?'

'On the couch.'

'Forget it; not gonna happen.'

'What about having someone posted outside?'

'What about patrol cars making frequent checks.'

'It's a deal. I'll phone them back and let them know it'll be enough just to keep passing by.'

'And let them know we won't be leaving again until Monday morning. That will make it simpler for them, not having to provide escorts.'

'All right, Pen; we'll batten down the hatches. I'll call them.'

'And then you'd better go to bed to recover. I'll get in as well, to make it easier to keep an eye on you.'

After Priestley had made the phone call to explain the plan, Penny bathed his skinned knuckles as though they were critical wounds. After yet another check that the lump on his head was no worse than before, she made him sit on the bed as she removed his clothes. Only his boxer shorts were allowed to remain, as he insisted he should avoid strenuous effort until it became certain his head injury was not life-threatening.

In the light filtering through the bedroom curtains, she undressed completely in front of him, still enjoying the novelty of being watched. As she slipped into bed, he closed his eyes as though he needed sleep. She dived slowly below the waves of sheets and fished around for his boxers' elasticated waistband. While removing his last item of clothing, she manually established he was up for more intercourse. To experience a position she had only ever seen acted in films, she knelt by him and rolled down a condom, before straddling him. He felt relieved he had been able to rise to the occasion, and experienced more relief shortly after.

They were both asleep when a phone rang. Marcus recognised it was playing his tune. He hurried out of bed to retrieve it. A conscientious officer was checking they were still alive and well. He thanked him for his diligence, and suggested they themselves should make regular phone calls to confirm their status. They agreed a schedule of six o'clock in the evening, then ten thirty, then nine in the morning.

As it was now after two o'clock, he convinced her she should shower and dress in case of any unexpected visitors, malignant or benign. Accepting the rationale, she hurried to the bathroom and took a quick shower.

He enjoyed a longer shower, wishing to have some time to himself. When he dressed and joined her in the kitchen, she invited him to select something from the items she had bought that morning in the supermarket. He chose fillet steak. She took it from the refrigerator and found it was meant to serve two people. Casually, as though a break from her vegetarian diet had little significance, she put the raw meat onto a dinner plate. After discarding all the packaging, she asked, 'Shall we have fried eggs and tomato?'

He understood her sacrifice. 'That will go well with the steak, but you could have something else entirely, if you prefer. I could have the other half tomorrow.'

She shook her head. 'I want to have the same meals as you. It'll be chicken tomorrow.'

After they had eaten and she was clearing away, he excused himself and phoned Helen from the living room. 'Hello, it's me.'

She sighed theatrically. 'Have you any idea just how meaningless those words are? Unless of course your intention is to provide me with a sample of your voice, so I can discern for myself who's calling.'

'Well, it's your lover.'

'Which one?'

He laughed quietly, not wishing to be overheard. 'I thought I'd let you know I'm perfectly safe and well, now.'

'I don't like the "now". What's been happening?'

'I was jumped by a few guys, but they shot off when

they realised I was more than a match for them.'

Her heart was racing. She sometimes wondered if his job was worth all the stress she suffered. 'Begin at the beginning and don't skip any details.'

'We had a plan to send DI Baker shopping on her own, to see if anyone attempted to abduct her. There was a whole team keeping her under surveillance, but nothing happened. What we hadn't considered was that they'd ignore her and try to abduct me instead. I drove to a park and went for a walk, until I was told Baker was back at her flat. Then, as I was heading back to the car, three blokes came at me with just a couple of clubs between them, so it's obvious they weren't intending to kill me. I sorted out the first two and was just about to deal with the third, when a fourth one whacked me from behind. It wasn't much, so I was still ready to defend myself, but they took off before they suffered any more injuries. One of them probably has a cracked rib or two; and another, maybe a fractured arm.'

She took a deep breath and let it out slowly. 'What if they try again? What protection is there in place now?'

'The two of us will be staying in her flat all the time. Local patrols are going to keep checking up on us. Plus, we have an agreed schedule for phoning in.'

'So, you were meant to be there to take care of her, and now you're the one that needs protecting.'

'Well, you could say we're taking care of each other. I mean, with two of us together, we're in a stronger position.'

'I'm not convinced it's enough. You need armed bodyguards, don't you? What if there's another attack and this time they come with guns?'

'You're worrying too much; they won't try anything

now.' He would have added, 'love,' but there were no longer any sounds emanating from the kitchen.

'I'm not happy about this, Marcus. You call me every hour on the hour to confirm you're all right.'

'Every four hours.'

'Every two hours.'

'Every three hours.'

'Starting at six?'

'Will do. Anyway, must go. She says I have to help with the washing up.'

Despite the strain, Helen managed a little laughter. 'Does she know it'll be your first time?'

'Perhaps I should drop a few pieces on the floor to prove my incompetence; then she might let me off kitchen duties. I'll talk to you later.'

'Bye, love.' She heard the call terminate, leaving her disappointed not to have heard an affectionate response.

CHAPTER 17

Penny found Marcus looking at her selection of books on the small beech shelf attached to the wall near the television. 'Are you wanting to sit and read?'

He selected one at random. 'It might help me relax; I've had enough excitement for one day. What do you normally do on a Saturday afternoon?'

She reflected on whether to invent something that would make her appear more interesting, but decided to tell him the truth. 'I often review cases I'm working on. Sometimes things can come to me when I'm not under pressure.'

'You're certainly dedicated, but don't you think you need a life away from work? Some way of relaxing?'

She smiled. 'I think I've found one.'

Rather than entering into a discussion regarding his future unavailability, he held up the paperback novel. 'Is this any good?'

'Give it a try, but I'm not sure it'll be to your taste.' She picked up another paperback and joined him on the settee, comfortably nestling up against him.

Relieved to have a way of quietly passing the time, he began reading, slowly at first, but picking up speed as he discovered its limited literary qualities.

He was well over half way through the slim novella when she asked if he would like a drink. While she was making their coffee, he looked again at the paperbacks arrayed on the shelf. There was a similarity to the titles, the cover designs and the thicknesses. He imagined some semi-automated factory somewhere, churning out romantic fiction. Before she could catch him inspecting them, he returned to the settee.

Seeing how much of the novella he had read, she asked, 'What do you think of it so far?'

He had already formed a low opinion, but preferred to keep it to himself, at least for now. 'I'll let you know when I've finished.'

By the final page, all loose ends were neatly tied up. He kept the book open in his hand to give him time to reflect on the story and its telling. Innocent girl meets pure boy. They fall in love. Some chance event causes them to lose contact. They suffer the slings and arrows of outrageous fortune, tossed by fate's cruel sea, until they wash up on different, distant shores. He marries, but his wife dies of cancer. She becomes a nun and takes care of hundreds of children. By another twist of fate they meet in some exotic, foreign field. He declares his undying love for her, but she protests that she is a Bride of Christ. They accept they are destined never to consummate their deep and profound love in any physical way. Then, the mother superior intervenes and tells her she should follow her heart. She rushes off to see him, but is told he has already departed on a ship heading for another continent. As she stands at the quayside, weeping bitter tears, he appears from out of the shadows and explains he could not bring himself to be parted from her. They agree to marry. The mother superior conducts the ceremony. Can she do that? Will it be legal? No one in the book raises any such doubts. They take the next ship and head off into the sunset. Everyone lives happily ever after. The End.

'Marcus? Are you re-reading the last page?'

'I always like to spend a few minutes thinking about what I've just read.'

'Well, tell me, what do you think?'

'It's very… touching.'

'I'm glad you like it.'

'How's your book?'

'I've read it before; it's one of my favourites.'

'What's it about?'

She closed it and put it on the nearby coffee table. 'A girl and a boy meet on holiday when they're both teenagers. They fall in love, but he's from a rough background and she's the daughter of a lord, so she never tells him where she lives, which is a castle. At the end of the holiday, she writes down her address on a piece of paper and folds it up. He puts it into his pocket, but his mother washes his trousers before he can read it, and all the ink washes out. He becomes a doctor and works with children in Africa, where he marries another doctor, but she dies from the disease they're treating out there. Then the girl he had met on holiday, who he finds out is an Honourable lady, that's with a capital aitch, meets him while she's working for a children's charity, and they realise they're still in love with each other. He asks her father for her hand in marriage, but he refuses because he's only a commoner. Then, he discovers a cure for the disease the children had been suffering from, and is given a knighthood, so the father changes his mind and says it's all right for them to marry. The ceremony is at the castle, where they live happily ever after.'

'Hmm, interesting. Is it by the same author as my book, by any chance?'

'Yes, she's written a whole series; I've got them all.'

'You obviously like that type of story. Do you relate to it, personally? Is there some famous doctor pining away in a hospital, just waiting to meet you again?'

She laughed. 'I don't think so. I had a boyfriend at school, but I'd guess he only goes into a hospital when he's been in a fight in prison. He's doing life.'

He realised she was being serious. 'Does that have anything to do with you joining the police force?'

'Not in the slightest.'

He put down his book. 'Then why did you join? I would like to know more about you.'

She shook her head. 'No, you might not like it.'

Believing that she really was wishing to reveal her background, he squeezed her hand for a moment. 'If you'd like to tell me, I'd like to listen.'

She took a deep breath and let it out slowly. 'When I was at school, everybody said they were having sex, so I let him do it to me. He banged away at me whenever he wanted, but I never enjoyed it. When we left school, he never bothered seeing me again. Then I read in the paper he'd been found guilty of murder; he'd been part of some drug dealer's gang. He should have been put away a long time before then.'

'And yet that didn't have anything to do with you joining the force?'

'Well, maybe it did, just a little. I wanted to see all the bad guys locked up.'

'Have you ever cut corners before, to get a result?'

She eyed him steadily. 'I wouldn't like to say.'

'When we first met, I thought you were a stickler for the rules.' She looked away. 'It's a good thing that most people obey the rules, otherwise there'd be utter chaos.'

'But you don't stick to the rules, do you.'

'I may have bent some in the past.'

'Well, I've bent some, too.'

'For instance?'

'I can't recall, offhand. Anyway, nothing like I've done recently. It's your bad influence.'

He felt convinced she had chosen to start breaking the rules as a way of showing her commitment to him, and not as a consequence of misconstruing his words. Feeling in some measure responsible, he gently coaxed her, 'I must ask you to rein back on the rule-breaking, Pen, before you get into trouble.'

Fishing for a compliment, she responded, 'Because you care about me?'

Accepting they were still in her make-believe world, he gave her what she craved. 'Of course.'

She climbed onto him, straddling him and gazing into his eyes. 'I gave up sex after I left school; I didn't know how nice it could be.'

Concerned she would soon ask for more of the same, he eased her off him. 'What's for tea?'

While she was preparing pepperoni pizza and salad, he wrote down the telephone calls they were scheduled to make, and then turned on the television. From the dozens of channels available he chose one dedicated to showing the latest news.

She brought him a can of chilled beer. He considered asking for a glass, but decided that would not fit with the image of the man she wanted him to be.

While eating together, she let him roam through the channels in search of something to his taste. Having no interest in dancing, baking, talent shows and quizzes, he found very little that he thought might be suitable for both of them. Had he been alone, he may have watched a programme about railway engines from the steam era.

She pointed to the dozens of DVDs in a rack by the television. 'We could watch one of those if you like.'

From his place on the settee he was unable to read the titles. 'Good idea; you choose.'

He sat through almost two hours of a film in which members of the same family had widely contrasting accents. The twin sisters who had been brought up together were particularly remarkable, one having a hint of Irish, the other being strictly Home Counties. A young man had imagined he had fallen in love with Home Counties, but eventually realised it was the Irish girl he really loved. Home Counties was bitterly upset, until she found the sympathetic ear of the young man's friend, and discovered almost instantly that she was now deeply in love with him. They had a joint wedding and everyone lived happily ever after.

As the long list of featured songs was scrolling up, she asked, 'What did you think of it? Wasn't it lovely?'

He smiled and nodded. 'Are there any humorous out-takes?'

She frowned at him. 'Of course not; it wasn't that sort of a film.' He grinned. 'Oh, you were joking.'

Though he found little on television to interest him, it remained turned on for the rest of the evening. After completing the last of their scheduled phone calls, she asked, 'Shall we go to bed now? I'm feeling tired.'

He was concerned she may not be tired enough to allow him to sleep. 'Yes, you go to bed; I'll stay up a bit and watch the football, if that's all right.' He would never normally have watched the programme live, as he much preferred to skip through all the studio debate and just see the matches. Thoroughly bored long before the programme had finished, he stuck it out to the bitter end. She had nodded off, so he eased down the volume.

Her eyes sprang open. 'It's late. You go first.'

In bed, he feigned a convincing sleep as she returned from the bathroom. Seeing he was wearing plain cotton pyjamas, she reluctantly put on a pair of her own. After slipping between the sheets, she cuddled up to him.

Following a good night's rest, Marcus woke to the alarm that was set to the time of the first scheduled call. Guiltily, he phoned Helen from the bed. Penny began to slip her hand down his pyjamas while he was speaking. He quickly terminated the call, using the excuse that he had another timed report to make.

Once certain it had disconnected, she grinned at him. 'Sorry, I couldn't resist it.'

He frowned hard at her. 'Don't ever do that again! I ought to pull your pants down and smack your bottom.'

Her grin broadened. 'I'm game.'

As he made the call to the current duty officer, she climbed out of bed, stood directly in front of him and began removing her pyjama top. He tried to hurry the call, as she slowly peeled off the lower garment. The officer asked, 'Are you certain everything is all right, sir? I'm detecting some stress in your voice.'

He tried to sound calmer. 'I must still be feeling the after-effects of yesterday's incident. Everything's fine here. I'll call you again in three hours.'

When he put down the phone, she stepped up to the edge of the bed. He reached out and gently turned her around. 'I told you what would happen. Now, stand still and take your punishment.' He touched her gently on each buttock with the flat of his hand.

'Is that it? I thought I was much badder than that.'

He gave her the softest of smacks, just enough to register the right sound. 'There, take that you bad girl. And next time I'm on the phone, just behave yourself, will you?'

She folded back the sheet and climbed in, lingering on top of him for a few seconds before returning to her own side. 'I've always liked the idea of spending a whole day in bed.' She checked the pack of condoms. 'Should I go on the pill?'

He eased her onto her back. 'Let's not discuss things like that; not today.'

After he had satisfied her desires, she fell fast asleep. He showered and dressed, and then caught up with the news on the television.

Later, he brought in her breakfast on a tray, before leaving to watch a politics programme. Disappointed to be alone, she went for a shower. When she had dressed, she found him channel-hopping. Believing him to be bored, she rummaged for a long novel he could read while she busied herself with washing and ironing.

After lunch, she snuggled up to him on the settee, while they watched a black-and-white film about a man who had returned from Africa and become caught up in an intrigue involving secret agents. He had seen the film several times before, but still enjoyed catching glimpses of Gresley A4 Pacific steam engines, the so-called *Streaks*. As she watched him concentrating on the screen, she thought how happily she could do this every weekend. He found he was missing his wife and children.

CHAPTER 18

On the Monday, Marcus woke to Penny's alarm and realised she had set it an hour early. She demonstrated her reason, that they would need plenty of time to start the day the way she wanted.

At the station, they were invited to an eleven o'clock meeting with Coker. When they presented themselves with a minute to spare, they found Watt and Yelland were also there, together with Philippa Hatchette, the Head of Human Resources. Coker began, 'Marcus, you appeared unwilling to accept a bravery commendation last week. Now I find you successfully fought off four men who attacked you on Saturday, so I assume you'll have no such reluctance this time.'

Priestley frowned. 'I only succeeded against two of them, sir. I was ready to deal with the third, when the fourth one struck me from behind, so I can only claim to have fought off two, or at most two-and-a-half.'

Coker sighed. 'But four of them ran away, and even if you don't count the van driver, that still leaves three. So you can't really object, can you?'

'Actually, sir, I feel I should. There were two big lads carrying clubs, but they didn't have a clue how to fight; they were obviously amateurs. Plus the guy on the motorbike was a bit weedy.'

'Even so, we need some good publicity and you're just the man for the job.'

'I do think we'd better leave things for now, sir, until the investigation has reached a satisfactory conclusion.'

'Well, when will that be?'

'As far as the original murder case is concerned, it's difficult to say. If we consider who had means, motive and opportunity, we don't have anyone who comes up with three cherries. Focusing just on means, legitimate purchasers of cyanide need a Home Office licence, but that would give us a very long list, starting with all the jewellers who use it for gilding. And anyway, it could well have been an illegitimate buyer. As to motive, we have only uncovered one rather tenuous link, relating to an old woman who was far too ill to have carried out the deed herself, being in a hospice at the time. She has since died, so we can't even question her any more. Her son could have vicariously adopted the same motive, only he was in America. And as to opportunity, there was just one suspicious sighting in the vicinity; that was of another old woman, carrying a shopping bag.'

'So we've nothing, then.'

'We may or may not have something, depending on whether we accept the attacks on DI Baker and myself are linked to the murder. If they are connected, then this indicates there is a conspiracy. So far, we have had two people who attacked DI Baker and four who attacked me. Including the murderer, that would make at least seven people operating together with a common cause.'

'And if we find the cause, we solve the case.'

'One would like to hope so, sir.'

'What would you say is the likelihood that there'll be another attempt to abduct you or DI Baker?'

'Like I said before, I think they're amateurs, so they may well have been scared off. That's unless there are more professional actors involved in the conspiracy who could be brought into play.'

'What if we were to make the two of you tempting targets? Might that flush them out?'

Hatchette interjected, 'That sounds too dangerous, Charles, deliberately putting officers' lives at risk.'

Coker responded, 'We'd keep them both under close surveillance at all times.'

Yelland commented, 'That's a resource-intensive process, sir. Even for one, it would require…'

Baker interrupted him and addressed Coker. 'May I speak, sir?' She continued without waiting to be given permission. 'The surveillance on Friday from when we left the station and went to DCI Priestley's home found no evidence of anyone on the lookout, so they probably don't know where he lives. On the other hand, they already know where I live. If DCI Priestley were to go home at any time, he could be followed, and then his family would be put at risk, and the number of people needing close protection would increase substantially. Therefore I respectfully suggest DCI Priestley should not be allowed to go home until this case is solved, to keep his family out of danger. My own place is already compromised, so it clearly makes sense for him to stay at my flat, along with me, thereby requiring only one location to be kept under surveillance. At other times, the two of us would stay in close proximity, providing a single focus for the work of the surveillance team.'

Coker replied immediately, 'Well done, DI Baker. I can see you've thought this through very carefully.'

Watt commented to her, quietly, 'Yes, well played.'

Coker continued, 'So that's settled, then.' He turned to Priestley. 'You can't go home for your things, so buy new stuff and claim it on expenses; I'll sign it off. Keep me informed of any developments.' The sweep of his hand indicated the meeting was now at an end.

Priestley walked with Baker back to his office. She closed the door behind her and began defensively, 'It was the right thing to do, Marcus; you know it was.'

He held her frightened-rabbit stare for a moment. 'Don't fret, Penny. I'd already thought along those lines and reached a similar conclusion, only I didn't want to raise the subject myself in case anyone made inferences I'd rather they didn't. I wondered if I might have to decamp to a safe house, but as you're obviously happy to entertain me, we're going to be sharing for a while.'

Her relief was palpable. 'So you're not cross with me for suggesting it?'

'No, not at all; you did it quite subtly, though the Chief Super gave me a questioning look. Make sure you don't treat me like anything but another colleague, won't you, while ever we're here. We'll go shopping after work; I'll have to buy some new clothes.'

She smiled. 'And condoms.'

He frowned. 'I can't claim those on expenses.'

'Should I go to the doctor's, instead?'

'You keep forgetting we'll only be living together until this case is over, and that might not be very long if we catch a lucky break.' He read her expression and knew she regarded that as an unlucky break. 'Let's get Liversedge back in here. You stay behind the scenes while I interview him with Neil.'

Baker left his office, consciously resisting giving a backward glance. Priestley phoned Witty and requested he arrange the interview with Liversedge.

Marcus checked Helen's schedule and phoned her during her short break. 'Hello, it's me, your husband.'

'I'm hardly likely to forget who you are.'

'But if I just say "It's me," you tell me off.'

'I never told you off; I simply pointed out the... Why are you calling? Is it to tell me you're now safe, again?'

'I'm letting you know that I'm keeping *you* safe by not coming home.' He waited for a response but heard only silence. 'The Chief Constable has instructed me to remain in residence with DI Baker, as we both need to be kept under close surveillance; otherwise it doubles the manpower we'd need to find. We weren't followed last Friday when I came home after work, so they don't know where we live, but I have to stay away in case they're watching where I go.' He knew he had rushed out his explanation, despite attempting to sound calm.

'Should I send some clean underwear over for you? What about socks and shirts?'

'The boss has authorised me to buy new stuff on expenses so there's no link back to you. And DI Baker has a combined washing machine and tumble dryer, which I'm sure she won't mind my using.'

'When are you going to stop calling her DI Baker? You're sharing an apartment with her, for God's sake. She may not be the easiest of people to get on with, but you need to make an effort to rub along with her.'

'You're right, of course.' He gave a nervous laugh. 'When we first met, I asked if I could call her "Penny", but she objected because she said it was too familiar. She eventually gave me permission, but it still feels a bit strained. I'll make a point of always calling her "Penny" from now on, no matter how formal she likes to be. Maybe then she'll start to loosen up a bit.'

'OK. And don't forget, you're an interloper at her place, so make sure you respect her personal space.'

'I'll try not to encroach.'

'So, how long do you expect this to last?'

'It's supposed to be until we've cracked the case, but if it starts to drag on, I'm going to request a separate safe house; I'm not sure how long I'll be able to stand being billeted with her.'

'She's probably thinking along the same lines, just wanting you out of there. As you're her guest, it's more your responsibility to keep things civil.'

'I'll make sure I'm on my best behaviour.'

'Yes, but don't go too far the other way. If it's like you're walking on eggshells with her, neither of you will feel comfortable, so just try to relax a bit. I know it'll be hard with her, but do your best. Anyway, I must go now. I have to deliver a lecture on human behaviour with a focus on conflict within confined environments; quite appropriate, really.'

'I'll call you this evening. Bye, love.'

He stood looking through the window and down the valley, but failed to see the beauty of the view as he began to despise himself for deceiving his loving wife.

When he refocused on work, he began by reviewing the latest forensic reports, which made him realise any progress would need to come from another source.

Witty collected Liversedge from reception at four thirty, the earliest time he had claimed to be available. Priestley joined them and was relieved to find there was no lawyer in tow, suggesting he intended to maintain his nothing-to-hide stance. In order to reinforce the idea that he was an unintelligent copper who depended on stock phrases and Political Correctness, he began, 'First of all, let me thank you most sincerely for providing a list of your mother's non-young female associates.'

Liversedge snorted disparagingly. 'Old women who were friends of hers, you mean.'

'Indeed, sir. I have to tell you that none of the ladies named on your list proved to be viable suspects.'

'I'm not surprised.'

'As to the boy who crashed a van into your car, so far we have been unable to identify any viable suspects, though we are continuing to investigate.'

'That's disappointing; I was rather hoping you might have tracked down the woman who's been demanding money with menaces. Could it be someone who knows something about the police investigation and thought she'd try her hand at a bit of blackmail?'

'We never discount any possibility, sir.'

'But are you actively investigating that angle? She could be one of your colleagues.'

Priestley displayed surprise bordering on shock. 'I am quite sure no one in the police service would ever commit such an act of criminality.'

'But if you've no other leads, it must be something worth considering, mustn't it?'

'I'll certainly make sure it's added to the list of things to be looked into, once we have the manpower.'

'Everyone's busy at the moment, then?'

Priestley leaned in conspiratorially. 'Very busy, sir. We have a lead that I'm not allowed to disclose to you, but if it goes the way I hope it will, we should be able to identify everyone involved in the conspiracy behind the murder of Mrs Batter. That's something to keep between ourselves, for now.' He raised his volume back to normal. 'The good news is, now that we have an idea of the scale of the operation behind the killing, it seems increasingly unlikely that your mother had anything to do with it. I'm sure you'll be pleased to hear that, sir.'

Liversedge nodded, unable to smooth the worry lines now etched into his face. 'Yes, I am pleased to hear it.'

'So we may have no further need to contact you, sir. Therefore, let me again express my thanks for your help, and to apologise most sincerely on behalf of the constabulary for any untoward suggestion made to you during the course of this investigation in relation to the possibility of criminal activity by your mother.'

'That's all right; I understand you have to do such things. I'll be off, then.'

'Sergeant Whittington will show you out.'

Witty escorted Liversedge from the building before joining Baker in Priestley's office. She fell silent as he entered. He asked, 'Have I missed it all? Are you down to the conclusions?'

Priestley waved him to his usual chair. 'Not at all, Neil; we haven't started yet.' He turned to Baker. 'You kick off, Penny.'

She put on her most severe expression. 'He looked worried at the suggestion we knew about a conspiracy. That must mean he's a part of it.'

Priestley commented, 'Not that we know the precise nature of the conspiracy, or how wide it goes.'

Witty interjected, 'But if he is part of a conspiracy, and he arranged for an anonymous caller to request a meeting in Meadowhall, then doesn't that mean that the blackmail is just a hoax? In which case, why would he want us to investigate the matter?'

Priestley responded, 'He has to act as though there *is* a genuine blackmail attempt, otherwise we'd know he's behind it. There clearly is a conspiracy, if we consider how the Meadowhall ploy was used to discover the identity of the most senior female officer, no doubt in the belief that women are softer targets.' He flashed a smile at Penny. 'Evidently they'd never met DI Baker.' She glowed with pride at the compliment. 'We don't know how many conspirators trailed Penny back to the station and then to her home, but there were two would-be abductors in that first attempt and a further four who had a go at me.'

Witty replied, 'But what if he's entirely innocent and the blackmail attempt is real? Wouldn't *that* make him push us into investigating it?'

Priestley looked at his watch. 'You're quite right to keep an open mind, Neil. Anyway, I'm sorry, but I'm going to have to cut this meeting short. The blackmail may end up serving as a distraction from our core case, so let's remain focused on the murder and abduction attempts. If Penny and I are the only potential sources of information so far identified by the conspirators, another shot at abducting us is a distinct possibility.'

Baker responded, 'Is our surveillance all sorted?'

Priestley replied, 'Not only is *ours* ready to roll, but we're also monitoring Liversedge as of the moment he left this building, though I doubt he'll show his hand.' He turned to Witty. 'You can get off now, Neil. Penny and I will be departing at eighteen hundred hours.'

Once Witty was out of earshot, Marcus explained to Penny, 'I had to halt the meeting; he was getting too close to what's been going on.'

Penny nodded. 'Yes, he's a bright bloke. Now, tell me what you'd really like for tea.'

He smiled. 'Vegetarian will be fine. Honest. What about a mushroom risotto?'

CHAPTER 19

After a monitored visit to the supermarket where they bought vegetarian food and men's underwear, Baker parked the car close to her home. They shared the bags from the boot and walked to the front door. She asked him to open it. He took another of the bags from her. 'You'll have to do it; I don't have my keys anymore.'

She stared at him accusingly. 'You've lost them?'

'No, I just slipped them to our guardian angel in the men's loos; if his team need to rescue us it would be better if they don't have to break down the door. The guy claimed to be disappointed; he reckons they all enjoy the adrenaline rush of smashing into a place with their guns drawn.'

'Guns?'

'I should have mentioned it earlier but I didn't want you fretting we're in more danger than we really are. Just in case our would-be abductors take it up another notch, the protection unit will be fully armed.'

'Does that mean you think we really are in danger?'

'I'm simply being cautious.'

They entered the flat and took the food into the kitchen. He headed for the bedroom to deposit his new clothes in the drawers she had emptied for him. When he returned, he found everything had been tidied away. Hopefully, he asked, 'Are we eating now?'

She shook her head. 'No; after.'

'After what?'

She took his hand. 'I've been wanting you all day.'

In the bedroom, he suddenly remembered something that had been troubling him. 'If our guys decide to check up on us in the night, it would be a good idea to look like I'm sleeping on the sofa.'

She ferreted out a rolled sleeping bag. 'Will this do?'

He took it from her and placed it behind the settee. When he returned to the bedroom she was removing her clothes with unseemly haste. He tried hard not to be too quick with her, knowing he really wanted to eat.

After the mushroom risotto, he turned on the news. He held his tongue when a woman performed such an adversarial interview that the male politician was barely able to get a word in edgeways; at home he would have aimed to deliver an amusing non-PC observation.

They watched a DVD of her choosing, punctuated only by timed telephone calls. Despite the many hurdles fate placed in the way of the civil rights lawyer and the outdoor girl with fashion model looks and ten thousand acres of woodland to protect, he remained certain they would win their court case against Big Business and coincidentally discover the path to true love.

She wanted them both to sleep naked, but he found her breath rippled his body hair and kept him awake. When he insisted he should wear his new pyjama top and matching shorts, she put on a T-shirt and leggings.

In the early hours of the morning he heard a sound that woke him and rendered him fully conscious. He shook her roughly. 'Penny. Pen. Did you hear that?'

'Hear what?'

'Someone's just forced the front door. Quick, put the light on.' She found the switch to the bedside lamp. He grabbed his police radio. 'Victor Charlie Three One, Victor Charlie Three One from Alpha Bravo, over.'

'Victor Charlie Three One, receiving.'

'Order is Vesuvius. Repeat, order is Vesuvius.'

'Victor Charlie Three One responding.'

Priestley turned off the radio and placed it under his pillow. 'Remember, we need to slow them down but not scare them off before the team arrives.'

They listened for a sound on the stairs but heard nothing. Suddenly, the noise Priestley had heard earlier was repeated, as the lock on the door to the flat was given the same treatment as the one on the outer door. He guessed it was some sort of air pressure device that had blown a hole through the wood where the lock had been. Though quick and efficient, he knew they had committed a tactical error by giving a warning that would have been absent if skeleton keys had been used.

Baker was about to fetch the baseball bat that was to be her defensive weapon, but Priestley stayed her arm. 'Change of plan; trust me. Just wait for them; then we may not have to fight at all.'

With the bedside lamp still turned on, they watched the door, ready for a sudden incoming charge. Instead, two men wearing full army combat gear entered slowly, pulling their night-vision goggles one-handed away from their eyes. In their other hands were guns pointed at the occupants of the bed. Priestley recognised that the semi-automatic held by the shorter intruder was a Browning of the type used until recently by the British army, whereas the taller one was holding a Glock 17, the army's replacement pistol, a lighter weapon made from plastic. Though the Glock was also standard issue in the police, his instincts told him the army connection was the more likely. He pointed to the dressing table and called out, 'My wallet's over there; just take it, and anything else you want. We won't tell anyone.'

The taller intruder responded, 'We're not here for your money. If you don't do anything stupid, you won't get hurt. Somebody wants to ask you some questions, so just come quietly and there'll be no bother.'

Baker spoke up, her reedy voice quivering. 'I can't go out like this; I need to get dressed.'

The taller one replied, 'Well, get some clothes on.'

She hissed through clenched teeth, 'I'm not getting changed while you're here looking at me.'

Restraining himself to avoid being overheard by neighbours, the shorter one growled, 'I'm standing here with a feckin' gun pointed at your feckin' head and you're feckin' telling me what you won't feckin' do? Are you a feckin' eejit?'

She repeatedly jabbed her right index finger toward his chest. 'Don't you fucking swear at me, you fucker.'

Priestley interjected in a conciliatory tone, 'If you just let her get changed in the bathroom she won't be any trouble.'

The shorter one passed his weapon to his partner and then peeled off a ready-cut piece of silver duct tape from a roll. 'Get up and come here, ya wee gobshite. And if you take it off…'

Priestley responded, 'She won't touch it; honest.'

Baker accepted the gag over her mouth and then collected up a pile of clothes. While she was getting changed in the bathroom Priestley quickly dressed in the bedroom. The taller one knocked on the bathroom door. 'Come on out.' After a few seconds he knocked again. 'If you don't come out now, I'm coming in.' She opened the door and exited, fully dressed. Without waiting for instructions, she re-entered the bedroom.

The shorter one turned her around and pulled her hands behind her back, where he fastened her wrists together with a cable tie. He barked out, 'Lie face down on the floor.' Then he turned to Priestley. 'You're a bit handy, aren't you; get on the bed, face down.'

Hoping to keep the mood as light as possible under the circumstances, Priestley quipped, 'You aren't going to bugger me, are you? You're not my type.'

The taller one stifled a titter before instructing his partner, 'Do his ankles as well, and then tape his mouth before he cracks any more jokes.' When Priestley was tied and gagged, the taller one ordered him to lead off.

Priestley hobbled down the stairs, swinging on the banister for support at each step. Baker followed close behind. The two abductors stayed back, holding their guns close to their bodies. At the outer door, the taller abductor came up behind Priestley and sliced through his ankle tie with a Stanley knife. 'You're going to turn left and keep walking until I tell you to stop. Got that?' When Priestley nodded, he instructed him to walk close to Baker as though they were a couple.

The four moved slowly in pairs to the first corner, where the taller abductor gave an order. 'Turn left.'

They were approaching another corner when a voice yelled out, 'Armed police! Put down your weapons.' Simultaneously, three members of the armed protection unit appeared from different hiding places. The shorter abductor began to raise his gun. An officer fired at him, a double tap to the chest. The man crumpled to the pavement, his gun falling harmlessly to one side.

The taller one immediately threw his Glock to the ground. Priestley was relieved it wasn't the Browning, as the older weapon lacked the Glock's safety features that would stop it from going off accidentally.

As officers secured the guns and removed the gags, Victor Charlie Three One established contact with control using Airwave Speak. He then informed them, 'One suspect to be taken into custody. The other one's down. Terminal force had to be used. I'm taking Alpha Bravo and Delta Indigo back inside.'

At the outer door, Victor Charlie Three One handed Priestley the keys to Baker's flat. 'We didn't need them in the end, but it was a good idea.'

Priestley accepted them, commenting, 'They're not much use, now; they did the upstairs one as well.'

Baker inspected the damaged door. 'When we fit a new lock, we'll have to do plenty of spare keys for my neighbours.' She led the way upstairs and into her flat. 'I need a cup of tea. Anyone else?' Knowing Marcus only drank coffee, her intention was to imply she was unfamiliar with his habits.

Three One accepted the offer. Priestley declined, and went to recover his radio from the bedroom. When he returned, Three One asked, 'How did it all work out in here, then? What happened when you were putting on a show of resistance?'

Priestley shook his head. 'I decided it was better not to, so when I heard a sound outside, I climbed out of my sleeping bag and got into the edge of the bed, so we wouldn't appear threatening when they came in.'

Three One nodded. 'If you're intending to make a statement to that effect, sir, may I respectfully suggest you cut the plastic ties off the sleeping bag first. At the moment, they're holding the zip in place, so it isn't actually possible to get into it.'

Priestley felt his colour rising. 'Thank you for that

suggestion; I'll do it right away.'

Baker arrived with two mugs of tea. 'You'll do what right away?'

'Do you have some sharp scissors?' She fetched a pair from the kitchen. He cut through the zip tags, and also the one displaying the price label, before turning to the officer. 'As I was saying, I decided it was better for us not to show any resistance, so when I heard a sound outside, I climbed out of my sleeping bag and got into the edge of the bed, so we wouldn't appear threatening when they came in.'

He nodded his head firmly. 'That's very believable.'

'You'll need to get your story straight, too, before IPCC come to investigate the shooting.'

'I don't see any problem on that front; we played it by the book and only did what was necessary. Now we need to get the two of you to a safe house.'

Priestley responded, 'One with two bedrooms.'

Baker interjected, 'Or just one room would be OK, if it would make it easier for you to provide protection.'

Priestley replied to her, 'We could manage in just one room, I suppose, if it had twin beds.'

She nodded as though in agreement. 'Or even one big bed, at a pinch… if it was the safest place.'

He shook his head. '"Twin beds" is where I draw the line.' A palpable awkwardness hung in the air.

Three One broke the silence. 'I'd suggest you pack enough things to keep you going for quite a while; you never know how long it'll be before you're back here.'

She put down her mug. 'I'd better empty the fridge; I don't want stuff going off and smelling the place out.'

They agreed Baker's car should be removed to the police station at Midshaw. She reluctantly relinquished her keys, feeling uncomfortable to be dependent on others for transportation. Priestley requested that his own car also be delivered to Midshaw.

Priestley and Baker were taken by unmarked police van to a farmhouse on the fringes of Hathersage in the Peak District. Though it was still night-time, the sky was light enough for them to see the fallow fields that surrounded the stone dwelling. An outside light was shining and yellow beams were filtering through the skylight above the outer door to the porch.

They carried their own cases from the van. As they approached, the door was opened wide, allowing more light beams to illuminate the pathway in front of them. A woman with the build of a prop forward stepped out to greet them with a smile, though no handshake. 'I'm June, and you're Julie and Augustus. Come inside.'

They followed her into the traditional farmhouse kitchen, its oak beams blackened by generations of accreted soot. Julie put down her case. 'I had to empty my fridge, so I brought everything with me. You don't mind, do you?'

June put the kettle on the Yorkshire range. 'Not a bit of it, love. You fetch it all in and I'll make a cuppa.'

June led Augustus to a bedroom. 'I've put you in here, and Julie right next door. Don't feel you have to mess up more sheets than you need to, though; it just makes more washing for me, and nobody else will be staying. Your man tipped me the wink.'

He put down his case. 'I think there's been a bit of a misunderstanding; we should have separate bedrooms. Erm, but, don't tell Julie what I just said, will you.'

'She's doing all the running, then, is she. Well, I'm down t'other end so I won't hear what you get up to.'

'Thank you, June; you're very understanding.'

They headed for the kitchen. As they heard the van drive away, Julie stepped in from the porch, struggling not to brush against the walls of the narrow passageway with her four bags of food. 'What shall I do with these? Is there a fridge I can use?'

'Don't bother yourself, lass; I'll sort it all out. You'll be picked up at eight, so breakfast at seven. I'll do your dinner for whatever time you want, only let me know if you won't be in; I don't like anything going to waste.'

'I have to let you know I'm a vegetarian.'

'That explains why you're so skinny, love; you need to get some meat down you, build yourself up. I'll bet Augustus eats plenty of meat; you do know the way to a man's heart is through his stomach, don't you? I always made sure my husband had proper food; he looked so healthy with his ruddy cheeks, right until he upped and died on me at just fifty-four. It was a heart attack.'

'I'm sorry for your loss. Erm, well, I don't mind eating meat if that's what you want to cook for us.'

'That's what I like to hear, a bit of common sense. Now let's get you two to bed.' She led her to the second bedroom. Before she left her she reprised her earlier comment to Augustus. 'These are thick walls and I'm down t'other end, so I won't be able to hear you.'

As soon as Julie was alone, she transferred her case to Augustus's room. He pretended to be puzzled. She extracted the box of condoms and held them up as though a prize exhibit. 'We'll need plenty of these.'

CHAPTER 20

Breakfast was served in the kitchen at seven o'clock sharp. June put down their crowded plates and left the two of them alone. Observing the amount of fat on the ham, Augustus considered how much he could trim off without giving offence. Julie exhibited no such concern as she cut out every last trace. He followed her lead until only the salty pink flesh remained. As he looked at the two eggs, the fried mushroom, the fried bread, the cooked tomatoes and the slices of black pudding, he consoled himself with the thought that his diet could probably stand the strain at the moment, considering how many calories he must be burning off.

With the exception of the fat excised from the ham, Julie devoured every last morsel of food on her plate. She wondered if her appetite was being driven by the vigorous love-making, or whether it stemmed from the excitement she felt following the danger she and her lover had been in. When that gun had been pointing at her head, she had been terrified; but now, looking back at the incident, she felt only the relief that it was just her tongue that had loosened, and not the grip of some sphincter muscle. What would he have thought of her if she had wet herself? But she hadn't, and so felt stronger for the experience. And now, living with him in a safe house like some underworld VIP, her overwhelming feeling was one of euphoria. With such mortal dangers being faced and overcome by the two of them together, she felt certain a happy ending was inevitable.

At eight o'clock, she was standing looking out of their bedroom window, watching and waiting for an unmarked police car. A red Royal Mail van hove into view and trundled along the rutted road. She suddenly felt a wave of anxiety wash over her. 'Look! There's a mail van coming! What if it's really more of them?'

He heard the fear and trepidation in her voice. 'It's probably just someone delivering the post, but check in with our guys anyway.'

As the call connected, she suddenly realised she was unsure who she now was: Delta Indigo, or Julie, or even herself. 'I'm Delta Indigo from the incident at...' She released her breath in a deep sigh. 'Yes, that's me. There's a Royal Mail van coming up the road.' She turned and smiled at Marcus. 'That's all right then. Thank you.' She put her phone back into her pocket. 'That's our limo arriving.'

To create the appearance of authenticity in the mind of any casual observer, the van had not been converted for passenger use. In the back was only empty space, except for four straps attached to the inner skin of the double panels. Isolated from the driver, they grabbed two straps each and held on tight. Having no view of the road outside, they were unable to anticipate changes of direction, and so were pitched about.

The vehicle came to a sudden halt. Moments later the rear doors were yanked open. They scrambled out and looked around, finding themselves in a corner of a mail sorting office car park. Recognising Craig Vardy sitting in a black BMW with the engine idling, Priestley headed for him. They jumped into the back seat, one from each side. Vardy roared off while they were still fastening their seat belts. Priestley called over to him,

'Hello, Craig. How are you doing?'

'Just great, boss. Can I light us up?'

Priestley laughed. 'You do know we're meant to be inconspicuous, don't you? Can you just try and stick to the speed limits?'

'I can certainly try, but this beast runs away with me if I don't hold it back.'

'Do you know DI Baker, officer Vardy? Penny, to her friends.'

'Hello, Penny, ma'am. I'm Craig.'

She recognised he was attempting to be both friendly and humorous. 'So I gathered. You're a bit of a speed merchant, then?'

'I would be, if certain officers would let me off the leash... naming no names.'

Priestley laughed again. 'You're not still going on about that, are you? If I'd let you go any faster, you'd have arrived before you set off.'

Craig pretended to be puzzled. 'Is that possible?'

When they arrived at the station, Witty was waiting at the front steps. As soon as they stepped out of the car he called over to them, 'I'm glad to see you're safe and sound. You're both to go straight to the Chief's office. I'm busting to know what really happened; any chance I can come along, too?'

Priestley nodded. 'Just follow us in as though you're invited. Do you know if anyone else will be there?'

'It would be easier to say who won't be.'

Priestley and Baker went directly to Coker's office. Superintendent Yelland was at the door to welcome them. As they entered, Coker gave a burst of applause; the others joined in enthusiastically, until he finally quietened them with the usual two-handed signal for hushing a room. 'Marcus, a hero again, and this time you can't say otherwise.'

'Well, sir, I'd like to make the point that DI Baker was far braver, the way she stood up to them.'

Coker looked impressed. 'Really? Come over here and explain, though we'll be reviewing your full report later.' Coker, Priestley and Baker sat down. There were insufficient seats for all the senior officers assembled, so they chose to stand rather than traverse the minefield of rank versus gender.

When Priestley described the sound outside the flat, Chief Superintendent Watt asked, 'Was it just you who heard it?'

He answered quickly, 'Yes, ma'am. DI Baker was in her bedroom at the time.' He knew that was really a lie, though it masqueraded as a literal truth. 'In order not to provoke them, I went into her bedroom.'

Watt asked, 'How did that avoid provoking them?'

He took a deep breath. 'I slipped into the edge of her bed, so that it looked like we had both been asleep and therefore would be unprepared for an attack.' Feeling Watt boring into his mind, he looked again at Coker. 'We got dressed, and…'

Watt interrupted. 'You got dressed in the bedroom?'

Baker interjected quickly, 'Not me, ma'am; I went into the bathroom to get changed.'

'And they allowed you out of their sight?'

'Yes, ma'am.'

Watt raised an eyebrow. 'These would-be abductors were incredibly polite and considerate.'

'I had to insist, ma'am.'

Watt echoed, 'You had to insist?'

Priestley explained hurriedly, 'DI Baker insisted

very forcefully, ma'am.' He grinned. 'I don't know what the two guys thought, but she certainly scared the hell out of me.'

Coker gave a chuckle, inviting the others to smile.

Priestley continued, 'They gagged us with duct tape and fastened our hands behind our backs with plastic ties. When we left the building, the armed protection team stepped in.'

Coker responded, 'Yes, we've seen their reports. But now, Marcus, tell us what you think it all means. Then we need to decide who picks up the questioning.'

'Well, it's all been very strange, this case, right from the start. DI Baker and I have laid a few false trails to make them, whoever they are, think we know what's behind the original murder; but frankly, we don't have a clue. That's why we needed to force their hand.'

'And you certainly did that. So, how do we go about questioning the guy in the cells, when we don't really know what it is we want to know, if you know what I mean?'

'I know my presence at the shooting incident would normally disqualify me from leading the questioning, but I would like permission to try and tease something out of him.'

Coker swung a glance at the officers standing around the crowded room. 'Any dissenters?' No one moved a muscle. 'All right, Marcus, go ahead; we'll review your written report with interest. Now, I brought everyone together so we could express our heartfelt appreciation for your bravery, which will be placed on record in the appropriate way.'

'And DI Baker, sir?'

'Absolutely. It's good for the police's image as a

whole to have a female officer showing her mettle.' He began to stand, triggering a matching movement from the other two. After shaking Priestley's hand, he did likewise with Baker. 'Well done to the both of you. Keep me informed, Marcus.'

Priestley was encouraged to lead the exodus. Watt caught his eye. 'Go to my office straight away.'

By the time she arrived, he had been waiting outside for several minutes. She invited him to follow her in and close the door. 'Sit down and tell me what really happened.'

He tried to look amazed, but slipped his face back into neutral when he realized his over-acting was to the standard of an Italian footballer who has just scythed down an opponent and is now explaining to a referee how it was all entirely accidental. 'It's very much the way I described it, ma'am.'

She held his gaze silently for a while. 'Maybe so, but if it is, then you must be holding something back.'

'I'm sure there are details I can put into my report that will describe events more precisely, ma'am.'

'That's not what I'm talking about.'

'Can you clarify what you wish me to explain?'

'Yes, Marcus, I can. There is nothing you have said, and nothing in the reports from the other officers, that explains why DI Baker has just been gazing at you like you're a god. Did you save her life, or something, and chose not to mention it?'

'There really hasn't been anything significant missed out of my explanation, ma'am.'

'In that case, I'm guessing she must have fallen for your charms.'

'Surely not, ma'am. She always gives the impression

she has no desire to interact socially with anyone, and I don't see why I should be made an exception.'

'Even so, Marcus, I'd say her mask is slipping.'

'Well, I promise you, I've never deliberately set out to charm her in any way whatsoever.'

'I believe you, but I do think you need to be on your guard with her if you're to maintain your unblemished record of keeping all female colleagues at a distance. And let me just remind you that you outrank her, which obliges you to handle her very carefully.'

'I'll be *extremely* careful how I handle her, ma'am.'

Suspecting he was making light of the matter, she frowned. 'I just mean RHIP is an unacceptable attitude in the force.'

'I'll bear it in mind, ma'am. If she ever attempts to seduce me, I'll be sure to raise the point with her and insist we discuss it at length.'

Watt sighed. 'I can't tell if you're being serious. Even though you're giving all the correct responses, it still seems like you're fencing with me. Why do I feel you're holding something back? If you'd simply said the two of you had been at it like knives, at least I'd have thought it might explain away my intuition.'

'In which case, ma'am, for your benefit, I'll explore that avenue at the first available opportunity.'

Watt's stern exterior collapsed as she delivered a dirty laugh. 'You're twisting my words.'

He smiled. 'Actually, ma'am, to be fair, I believe I may have seen some evidence that she quite likes me, which in some ways is a good thing, as we're going to be bottled up together for I-don't-know-how-long.'

'Well, don't tell me where you're currently staying; it's all being kept on a strictly need-to-know basis.'

'I'm glad to hear security is being taken seriously. Now that it's escalated to an armed attack, we need to push the case forward as fast as we can. I'll interview the guy this morning, once I've been briefed on exactly where things stand on the investigation.'

'In which case, I'd better let you go. But do keep me informed.'

Priestley and Baker held a plenary session, involving all available members of the team. They agreed their best hope was to establish the backgrounds of the two assailants and see how they might be linked to anyone else involved in the case. Neither gunman had carried identification. The dead man had a tattoo on his right shoulder; Priestley asked to see a photograph of it. Reading the inscription "Death From Above", he asked, 'Has anyone contacted the British Army? The guy was probably in the Parachute Regiment.'

A detective spoke up. 'That's what I thought too, sir, so I've made a start.'

Baker snapped at him, 'Then why didn't you say so, earlier?'

He examined the carpet tiles. 'Sorry, ma'am.'

Priestley asked the assembled team, 'Does anyone know if the guy in custody has any tattoos?'

A different male detective responded, 'He has the letter "A" over his heart, but that's all.'

Priestley asked the reprimanded detective, 'Do you have a theory on that, as well?'

Relieved to appear useful, he replied quickly, 'His blood type, sir.'

Priestley nodded. 'That's a viable theory. Anything you'd like to add?' The man shook his head, fearing to negate his positive contribution. Priestley addressed the wider audience. 'Having your blood type tattooed over your heart is nowhere near as prevalent as it used to be. It now takes just a matter of minutes to perform ABO blood typing, so only someone who might reasonably expect to need blood urgently would consider having it done. That suggests someone in the military, except the information would also be on their dog tags. It takes a cautious man to have a tattoo done in case his tags are lost, which indicates a contradiction of sorts; you don't normally find cautious men joining the armed forces for combat roles.'

Baker asked, 'Does that internal contradiction affect how you'll interview him?'

Not wishing to appear too friendly toward her, he held his usual smile in check. 'Perhaps, but I may be in danger of reading too much into the tattoo. Maybe he's just a fan of *The A-Team*.'

When she laughed at his joke, he noticed a number of detectives turn and look at her with expressions of surprise; he made a mental note to discuss with her how she must avoid revealing their clandestine relationship. Addressing the entire room again, he continued, 'If one of them was in the Paras, it's a fair bet the other one was as well. Was or is; compulsory retirement age has been pushed back by five years to sixty.' He turned to the first detective. 'Chase that up. Ask for help if you need it. I'm holding off interviewing the gunman until I know more. And by the way, the dead man was almost certainly Irish. Meeting adjourned.'

He spoke quietly to Baker. 'Let's have a chat.'

Marching briskly, he avoided speaking to her again until they were ensconced in his office with the door closed. He began, 'Have you heard of Oklahoma?'

She raised her eyebrows. 'The US state?'

'The musical. There's a song in it: *People will say we're in love.*'

Her face beamed as she responded, 'And are we?'

'People might think so if we aren't careful. The lyric has a line about not laughing at my jokes too much.'

'Oh, I see. I'm trying to be my usual self, but I feel so different. Do you think anyone's noticed anything?'

'Some of the team looked a bit surprised when you laughed out loud. Plus, Watt's had a word with me, because she thought she could read some sort of hero-worship in the way you were looking at me. Her first guess was that I'd saved your life but didn't want it on record. Her second was that you'd fallen in love with me. I denied both, of course. If we're to keep people from suspecting, you need to remember how you used to be, and to act the part.'

She nodded. 'I'll try my best, but I can't forget that we'll be sleeping together again tonight.'

'Well, we need to put such thoughts aside and focus on the case.' He rapped the desk with his finger-ends. 'Find out the identities of the assailants and inform me as soon as you have something. Dismissed!'

She giggled. 'I do love it when you're masterful.'

CHAPTER 21

Shortly after ten o'clock, Priestley took a call from the pathologist. 'Good morning to you, Chief Inspector.'

'And the day's felicitations to you too, Dr Patel.'

'I hear you had a narrow escape when rescuing a fair damsel, Marcus.'

'Someone's been feeding you rubbish, Paal. I'll tell you all about it later, once I'm cleared to speak.'

'You mean, once you've all agreed the same official story.'

'How can you be so cynical; you must know that all serving officers operate to the same high standard of truthfulness.'

'Yes, of course, without exception; it was foolish of me to suggest otherwise.'

'Is there a point to this conversation, Paal?'

'Indeed there is. I've conducted a post-mortem on your assailant.'

'Don't tell me, let me guess: the cause of death was two bullets to the chest.'

'It takes all the fun out of it when you guess what my conclusion is.'

'Well, thanks for confirming it. Goodbye.'

'Goodbye.' Patel waited several seconds, the silence acting as a punchline. 'But here's what you don't know: I found light chain proteins in his blood.'

'Did you indeed; I'm so pleased for you.'

'His immunoglobulins were incomplete.'

'How unfortunate for him.'

'His condition was severe.'

'I certainly never saw him smile.'

'Do I need to spell it out to you, Marcus?'

'Indeed you do.'

'He had multiple myeloma. His predictive lifespan had suffered curtailment long before your colleague terminated his vitals. There had been a prior medical foreshortening of his anticipated existential duration.'

'And in English?'

'He was a dead man walking.'

'Well, I'm glad we got there in the end. Seriously, that's actually very interesting.'

'I thought it might be. By the way, is it your turn to come to us, or is it us to you?'

'I think Helen and I are due to play host next, but I'm unavailable for socialising at the moment. Just in case there's another attempt to abduct me, I'm being kept in protective custody every night from now on. It's a bit of a bummer, to say the least.'

'I'm sorry to hear that. Well, I'd better let you go.'

'Yes, back to the grindstone. Thanks for letting me know about the bone marrow cancer.'

'I thought you didn't understand?'

'I like to keep my cards close to my chest.'

After Priestley had terminated the conversation he immediately phoned Baker. 'Are you free for a meeting right now? I've just learned something significant.'

'Can you give me ten minutes? There's something I'm chasing up that could prove very useful to us.'

'In ten then.' He registered how differently she had reacted; instead of coming at once, she had confidently put him off. Though she may have had good reason, he hoped colleagues had not noticed her changed attitude.

While waiting for her, he read through the interim post-mortem report that Dr Patel had e-mailed him after their conversation. Though the full tox screen results would take several weeks to arrive, the interesting finding was already on record. He pondered on possible reasons why a dying man might attempt the abduction of two police officers.

Half an hour later, Baker bustled into Priestley's office bearing two mugs of coffee. 'Sorry I'm late; it took a bit longer than I'd expected. Shall I go first, or will you?'

He suppressed his immediate misgivings about the implicit familiarity behind arriving late and choosing his drink for him. 'Ladies first.'

'Right. I'll tell you what we've found out so far. The dead guy was Padraic O'Leary. He was in the Paras, just like you said, and left nineteen months ago.'

'What reason?'

'Sorry, I don't have that yet; his records are being sent to us from Glasgow. I'll give them a call.'

'My guess is it'll be on health grounds. I've been on the phone to the pathologist, who says he had a terminal medical condition.'

'I wonder if that's significant to the case.'

'I find it difficult to believe it isn't. Do you have any other background on him? Any recent criminal activity? Mental health issues?'

'Nothing's shown up.'

'All right. What about our guy in the cells?'

'He's refusing to tell us anything. Something strange has just happened, though: he's asked that the senior male investigating officer interview him straight away. We don't normally get requests like that.'

'It's certainly unusual, but I'm not entirely surprised; he obviously knows something about how we operate. My guess is, he wants to make sure the person who interviews him knows the full background to the case, in the hope that they'll disclose whatever it is that he wishes to know; after all, you can only let something slip if you know it in the first place. One way he might be looking to gain some insight is simply by hearing what questions he's asked. Obviously, we sometimes already know the answers, but a clever interviewee may be able to sort the wheat from the chaff. I'll have a go at him to find out what he has to say for himself. Has he requested a lawyer?'

'No, he specifically said he doesn't want one yet.'

'That suggests he intends to rely on his own ability to navigate the questions. He's starting to sound like he could be quite a formidable foe. How are we doing on finding out who he is?'

'We've taken fingerprints, and a swab for DNA, but it all takes time.'

'Do you remember the *Charlie Hebdo* incident back in twenty fifteen? The French harvested DNA from a balaclava, and three hours later they'd identified the terrorist. Why can't we have that sort of service?'

'Well, our man isn't going anywhere, so there's no real need to put a rush on it.'

'I suppose you're right. You do realise we're going to be cooped up together until we break this case?'

'Yes, I'm fully aware of that benefit; I'll be sure to tell them to take as much time as they like.'

He found himself unable to hold back a smile. 'That isn't what I meant.'

She smiled back. 'Even so.'

While an audience assembled to watch the interview on the largest monitor, Priestley explained to Witty why he would be conducting the interview alone. 'I'm going to have to play it by ear, and I may suddenly need to change tack, so it wouldn't be feasible to work out a strategy in advance. Plus, I think he may be looking to take me on, *mano a mano*, to prove himself.'

Priestley was already seated in the interview room when the prisoner was brought in wearing handcuffs. Seeing an opportunity to challenge his masculinity, he instructed the accompanying officer, 'Take the cuffs off him and then you can leave us.'

The prisoner rubbed each wrist but said nothing.

Priestley began, 'I'm the senior investigating officer. You wanted to talk to me.'

'And you are?'

Believing the question was genuine, he felt relieved to know the man was currently unaware of his identity. 'I understand you've refused to disclose your name. There's a *quid pro quo*; you tell me yours and I'll tell you mine.'

'I'm John Smith.'

'And I'm Billy the Kid; delighted to meet you, John. Of course we met earlier, but you failed to introduce yourself on that occasion.'

'Yes, that was rather rude of me.'

'Not quite as rude as pointing guns at my colleague and myself.'

'I deny that allegation. At no time did I point my gun at either of you.'

Priestley recognised it was the start of his defence. 'Your mate did.'

'My mate?'

'Yes, your mate from the Paras.' He hoped there was sufficient ambiguity in the assertion to mislead him into believing they knew the two of them had been together in the army, if that were true. He pushed the deception further. 'Padraic O'Leary. Or have you forgotten his name, as well as your own, John?'

'Well done, Billy. It didn't take you long to find out we were in the Paras together, but how did you do it? We'd removed all our clothes labels and any ID.'

'Tattoos can be such a giveaway.'

'But I don't have any tattoos, apart from the "A" for Anthea, my wife.'

Priestley avoided reacting to the disclosure, quickly moving to the next question. 'I've never had one done, myself; I don't like the idea. Do they hurt, much?'

'Not as much as being hit by a metal bar, I'd guess. You cracked two of his ribs, you know.'

'I'm sorry to hear that. Is the hospital taking good care of him?'

The man gave a sly smile. 'Do you think I'm a fool? You're fishing, aren't you.'

Priestley, delighted with how the man was leaking information, hoped to convince him he was performing well. 'Yes, but I have to try, don't I.' His phone buzzed. 'Excuse me, John.' He read the text message. 'Sorry about the interruption. Where were we?'

'You were fishing and I wasn't biting.'

'Oh, yes, I remember. The injured guy, he wasn't very handy, I have to say.'

'Well, he wouldn't be, would he.'

'No, not like you and Padraic; you looked like you really knew what you were doing.'

'You get top quality training in the Paras.'

'Do you miss those days, Barry? I mean John?'

Barry allowed himself a smile. 'You let that slip, didn't you. I'll come clean with you if you tell me what you know about me. Is it a deal?'

'*Quid pro quo* again? You chose to say nothing at the First Account Interview, so before we move onto the Disclosure and Challenge stages, perhaps you'd like to give it another try and tell us what happened.'

'That's a bit pointless, isn't it? You were there.'

'Even so, it's your opportunity to have your say.'

'OK, there is something I want to put on record: there was never any intention to hurt either you or your girlfriend.' Priestley suppressed his powerful desire to interrupt with a correction. 'We only had the guns so you wouldn't put up a fight; we were really carrying them for your sake.'

As Barry was obviously waiting for a response, Priestley replied, 'There is a sort of logic to what you say, but it's for others to draw their own conclusions.'

Barry nodded. 'We would have brought you back safe and sound if only you hadn't laid an ambush. So, how did you know to expect us?'

Priestley shook his head. 'That's something we can talk about on another occasion.'

'But I've been telling *you* things.'

'This interview is all about you having your say.'

'In that case, I've nothing to add. And next time, I'll have a lawyer present.'

'That's your prerogative. Interview terminated with Barry Blackstone at...' He looked at his watch and recorded the time.

Blackstone frowned. 'You knew all along.'

Priestley gave him a wink.

Following the interview, Priestley went into the MIR and called out, 'Who discovered his identity?'

Witty stretched up an arm like an eager schoolboy. 'Me, sir.'

'Thank you, Neil. Would you like to explain how?'

'I had a lady at Army Records on speed dial from earlier. When I asked her to check for someone who had been in the same battalion as Padraic O'Leary and was married to an Anthea, she said there weren't any current matches, but there was one who had had a wife of that name, except she died in February. She sent me a photo which confirmed it was our man. I texted you his name and battalion; should I have mentioned he was widowed, as well?'

'No, it's fine; it would have been too tricky to try to factor that into the interview.' He caught Penny gazing at him in her adoring way. 'DI Baker, will you organise a detailed search on Barry Blackstone. I want to know everything about him, right back to his conception. Provide me with interim reports, every hour on the hour, without fail. I'll leave you to get on with it.' He marched away without a backward glance.

Priestley noted Baker arrived on time to present her first report. He asked, casually, 'How are you feeling?'

'We missed a lot of sleep last night; I'll be glad to get to bed.' She gave him an encouraging smile.

'We'll knock off at four.'

'It was nice of you to ask me to come and see you every hour.'

He frowned. 'I wasn't trying to be nice; I want to know what progress you're making.'

She nodded. 'Yes, of course; I believe you.'

'So, what have you found?'

'Barry Blackstone doesn't have a criminal record. There isn't even anything as a juvenile.'

'What about his background? Where was he born? Who are his parents? Where does he live? We really need to know everything about him if we're to get inside his mind and work out why he might have tried to abduct us. Let's forget about hourly reporting; just give me everything at three thirty.'

She showed her disappointment. 'OK. We shouldn't really be seen together all the time, I suppose.'

At precisely three thirty, Baker gave a brief knock at Priestley's open door and walked in with a set of notes. She flopped into a chair, commenting, 'I'm feeling really tired. I think the adrenaline rush has all gone.'

He smiled sympathetically. 'We'll catch up on sleep, tonight. Now, what do you have on Barry Blackstone?'

She read from her notes. 'Born in Leeds. Brought up in the Hunslet area. Went to school there, primary and secondary. Good at sport. Not academic. Left school without qualifications. Worked in the building trade. Joined the army at nineteen. At twenty, he married a local girl, Anthea; she was eighteen. They didn't have any children. In February, she died in a car crash while working as a district nurse.'

He reached over and accepted the printed sheets she was offering him. Scanning down, he read additional details, including the names and addresses of parents and schools. 'When did he have the tattoo done?'

'Sorry, I haven't got that; I'll get someone onto it right away.'

He grinned. 'I wasn't being entirely serious.' After a pause for reflection, he continued, '…though it might be interesting to know if it was done before or after she died. I'm going to have another chat with him before we go; I'll drop it into the conversation.'

'You make it sound all very friendly.'

'I'm not intending to do any formal interviews with him; there could be a benefit in my not being associated with the charging process. He may be more relaxed if I only want a chat, and I might understand his motivation better that way.'

'Will it just be you on your own again?'

'Yes, that's my plan; or do you think differently?'

Pleased to be asked for her opinion, she waited for a few seconds before giving the response that had come to her immediately. 'You're obviously very good at this psychological approach, but it isn't something that can be built into procedures; most officers don't have the ability to gain insights that way. If it were me, I'd be trying to follow the official rules; but for you, I'm sure it can work best if you do things your way.'

'Well, it might work, but there are no guarantees. I'll go and see him now.'

'But he said he wants a solicitor present for all future interviews.'

'He may not have a problem with me if I make it clear I'm just there for a natter.'

'OK, then. I'll watch what happens.'

CHAPTER 22

Priestley watched on the monitor as Blackstone entered the interview room. When he joined him soon after, he sat opposite and asked, casually, 'How are they treating you, Barry? Is everything all right?'

Blackstone responded smartly, 'I've got a lawyer who says she should be here for all my interviews.'

Priestley nodded. 'I'm sure she will only have meant all *formal* interviews. Would you like a drink?'

'Yes, I'll have a beer.'

Priestley gave a short laugh. 'Tea or coffee?'

'Cup of tea, I suppose. White, one sugar.'

Priestley addressed the attendant constable. 'Do you mind? And I'll have a strong black coffee, no sugar.' The officer accepted the instruction unquestioningly. After he had left them, Priestley grinned at Blackstone. 'I need the caffeine to keep me awake, after my sleep was so severely interrupted last night.' He sensed little hostility in Blackstone's gaze.

'Sorry about that, but if you let bygones be bygones, I'll be on my way.'

Priestley gave a longer laugh. 'You know you're going to be charged, don't you; but I have to say, you seem very relaxed about it.'

'I'm sure I've known a lot worse situations than the inside of a prison cell.'

'You've seen some hard action, then?'

'Yes, all my life. My infants' school was so rough, they used to check all the kids at the gate for weapons.'

Priestley nodded. 'And confiscate them.'

Blackstone shook his head. 'No; to give you a knife if you didn't have one of your own.'

Priestley laughed long and hard, even though he had heard the joke before. 'But you've always kept your nose clean, haven't you.'

Blackstone winked, slowly and deliberately. 'Either that, or they never caught me.'

Priestley spoke as though responding seriously, yet ensuring the edges of his mouth turned up to indicate he was continuing their humorous banter. 'You can ask for the rest of your offences to be taken into consideration.'

'No need; they're all too far in the past.'

'So, you've been a good guy for a long time. What was it that put you on the straight and narrow, then?' Blackstone fell silent. Priestley continued to look at him, determined to express genuine interest.

The constable returned with their drinks. Priestley thanked him and then asked him to leave them alone. With no more than a brief questioning look at Priestley, he did as requested.

Blackstone blew on his tea before taking a sip. 'It isn't good for you, drinking liquids that are too hot; my wife told me that. Joining the army changed me, like you'd expect; but so did she. You can see girls in town every night of the week getting drunk and throwing up like they're proud of themselves to be doing it, but Anthea was different; she was more likely to be the one taking care of them. She always wanted to be a nurse, so that's what she trained to do, after we got married; that was on her eighteenth birthday.'

Priestley heard the catch in his voice and saw his eyes glisten. 'It sounds like the two of you were meant for each other.' He hoped his own recent exposure to romantic films and books had not pushed him to lose his credibility by implicitly referring to love.

'That's exactly how it was. She was a perfect lady; at home, she wouldn't even let me swear. It turned out she couldn't have children. I'm supposed to say, "We couldn't have children," but you know what I mean. If anything, it made us even closer. We were very happy until that bastard took her away from me.'

'Who was that? What do you mean?'

'Well, it wasn't another man, not in that way; she would never have gone off with anyone. No, it was a bloke in a Porsche who smashed her Micra into a tree. God knows what speed he was doing. It was such a bad crash they wouldn't even let me see her body.'

'I can't begin to imagine how you could cope with something like that, Barry.'

'I didn't cope; not really. I got pissed up and never wanted to be sober again. That's when I had her initial put on my heart, even though I'd promised my mother I'd never have any tattoos done.'

'Did you receive help on coping with your loss?'

'Only after me and the army agreed to part company. I'm now an expert on the subject.'

'Social workers can be very helpful at such times.'

'It wasn't a social worker that helped me; it was Padraic. He told me all about his own grief, and about the five stages on the Kübler-Ross model. You won't have heard of it, I don't suppose.'

Though familiar with the concept, he responded, 'No, tell me all about it.'

'The first stage is denial, then anger, bargaining, depression and finally acceptance. It's supposed to be for terminally ill patients, though I'd say some of it also applies to people who've just lost someone. But it isn't everything, though; there's another stage.'

'And what's that?'

Blackstone winked. 'Now, that would be telling.'

Priestley recognised the limit of his confidences had been reached. 'Well, I'm getting off home now for an early night. You should try and get some rest yourself.'

Blackstone stared at him. 'Why aren't you angry with me? When we burst in on you and your girlfriend like that, I could see she was terrified; I honestly hope she'll eventually get over it.'

'She's very resilient.'

'But why weren't *you* frightened?'

'I guess my attitude is similar to yours about being in here: I've known worse.' Realising he had disclosed something he had not intended, he quickly terminated their conversation. 'Right then, Barry; I'm off. If you want to chat to me about anything, just let someone know.' He opened the door and called for the constable.

After leaving the interview room, he found Baker in the MIR, where he asked her, 'Have you started making inquiries about the car crash?'

Having failed to consider the matter, she responded quickly, 'Just about to, boss.'

'Tell me when you have something, and then we'll talk about what else came out of that discussion. By the way, we're being picked up at ten past four.'

At four o'clock he phoned Helen from his office. 'How are you? How are the children?'

'We're fine. And yourself?'

'Missing you all. When we're finished, let me talk to them.'

'Shall I fetch them now?'

'Not yet. I just wanted to ask you something about the Kübler-Ross five stages of grief. Has anyone ever suggested a sixth stage?'

'Not to my knowledge; after all, what can there be beyond acceptance?'

'What if it was not relating to a terminal illness, but to coping with someone's sudden death?'

'That isn't really the same situation. There's shock, disbelief, physical and mental draining. One typical response is the adoption of the belief that the deceased had been a wonderful person, but eventually it changes into a more honest realisation that they were who they were. The common end-point is acceptance, though that can still be accompanied by sudden moments of intense sadness. Some clinicians conflate reactions to natural deaths with battlefield PTSD, but I would say that's unhelpful. After all, apart from the death itself, there's very little similarity between someone dying of old age and someone being ripped apart in a fire-fight.'

'In that case, I'm left with a puzzle. The latest guy who tried to abduct me has mentioned an extra stage of grief, but he won't tell me what it is. It relates to his wife dying in a car crash. Any ideas?'

'I assume we're not talking supernatural, spiritual, a gypsy's curse, revenge from beyond the grave.'

'No, the guy seems very down-to-earth.'

'What about building a physical monument to her? Or creating a charity in her name?'

'I'll certainly look into those possibilities, though if it were a charity he'd be wishing to publicise it rather than keeping it a secret.'

'I'll give it some more thought. Now, would you like

to talk to Alice first, or Edwin?'

'I'll start with my little chatterbox.'

'All right; I'll fetch her.'

After listening to Alice and talking to Edwin, he spoke once more with Helen. 'Should I call you again? We don't need to schedule calls anymore; I won't be in any danger.'

'Just phone me before you go to bed.'

'I'm having an early night to catch up on sleep.'

'That's a good idea. Talk to you later.'

Witty arrived at Priestley's office just before ten past four and gave a rat-tatta-tat-tat on the door. 'I'm your first chauffeur of the evening.'

'How many will I have?'

'That's on a need-to-know basis, and apparently I don't need to know.'

Priestley stood to leave. Witty set off and called on Baker in the MIR. 'Time to go, Penny.' Priestley joined them as they headed for the door to the underground section of the car park.

Witty commented dispassionately, 'To make sure no one sees you leave, you both need to cram into the boot. It won't be very comfy, but it's only a short journey.'

Baker responded, 'Is that really necessary?'

Priestley replied to Witty, 'If anyone's getting the boot, it'll be you.' He turned to Baker. 'Neil was only winding you up.' Witty grinned.

In the back seat, Baker asked, 'Should I duck down? Then no one can see we're both in here.'

Witty responded immediately, 'Yes, do that. Only, if anyone does see you, it might look like you're giving him a blow-job.'

She leaned forward from her position behind the

driver's seat, and hissed in Witty's ear, 'If you come out with one more wisecrack, I'm going to report you to a superior officer, such as the one sitting next to me.'

Priestley saw Witty's grimace through the rear-view mirror and decided to act. 'For showing disrespect, I'm giving you a punishment; make sure both our cars are so clean I can see my reflection in them.'

Unsure whether this was still part of the banter, Witty replied, 'Yes sir. Of course sir,' before adding, just loudly enough to be heard, '…three bags full sir.' Baker looked at Priestley, who gave a tiny shake of his head to indicate no further action was necessary.

Witty drove them to a BT facility and parked close to what appeared to be one of their vans. The same man as had that morning driven the Royal Mail van was now opening its rear doors. The two passengers climbed into the back and held onto the straps.

At the farmhouse, June opened the front door and welcomed them in. She asked, 'What would you like to do about food?'

Before Augustus could respond, Julie spoke up. 'We missed our beauty sleep last night, so we were thinking we'd have a nap and then get up to eat. Would eight o'clock be all right?'

June responded to her, 'That's just fine, love; you get off to bed.' She turned and left them to find their own way.

Augustus suggested, 'Maybe you should go to your own room if you're tired.'

Julie giggled, 'I'm not that tired.'

CHAPTER 23

In the morning, Priestley and Baker were collected by Royal Mail van for transfer to traffic pursuit officer Craig Vardy, who in turn delivered them to the station.

Witty joined them for their start-of-day meeting. He began, earnestly, 'Were your cars shiny enough, then? I had to come in early, especially.'

Baker looked puzzled. 'What are you on about?'

'Don't you remember? I was ordered to clean both your cars.'

She drew her head back to look up at him more directly. 'Can't you tell when someone's just having you on?'

Priestley pointed an index finger alternately at Baker and Witty, as though introducing them to each other. 'Pot, kettle. Kettle, pot.' The two exchanged grins.

Witty became serious. 'Barry Blackstone's wife died in an RTC near Colchester, just off the A12. Her Nissan was struck by a Porsche and catapulted into a tree. She died instantly on impact. The other driver, a Mr Yasser Khan, was prosecuted but found not guilty. His defence was that his car skidded on black ice and he was unable to change speed or direction. He had a very expensive lawyer who convinced the jury it was an accident beyond his control.'

'There's a job for you, then: review the evidence and see whether you think the jury got it wrong.'

'I thought you might say that; I've arranged for the case notes to be sent up.'

'Good man. Did Blackstone have anything else to say for himself after we left, yesterday?'

'Yes: he'll be pleading not guilty to all charges, which is a bit rich considering how he was carrying a firearm and pointed it at the two of you.'

'Hold on, Neil.' He turned to Baker. 'I've had a note saying I'm being called to give testimony at an internal inquiry about the shooting incident. You'll be getting a summons, too. We shouldn't discuss our recollections in advance, but I just wanted to say that Neil wasn't present and therefore we shouldn't allow his personal interpretation of the incident reports to colour our own judgement.'

She frowned. 'Are you trying to tell me something?'

He shook his head slowly. 'No: quite the opposite. I'm simply saying, don't let anyone tell you what you saw; just rely on your own memory.'

'But the fact that you didn't let Neil's interpretation stand suggests you don't agree with it.'

'We need to end this thread.' They fell silent.

Witty began again. 'Blackstone also asked to speak in private to the other officer who was present at the flat.' He turned to Baker. 'I told him it wasn't possible. For one thing, you'd already left by then.'

Baker looked intently at Priestley. 'What do you think? Should I go and see him?'

'I'm not sure. Why would he want to see you? Is it so that he can identify you, if you give your name?'

'Does that matter? He already knows who you are.'

'No, he doesn't; I didn't tell him. And we shouldn't, in view of the security concerns.'

'Well, I'm prepared to talk to him.'

'All right. Maybe I should come with you.'

Witty interjected, 'Actually, he was quite specific on that point: it has to be with the lady on her own.'

Baker responded, smiling, 'How nice of you to call me a lady, Neil.'

Witty frowned. 'It wasn't me calling you a lady, it was Barry Blackstone. That was his word.'

'In that case, I'll go and hear what he has to say.'

Witty observed, 'It might be dangerous. Do you want him cuffed to the table?'

Priestley commented, 'Don't go taking risks, Penny; make sure there's someone outside, ready to intervene. But something tells me he isn't a threat to you. What do you think?'

'If he thinks I'm a lady, I think he'll be a gentleman. And he may be more willing to disclose information if he's relaxed, so I'll do what you did and just chat with him without the cuffs on.'

'All right. I'll watch on the monitor.'

In the interview room, Baker positioned herself well back from the desk as she waited for Blackstone, to give herself more time and space to react if he should turn violent. Blackstone entered unaccompanied, an officer closing the door behind him as instructed. He remained standing until Baker invited him to sit.

She began, 'You wanted to talk to me, Barry.' She thought use of his first name would set the right tone, but had failed to recognise how anxious she felt, and consequently stumbled over her words.

'Yes, that's right. I just wanted to apologise to you. It must have been so frightening for you when Padraic pointed his gun at your head, though you can be certain he never intended to use it; we were only wanting to take you somewhere to answer some questions.'

'I do wish I could believe that, Barry; but outside, he was all ready to shoot a police officer.'

Blackstone looked intently at her. 'Was he? Was he really?'

'He raised his gun.'

'But did he point it at any of them?' She fell silent as she tried to think back to the incident. He continued, 'Anyway, there was something else I wanted to say to you: there won't be any further attempts to abduct you, so there's no need to worry about that.'

She held his gaze, trying to decide whether she could believe him. 'How do you know that?'

He smiled. 'Believe me, I know.'

'Is there anything else you'd like to tell me?'

'I think I've said enough; don't you?'

She called for the officer to take him back to his cell, before going to see Priestley. He asked, 'Do you think he meant it about no more abduction attempts?'

She shook her head vigorously. 'It could just be a way of getting me to drop my guard. Besides, he only said there'd be no more attempts to abduct *me*; he never mentioned *you*. It would be stupid not to maintain the current security arrangement.'

'I thought he seemed very plausible.'

'It's too big a risk. No, we should definitely continue to stay where we are until the case is cracked.' As she said it, she knew she really thought Blackstone could be taken at his word, but had no intention of losing Marcus quite so soon.

'Well, all right, if you say so; but let's agree to keep the situation under review.'

She tried to sound reasonable. 'Of course. If we *both* agree the security precautions are no longer necessary, then we'll drop them straight away.' Before he could revise the terms of the agreement, she continued, 'I'll go and check on Neil's progress with the RTC.'

Later, Witty arrived with Baker at Priestley's office to report his findings. 'The evidence seemed pretty strong to me. No one else experienced black ice on that stretch of road. Khan claimed he was braking on a bend when his car began to slide. The collision investigator examined the brake-light bulbs and found there was no distortion to the filaments, indicating they were not illuminated at the time of the accident, which was evidence that the brakes were not being applied. His interpretation was that the vehicle was travelling at a speed substantially in excess of the legal limit for that road, and when the driver over-steered on a left-hand bend he tried to compensate by applying right-hand steer. His car was then spat across the road on the off-side and directly into the oncoming vehicle.'

Priestley commented, 'Taking into account he was in a Porsche, that all fits with a scenario of a macho driver who was going too fast.'

Baker added, 'I don't see how a jury couldn't find him guilty.'

Witty responded, 'His lawyer brought in her own so-called expert on filament distortion. In the end, the jury didn't know which expert to believe. Without that vital evidence to support the prosecution, the guy got off.'

Priestley reflected, 'The relaxing of double jeopardy laws hasn't gone far enough to allow a retrial, but it might be interesting to talk to the driver and see if he has anything more to say for himself.'

Witty shook his head. 'That won't be possible.'

Priestley asked, 'Why not?'

'He's dead. Shot twice in the head from close range with a nine millimetre.'

'Were the casings found?'

'Yes.'

'See if the cartridges in Blackstone's Glock are the same type.'

'I can't.'

'Why not?'

'Because his magazine was empty.'

Priestley snapped, 'Why didn't you say so earlier?'

'Sorry, I was still getting there, boss.'

'And was O'Leary's Browning empty as well?'

'No, it had a full complement of thirteen.'

'Were the bullets recovered from the Khan killing?'

'Yes.'

'Were they badly deformed?'

'One of them wasn't.'

'Get ballistics matches done with both the Glock and the Browning. Do you know if the Khan investigation had Blackstone as a suspect?'

'I'll find out.'

'Come and report back when you have something.'

After the meeting, Priestley checked his schedule. His presence was requested by the inquiry into the killing of Padraic O'Leary. He knew that his testimony would not be exactly what they wanted to hear. When the time came, he headed for the interview room.

The leading officer went through the formalities. She appeared earnest and respectful as she looked at him across the table. 'In your own words, DCI Priestley, tell us what happened from the moment you exited the apartment building and stepped onto the street.'

Priestley wondered why it was necessary to ask him

to use his own words; after all, whose would they be if he were the one speaking. But then, perhaps she had previously interviewed officers who gave such similar versions of events that she assumed they had agreed their wording in advance. Well, he had conscientiously avoided any such collusion. 'I exited the building and stepped onto the pavement.' He realised how his words were uncomfortably similar to hers. 'I turned left and walked slowly so that DI Baker could catch up with me. We then walked side-by-side to the first corner, at which point we turned left, as instructed by a voice from behind us.'

'Did you recognise the voice?'

'It was the man I now know to be Barry Blackstone.'

'Go on, sir.'

'We were continuing toward the next corner, when one of the officers from an armed protection unit called out, clearly and distinctly, "Armed police. Put down your weapons." He and two other officers then emerged from three different places of concealment.'

'Do you know who gave the command?'

'Having the previous day conversed with the officer, I was immediately able to recognise his voice. It was Victor Charlie Three One.'

'Continue, please.'

'The man I now know as Padraic O'Leary raised his gun, whereupon an officer shot him twice in the chest.'

'Describe that in more detail, if you will. Where did O'Leary point his gun before he was shot?'

'He was still raising it when he was fired on.'

'What do you think O'Leary's intentions were?'

'Answering that would involve my speculating.'

'Indulge us please, sir.'

He had hoped the questioning would allow him to avoid saying what he really thought, but saw no good reason to hold back any longer. 'Let me say, first of all, that O'Leary's movement was consistent with raising his gun to fire it. The only question is, fire it at whom. It was my impression that the intended target may have been himself, as the arc of his arm remained close to his chest at all times.'

'So are you saying, when Victor Charlie Three Two shot him, he may have been about to shoot himself?'

'I'm only suggesting it as a possibility. To my mind, the officer who fired was behaving perfectly correctly when he interpreted the action as precipitate to the discharge of the weapon.'

She responded abruptly, 'It's up to us to decide how to interpret what happened.' Realising she had spoken inappropriately, she put on a slightly less butch voice. 'Thank you for your testimony.'

As he left the room, he saw Baker standing outside. She raised her eyebrows questioningly. He shrugged noncommittally. She knocked and entered.

When asked about the actual shooting, she gave an unnuanced explanation. 'As he was raising his gun, an officer shot him before he could fire.' When asked who might have been the intended target, she suggested Victor Charlie Three One, as he was the only officer who had spoken and so was the most prominent.

After Baker had finished giving her testimony, she went to see Priestley to compare answers. He admitted there was one difference. 'I thought he might have been about to shoot himself in the head.'

She sucked in air noisily. 'I didn't think of that; but now you mention it, he didn't point it at anyone else.'

Priestley looked thoughtful. 'Perhaps I should have said that his arm movement was almost slow enough to be encouraging one of them to shoot him first, though that could just have been my imagination. If he'd really wished to make one of them fire at him, he could have pointed his gun directly at them, but then that might not have left him the alternative option of shooting himself. I think I shall raise the possibility with the inquiry team that it was suicide by inviting lethal fire.'

'I'd have thought they only wanted to gather enough evidence to indicate the officer acted correctly.'

'I hope you're right, and that they're not looking to hang him out to dry, but I'm honour bound to tell them what I think may have happened.'

'They won't like you changing your testimony.'

'It isn't so much a revision as an addendum.' He left a brief telephone message to the effect that he had a small addition to make to his earlier statement.

When he put down the telephone, Baker commented, 'This case is unlike anything I've ever known before. What do you think is really going on?'

'That empty magazine was certainly a turn up for the books, especially as the other's gun was loaded. When we have more information about...' His words were interrupted by the ringing of his desk telephone.

'Marcus, it's Pippa. Is Penny Baker with you?'

'Yes, as it happens.'

'I've arranged for her to have an initial counselling session this morning, as in right now. It's on-site, so she won't need a security detail. Could you send her to me and I'll do the introductions.'

'Has she asked for counselling?'

'I assume it's essential under these circumstances.'

'But "assume" makes an "ass" of "u" and "me". Am *I* expected to have counselling, as well?'

'You're the exception that proves the rule.'

'In that context, "proves" means "tests". One could argue it relates to proofing rather than proving.'

She sighed loudly. 'Just send her up, Marcus.'

After he had explained to Penny about the call, she asked, 'Have you ever had to see a counsellor?'

He shrugged. 'A few times.'

'Well, what should I say to them?'

He returned her question. 'What do you think you should say to them?'

'I could tell them the truth; that I was so frightened I nearly pissed myself.'

He stared anxiously into her eyes. 'I never realised you were as worried as that.' He wanted to put his arms around her to make her feel safe, but knew that was not an appropriate response in the office. 'I'll do my best tonight to help you get over it.'

She smiled contentedly. 'That's the kind of therapy I really need. So, what do I say to them? What would you say if it were you?'

'I'd say I've become a Buddhist and so I know that each life is merely a stage on the path to enlightenment, and therefore it is only how I live this life that matters. The problem with Buddhism is you're supposed to give up all your earthly desires. Maybe bushido, the way of the warrior, would be better. I'd claim to be a samurai who thinks on death every day, and so yesterday was no different to any other day. But don't let me put ideas into your head; if you believe you need help to cope with the trauma you suffered, you should definitely have a one-to-one with the counsellor.'

'You don't think I should admit I'm the happiest I've been in my whole life and I don't need any help?'

'That would lead to questions as to why you're so happy, which would be somewhat problematic.'

She smiled as she stood up. 'Don't worry; there are some things I'll always keep secret.'

Philippa Hatchette opened her office door wide and smiled sympathetically. 'Hello, Penny. Come and have some tea and biscuits.' Baker followed her inside.

A tall, black woman in an astonishingly bright dress stood to greet her. 'I'm Gbemisola. I'm here to offer you counselling, to help you get over the shock of your recent traumatic experience.'

Baker shook hands with her. 'It's nice to meet you, but I'm sorry to say you've had a wasted journey. You see, I'm already receiving counselling.'

Hatchette interjected with a slight hint of annoyance, 'I wasn't aware of that. Who arranged it?'

Baker turned to her. 'It's an informal arrangement with someone who has himself suffered similar trauma in the past and is therefore uniquely placed to offer appropriately focused advice and guidance. So, if it's all the same to you, I'll get right back to work.' She bent down to the plate of biscuits on the coffee table and picked up one that was wrapped in gold foil. 'But thanks for the bicky.' She smiled before walking out.

Hatchette immediately telephoned Priestley. 'Will you stop stopping me from doing my job, Marcus? Your latest acolyte has just declined counselling, so I've a lady here who has now had a wasted journey.'

'Well, perhaps I should come and see her?'

She snorted. 'And then she'd be the one needing counselling. Don't think I've forgotten what happened with that sweet American chap.'

'That's really unfair, Pippa. As I recall, all I did was explain that, to understand fully what it's like to be a survivor from a two-day non-stop gun battle, you have to have experienced it yourself. I never expected him to go off and fight in the Middle East.'

'Well, be that as it may, you're not coming near any more of them. If ever it's necessary, I'll have to handle you myself. And if DI Baker has a breakdown under your guidance, you'll have me to answer to.'

'All right; I'll be sure to let you know if I think she's suffering from abnormal stress.'

'Promise?'

'Promise.'

By the time the conversation was ending, Baker was standing at the door. 'Who are you talking to and what are you promising them?'

'What did you say to Philippa Hatchette?'

'Only that I already have someone who's giving me counselling.'

'You didn't mention my name?'

'No.'

'She assumed it was me.'

'Well, she got that right. I've brought you a bicky, by the way; I didn't want to look ungrateful by leaving empty-handed, only I don't wish to put on any weight.'

'Much appreciated. Now get back to work.'

She attempted a curtsey. 'Yes sir.'

CHAPTER 24

In the late afternoon, Witty went to Priestley's office with Baker, for them to hear the fruits of his research. 'I've spoken to DCI Vinnie Essex, who's leading the inquiry into the Khan killing.'

'Not a name I know. What's he like?'

'I thought he seemed rather self-important.'

'Did he have Blackstone on his list of suspects?'

'He did, but it was a long list. Khan had his thumb in a number of unsavoury pies. He was a landlord with several low quality, high rent properties, and not only was he pocketing the inflated housing benefits he arranged for his invariably single female tenants, but he also collected their earnings from the sex industry. Plus, he liked fast cars, and had a side line in exporting them, which he bought by placing orders on a steal-as-you-go basis. Khan's death has led Essex to set up several other major investigations which he expects will run well beyond this year.'

'What about the murder case itself?'

'Blackstone was investigated thoroughly. He had a cast iron alibi, or should I say top brass. There was an inquiry at his barracks into his behaviour following his wife's death; at the time of Khan's murder he was being interviewed by three senior army officers.'

'How convenient for him; so, another prime suspect with a perfect alibi.'

'Essex said his likeliest suspects are the Bulgarian and Romanian gangs who are currently fighting it out for control of Khan's prostitution business.'

'If it turns out it was a hit by one of those gangs, it would almost certainly put Blackstone in the clear.'

'That's why I asked him to keep me informed, but he was a bit sniffy about it. I think it came down to our difference in rank. He said he'd instruct his sergeant to let me know of any significant developments.'

'It sounds like we can't rely on that happening. Just leave it with me; I'll have a word with him.'

'If you find out the name of his sergeant, I can keep chasing it up.'

'All right; thanks, Neil. Now, what about ballistics?'

'Results are due in the morning.'

'That just leaves one big puzzle for now: how was Blackstone able to say there'll be no further abduction attempts? Who has he been speaking to?'

'Only his lawyer.'

'One from the list?'

'No; it was Miss Garnet Hilton-Ikeda.'

'What is she doing getting involved?'

Baker interjected, 'Isn't she the one demanding the law be changed on the right to die?'

Priestley responded, 'Indeed she is, which makes me wonder what her interest is in the case.'

Baker commented, 'She obviously doesn't only do Human Rights work, then.'

Priestley shrugged. 'Unless this case is about Human Rights and we just can't see it yet. Let's have a think.'

Eventually, Witty broke their meditation. 'Am I OK to knock off for the day? Lily isn't feeling very well.'

Priestley stood up, triggering the other two to do the same. 'Of course you can, Neil. You should have said, earlier. We'll be working late, but only because there's nothing much to do at our hideaway.'

Witty looked sympathetic. 'You'll be relieved when you can get back to normal.'

Priestley responded emphatically, 'I certainly shall.'

After Witty had left, Penny closed the door and went to the window to stand close to Marcus. 'You sounded like you meant that. Aren't you enjoying being with me every night? Is there something more I can do for you?'

He tried to allay her fears. 'How could I not enjoy being with you; speaking of which, if you have some exotic ideas, we'll try them out later.'

She knew he was aiming to be humorous, so tried to respond in kind. 'I'm still a novice at this, but I'll think of something kinky.'

He grinned wickedly. 'Should I bring some cuffs?'

She laughed unconvincingly. 'If you like. You know I'd do anything you ask; anything at all.'

He felt a need to break the underlying tension. 'In that case, there is something I'd like you to do for me.' After pausing for effect, he continued, 'Review all the evidence on Khan's actual killing. I'm not a believer in coincidences, so the timing to me suggests Blackstone was behind it. With the nine millimetre slugs, we may be able to make a match to one of the guns used in our attempted abduction; but even if we find we don't have the murder weapon, I still believe there must be some sort of connection to his wife's death.'

She frowned. 'Couldn't we just wait for the ballistics test results in the morning and knock off early?'

'Let's compromise; we'll finish at seven, or earlier if you feel you've done everything you can. For now, you should focus on the actual hit. Did anyone notice any suspicious characters hanging around at the time, such as a fourteen-year-old boy wearing a hoody?'

She grinned. 'I'll check to see if there's any reliable eye-witness testimony.'

When Priestley was alone, he phoned his wife. After saying how much he missed her, and admitting he had no clear idea of how long their separation would need to continue, he ran through his thoughts on the cases. She supported his hypothesis regarding the connection between the death of Blackstone's wife and the murder of Khan, but had nothing further to add for now. The children took it in turns to speak to him. Both seemed to have accepted his absence without undue concern; for just a fleeting moment he selfishly found himself wishing they would miss him more than they were.

Next, he tried to speak to DCI Vinnie Essex, but had to settle for leaving a brief message on his voicemail. Ten minutes later he received a call back. 'DCI Essex here. I've already told your DS that my DS will be in touch if there are any developments.'

'Yes, and it's very much appreciated, only he forgot to ask for your DS's contact details.'

'He didn't forget to ask, but I don't want people here having their work interrupted by unnecessary phone calls. When we have something for you, someone will be in touch. Is that all you wanted?'

'Not entirely. It's possible we may have a lead, but it isn't definite yet. There's a connection with the army.'

'You're wasting your time with that line of inquiry. We had someone in the frame, but he had a rock-solid alibi. If that's everything, I've another call waiting.'

'Then I'll let you go. Best of luck with your inquiry.' Priestley heard the line go dead.

A little before seven o'clock, Baker came to report

her findings to Priestley. As she closed the door behind her, she began, 'I have reliable descriptions of Khan's killer and his accomplice.' Knowing his interest would be piqued, she took her time walking over to her seat.

He knew she was coquettishly keeping him waiting. 'Come on then, what did they look like?'

'Well, for a start, they were virtually identical.'

'Do you mean they were twins?'

'Not exactly.'

'Give me their descriptions.'

'Average height, average build, dressed entirely in black leather.' She waited for his curiosity to mount. 'And they were wearing maroon crash helmets with dark visors.'

'Do you mean they were in motorcycle gear?'

'Yes. It was a ride-by killing. Khan stopped at lights in his coupé and a motorbike came up alongside with two men on it. The pillion passenger calmly fired two shots into Khan's head, and then they waited for the lights to change before riding away.'

'They waited for the lights?'

'That's what the witnesses said.'

'Well, obviously they respect the Road Traffic Acts. I have to say, it comes as something of a relief to learn they're essentially law-abiding citizens.'

She flashed a brief smile at his humour. 'It sounds like a Russian-style hit.'

'The Russians don't have a monopoly on ride-by shootings. Gang members from anywhere in the former Soviet Union must be seen as contenders; or the Balkan Peninsula, including Bulgaria and Romania.'

'So perhaps Blackstone isn't connected to it.'

'I'm tempted just to go and ask him and watch his

reaction, except I think for now it's better he doesn't know we have suspicions about him being involved.'

'In that case, if there's nothing else we can do tonight, shall we get off?' She put on a cheeky grin.

He read her alternative meaning. 'Undoubtedly!'

Plummer knocked at Priestley's door and began to open it. To avoid any suggestion that she was entering without permission, he quickly called out, 'Come in!'

Baker snapped at her, 'Don't you know you should wait until you're asked?'

'Sorry, ma'am; I'm obviously too keen today.'

He detected the insincerity in Plummer's response. 'What is it, Lin? You know we're just about to set off for our safe house.'

'And that's why I'm here, sir. I'm the one who'll be giving you a lift, as soon as you're ready.'

'Well, we're almost ready now. We just need to wait for Penny to check for final messages back at her desk.'

Baker took the hint. 'I don't expect there'll be any.'

When Lin was alone with Marcus, she asked, 'How much longer are you going to be locked away with her? Why don't you ask me to do your protection duty? You could stay at my place and you'd be just as safe there.'

He sighed heavily. 'If only I could, but you know the set-up.' He waited to see if she took the bait.

'Actually, I don't. My instructions are to drop you off at a certain BT depot. Where do you go after that?'

'Sorry, Lin, but it's on a need-to-know basis.'

'Don't you trust me?'

'Of course I do, but you might let something slip accidentally.'

She gave him a hard stare. 'How are you getting on with her? Is she still as uptight when she's off duty?'

'I think I can honestly say she's starting to relax in the evenings.'

'Whereas I'm getting more frustrated…'

'Shhh! She's coming back.'

Baker marched in. 'No messages. Let's go.'

At Lin's car, he suddenly feared Baker would say something too intimate that Plummer would overhear. 'Penny, you sit in the front with Lin. You can navigate if she gets lost.'

The women turned in tandem and glared at him. Lin snapped, 'Are you saying I'm incapable of following simple directions without help?'

Penny added, 'Or are you saying it takes two women to read a satnav?'

Having achieved his objective, he smiled inwardly. 'Everyone knows women can't do navigation. Besides, it makes me feel more important, sitting in the back on my own.' Knowing their claws were still out, he added, 'Lin, the next time you're driving me, would you mind getting yourself a peaked cap? I like the idea of looking as though I have my own personal chauffeuse.'

He climbed into the back, next to where Penny was standing, blocking her from following. She flounced into the front passenger seat and slammed the door.

As Lin depressed the accelerator, he prepared to defuse the tension. 'I was only jo…'

Lin cut him off. 'With respect, sir, just shut it.'

Baker echoed, 'Yes, just shut it, sir.'

As they travelled in silence, for once he felt relieved to be shunned.

CHAPTER 25

In the morning, at Penny's insistence, Marcus reached for another condom packet. He recognised they had ploughed their way through an entire box of twelve in little more than a week and were down to the final one. He told himself he really needed to get away from this situation, if only for the sake of his blood pressure.

At breakfast, June loaded two plates with fried food and clattered them down in front of her guests. 'This is what you need, Julie, to get some flesh on your bones.'

Julie nodded in agreement. 'Thanks, June.'

As soon as June had left them alone, Julie pushed her plate up against Augustus's. 'You need to cover for me.' She transferred two sausages, a slice of bacon and one of her fried eggs.

He stared at the daunting mountain he felt he had to consume, and decided he would rather accept the risk of another abduction attempt than allow his weight to get out of hand. 'You really should make the most of this food while you can; tonight will be our last night here.' He saw how shocked she looked. 'The powers-that-be have been pressuring me to stand down the protection detail; they don't believe the expense is still justified. I've resisted up to now, but the writing's on the wall.'

'But surely it doesn't cost much for us to stay here. If it's just a matter of budgets, I'm happy to pay for us.'

'It isn't so much the cost, as the operational aspects, having to provide four vehicles and drivers every day to ferry us back and forth. They wanted us out today, but I said they should wait and see what happens in court.'

'Why didn't you tell me this earlier?'

'I know how much you're enjoying being here, so I thought I'd protect you from the bad news for as long as I could.'

'But tonight's going to be our last night?'

'It is, unless something occurs today that changes people's perceptions of the threat level.'

'What happens to me? Do I go back to my flat?'

'If you're the least bit concerned you're still at risk, I'll make sure some solid protection is put in place.'

'I'll have to have a think about this. Maybe we could just stay at a bed-and-breakfast somewhere?'

'Let's talk about it later.'

At the station, Priestley and Baker held a progress review with Witty. Blackstone was due to appear before the magistrates that morning for a bail hearing. In view of the abduction attempts, the two senior officers had no wish to risk revealing their identities by attending, so Witty was delegated. Priestley instructed him first to chase up the ballistics tests, as a clear connection with the Khan killing would support their opposition to bail.

After the meeting, Priestley closed his office door and telephoned Yelland. 'I'm needing a favour, boss.'

'Big or small?'

'It's a matter of perception.'

'That's not the straightest answer I've ever heard. You'd better come and see me and we'll talk about it.'

In Yelland's office, Priestley began, 'I'd like you to cancel the current protection arrangement.'

Yelland frowned. 'If you think the threat has passed, you could do that yourself. What do you need me for?'

'I'd like you to appear to be behind it, so DI Baker

doesn't blame me. Our working relationship is difficult enough without adding more fuel to the fire.'

'What exactly is the situation between you two?'

'Everything seems fine on the surface, but there's an awkward undercurrent that's doing my head in. While ever she believes she's in danger of abduction, we need to provide her with a safe place to stay; but I'm damned if I'm going to be cooped up with her any longer.'

'So, do I cancel the current set-up straight away?'

'No, make it with effect from tomorrow. Have us picked up in the morning with the usual routine so we can move our things out, and then we'll go with a new arrangement, whatever that is.'

'Does she know what you're up to?'

'I've already told her that tonight's the last night because of revised risk perceptions from above. Now I'll let her know you're the one winding it down.'

Yelland grinned. 'Let me guess what you're going to say. "That tight-fisted bastard Yelland doesn't want to spend his budget." Is that how it begins?'

'I might not say "tight-fisted", sir.' He grinned back.

'Well, my shoulders are broad enough, but I will have to run it by Babs. If she believes there's still a credible threat, we'll have to put something substantial in place to protect Baker.'

'Thank you, boss. It'll be such a relief to get away from her; she's so needy.'

Yelland went to Chief Superintendent Watt's office and relayed the conversation he had had with Priestley. He added, 'Despite what he said about getting on well enough with her, I'm convinced there must be some friction there. What do you think?'

She smirked. 'I think he's been telling you a load of

old codswallop. I've seen the adoring way Baker looks at him. My guess is she's made a pass at him. Being the upright fellow that he is, he'll have brushed it off; but now he's desperate to put distance between them before she can try again.'

Yelland smiled as he nodded. 'Yes, that does have the ring of truth about it. Well, we'd better rescue the stout chap before she tries again to seduce him.'

'You're thinking, with immediate effect?'

'It sounds like he has the situation under control, so I'll cancel the safe house as of tomorrow, if you agree.'

She looked thoughtful for a moment. 'But what if there is still a significant threat out there? We'd look foolish if either of them we're abducted straight after we'd withdrawn their protection. We need a Plan B.'

'Maybe they could simply stay with colleagues?'

'The last thing we want is to have families brought into the equation; imagine what would happen if a child were to be kidnapped. Singles only, I'd say.'

'Yes, that would be sensible. I'll make enquiries.'

'If the request comes from too high a rank, it may put undue pressure on potential volunteers. Assign a sergeant to ask, and make it clear anyone can say no.'

'I'll put DS Whittington onto it.'

Yelland called in on Priestley. 'Watt has agreed to dropping use of the safe house from tomorrow morning, but she wants it replaced with a Plan B. You and Baker are to stay separately with single colleagues, always assuming anyone is willing to put you up. To avoid any suggestion of duress, Witty can do the asking around.'

'I'll raise it with him once he's back from court; he's at Blackstone's bail hearing.'

'That should be a formality, shouldn't it?'

'One would hope so.'

Later, Witty called in on Priestley. 'I've some bad news, boss.'

Priestley saw his worried frown and imagined the worst about Lily's pregnancy. 'What is it, Neil?'

'Blackstone's been given bail.'

Priestley's anxiety dissipated. 'Oh, is that all.'

'I didn't think you'd be quite so calm about it.'

'I've come to accept that sort of thing. Was there any particular reason behind it?'

Witty continued to look troubled. 'You could say that. His lawyer divulged rather more of their intended defence argument than we might have been expecting. This is how she put it. Blackstone first began suffering from symptoms of PTSD following his wife's death in a horrific traffic accident. One of the ways in which it manifested itself was an immediate dependency on alcohol. This led to his judgement becoming impaired. Consequently, when a former colleague asked him to help someone who was being blackmailed, he agreed to do so. The colleague was Padraic O'Leary. The two of them visited the home of a police officer they had reason to believe may either be the blackmailer or who knows their identity. In the hope of avoiding actual violence, they took guns with them to suppress any attempt at resistance. However, so as not to have any unfortunate accidental discharge of either weapon with potentially harmful consequences, it was agreed the guns would not be loaded.'

'Except, O'Leary's gun was loaded.'

'That fact was unknown to Blackstone.'

'They're certainly putting their best gloss on it.'

'But that wasn't all; a bit of hearsay was allowed.

The blackmail victim alleges that only the police would have had information which could have led someone into mistakenly believing they were guilty of some crime, the nature of which is unknown to Blackstone. As a result, the blackmail victim wished to interview the officer who was in charge of the investigation, in order to discover which member or members of the police force were behind the demand for hush-money. O'Leary was shot dead by the police in an ambush, thereby silencing him. It may therefore reasonably be concluded that Blackstone will be in danger while ever he is in police custody. Consequently, it is respectfully requested that Blackstone be granted bail without the placing of any unduly onerous restrictions, and without any tagging that would enable the police to locate him.'

'That's clever, Neil. They've turned it around so it's the police who are the criminals, and the accused was merely acting on behalf of an alleged victim of police corruption.'

'I know it might sound flimsy, but the magistrates certainly bought it. Blackstone is bailed with minimal conditions.'

'If he's on the loose, I think that means Penny and I will need to remain under the radar for quite some time. Unfortunately, we have to move out of the safe house tomorrow.'

'You could book into a hotel as Mr and Mrs Smith.'

'Whoa, there's a massive misconception there, Neil; no way am I staying in the same hotel room as Penny. It's bad enough sharing the same safe house with her, with separate bedrooms; she's not exactly easy to get on with. No, I want somewhere well away from her. Watt proposed we find a couple of single colleagues who are willing to put us up. They'd be able to claim an overnight expenses allowance as a financial incentive, in addition to the inestimable pleasure of playing host. Yelland recommended you should be the one to make enquiries, so that no one would feel the same pressure to volunteer as they might if Penny and I were doing the asking ourselves. Do you have any suggestions?'

'Well, there's always Lin.'

'I couldn't possibly stay with Lin.' He realised he should have thought longer before responding.

Witty did a double-take. 'I didn't mean you; I meant Penny.'

He tried to laugh it off. 'Just joking! And what about a host for me? You can't volunteer yourself; it has to be someone single, so there are no family members who could be put at risk.'

'I'll have a think.'

'No rush; it isn't until tomorrow. So, what's going to happen about the allegation of police corruption?'

'It's already happening. An investigation team is on its way, as we speak.'

'In that case, get hold of Penny and send her in here. The two of us had better have a one-to-one.'

'That's what I hoped you say. She may not know about the allegation, yet; I didn't dare tell her.'

'Quick as you can, then.'

'I heard about you being put forward for two bravery awards; I reckon telling her about this should be worth a third.'

Waiting for Baker, he wondered whether she would regard the investigation into police corruption as more worrying than any potential abduction.

Baker arrived out of breath, not from the physical

exertion of hurrying, but due to omitting to breathe, as she began to fear the worst: that Marcus intended to finish their affair. Witty had only indicated there was some bad news that had to come from Priestley himself.

Her hand slipped as she hastily swung the door to close it behind her. Witty heard it slam and guessed she was having a temper tantrum.

Baker froze at Priestley's desk. Seeing the fear in her eyes, he spoke softly. 'Sit down, Penny; I have some bad news.' She felt her way to a chair, unable to break eye contact. As he explained about the court hearing, he saw her visibly relax. At the end, he asked, 'Have you ever been the subject of an anti-corruption inquiry?'

She shook her head. 'I've given testimony plenty of times, but I've never been accused of anything.'

'Well, there are a few things you need to consider. For a start, they'll lie through their teeth to try to trap you into saying something incriminating; unlike people like us, who are as honest as the day is long.'

'But I've done some things that…'

He cut her short. 'You need to get it into your mind that you haven't done anything wrong whatsoever. If there's something you don't want them to know, you have to hide it in some deep recess of your brain, as though you yourself don't even know it's there.'

'That sounds good in theory, but how do I make it work in practice?'

'You put together a complete picture of everything that has happened so far, based on how you wish it go down in history. You know nothing beyond having been the subject of two abduction attempts, which you believe were a consequence of your leadership rôle in a murder inquiry. As a result of that, you are currently staying at a safe house.'

'I thought we were being de-prioritised?'

'It's been proposed we stay separately with single colleagues, but I'm now thinking I ought to talk up the risk factor. I'm going to argue you should be moved to a distant safe house. When you speak to AC today, tell them you know nothing beyond what's on record, and that you may be unavailable for further interviews, as the protection consideration will take precedence. That should piss them off nicely, so expect a come-back. You just stick to the party line: that you don't believe there's any blackmail going on and it's just a ridiculous smokescreen laid down by a smart-ass lawyer. As to the suggestion that O'Leary was shot deliberately as part of some cover-up, again it's beyond belief. You know, of course, that you're entitled to be questioned only by higher ranking officers; but if you refuse to answer questions from other ranks, you can give the impression you have something to hide, so just answer anyone who asks anything. Always remembering of course that you know nothing whatsoever about any police involvement in blackmail, or a plot to bump off O'Leary.'

'Should I claim I'm suffering from PTSD, so they don't pressure me too much? After all, I've been the subject of two abduction attempts, and I was right there when O'Leary was shot.'

'It would certainly be an option for some people, but I think the Queen Elizabeth attitude is more your style.' He delivered his words in a lilting, quavering manner. '"I know I have the body of a weak and feeble woman, but I have the heart and stomach of a king."'

'The Queen said that?'

'Yes... Elizabeth the First, as part of a motivational

speech to inspire her troops when the Spanish Armada was coming. It might earn you their respect; you know, a woman bravely refusing to be cowed by firearms in a man's world. Not that it is any more, if our continental neighbours' defence ministers are anything to go by; the majority are women. But simply continuing to plead ignorance may be the best way of handling questioning in the face of mounting hostility.'

'You assume they'll be hostile?'

'I can almost guarantee it.'

'What sort of defence will *you* put up against their interrogation techniques?'

'It's better that you don't know, to avoid us seeming too similar. I've previously suffered so much more than anything they can do, it'll be like water off a duck's back. While ever they're here, it's best if we don't have any one-to-ones, or they'll assume we're in cahoots.'

'But we're staying together tonight, aren't we?'

'If they ask whether we're at the same safe house, just tell them all such details are highly confidential.'

She pursed her lips. 'I'm going to miss you so much, every night we're apart. I'll be glad when they're done, and we can see each other whenever we want, without having to look over our shoulders all the time.'

'They do have a habit of putting in place long-term surveillance operations, in case they missed something in their original inquiries. That means it could be a very long time before we can safely see each other. Also, they monitor communications, so we can't even talk to each other on the phone or over the internet.'

'This is going to be so hard for us, isn't it; but it'll make everything even better when we can see each other again. Absence makes the heart grow fonder.'

He thought of the contrary expression, 'Out of sight, out of mind,' but admitted to himself he would miss her, though he knew it would be nowhere near as much as she would miss him.

Seeing Yelland outside, Priestley stood and walked to the door. As he opened it for Baker to leave, he delivered a few final words loudly enough for Yelland to overhear. 'They could be here any time; just make sure you're completely open and honest with them.'

As Baker was leaving, Priestley spoke to Yelland. 'Did you want me for something, Richie?'

Yelland stepped inside and closed the door. 'Just a quick chat, Marcus. I've been briefed on the Blackstone defence; will AC find anything to worry us?'

He decided this was not a time for levity, so made no distinction between the concepts of what might actually exist and what AC might find, worrying or otherwise. 'To the best of my knowledge, nothing has been going on that should give us the least concern. The shooting was clearly justified, so the suggestion that it was part of a cover-up is total nonsense. As to the allegation of blackmail by someone in the police, it's too ridiculous to be taken seriously. But we have to be seen to be whiter than white, so we'll go through the motions.'

'All right; we'll try and have them in and out as fast as we can.' He stood to leave.

'Erm, there's something I've been thinking about: it's the protection arrangements for DI Baker. I believe the best solution would be for her to be taken off the case and moved as far away as possible.'

Yelland nodded. 'I understand where you're coming from; leave it with me and I'll do my best.'

CHAPTER 26

Later that morning, Priestley received a call from Watt to come at once to her office. When he asked for an indication of the reason so that he could prepare himself mentally, she declined to give even the slightest hint. With a feeling of trepidation, he climbed the stairs two at a time. As usual, her door was closed, so he knocked and waited. Hearing the bellowed 'Enter,' he stepped inside and accepted her motioned invitation to sit. She remained silent, so he began, tentatively, 'Ma'am?'

She raised her eyebrows at him. 'Richie says you want DI Baker off the case and sent packing.'

He drew in his lips as he considered how to respond. 'I wouldn't wish to be seen to be disagreeing with him, but I do think there's a substantial element of license in his interpretation. In view of the two attempts to abduct DI Baker, I believe it would be appropriate for her to be removed to a distant place of safety.'

She allowed a wide grin to soften her strong jawline. 'Would that be for her safety or for yours, Marcus?'

He decided a shy, silent smile was the best response.

'I won't tell you what's been arranged, so you aren't directly implicated; but I will say it may be the perfect solution. I'll be informing her she's being reassigned, and that it's highly confidential, so I'm sure she'll rush back and tell you all about it. Leave it open as you go.'

'Thank you, ma'am... I think.'

Baker was next to be summoned. She stood in the open doorway, unsure whether to knock or to cough.

Watt looked up. Softening her voice, she called out, 'DI Baker. Penny. Do come in and sit down.'

Baker sat erect on the high-backed chair, stiff and prim, hands crossed in her lap, expecting bad news.

'Penny, you've been through such a lot recently, and we're all terribly concerned about your wellbeing. You have survived two serious abduction attempts without the slightest suggestion of becoming stressed, for which you must be congratulated. But if there were to be a third, I'm sure you can appreciate how badly that would reflect on your ranking officers, both here and in Derby. We have therefore held an in-depth discussion on the subject of your protection, and have concluded the best solution is for you to be taken off the Blackstone case and to be reassigned to work at a more distant location. Of course, everyone here will be terribly sorry to lose you, but your safety is paramount to us. Now, before I give you the details, tell me how you feel about this?'

Recognising it was a done deal, Baker saw no point in appearing to be anything other than enthusiastic. 'I'm deeply grateful to you and to everyone else who has seen fit to put my safety above operational needs. When am I to take up my new responsibilities?'

'You have an interview at midday with AC, and I've asked them to make it as brief as possible. Tidy your things before then, so you can leave immediately after. As per the current arrangements, you'll stay at the safe house tonight, and then tomorrow you'll set off for your new assignment.'

Baker found she was already speaking before she had thought through her questions. 'Will DCI Priestley be at the safe house as well? Will he also be assigned to the new case? Will we still be working together?'

Watt felt convinced her earlier suspicions were now proven. 'DCI Priestley will retain his current duties. He will be subject to different protection procedures after tonight; I'm sure you will appreciate it would be best if as few people as possible know exactly what they are.' She observed Baker failing to mask her disappointment.

'I understand perfectly, ma'am. What can you tell me about my new assignment?'

'A young homosexual man from Chesterfield was found murdered in Green Park. The investigation is already fully underway. You would be there in more of an advisory capacity than as an active participant. The team is based at Paddington police station, and you're booked into a hotel quite close by on Oxford Street.'

'You wouldn't normally assign someone of my rank to watch another force at work, would you, ma'am?'

'The circumstances do warrant it in this case. It may be a hate crime, but there is another distinct possibility: there may be a political connection to the murder. The young man's great-uncle is a long-serving Member of Parliament who exerts a substantial degree of influence. You'll need to be at your most diplomatic.'

'I'll do my very best, ma'am.'

'Good. Now, practically speaking, your car is almost certainly known to the people we believe are behind the Blackstone case; it would therefore make sense to leave it here, so that no one can tail you.'

'Am I authorised to obtain a hire car?'

'Yes, if that proves necessary.'

'What about for the journey to London?'

'I think the train would be most convenient, down to St Pancras and then an hour on the tube to Heathrow.'

'Heathrow? Why Heathrow?'

'To get your plane to Australia; it sets off tomorrow night just before ten. Sorry, didn't I say the murder took place in Sydney?' Watt had watched her closely to see how she reacted, and was impressed with the way she had taken it squarely on the chin without flinching.

'So you're basically sending me as far away as you can. I'm grateful, ma'am; it will certainly make it much harder for anyone from around here to abduct me.'

'That's settled, then. You'll be issued with a special visa for entering the country. There are no inoculation requirements. Anything else?'

'Is DCI Priestley aware of my assignment, ma'am?'

'No, it's firmly on a need-to-know basis.'

'May I tell him? I'd really like him to know.'

'If you so wish; but no one else. Any questions?'

'No, ma'am. Thank you for your support.'

Baker went immediately to Priestley's office. As she told him she was being taken off the case, he gave an excellent performance of being surprised. When she stated she was being sent to Australia, his amazement became genuine. After briefing him about the Sydney case, she concluded, 'When I get back home, we'll have to make up for lost time.'

He shook his head. 'You'll probably have picked up some hunk of an Aussie on Bondi Beach and forgotten all about me, before your first week's out.'

She laughed lightly, attempting to hide her feeling of trepidation. 'Maybe I'll pick up a new guy every day and throw them back into the sea every night.'

He smiled. 'You'll have to pack your cossie.'

'I'll have to pack everything. Can you come home with me this afternoon and help?'

'Sorry, it won't be possible; I'm being interviewed

by AC at two. Besides, you need an armed escort, even if it's only for the sake of appearances.'

'It all seems very OTT. Anyway, must dash; it's my turn at twelve.'

'Ask Neil to come in, will you? I'll fill him in on what you're up to.'

'Sorry, but you're not allowed to tell him; Watt told me it's on a strictly need-to-know basis. I even had to ask her permission to let *you* know. I'd have told you anyway, of course.'

'So I can't tell Neil?'

'Yes, you can tell him, but only unofficially.'

She hurried off. Witty arrived shortly after. Priestley invited him to enter and close the door. 'Thanks for the ballistics report, Neil; it didn't surprise me in the least that O'Leary's gun was the one used to kill Khan. Now, I have some top-secret information I can only disclose to you unofficially: Penny's been assigned to a murder case in Australia.'

'What's the thinking behind that?'

'Sending her somewhere she won't be abducted.'

'So Lin won't need to put her up, then.'

'Obviously not. Did you find a place for me to stay?'

'Not yet; there aren't many genuinely single blokes, when it comes down to brass tacks.'

'In that case, you can just forget about it; I'll arrange something myself.'

'Are you sure? I can keep trying.'

'No, honestly. I'll work something out, but I won't be able to tell you about it, officially or unofficially; that way, no one could beat the information out of you if they grab you off the streets.'

'Thank you for that comforting thought.'

'Could you ask Lin to come and see me; I feel it's only right to explain in person why her generous offer of providing sanctuary has been turned down.'

Plummer hurried to Priestley's office, rapped at the open door, closed it behind her and sat down uninvited.

He began, 'I can only let you know this unofficially, so don't go telling anyone else: Penny is being assigned to a case in Australia to put her out of harm's way. That means, of course, she won't be taking up your generous offer of staying at your place. I, on the other hand, still need accommodation. Does your offer extend to me?'

Her face lit up. 'Fantastic!'

He smiled. 'This time, when I say you're not to tell anyone else, I absolutely mean it.'

'Not a word shall pass my lips.'

'I'm staying somewhere else tonight, but I'll move in tomorrow.'

'Brilliant!'

'Now, take that grin off your face before you leave my office; people may misinterpret.'

'Or interpret correctly.' She stood and spun around, making her ponytail swish from side to side.

He watched her as she sashayed away.

Later, the Police Federation representative arrived at the station, shortly ahead of the first meeting with AC. The rep located Baker and introduced himself formally as DCI Lawton.

She shook his massive hand as firmly as she could. 'I'm pleased to meet you, but I'm sorry to say it's going to be a waste of your time. This thing about blackmail is just a lawyer's trick.'

He gently released her hand. 'Don't be too hasty to rush to judgement, DI Baker. How do you know one of your team hasn't been trying it on? Is every single one of them a hundred per cent trustworthy?'

'I've no reason to believe otherwise. I've known all of the team from Derby for quite some time, and I'd say there isn't a wrong 'un among 'em.'

'And local officers assigned to the case?'

'They all seem as straight as a die.'

'Well, let's get it over with, then.'

'I'm Penny, by the way.'

'I'm Bill, but don't expect any informality during the interrogation; sorry, interview.'

Finding the reserved room vacant, they sat side-by-side and waited. To fill the awkward silence, he stated the obvious. 'The anti-corruption team hasn't arrived yet. You'd normally have to go to them, but they're the ones having to travel because of your protection issue.'

Ten minutes after midday a young female officer with fiery red hair burst into the room, out of breath. 'Sorry I'm late sir, ma'am.' She glanced around, though it was evident there was no one else present. 'I'm DC Fiona MacDuff. Where are the others?'

Lawton growled, 'Even later than you.'

She plonked herself down. 'Sorry, again; someone screwed up. We thought you were coming to us.'

He looked pointedly at his chunky black wristwatch. 'There is a credible threat to the life of DI Baker, so she must be kept under an assigned protection detail. If you have any questions before she has to drop out of sight, you'd better get started straight away.'

MacDuff stayed focused entirely on Lawton. 'I can't do that, sir. DI Baker is entitled to be questioned by an officer who is at least one rank superior.'

Baker leaned over to her and smiled. 'Yes, we all

know the rules, Fiona, but I don't mind you asking the questions. After all, I don't know anything, so it really doesn't matter who's doing the asking.'

Fiona smiled back. 'That's extremely helpful of you, ma'am… but I'm not prepared. I'm new, you see.'

Lawton rumbled, 'Don't you fret. I've been to lots of these interviews; I'll keep you on track. Now, let's get started. You're part of AC-7, right?' She nodded. He pressed the recording button. After the machine had given a continuous tone for a quarter of a minute, he began, 'DI Penny Baker and Federation Rep DCI Bill Lawton, in the presence of…'

As he pointed to the microphone, she took the hint. '…DC Fiona MacDuff from AC-7.'

He continued, 'DI Baker is being interviewed in connection with an allegation of blackmail relating to an unidentified member of a murder investigation team. She is not herself a suspect in relation to any allegation concerning discipline, misconduct or crime. That is correct, isn't it, DC MacDuff?'

Accepting his direction, she responded, 'Yes, sir. May I ask, ma'am, what you know about the blackmail allegation?'

Baker shook her head. 'Nothing at all, beyond Barry Blackstone's lawyer raising it at the magistrate's court.'

'Are you in any way connected with the blackmail?'

Lawton interjected, 'Alleged!'

Baker turned to him. 'It's all right, Bill; she's doing her best.' She smiled again at MacDuff. 'But he is right. I'm sure there isn't any blackmail going on, and it's just a lawyer's trick.'

MacDuff blinked a few times as she considered how to proceed. 'Is it possible a member of your team is involved in the alleged blackmail?'

Baker raised her eyebrows. 'The blackmail would have to be real for a member of my team to be involved in it, but I know what you mean. I'd therefore like to go on record as saying I've known them all for quite some time and believe every last one of them to be entirely honest and trustworthy.'

'Thank you, ma'am; I'm sure they appreciate your support. What about the local officers? Do you have any suspicions about any of them?'

'They all seem as straight as a die.' Realising she had earlier given the same response to Lawton, she hoped the repetition had not made her sound rehearsed.

'What about DCI Priestley? How well do you know him?'

She found herself blushing. 'He seems very upright.'

Lawton noticed her reaction. 'I think we can finish there, can't we, DC MacDuff? Clearly, DI Baker has no knowledge relating to the blackmail allegation.'

Responding to Lawton's vigorous nodding, MacDuff spoke into the microphone. 'Thank you for your help, DI Baker, and your assistance, DCI Lawton. Interview terminated.'

After leaving the interview room, Lawton invited Baker to accompany him to the car park. He took out a half-empty packet of cigarettes and offered her one, which she declined. As he drew heavily on his first fag for more than an hour, he asked, 'Off the record, do you think any of your colleagues is involved in blackmail?'

She responded confidently, 'No, I really don't.'

He looked intently at her. 'Does that include DCI Priestley?'

She tried to hide her concern. 'Certainly it includes

DCI Priestley. Why have you singled him out? He has to be the least likely to do anything wrong.'

Lawton shrugged. 'You looked a bit flushed when DC MacDuff asked about him.'

Baker shook her head repeatedly. 'If I did, I don't know why. He's completely honest and trustworthy; I'd happily trust him with my life.'

'That's good to hear. It's his turn at two, but I don't expect it to go anything like the interview you've just had; MacDuff let us push her any way we wanted.'

Baker left him to enjoy his cigarette. When it was almost spent he flicked it along the ground and watched a few strands of tobacco glowing for a moment. His hand automatically dipped into his pocket for another, but he resisted the temptation. He decided to speak with Superintendent Yelland, someone he had known for many years.

In Yelland's office, after a few pleasantries, Lawton asked, 'Have you any idea why DI Baker might have had cause to blush when asked about DCI Priestley?'

Yelland grinned. 'Rumour has it she has the hots for him, but he's having none of it. He's happily married, you see.'

Lawton became more relaxed. 'Is it still possible he's mixed up in blackmail?'

Yelland shook his head. 'You can rest assured on that point, Bill; Marcus is as straight as an arrow.'

CHAPTER 27

Lawton met up with Priestley in his office. Once he was confident they were both as well-prepared as possible, he asked, 'So, Marcus, what do you think? Is there any actual blackmail going on?'

Priestley shrugged his shoulders. 'It doesn't mean there isn't any, just because I'm totally unaware of it. I will say, though, that I don't doubt the local officers, not even for a moment; but there have been plenty of others I haven't met before, working on the case. Did DI Baker have anything to offer on that front?'

'Similar to yourself: she has complete confidence in all the officers she already knew. I'd say it's beginning to look like there's nothing behind the allegation.'

'So it would seem. All right, time to face the enemy. How did DI Baker fare, by the way?'

'It was a walk in the park. There was only Detective Constable Fiona MacDuff there to do the interview; the others hadn't arrived yet.'

'Shouldn't you have waited?'

He laughed, a rumble coming from deep within his barrel chest. 'It was too good an opportunity to miss; the poor girl never stood a chance. All the same, I'm glad DI Baker had nothing to hide.' He observed how Priestley reacted. 'Just one word of advice, Marcus: when her name crops up, try not to blush... like you're doing now.'

Priestley stretched a hand across his face to cover his cheeks. 'Thanks for the warning. There's nothing...'

Lawton interrupted. 'It's all right, I know how it is: she's been chasing you and you've been running away. I must say, though, getting her sent to Australia seems a bit extreme.' He began to laugh.

Priestley joined in. 'I did enquire about tickets to the moon, but they're still a bit pricey.'

Vestiges of their shared humour remained visible as they entered the interview room. Priestley looked at the two officers sitting behind the desk, a scrawny man and an attractive redhead. The man rebuked him, revealing a guttural Scottish accent. 'You shouldnae ha' that grin on your face when you come to see me, DCI Priestley. I'm here to put the fear of God into you, man.'

Priestley widened his eyes and looked heavenward for a few moments, to suggest he was seeking divine guidance. 'I rather believe that's the prerogative of the Almighty, sir; but perhaps you're his emissary. Does that make you an angel? Or possibly a cherub?'

'Are you trying to be funny?'

'It's what passes for humour among we Sassenachs.'

'Well, this interview is not a cause for levity; let's get on with it.' He motioned them to sit, before jabbing at the recording button. 'AC-7 interview of Detective Chief Inspector Marcus Priestley in the presence of his federation representative…'

Lawton leaned toward the microphone. 'Detective Chief Inspector William Lawton.'

MacTavish continued, 'Interview by Superintendent Alistair MacTavish with Detective Constable Fiona MacDuff. This interview is in connection with an allegation of blackmail against an as yet unidentified police officer.'

Lawton interjected forcefully, 'The use of the term

"as yet" may be interpreted as indicating such a person or persons exist, which is inconsistent with the use of the word "allegation". If the allegation is unfounded then there can never be a police officer who fits the bill. May I respectfully recommend that the terms of the interview be clarified to the extent it be recognised it is only regarding an *allegation* of attempted blackmail, and that there may or may not be one or more police officers who are in any way associated with...'

MacTavish interrupted him. 'You are here to offer advice to DCI Priestley, not to attempt to define the parameters of this interview with the suspect.'

Lawton immediately fought back. 'If DCI Priestley is a suspect, then you must issue a Regulation Fifteen notice in accordance with the Police Regulation Act...'

MacTavish held up a hand to stop him in mid-flow. 'You don't need to quote acts and regulations to me, DCI Lawton. When I said "suspect" I didn't mean DCI Priestley is a *suspect* as such...'

Lawton stopped him from clarifying. 'Let it be put on record that DCI Priestley is not a suspect. Accepted and agreed?'

MacTavish glared at Lawton. 'Accepted and agreed. For now, I'm just gathering information. Or at least I would be if you didn't keep interrupting me. And I'll thank you to address me as "sir", DCI Lawton.'

Lawton sat back comfortably. 'May I request a short adjournment, sir?'

MacTavish snorted. 'What can you possibly need to discuss with DCI Priestley? I haven't asked him any questions yet.'

Lawton spread his arms and hands expansively. 'Actually, sir, it was you I was wishing to speak to.'

MacTavish eyed him suspiciously. 'I can't imagine what for, but I accede. Interview suspended.'

Lawton pressed both hands onto the table to lever himself up. When MacTavish rose to his feet, Lawton invited him to lead the way into the corridor. With the door closed behind them, Lawton began, 'What's up with you today, Ali?'

MacTavish glowered. 'I listened to how you took over the interview with DI Baker and then closed it down; that was very naughty of you, Bill.'

Lawton grinned. 'I suppose you're right, but it was obvious Baker knows nothing, so no harm done, eh?'

MacTavish shook his head. 'I'd agree with you if it wasn't for the fact that the wee lassie went red in the face when DCI Priestley's name came up, according to Fiona. Or was she mistaken?'

'No, she's quite right, though at the time I didn't think she'd noticed. So, is *that* why you're gunning for Priestley?'

'Aye, it is, for one thing. But there's another reason. We've been scanning through personnel files at a rate of knots, and on first reading the only officer on the case with the balls to set up a sting is him.'

'In that case, I'll let you in on a bit of office gossip that could shed some light on Baker's reaction. Rumour has it she's been mooning over him. He's happily married, so he hasn't given her any encouragement, but…'

MacTavish completed the sentence for him. '…the lassie is still smitten. Well, if so, her reaction may have nothing to do with this blackmail allegation, but I do need to satisfy myself on that score. Shall we call a truce until I've got to the bottom of things?'

'Sure thing, Ali. Will you be going to the Black Bull tomorrow night?'

'Aye, if you're buying.'

'You tight Scotch git, it's your round.'

MacTavish covered a laugh with a cough. 'Maybe you're right. Let's get back in; I expect your man's now fretting about what's going on.'

They returned along the corridor to the interview room. MacTavish began to open the door, but stopped when he heard Priestley say, 'You really do have the most gorgeous red hair, Fiona. And you promise me it didn't come out of a bottle?'

When he heard Fiona giggling her response, 'I could pr…' he barged in noisily, halting her mid-word.

Lawton followed him in and closed the door.

MacTavish stared hard at Priestley. 'When you're finished charming DC MacDuff, DCI Priestley, I'd like to get on with the interview… if that's all right by you.'

Marcus waited for Fiona's smile to fade before he adopted a serious expression. 'Certainly, sir.'

MacTavish restarted the recording, again specifying the purpose and time. After handing out copies of a file, he listed the contents out loud.

Priestley flicked through the pages and then looked up at MacTavish. 'It's a bit thin isn't it, sir?'

MacTavish ignored his reaction. 'Turn to the fourth document, an eye-witness statement regarding an RTC. Some young lad crashed a van into a car and then legged it. Tell me what you know about that.'

Priestley frowned theatrically. 'With respect, sir, I don't know why this is even in the file. To the best of my knowledge, we are here in relation to an allegation of blackmail deriving from the Blackstone case.'

MacTavish drummed the bunched fingers of his right hand hard on the desk. 'The car that was crashed into was owned by Aden Liversedge whose name features in the Sylvia Batter case, and who has claimed someone has been attempting to blackmail him.'

'I'm aware of that, sir, but the blackmail allegation against the police relates to the attempted abduction of DI Baker and myself by Barry Blackstone. You appear to be implying the two are connected.'

'Indeed I am, DCI Priestley. I dislike coincidences, so if two connections to blackmail happen together, my first question is: how are they related? Are you saying you haven't made the link yourself?'

'I have, sir, but I recognise it's merely supposition. As far as I'm aware, Blackstone has not identified the person who claimed to have been blackmailed, and who enlisted the help of his late friend Padraic O'Leary.'

'How's your maths? What do you get when you add two and two together?'

'Five, sir; it's called synergy.'

MacTavish sighed loudly. 'Are you refusing even to answer the simplest of questions?'

'I'm certainly not withdrawing my co-operation, sir. I was merely trying to suggest that not everything is as simple as adding numbers.'

'Do you have any family?'

Lawton interjected, 'I'm not sure I can see what relevance that has, Superintendent.'

Priestley added, 'I would have expected you to have consulted my personnel file prior to this interview, sir.'

MacTavish glared at Priestley. 'We have, and it says you have a son and a daughter. Does your son know how to drive vehicles such as cars and vans?'

'Only in theory, sir.'

'So you didn't recruit him, then, to crash a van into Blackstone's car?'

'I would never ask him to put himself in danger in any way whatsoever. But why would you imagine he might have been the driver of the stolen van?'

'Because he's the right age to fit the description of the lad who was driving, and the eye-witness said it looked deliberate.'

'Could we return to some maths, sir? What do you get when you take five from thirteen?'

MacTavish jerked back. 'Oh, he's only eight, is he; I was told he was older.' He glared at MacDuff, inviting an apology.

She looked at the floor and mumbled, 'Sorry, sir.'

Priestley added, as though helpfully, 'He is coming up to nine, though.'

MacTavish sighed, before continuing, 'Anyway, you know as well as I do how many lads not much older than eight have been arrested for drunk-driving; and you're a big fellah, so I'm guessing your son could look a lot older than he is.'

'Well, sir, I'm impressed with the way you've strung so many tenuous links together; but in the end, you're clearly barking up the wrong tree.'

'And why is that, DCI Priestley?'

'It's the size of the blackmail demand that's the problem; fifty thousand pounds, we're told.'

'Aye, it's a large sum.'

'That rather depends on who you are. I remember a lawyer arguing in court that a million pounds given to a political party was a *very* large amount, but the donor, a multi-billionaire, declared it was no more than a pee in the ocean to him. I'm paraphrasing, of course. But if you scale things down, you'll find my personal wealth is more than sufficient to regard fifty thousand pounds as an inadequate sum to warrant my engaging in any blackmail attempt. Have you not undertaken the usual financial background checks, sir?'

MacTavish hit himself on the chin a few times using the index finger side of his fist. 'We've barely had the time to understand what the allegation is; we had to move quickly, now DI Baker is dropping out of sight. But I'm getting the message that you're not implicated. Can you suggest who might be? What about DI Baker?'

Priestley caught the impression that MacTavish was looking a little too earnestly at him, so interpreted it as a key question. He allowed a rueful smile to take hold, before responding, 'What about DI Baker indeed, sir. I'm unclear if there is an actual question, there.'

'Could DI Baker have arranged for some lad to crash a van into a car, if she's behind the blackmail?'

'Anything is possible, like being struck by lightning three times while staring at the night sky as an alien flying saucer abducts a burglar who's just broken into a stately home and stolen a Renoir that had...'

MacTavish finally interrupted. 'You're saying it's really not at all likely?'

'Indeed I am, sir; she would never break any rules.'

'Then I guess we'll have to keep looking.'

'May I respectfully suggest, sir, that you don't waste your effort; at least for now. Liversedge received an untraceable e-mail demand for blackmail money. It could be some sort of phishing scam, or he could have arranged it himself, but he claims it must have come from someone with inside knowledge of the Batter investigation. Then we have Blackstone attempting to abduct two police officers, and saying he was helping out a friend of a friend who was being blackmailed by the police, so a link between the two cases is not an unreasonable inference. Now, considering the number of people involved in the abduction attempts, there's quite a web of connections.'

'Aye, there is, right enough. *What a tangled web we weave when first we practise to deceive!* Walter Scott.'

'Very good, sir. But my point is, though *we* can clearly see the connections, I can well imagine a jury being persuaded by some glib lawyer that they're unrelated. That would leave Liversedge an innocent victim of an RTC with no connection to either the Batter or the Blackstone cases. Similarly, looking at the Blackstone case in isolation, there's no evidence that any police officer has been involved in any blackmail attempt. You would therefore be investigating a legal non-event. That's why I think it makes sense to park your enquiry, until and unless there is some provable offence to warrant your searching for corruption in our ranks.'

'Just because a jury might not believe there's a link, that doesn't stop us from investigating as if there is.'

'Quite so, sir; but without a supporting court case, I seriously doubt you'd be able to make real progress. As I'll be continuing to work the allegedly related cases, I'd be happy to let you know of any developments that suggest your team might have something or someone they can get their teeth into.'

'I appreciate your offer, but you must recognise it's entirely my decision as to what should, and what should not, be investigated by my team.'

'Indeed so, sir.'

'Very well, then. In view of the lack of evidence at this present time to link DCI Priestley to the blackmail allegation, I'm terminating the interview.'

Afterwards, Lawton returned with Priestley to his office. 'Well, Marcus, it seems AC's inquiry has fizzled out before it got started. Their dossier was pathetic, though I'm sure it was because they had to rush it, what with DI Baker going off to Australia.'

'I suppose so. By the way, how did *you* know about her posting? It was supposed to be confidential.'

'I overheard a couple of WPCs discussing whether they should arrange a farewell party for her.'

'So it's common knowledge?'

'Certainly sounds like it. Anyway, must go. If the blackmail allegation takes off in court, I'll be seeing you again.'

'Right. Many thanks for your support.' They stood and shook hands.

Lawton headed outside and found the darkest corner of the car park, where he furtively smoked a cigarette. He watched MacDuff go to her car and drive away. Seeing MacTavish leaving the station, he strolled over. 'Where's it going from here then, Ali?'

MacTavish checked that no one was near enough to overhear. 'Unless something comes up in court to move things forward, we've better things to do than search for a hypothetical blackmailer.'

'That's my thinking, too. See you tomorrow.'

'Aye. Cheers pal.'

CHAPTER 28

Priestley checked his watch again; it was a quarter past five and Baker had not yet returned to the station. He phoned her. There was a pause before she answered. Hearing the hum of traffic, he asked, 'Are you driving?'

There was an unnatural break before she responded, 'Yes. I should be there in ten minutes.'

'I'll let you focus on the road.'

'I can talk; I'm on hands-free.'

'Even so, you know the stats.' He hung up without waiting for a response.

Baker lugged her two heavy suitcases into the office. Taken by surprise when her colleagues burst into a round of applause, she glanced behind her in case it was intended for someone else. A banner with the words *Bon Voyage* in multi-coloured letters was hanging above a table on which stood a large round cake, an aeroplane in RAF livery gracing the white, smoothly-iced surface. She looked at all the smiling faces and knew in the past she would have interpreted them negatively, that they were happy to see her leave; but now she felt there was an element of warmth behind them, and attributed it to how much she had changed since beginning her affair with Marcus. Her eyes sought him out; he was standing next to Yelland at the back of the room. She called out a cheery, 'Thank you all ever so much,' as she headed straight for him.

Watt stepped forward. 'If this is your idea of keeping an assignment confidential, Penny, I can't imagine what would have happened if I'd asked you to broadcast it!'

Everyone laughed dutifully. Baker veered off and headed for Watt. 'Thank you for this, ma'am.'

Watt shook her head. 'It was your team who had the idea; I didn't even know they knew.'

Everyone crowded around as Baker picked up the knife. She cut a wedge, placed it on a white paper plate and handed it to Watt. Yelland being next in rank, she gave him the second piece. As she passed the third to Priestley, she made sure her fingers touched his for a moment. He pretended not to notice. She wielded the blade rapidly and demolished the rest of the cake, taking a tiny piece for herself and leaving everyone else to choose their own. The colleagues she had known the longest asked the expected questions about her new assignment; she insisted she was unable to disclose the confidential details.

Realising some of the officers were keenly awaiting her departure in order that they could themselves leave, she asked Priestley what time they would be going.

Witty was standing nearby and interjected, 'I'm the chauffeur, so just give the word.'

Before Priestley could respond, Baker indicated her own preference. 'Shall we go *now*?' He assented.

Still wearing her genuine smile from receiving a fond farewell, for the first time in her life she delivered goodbyes as though an extrovert. She imagined herself a famous film star, the centre of attraction for her devoted fans. When Priestley grasped the handle of the larger case, she grabbed the smaller, knowing such an action was inconsistent with that persona.

After being transferred to the Royal Mail van, they were in due course deposited at their hideaway. June met them at the door. 'This is your last night here, then. I won't ask where you're off to next.'

Julie laughed. 'And you probably wouldn't believe me if I told you.'

While the evening meal was being prepared, Julie repacked her suitcases and left one of them unfastened, ready to take the final items in the morning.

After Julie and Augustus had polished off their roast pork, potatoes, carrots and peas, June returned to the kitchen and made custard from raw ingredients to go with their jam roly-poly; enhancing the yellow colour from the egg yolks with an overly generous sprinkling of turmeric, it glowed like radioactive uranium glass.

They retired to their room with heavy stomachs. As the Australian posting was very much a journey into the unknown, Penny asked a series of rhetorical questions. At nine o'clock they settled quietly to watch television. At ten o'clock the news began; he thought how little the international situations had moved forward since the previous day's reports. She watched intently, believing this would be her last contact with English civilisation for quite some time. Half an hour later he switched channels for politics and current affairs. Appalled by the ingrained liberal left leaning bias that rendered the presenter incapable of posing unprejudiced questions, he hit the mute button. 'Shall we have an early night?'

She took his hand and raised it to her lips, where she delivered several kisses to his fingers. 'I'm really going to miss you.' She hoped he would respond in kind.

'I'm sure you'll be far too busy with other things to even think about me.'

Though knowing how needy it would sound, she nevertheless tried again. 'Will you miss *me*?'

Hearing an unmistakably plaintive edge to her voice, he gave her the succour she so desperately craved. 'You know I will, Pen, in so many different ways.'

She adopted a cheeky grin that now came naturally to her. 'How many different ways? I've lost count.'

After a little while in bed together he reached for the condom box that now held only the thirteenth packet, which he extracted with mixed emotions. His feeling of guilt at deceiving his wife came with a sense of relief that this would be the last occasion he would ever have sex with Penny. He had to admit to himself just how much he had enjoyed their shared intimacy, and in no sense did he feel he had taken advantage of her; on the contrary, his sincere belief was that she had wanted something and he had generously obliged her.

Still feeling full from the stodgy pudding, he happily accepted her suggestion that she straddle his supine body.

Afterwards, she checked his face for approval of her performance. He kissed her repeatedly, realising just how much he would miss her. When he suggested they take a shower together, her face shone with delight.

In the morning, she gently shook his arm to persuade him to wake. He asked, 'What is it?'

'One last time before I go?'

He sighed. 'I can't.'

She slipped her hand down the bed and grasped his lie in her hand. 'Yes you can.'

'I mean, I can't because we've run out of condoms.'

'Damn!' She hesitated for just a moment. 'I could give you a blow-job.'

'I don't think so.'

'What about a hand-job?'

'Are you an expert at it?'

'I'm sure I will be, once I've given it a try.'

'So you're an absolute beginner.'

'Well, yes. What else could we do? Would you like to fuck my ass?'

He felt shocked. 'Would I like to *what*?'

'Have my arse?'

'No, I wouldn't. Why would you imagine even for a moment I *would* like to?'

'I thought some men enjoy that type of thing.'

'Yes: homosexuals. In some Catholic countries the heterosexuals have to make do with that way as well, when a woman wants to avoid pregnancy but won't use contraceptives. I once heard someone from Chile refer to it as "doing it like a girl from Argentina".'

'So, shall we give it a try? It can't be that different for you, can it?'

'I have no idea, but I don't think you should ever be offering yourself up that way; as a woman, you aren't respecting your body if you let someone bugger you.'

'Well, what about normal sex without a condom.' He found himself deeply disturbed by the thought that she would risk becoming pregnant for the sake of a little pleasure. She misinterpreted his silence. 'So that's what you'd really like. In that case, I'll go on the pill.'

He ignored her suggestion. 'Let's just deal with your needs, shall we? And don't worry about mine; you've given me so much pleasure this past week, I could do with a rest.'

'But I want to please you.'

'And you will please me, if you have your best ever orgasm. Now, just remind me how you like it. Is it like this?' His fingers began to work their magic.

Her moistening prelude was suddenly flooded by a superabundance of hot liquid. She desperately begged him, 'Don't stop,' until her repeated pleading changed to the opposite, with each 'Stop' punctuated by a sob. As he gently wound her down, she whimpered, 'Please stop now; I've had enough.' After one final caress, she sighed contentedly. Only seconds later she whispered, 'What about you?'

He kissed her tenderly on the lips. 'You've enjoyed it enough for the both of us.'

After a polite interval, he left her dozing and went to the nearer bathroom that she always shared with him, even though her own official bathroom was much nicer. As he was about to step out of the shower cubicle, she rushed into the room and blocked his way, gazing up at him with pulsating eyes. 'Will you wash my hair?'

He made room for her in the shower and applied the shampoo, working up the lather on her head. After rinsing it away, he repeated the process. This time, he used his hands to chase down the foam over her entire body, caressing every little bump and hollow, until finally running the bubbles off her toes. As he did so, he imagined it would be the perfect ending for her, to remember how it had been between them.

In the kitchen, Julie queried why they had two extra sausages each. June explained, 'They would have been left over; I'm not expecting anyone.' Augustus found he was craving fruit and cereal, and wondered how often her husband had felt the same.

After breakfast, they finished the packing. When the BT van drew up, they took their leave of June.

In due course, they transferred over to Vardy's car. He asked Penny, 'How long will you be in Australia?'

She glanced at Marcus for a moment. 'Too long!' Realising her response must have sounded brusque, she added, 'I really don't have any idea, but it's bound to be long enough to miss everyone.'

Marcus quickly redirected the conversation. 'Will you be taking Penny to catch her train, later?'

Vardy replied, 'Yes, unless she wants to go now.'

Knowing she was perfectly capable of responding for herself, nevertheless Marcus solicitously asked her, 'Would you like to go straight away?'

She nodded. 'There's no point in going in to work; I've already said my goodbyes.'

Vardy dropped them at the station's main entrance and went to park in the Transport Police reserved area.

Penny and Marcus wheeled one suitcase each along the platform to the buffet, where they sat opposite each other at a small table. He fetched them both a coffee. Fingering his cup, he asked, 'Have you ever seen that old black-and-white film, *Brief Encounter*?'

She reflected for a moment. 'I've heard of it. Why?'

'Near the end, Celia Johnson and Trevor Howard are in a railway station refreshment room just like this one. They're saying goodbye to each other before they have to part forever. He's going to South Africa…'

'…whereas I'm going to Australia. We could watch it together when I'm back, if you like.'

He gave the briefest of sad smiles, wishing she had read more significance into the scene. 'You might not like it. The ending isn't an especially happy one, though it could have been far worse. The first time I saw it, I thought she was going to throw herself under the train, like in *Anna Karenina*.'

'That's another old film, isn't it?'

'It's a book by Leo Tolstoy, though it's been made into a film more than once. Maybe you should read it if you have a lot of time on your hands down under.'

'Perhaps after this one I'm taking for my journey.' She showed him a large novel with a Christmassy title and a photograph of a steam train on the front cover.

'Maybe you'll be too busy to read anything, once you're working the case.'

She shook her head. 'I don't expect to be doing very much at all; I know I'm only being sent there to keep me out of danger. I've been told not to communicate with anyone in the UK except through official channels, and not to divulge where I am in case there's a leak; so, don't expect to hear from me until I'm back.'

'Well, that may be for the best; you can absorb the culture of the place better if you're not spending all your time thinking of England.'

'I'm certain I'll be thinking of you all the time.'

'Surely you won't. As the saying goes, out of sight, out of mind.'

'But, like I said to you before, absence makes the heart grow fonder.'

He accepted the stalemate and fell silent.

The train was punctual for its brief stop. He carried the larger suitcase on board and stowed it in the rack. She declined his offer of help with the second case.

He returned to the platform to say goodbye at the door. She stepped off after him. Concerned they may be observed, he offered a formal handshake to signify her official departure. She brushed it aside and grasped his neck, pulling him down to kiss him firmly on the lips. He responded quickly before breaking away, hoping no one had noticed them. Seeking to justify the brevity of the kiss, he commented, 'It'll be going in a minute.'

She climbed aboard and stayed at the door. When the train began to move, she mouthed through the glass, 'I love you.' He waved until she was out of sight.

As he returned to his driver's car, Vardy stepped out from the Transport Police office and called over to him, 'You've never kissed me goodbye, sir.'

He tried to look unruffled. 'You were watching?'

'Yes, I saw it all on the monitor. You were going to shake her hand, but she kissed you instead. Looked like she took you by surprise, boss.'

'Yes, indeed. I suppose she must have been feeling anxious about going so far away, and wanted to behave like she had someone to say goodbye to. I should have let you take her suitcase.'

'I really don't think the missus would approve of me kissing other women.'

'Neither would mine. Do you mind not mentioning it to anybody? I know it's a good bit of gossip, but people might start reading things into it that aren't there.'

'Sure. I know I wouldn't appreciate it if it were me.'

'Thanks, Craig. Let's get off, then.'

At the police station, Priestley informed the team that staffing levels would be reduced even further over the coming weeks, unless a new line of enquiry came to light. Those already listed for redeployment were asked to tidy up any loose ends from their various strands of the investigation.

Priestley returned to his office. Yelland called in to see him. 'What are we going to do with *you* now? Do we need to send *you* to some far-flung corner of the world?'

He grinned. 'Anywhere but Australia, Richie.'

'I understand you've organised your own safe house. Do I get to know where it is?'

'Just one officer is aware, for maximum security.'

'I can't fault you for being safety-conscious. How long do you expect it to be needed for?'

'It could be longer than we might have hoped, seeing as the defence is arranging a psychological assessment to bolster the claim that Blackstone was suffering from post-traumatic stress disorder.'

'Yes, I was aware of that. I expect we'll get one of our own tame psychologists to argue the other way.'

'Expert assessments are meant to be independent.'

'So I've heard, but we both know that isn't how the game is played.'

'What if it's argued his judgement was so impaired he shouldn't be convicted of anything?'

'That way lies madness! If we were to accept such a line of defence, we'd have bank robbers claiming they only did a blag because their judgement was impaired. No, it's OK to take PTSD into consideration, but it isn't OK to treat it as anything more than mitigation.'

'For the extent of the PTSD to drive the level of the mitigation, we're dependent on having a sensible judge. Do you have any idea where we can find one of those?'

'How can you be so cynical about our legal system? Once you have the answer to that, explain it to me, so I can strive to achieve your level of doubt.'

Priestley smiled. 'To be fair, most of the judges I've come across have been quite reasonable. Sometimes it's the law that's at fault.'

'But we have to uphold it to the best of our ability. Anyway, what are we going to do with you next week?'

'Let me have a think about it over the weekend.'

'All right. By the way, if your safe house is actually the Hilton, don't expect me to authorise your expenses.'

'I can't submit invoices for sign-off; that would give away the location.'

'So you want cash-in-hand, do you? It's all highly irregular, but I'll find you a few hundred quid to cover you for the next three nights, out of the slush fund we no longer maintain.' Yelland winked theatrically.

'It isn't strictly necessary, but if you wish to give me three ton, I'll be happy to put it to good use.'

'Make the most of it, Marcus. Come Monday, we'll have to put an arrangement in place that can withstand scrutiny by the auditors.'

Later, Yelland returned to Priestley's office with a brown envelope containing three hundred pounds. Once he had left, Marcus called Lin to come and see him. She entered and closed the door. Disappointment registering in her voice, she asked, 'Don't tell me you've had to call it off?'

He grinned. 'No, quite the opposite: I've been given some cash, off the books, enough for a weekend in the Lake District. What do you think?'

'Leave it to me; I'll arrange something. We'll set off this evening and come back Sunday night.'

'Great. Now, stop smiling before you go.'

CHAPTER 29

The last time Lin and Marcus had been to the Lake District together was to celebrate her birthday. The rain had fallen unceasingly, not untypically for October, so they had taken refuge under the bed covers for the whole weekend, only surfacing for food. This time, the weather was better for walking, so Marcus intended to enjoy the outdoor air.

After a pleasant meal in the pub close to the B&B where they were staying, they took a stroll to enjoy the scenery. Before long, she grasped his arm. 'Let's get back. You've been doing without for quite a while now, hiding away, so I'm going to make it up to you.'

He responded enthusiastically to avoid implying her assumption was incorrect. 'Fantastic!'

'I hope you haven't forgotten how it works.'

'It's like riding a bike.'

She feigned amazement. 'That's a technique you've never tried with me before.'

He laughed. 'You know what I mean.'

Throughout the weekend, though Marcus wished to go walking in the hills to enjoy the stunning views of the tranquil waters, Lin insisted they spend much of their time in bed. Determined not to suggest he was unappreciative, he performed to the best of his ability.

On the Sunday evening, they drove back to her flat. That night when they slipped between the sheets, he turned away from her. She tugged him back around. He sighed wearily, 'I need some sleep.'

She climbed on top. 'A bit of exercise will help.'

He pushed her onto her back. 'In that case...'

When they had both enjoyed the experience, he lay down and started thinking with his mind instead of his hormones. 'I must stop being disloyal to Helen. It's time Lin found someone available. She's only twenty-two and I'm thirty-six; she needs someone her own age. If I keep on like this, I'm going to have high blood pressure and a heart attack.'

As he repeatedly cycled through reasons he should stop being with Lin, he found counterarguments began to undermine his resolve. 'The relationship came with no strings attached, so no one would suffer if the affair were never discovered. *She* had seduced *him*, so he was innocent of abusing his position and therefore under no obligation to end their affair. She had wanted someone unavailable so she could remain happily single; he was therefore being supportive. He would never wish to hurt her feelings by calling a halt to their intimacy.'

Without resolving the dichotomy, he finally drifted off to sleep.

In the morning, she woke him by repeatedly running one hand down his body; she knew not to run it up, as the hairs on his chest resisted the movement and he found it less pleasant. Her hand checked his inclination. 'Let's start the day with a bang.'

He felt convinced he should talk to her about their lack of a future together. After reflecting on this for a moment, he decided it would undoubtedly be better to discuss it afterwards. As they made love, he could think of nothing but how much he enjoyed being with her.

Not long after they were both satisfied, she checked the time. 'We'd better get going right away.'

He refused to budge. 'We need to be late, to suggest you've collected me from somewhere else.'

She climbed out of bed. 'In that case, let's have some breakfast.'

He left her to shower alone, before taking his turn. When he came out, he found breakfast was prepared. At the table, he took a bite of toast and orange marmalade, and then washed it down with black coffee. 'I wish it could always be like this, but we both know it can't. I know we've talked about it before, but don't you think it's time you chucked me? I'm too old for you, and you need someone you can be with every day, not someone who has to fit you in with his family life.'

She stopped chewing and flushed down a large piece of toast with fresh orange juice, making her gag a little. 'We've already had this debate, so I don't know why you're mentioning it again. I don't want someone who is always with me; I want my freedom.'

'But I'm taking advantage of you.'

'No you aren't.'

'Well, it feels like I am, what with you being so young and beautiful.'

She stared at him. 'Are you trying to find an excuse for finishing with me?'

He felt like a mesmerised rabbit caught in her big blue headlights. 'No, of course I'm not, Lin; I'm simply giving you the opportunity to end it without us having to have some awkward scene.'

'But this is turning into an awkward scene, isn't it? Don't ever mention it again, all right?'

'Sure, Lin. I'll leave it up to you to ditch me as soon as you think I'm passed my "Best Before" date.'

She refused to respond, instead reflecting on how

much she loved him and how certain she was she would never end their affair.

She drove them to the station. He went inside and checked his in-tray, but found nothing that might move the investigations forward. In his inbox was a formal e-mail from DI Baker stating her safe arrival; he clicked on the request for confirmation of receipt, intending to let it act as his only response. Immediately recognising it represented too abrupt a termination of their intimate relationship, he followed it up with a brief note.

Looking through the window at the view down the valley, he reflected on why he wished to return to living at home. Though he tried to argue his primary motive was the longing to be back in the bosom of his family, he had to accept that that was self-deception, knowing what he most desired was an undisturbed night's sleep. He knew he would first need to persuade Yelland, so telephoned him to request a meeting.

As he entered Yelland's office, he delivered a breezy 'Good morning, Richie,' before closing the door.

Yelland took a moment to scan his face and assess his underlying mood. 'Good morning to you, Marcus. Are you here for more funding?'

Priestley smiled as he shook his head. 'No, thank you. I've reassessed the risk and come to the conclusion that it's safe enough for me to return home.'

Yelland took his time considering his response. 'I'd been wondering about packing you off to college. You could give them the benefit of your vast experience, while relying on their standard security arrangements.'

'Those who can, do; those who can't, teach.'

'That's a bit unfair; I know some good people there who give useful training sessions.'

'Even so, it isn't really me. Besides, I'm missing my family.' He gave a sly grin. 'And home comforts.'

Yelland grinned back. 'Yes, it must be hard, having to go without. And college wouldn't be great for us, either; we'd have to reallocate all the cases you're supervising. Well, home it is, then; but if you change your mind, you only have to ask.'

Back in his office, he telephoned Lin. 'I've just been speaking with the Super; the latest risk assessment has concluded I can safely return home, so...'

'Can't you appeal against it? The situation hasn't really changed.'

'Careful what you say; can anyone overhear you?'

'I'll come and see you right away.'

She entered his office and closed the door, starting to speak before she had reached the chair facing his desk. 'If we don't make any claims for expenses, I don't see why anyone has to know where you spend your nights.'

He waited until she was seated. 'It's more to do with what the official assessment is. While ever I'm staying away from home, they have to make daily reports to those higher up the chain. It was fantastic being with you all weekend, but I'm sorry to say they won't allow it to continue.'

She glared at the desk before looking up at him. 'Who exactly decided?'

He shrugged. 'Officially it was a collective decision, but no doubt someone up above is driving it. Anyway, there's no point in arguing the matter; we just have to accept it.'

'I suppose I knew it was too good to last.'

When Lin had left the office, he telephoned Helen. She was relieved to know she would soon be having him home, but questioned the logic of the changed risk analysis as there had been no substantive alteration to the underlying parameters. He replied simply, 'Ours is not to reason why.'

She responded softly, 'Don't continue that quotation, love; just tell me you're sure we'll all be safe.'

He lightened his voice. 'I'm quite certain we will. The original analysis obviously overestimated the threat to me, and by extension to you, Alice and Edwin, as the main abductions were clearly focused on DI Baker.'

'And she's safely out of the way, now. Well, so long as we aren't putting the children at risk, I couldn't be happier to have you back.'

He cooed, 'I've really missed being with you.' Though certain this was true, he knew it was not as true as it might have been.

'Come home early, then, and I'll give you a suitable welcome.'

He heard her giggle before the line went dead.

After an uneventful day, he set off for home, pleased to be driving his own car for the first time in over a week. His frequent checking in the rear view mirror supported his belief that he was not being followed, though for greater certainty he included a repeated circuit that would have revealed anyone trailing him.

Helen opened the door as he drew up onto the drive. Inside, she kissed him as though he had been away for a year. 'Hello, love. It's so nice to have you back.'

'It's so nice to *be* back.' He kissed her again, before asking, 'Are they upstairs?'

She smiled sweetly as she tugged him by the arm. 'I've packed them off for the evening. As you haven't been getting any, I'm giving you a special welcome.'

He felt his smile faltering. 'Great idea, love.'

In bed, she expressed her enthusiasm with a degree of physicality he did his best to reciprocate.

Afterwards, he told himself he should have a check-up to see if his blood pressure was becoming a problem.

As he slept soundly, she stole out of bed. Not even the sound of her shower troubled his slumber.

Eventually, she gently shook him awake. 'I've been and fetched them. You'd better have a shower before you come down.'

After drying and dressing, he went down to the kitchen and found all three of them sitting at the table. Alice jumped down and threw her arms around him at waist height. He hoisted her up and kissed her. 'Have you missed me, sweetheart?'

She hugged his head. 'Yes, Daddy.'

He stretched out his neck to obtain a better view of Edwin. 'And have you, my love?' He expected only to receive limited confirmation.

Edwin slipped off his chair and hugged him and Alice at the same time. 'Yes, I have. You aren't going to go away again, are you, father?'

Marcus heard the concern in Edwin's unexpectedly formal mode of address. While holding Alice with one arm, he hugged his son even closer with the other. 'I don't have any plans to be off anywhere, but sometimes I have to do my duty and go where I'm sent.'

Helen untypically rushed up to them and put her arms around all three. 'It's nice to have a family hug.'

Marcus felt it was the nearest thing to heaven he could ever experience, having all three of them so close to him. His greatest fear was losing them because of his relationships with other women. At least he was back to just the one affair, he told himself.

After dinner, Edwin asked his father if they could play Risk, the board game.

Helen was stacking used crockery in the dishwasher. Marcus called over to her, 'What about you, love? Do you have time for a game?'

She twisted around. 'Yes, let's all play.'

Edwin fetched the Risk box and began to lay out the board on the kitchen table.

Once the set-up was complete, Helen joined them. Marcus considered offering some initial tactical advice to the children, but knew it would serve only a limited purpose until they had specific objectives in mind. As the game progressed slowly, he realised the others were only undertaking minor skirmishes with each other, and he was being excluded from their internecine warfare. He marched through Asia and wiped out all of Helen's armies, just as she had hoped, thereby allowing her to get on with her work.

Seeing little alternative on this occasion, he quickly destroyed Edwin's armies before dealing with Alice's. As he completed the rout, he thought he had never seen his children look so pleased to lose a game.

CHAPTER 30

Since the Blackstone hearing in the Magistrates' Court, the Crown Prosecution Service had diligently prepared a case against him they believed would be watertight. Being a victim of the attempted abduction, Priestley would only be attending the Crown Court when called to give evidence. On the opening morning of the trial he took a phone call in his office.

'Marcus, it's Sally Mansfield. I thought I'd let you know how things are progressing.'

'It's a bit early for a progress report, isn't it? Has something already happened?'

'Let me ask you a question: how do you think Barry Blackstone was dressed this morning in court?'

'Dark suit, white shirt, plain tie, black shoes?'

'As per conventional received wisdom, to suggest he's an upright chap who doesn't deserve to be in the dock. What if I told you he's wearing combat boots, camouflage trousers and commando-style olive-green jumper with canvas patches at the shoulders?'

'Asserting his army credentials, I suppose.'

'Now factor in how he's shaved only one side of his face, leaving the other covered in two-day-old stubble. And his eyes were darting all over the place.'

'It sounds like the defence might be preparing to put forward an insanity plea under the Criminal Procedure (Insanity and Unfitness to Plead) Act 1991.'

'What a clever boy you are, Marcus. Next thing, you'll be quoting me the history behind the legislation.'

'You know I do like history. Didn't it begin with the 1843 House of Lords ruling in the M'Naghten Case?'

'That's correct. The McNaughton Rule is based on the presumption that a defendant is sane and therefore responsible for their criminal behaviour. In 1883 we had the Trial of Lunatics Act, and in 1983 there was the Mental Health Act, so I suppose in 2083 there'll be another suitably named piece of legislation.'

'Maybe the Taking Good Care of People Who Did Bad Things (Because Society Didn't Look After Them Properly When They Were Children) Act.'

She laughed. 'Well, whatever it is, I won't be around by then to be concerned about any sanity clause.'

Believing she may have set him up to make a joke, he responded, 'Do you still believe in Sanity Claus?' He heard her titter. 'It's an old gag by one of the Marx Brothers.'

'Yes, that certainly sounds like Karl.'

'I think it was actually his twin brother, Chico.'

She chuckled. 'But seriously, Marcus, if the defence is successful in arguing that Blackstone was suffering from a temporary disease of the mind which left him unaware that what he was doing was against the law, he could be committed to a psychiatric hospital for just a short stay, before he's released back into society to pick up again where he left off.'

'We should fight that, because there's no way he's off his head; I've spoken with him and I know he's as sane as you or me. Well, as sane as me, anyway.'

She laughed again. 'Don't worry, we'll be contesting it if that's their game. I could update you over lunch? It's been ages since we last went to the pub together.'

'Ah, those were the days, before liquid lunches were

deemed unprofessional; but that's all in the past.'

'I can't tempt you, then.'

'Oh, I wouldn't say that, Sally.'

She giggled. 'Must dash; I'll call you later.'

As he replaced the receiver, it rang immediately with a queued call from an unfamiliar number. He answered it formally. 'DCI Priestley.'

'Marcus.'

'Hello?'

'Marcus, it's me.'

'Penny! How wonderful to hear your voice again.'

'God, I'm missing you.'

'Do you mean you haven't been picking up bronzed Aussie hunks lying around on Bondi Beach?'

'I'd first have to find a Straight one! The blokes here reckon all the beach bums have strange *proclivities*. I'll tell you all about it when I get back.'

'I'm really looking forward to meeting up with you again and having a good long chat.'

'It isn't your conversation I'm wanting.'

'This call may be monitored for training and quality control purposes.'

'Oh! I'll phone you again when I get the chance.'

He replaced the receiver. Though he was confident AC had not been recording his calls, he knew it was a good excuse for discouraging her from attempting to resurrect their relationship with intimate conversations.

Later, he took another call from Sally Mansfield. 'Marcus, the defence are offering a plea of Guilty with Diminished Responsibility.'

'And are you accepting it?'

'Not while ever we're pushing the conspiracy angle. You do know we don't have anywhere near enough to establish a clear link with the Khan or Batter killings? The most we can do is sow some seeds of doubt.'

'All right, Sally; let me know how it goes.'

'We could meet up this evening, if you wish?'

'I'd really like that, but I'm already fully booked.'

'Another time, then. See you, Marcus.'

'Yes, another time. See you, Sally.'

He decided to review the cases again in the hope of identifying a previously overlooked connection.

Blackstone had attempted an armed abduction with O'Leary. They had served in the Paras together.

Blackstone's wife had been killed by Khan. After the Crown Court had let him off, he was shot dead by a motorcycle pillion passenger using the same gun later found in O'Leary's possession during the attempted abduction. Working assumption: O'Leary killed Khan. Motive: he was acting in support of Blackstone.

The motorbike rider and passenger wore matching maroon helmets, the same colour as berets used in the Paras. Tenuous working assumption: the rider was also a mate of Blackstone or O'Leary from their army days.

Hypothesis: powerful bonds built in the army can carry forward into civilian life and be strong enough to warrant murdering someone on behalf of a mate.

Barring a huge coincidence of there being a second blackmailer, the assumption is that the abduction was attempted on Aden Liversedge's behalf; consequently, the idea of supporting a mate has been extended beyond the confines of the army.

Question: what other type of relationship might have induced an ex-Para to offer help to an outsider?

Lucy Liversedge and Padraic O'Leary had some form of cancer; how might that have connected them?

Priestley saw a glimmer of hope and called Witty into his office. 'I've another line of inquiry for you to pursue. Liversedge's mother and Padraic O'Leary both had cancer; check if the two of them are linked in any way. They're both dead, so we shouldn't get the usual doctor-patient confidentiality problems, but if anyone tries to block you, just get a warrant.'

'It sounds like a long-shot, boss.'

'Maybe it is, but we need to search for any possible connection. Did they attend the same hospital? Were they being treated by the same doctor? Were their appointments on the same day? Would they have been in the same waiting-room? Did they use the same pharmacy, either the hospital's or a different one? Did Aden Liversedge ever accompany his mother to her appointments? Did Barry Blackstone ever accompany Padraic O'Leary? Is the connection we're looking for between Liversedge and Blackstone, or between him and O'Leary?'

'What level of resources should I allocate to this?'

'As many officers as you need; the case has already gone to court, so we need a quick result.'

'I'll get on it straight away.' He hurried out.

Priestley returned to his contemplation of possible connections.

Yelland walked past Priestley's open door and found him staring out of the window. 'Have you nothing to do, DCI Priestley? I can always find you something.'

Priestley shook himself out of his meditation. 'I was thinking.'

Yelland pretended to be dismissive. 'I didn't get to be where I am today by thinking.'

Priestley grinned. 'Ah, you're more of a doer.'

'I hope you don't mean *dour*!' He adopted a severe expression for a moment. 'I suppose someone in the force has to break the mould and do some thinking, so it might as well be you. Have you something to share?'

'I've refocused our investigations to look for any cancer-related connection between Lucy Liversedge and Padraic O'Leary, and then to see if Blackstone and Aden Liversedge can be linked in.'

'It may not be a direct connection; I'm thinking O'Leary killed Khan for Blackstone, and someone more remote killed Sylvia Batter for Aden Liversedge.'

'I thought you weren't in the habit of thinking, sir?'

'I forget myself, once in a while.'

'Well, I've been thinking there might be some sort of beggar-my-neighbour organisation in play, whereby someone takes on a task for someone else and in return yet another person takes on a task for them. Liversedge may already have completed his task; but if not, he would still have one to do. He's a computer guy, so he's more likely to be asked to do something techie than physical. If it isn't too late, I believe we should put him under the closest possible electronic surveillance and keep a lookout for him doing anything unusual.'

'I'm glad we're thinking along the same lines. All Great Minds Think Alike.'

'But Fools Seldom Differ.'

'Let's go with my interpretation.'

'I'll put surveillance in place immediately, and hope we find something before the Blackstone case is over.'

'We can but try. Keep me informed.'

The working day was almost over when Priestley heard Witty's rat-tatta-tat-tat. He looked up from his desk and saw the self-satisfied smile. 'You look like the cat that had the cream.'

He licked his lips. 'We've found a clear connection.' As the bearer of good tidings, he walked in confidently and sat at the desk without being invited.

'Let me have it.'

'Lucy Liversedge and Padraic O'Leary went to the same hospital. Though they didn't have any doctors in common, they did both attend the same support group, according to the nurses. It isn't just for cancer, by the way, but for any terminal medical condition. They're sure Aden Liversedge has been there with his mother, and that O'Leary was a regular. I've asked for complete hospital appointment and support group attendance records, but I'm meeting some resistance. Anyway, I'm confident we'll prove the connection in the end.'

'That's great! I'm going to feed it to the CPS and see what they can make of it. They may be able to convince a jury there's a whole web of connections behind the attempted abduction.'

'I'm not sure the CPS will buy it, boss; I always find they want nothing but solid facts to take to court. You'll have to charm them.'

Priestley sighed heavily. 'You may well be right; I'll give it my best shot.'

Once Witty had left, Priestley closed his office door before phoning Mansfield on his mobile. 'Hello, Sally. I've some information for you, and I suppose you could say I'm wanting a favour. It's complicated. Perhaps it would be best if we met up. Have you eaten, yet?'

'No, but I thought you were busy this evening?'

He sensed she was smiling. 'I'll cancel with them. How would you like to try a new Chinese place?'

'I love Chinese. Pick me up at home, seven o'clock.'

'I don't have your address.'

'I'll text it. We're almost neighbours, you know.'

'No, I didn't know.'

'Seven, then.' The call terminated. His phone buzzed to indicate receipt of a message. He read the address, and then sent a text to Helen to let her know he would be dining out.

Later, at home, he explained to Helen that the meal had been arranged to facilitate a working meeting.

He arrived at Sally Mansfield's semi-detached house a calculated eight minutes late. As soon as he had rung the bell, he saw a boy in his early teens rush to the door and scrutinise him.

Confident that this was the long-expected caller, the boy tried to say 'Hello.' A cracked word emerged from his larynx at the second attempt.

Marcus recognised the sound of a voice that was still breaking. 'I'm here to collect Mrs Mansfield. Do I have the right address?' The boy nodded. 'I'm a bit late; I'll wait in the car.'

The boy opened the door wide. 'Mum says you're to come in.'

Marcus followed him into the living room. The boy turned and left without another word. Marcus remained standing. Looking out through the window, he thought the yellow ribbon encircling the tree by the kerb would prove an ineffective amulet against its replacement by the road maintenance planners. With Sheffield boasting more trees per person than any other city in Europe, he knew residents certainly took their protection to heart.

The door opened and Sally breezed in, her perfume contriving to reach his nostrils before she was within anticipated sniffing distance. He slowly looked her up and down, impressed with the way she had squeezed her broadening body into a slim, gold dress, though her bust appeared to be in danger of breaking free. 'Hello, Sally. You *are* looking nice. I mean, you always look nice, but I don't normally see you dressed up. Are you going somewhere special after we've had a bite to eat?'

She giggled. 'Come off it, Marcus; you know I'm all dressed up for you. How often does a divorced woman with four children get treated to a meal out.'

'I'm paying, then.'

'You mentioned something about a favour. Well, favours cost money… mostly.' She winked.

'I didn't know you had four children.'

'What sort of a favour is it?'

'They're all still at home, no doubt.'

'Is it a court case favour or a favour favour?'

He capitulated. 'Court case.'

'Well, there's nothing wrong with mixing business with pleasure. Shall we get off?'

He imagined just enough ambiguity in her huskily delivered suggestive question to allow him to take it at face value without appearing to be declining an offer. 'Yes. It isn't far, but parking may be a problem.'

As he opened the car door for her, he glanced up and saw four young faces at a window. Layered above the boy and a girl were two more girls craning their necks.

It was early enough in the evening for the restaurant to be deserted. The deep red flock material that lined the walls gave Marcus a sudden impression of intimate shadows. They chose the table in the furthest recess for added privacy in the event of an influx of customers.

She glanced at the menu and proposed they share a set meal for two, which he readily accepted. When he explained he would abstain from alcohol in support of sober driving, she withdrew her request for wine.

They kept the conversation light, talking about past cases and former colleagues. When the various dishes were almost empty, she leaned across to him. 'Will you be asking your favour before or after the sweet?'

He frowned. 'Is that a significant milestone?'

She smiled. 'Don't look so worried, Marcus; I know this is only work, but let me enjoy it all the same.'

He smiled back. 'It is nice, having a chat like this, but I'd better explain. In a way, it isn't even a favour, seeing as we share the same objectives as far as the prosecution of villains is concerned. I have a weak argument you might normally refuse to take to court, but I'd really appreciate it if you'd give it a go.'

As he detailed the tenuous hospital connection, she closed her eyes to display her green eye-shadow. He waited in silence. She opened them again, looking first at the dangling red lampshades, before gazing at him. 'Well, Marcus, you know I'd be happy to push anything for you, but I'm not the one who stands up in court. I'll certainly do my best to persuade our man to give it a shot, but you have to be prepared to be disappointed.'

'It's enough to know you'll try.'

'Oh, I shall, I promise. Now, what about a sweet?'

'You choose first.'

She giggled. 'I hoped you'd say that. I'd like the Ice Cream Mountain.'

'But that's for two.'

'Yes, I know. We can share it.'

Though the restaurant had been filling up steadily, he thought their location was sufficiently private for the intimacy of a shared sweet to remain unnoticed.

When the volcano of coloured ice cream balls with streaks of red, green and brown lava arrived in its broad glass bowl, she moved to the chair next to him so that they could share it more easily. He waited for her to make the first impression on the mountain peak. Once she had begun, he started to sculpt an arête by carving away the nearer side. She playfully interfered with his plan by scything across his precipice, before scooping up the shattered remains of his artwork to create a high mound on her long spoon. As she enticingly floated it toward his lips, he recognised he was faced with a choice of embarrassing options. Declining her offer might lead to some awkwardness. Accepting just a little of it could result in her proceeding to feed him in the style much favoured by Italian couples. He therefore chose to take it all in one go.

One of his neighbours from home, a Mrs Catherine Chatterton, tapped him on the shoulder.

'Hello, Marcus... and friend.'

He gulped down the ice cream, feeling it burn cold all the way to his stomach. 'Hello, Catherine. Let me introduce my colleague, Mrs, erm, Mansfield.'

Mrs Mansfield stretched out a hand. 'Sally.'

She touched it briefly. 'Catherine. Pleased to meet you.' She gave Marcus a prolonged wink, having seen past his attempt to suggest unfamiliarity by hesitating over her surname. 'Don't let me interrupt you.'

He smiled and nodded as he made a mental note to inform Helen that his meeting had been a tête-à-tête, before Catherine could leak the information to her.

Certain they were now being watched, he raced his way down his ice cream slope, while she merely picked at hers. When he suggested coffee, she declined, having recognised that the occasion had lost its intimacy.

He drove her home and walked her to the door. She invited him in. He replied, 'I need to explain to Helen, before the bush telegraph sends the wrong message.'

She grabbed him tightly and planted a luscious kiss on his lips. 'Don't forget to wipe off my lipstick.'

When he reached home, Helen welcomed him at the door with a frosty smile. 'And exactly who is this Mrs Sally Mansfield you've been wining and dining?'

He tried for hurt innocence. 'It was only dining; we didn't have any alcohol.' Seeing she was maintaining the hard smile that required him to explain further, he added, 'She works for the CPS. I was trying to persuade her to push a shaky argument in court.'

She gasped in mock-shock. 'Using your charm to get your way, you tart!' He laughed. 'Catherine came over to ask if I'd seen her cat; not her best excuse ever. If only she knew how great things are between us, she wouldn't waste her time with malicious gossip.'

He kissed her tenderly on the lips. 'Well, just in case you *are* in any doubt, let me take you upstairs.'

She giggled. 'And that's not your best excuse, either; but it's good enough.'

CHAPTER 31

In the late afternoon, Priestley was gazing out of his office window and up the hill to the rocky promontory known as Carl Wark. Shadows were framing weathered boulders with black and grey outlines within an overall wedge shape. He wondered if some ancient tectonic upheaval had caused the outcrop to erupt at that relative angle to the flat earth. Only, it had long been known that the earth was not flat. Except, for the breadth of landscape in front of him, the curvature of the earth would be minimal. And what were the geological forces that had sculpted the millstone grit? The weathering must surely have been driven by the shape of the valley.

His reverie was broken by the ringing of his phone. He shook off his daydreaming and read the Caller ID, before answering it formally. Sally Mansfield chirped back, 'Marcus, I thought I should let you know how things have been going in court. Let me treat you to dinner tonight.'

Though he enjoyed the easy working relationship they had, he knew she was far too keen on him. 'Much as I'd like that, two successive evenings is not a good idea. That neighbour of mine was dripping poison into Helen's ear before I reached home.'

'Did you have a row?'

'No; she accepted it was a working meeting.'

'If it was, it was the nicest one I've ever had.'

'But the pleasure may be lost by repetition.'

'Not for me it wouldn't, Marcus.'

'Even so, I'm taking Helen out this evening, so she doesn't feel neglected.'

'Another time, then?'

'Yes; sure. Anyway, how it's going it court?'

'It's going very well. Judge Jefferies has been giving us much more leeway than I would have expected. Miss Garnet Hilton-Ikeda has been objecting to everything, but good old Jeffers has been knocking her back every time. Putting conspiracy on the charge sheet may have seemed wildly optimistic, but he's allowing us to run with it. The possession charge is obviously rock solid, but the concomitant conspiracy to murder looks weak, as his gun wasn't loaded. The lesser firearms charges may be put aside; even at the best of times it's difficult to succeed with inchoate offences when there's a more substantive case to be considered.'

'Well, at least the judge is permitting you to put your arguments forward. I won't be too disappointed if we lose with the conspiracy charge; I appreciate our case amounts to little more than speculation.'

'I doubt there are many juries that would find him guilty of conspiracy, but serendipitous verdicts do come along every once in a while, though they're usually the other way, where an obviously guilty party gets off. Perhaps we should treat *any* conviction as a successful outcome. I suppose it's too early to consider how you and I might celebrate getting a good result?'

'Let's put that question aside for now. Should I be preparing a victim statement? I could tell the court how traumatised I still feel by the whole experience.'

'You may be a good actor, but you're not that good! What about Ms Baker? Will she want to give it a shot?'

'I can't say I know her particularly well, but it's my

impression she'd never admit to being traumatised by anything.'

'We'll leave it at that, then. I'll keep you informed.'

Priestley's end-of-day check on his team's progress established they had uncovered no significant leads. The electronic surveillance on Liversedge was proving particularly disappointing, as his visible online activity was so low as to suggest he was using communication applications which kept him under the radar. There was speculation that certain data streams indicated he was using the dark web with an unbreakable protocol.

Before leaving the station, Marcus telephoned Helen to ask her if she would like to eat out. Reluctant ever to use a babysitter, she responded, 'Just because you were off with some woman yesterday, it doesn't mean you have to take me out this evening to make up for it. Anyway, there's no one to look after the children.'

Though convinced she would not alter her decision, he emphasised his sincerity by trying again. 'Are you quite certain Amanda couldn't help out?'

She considered various options. 'I'll try and arrange something. Are you coming back right now?'

'Yes, I'm just about to set off. I'll see you soon.' He picked up his jacket and headed home.

Helen opened the door as he parked on the driveway. When he stepped inside, she informed him of the plan. 'Amanda has the children. We'll need to collect them by eight thirty, so we'll go out at seven.'

He asked, 'Have you booked somewhere?'

She replied without hesitation, 'We're going to that Chinese restaurant you went to yesterday. There's no need to book, this early.'

Instinctively feeling he should discourage her from

choosing the same restaurant, he responded, 'Are you certain you want to go there? I think of it more as the kind of place for having a quick bite with colleagues. We should go somewhere special.'

She stared him down. 'That's where I want to go.' To terminate the discussion, she headed upstairs.

When he found her dressing up, he initially accepted that dining out on a weekday was a rare enough event to justify it. But after a moment he began to wonder if she was being a little competitive, and thought about asking her what their neighbour had said regarding his guest of the previous evening.

Though he liked seeing her in high heels, he knew it meant she expected him to drive them to the restaurant, despite it being within fairly easy walking distance. He would therefore have to have another alcohol-free meal, which meant she would also abstain, in accordance with their agreed attitude toward never drinking alone.

In the car, he reset the tachometer so as to establish the precise distance; by calculating their walking time, he could in future argue they might go on foot and thereby avoid the alcohol restriction.

The waiter recognised Marcus and invited him to the quiet recess he had occupied previously. Helen chose a set meal for two. Aware of the time, they ate it all at a fair pace. The waiter asked if they would like a dessert. Helen replied, 'We'll share an Ice Cream Mountain.'

When it arrived, he waited for her to start scooping. As she transferred from the seat opposite him to an adjacent one, he correctly guessed what she would do next. The mound she collected on her long spoon was small enough for him to accept it in one mouthful. He returned the compliment. She asked, 'Is this how the two of you ate yesterday?'

He shook his head. 'I didn't feed her at all, and she only did it with me just the once for a laugh.'

'That's not what I heard.'

'Believe me, it's what happened.'

She checked for signs of mendacity. Satisfied, she responded, 'I do believe you, love; I knew Catherine was exaggerating when she said you'd fed each other.'

'It's more than an exaggeration; it's a downright lie.'

'Shall I keep feeding you, then?'

'I'd rather not, if you don't mind. There's an art to choosing just the right combination of different flavours for each spoonful. To do it perfectly you'd have to be able to read my mind.'

'And you think I can't?'

He laughed as he took her hand. 'Can you read my mind now?'

She smiled. 'Of course I can, but we need to collect the children soon, so you'll have to wait 'til tonight.'

Being tight for time, Helen decided they should do without coffee. They left right on schedule.

At home, Edwin argued he should be allowed to stay up late, his normal bedtime having already passed and therefore standard weekday rules no longer applying.

Helen, feeling guilty at having doubted her faithful husband, was intending to assuage her conscience by inviting him for an early night. She packed Edwin off to bed, refusing to debate his argument that he should be allowed to stay up an extra hour because he had been out of the house during the evening.

Soon after, she checked and found Edwin had fallen fast asleep. Though confident it was unnecessary, she looked in on Alice to confirm she was also slumbering.

Downstairs, she sat next to Marcus on the settee and whispered in his ear, 'It's your bedtime, now.'

Always delighted when she took the initiative, he responded in a childlike voice, 'Can't I stay up a bit later, Mummy? Another hour?' To avoid her taking him literally, he quickly stood up and stretched out his arms to receive her hands.

She allowed him to pull her to her feet. 'You can stay up as much as you like.'

He gasped in pretend-shock. 'Naughty.'

She pushed him to the door. 'I will be.'

In the morning, when she slipped out of bed after stopping her phone's alarm call, he reflected on how the neighbour's lies had done nothing to dent their magic. As he recalled certain inconvenient truths, he hoped, if they ever came to light, that they would also fail to damage the loving relationship he had with his wife. Once again he reminded himself he must in future remain faithful to her... except of course where he was powerless to resist. And anyway, she would always understand and forgive him.

At work, after a frustratingly uneventful morning, he received a phone call from Sally Mansfield. 'Marcus, you won't believe this.'

'Don't tell me then.'

'What? Why not?'

'Because I have it on high authority I won't believe what you say.'

'Have you already heard about it? Is that why you're messing with me?'

He laughed briefly. 'I haven't heard anything. Is it something important?'

'It is indeed. See me at the Wigan Penn for lunch.'

'Is it confidential? If it is, shouldn't we be meeting somewhere private?'

'It isn't confidential; it's what's happened in open court. Can you come right now?'

'If you're serious.'

'I am serious. Prepare to be surprised.' She ended the call.

As he hurried out to his car, he wondered if it was even theoretically possible to prepare to be surprised.

The pub was busy with the usual court day clientele; separation of prosecution and defence teams did not extend to lunchtimes. He peered inside the Dickensian establishment with its brown low ceiling and oak beams adorned with horse brasses. The rich smell of hot steak and kidney pie reached his nostrils slightly ahead of the rather more subdued perfume Sally was wearing today. She gripped him firmly by the shoulders so he could not escape the kisses she delivered to each cheek.

'Marcus, sweetie, so glad you could come.'

Recognising the gushing delivery was for the benefit of her colleagues, he supported her credibility with two kisses of his own. 'Sally, angel, how could I resist?'

She motioned to her four companions at a cosy table set for six. 'Come and join us.' As he approached them, she made introductions on a first name basis. 'Marcus, meet Irvine, Philippa, Genevieve and Martin.'

He guessed the order was in descending rank. After a handshake from Irvine and waves from the others, he accepted Sally's direction and took the seat next to the one she had reserved with her jacket.

Playing the part of attentive hostess, she ensured his order for steak and kidney pie was added to their table's list, before pressing him to accept a half of bitter.

He took a mouthful and savoured it before gulping it down. 'Well, Sal,' he had chosen to use a contraction to bolster the implied strength of their relationship, 'you sounded excited about something on the phone; how much longer are you going to keep me in suspense?'

She swept her hand toward the head of the table. 'I'll let Irvine explain it to you.'

Seeing Irvine flex his shoulders as though preparing to make a speech, he flashed him a brief smile. 'I can't imagine what's happened, Irvine.'

The barrister scanned the party to ensure everyone was paying close attention, even though most of them had witnessed the events themselves. 'I was attempting to make a strong case out of weak evidence. Possessing a firearm with intent to cause fear of violence was solid enough, though the lack of ammunition had dimmed that particular beacon.

Priestley asked, 'Did the presence of ammunition in the other firearm give you any scope on that front? He did hold both the guns at one time.'

Irvine shook his head. 'Unwitting possession could have been argued against that line of attack. Though there have been miscarriages of justice aplenty where someone has given a lift in their vehicle to a person in possession of drugs, the fact that the defendant himself had a weapon which was devoid of ammunition would have provided an adequate parry to any thrust on my part. Rather than lose that particular skirmish, I was keeping my powder dry for the larger battle.'

'You mean the conspiracy argument?'

'Indeed I do; if successful, it would undermine their entire defence. My suggestion of a broad conspiracy that connected Blackstone with the death of Mrs Batter was greeted with a howl of derision by Miss Ikea.' He checked that his cutting corruption of her name had been recognised as wit rather than an error. Pleased with the grins of appreciation, he directed himself again to Priestley. 'His honour the judge took exception to her attitude. She requested a short recess to gather herself... or so I thought at the time. But then, she asked the permission of the court to introduce a new witness. I had no objection, believing I had them on the run with my rhetoric.' He reached for his sherry and took a sip, his eyes looking over the rim to check that he was still the centre of attention. 'This new witness turned out to be an elderly woman, who explained, under oath, how she had taken the life of Mrs Batter. Under cross-examination, she stated that she had acted entirely alone and had no knowledge whatsoever of the defendant, nor of his deceased partner-in-crime, nor of Mr Liversedge whom we were seeking to ensnare.'

Priestley deliberately opened his eyes wide to reflect his genuine surprise. 'That *is* a turn-up for the book.'

'Indeed it is, Marcus. So, though we were obviously misguided in attempting to bring Mr L into the bear-pit, yet we solved an entirely different case.'

Priestley nodded. 'So it would seem, Irvine; always assuming she wasn't lying.'

'Why would she lie if by so doing she was admitting to being involved in an unlawful killing?'

'Did she admit premeditation?'

'No, but that was largely due to Miss Ikeda limiting her new client's evidence to avoid self-incrimination.'

'So it's possible we were on the right track and this was a diversionary tactic to head you off.'

'It did cause me to change my line of argument.'

'Miss Ikeda may have switched the points, so to speak, just as you had raised a full head of steam.'

'Oh, I do like that analogy, Marcus! Perhaps I shall reinvent it as mine own.'

The others provided a chorus of restrained laughter.

Sally tugged Marcus's arm. 'I'll be your contact for this new case; it's intriguing, isn't it.'

'Yes, indeed. Ah, here comes our food, if I'm not mistaken. Well, I'm sure you've all earned your corn today.'

The round of self-congratulation was interrupted only by the laying of claims to three steak and kidney pies and three assorted salads, one vegan.

While they ate, the conversation divided into pairs. Sally raised her voice a notch as she ostensibly declared to Marcus, 'This is the second time we've dined out together in three days; it's starting to become a habit.'

He smiled but said nothing.

With little time to spare before the afternoon session in court, all the food was consumed with a fair degree of haste. Irvine rose majestically, the others taking their cue to follow in concert. It reminded Marcus of a time he used to sing in a choir, when the conductor, by an almost imperceptible movement of one baton-wielding hand, would bring everyone smartly to their feet.

Sally walked outside with Marcus and grasped his arm to bring him to a halt. Leaning in close to his ear, she breathed, 'It was exciting in court. Do you have any ideas for what *we* could do for some more excitement?'

He turned his head so he could face her directly. 'What *can* you mean, Mrs Mansfield.'

She giggled. 'Anything you want me to mean.'

He shook his head. 'Don't be naughty, Sally.'

'We'll be seeing a lot of each other while you're investigating this latest development.'

'But there's seeing, and there's seeing.'

'Well, we'll see what it is that is to be seen.'

'Give me a call when you're out of court.'

She stretched up and pecked him on the cheek, before whispering in his ear, 'I'm looking forward to working *really* closely with you.'

He held her by the shoulders, out of kissing range. 'You do know I'm happily married?'

She gave him a slow wink. 'I like a challenge.'

He lowered his gaze and shook his head despairingly in rebuke. 'Then you'll need to prepare yourself for failure; I've always regarded my wedding vows as sacrosanct.' Having been trained to understand that the best way of being convincing was to believe one's own lies, he realised what an expert he had become. And yet, as he began to chastise himself for his duplicity, he still felt there was an underlying essential truth to his claim of fidelity... in between the lapses. 'I'll be late for a meeting. See you seen.'

As he hurried away, she watched him until he turned a corner and disappeared from view.

CHAPTER 32

Sally Mansfield called on Marcus Priestley in person at the station once the trial had reached a conclusion. She asked, 'How did you feel about the outcome?'

He shrugged. 'It was what I was expecting: guilty of the provable offences and not guilty of the rest.'

'We'll see where the judge's sympathies lie when it comes to sentencing. Possession of a firearm alone should warrant at least five years.'

'Judge Jefferies isn't exactly known for his empathy, but he could decide there are enough mitigating factors to depart from the minimum sentencing guidelines. If he accepts Blackstone genuinely thought that DI Baker and myself were blackmailers, that both the guns were empty, and that they were only bringing them as a show of force for meeting two potentially violent criminals, then he could be going down for a lot less.'

'But he will definitely be going down; the judge has warned him to expect a substantial custodial sentence. He's also called for a further psychiatric evaluation to help him understand the extent of the PTSD. He may find grounds for leniency.'

Priestley eased back into his chair. 'Well, Sally, it's all over now. So, what brings you here?'

'The Black Widow.'

'You mean Elsie Crompton?'

'The very same. As I see it, we have two possible ways ahead. One is to take her statement at face value. The other is to disbelieve her and to resurrect your old conspiracy theory. We failed with Blackstone, so what makes you think we might succeed with her?'

'I'm not at all confident we would succeed, but I just can't bring myself to request her prosecution based on a pack of lies about a pack of cards.'

'What makes you so sure she's lying?'

'Try and imagine it. Mrs Batter invites her to visit. Once there, she asks her to help her to die. Then she's to stuff the Queen of Clubs into her mouth, as a belated apology to Lucy Liversedge for cheating her out of that trophy; the same one that she's kept all these years and could have simply given to her if she'd really wanted to, though of course that wouldn't have made her the official winner. A genuine apology would have been made in person; not with a deathbed gesture.'

'You can convince me easily enough, but that sort of reasoning wouldn't stand up in court. So, we need to consider what to do about her. If she really did assist Sylvia Batter in committing suicide, then we should be charging her under Section two of the Suicide Act. We have clear evidence of how Mrs Batter died, and Mrs Crompton's statement is entirely consistent with that. Why do you believe she wasn't a victim of assisted suicide?'

'Is the CPS still allowed to use terms like "victim" and "commit suicide"? I heard someone on the BBC saying such words aren't Politically Correct.'

'God save me from Political Correctness, Marcus. I'm quoting the DPP, who states they're the appropriate descriptions in the context of criminal law. So, answer my question. After all, the facts do appear to fit.'

'The facts support the admitted method of killing, but the idea that Mrs Batter wanted to die just doesn't stack up. Speaking to people who knew her, we found no evidence she wished to end it all.'

'And yet Crompton didn't need to come forward and admit her guilt; after all, you were never going to track her down, were you.'

'Probably not, which convinces me she only came forward to undermine the case against Blackstone and thereby discredit the conspiracy theory.'

'Well, we can't just leave things up in the air. What are you intending to do about her?'

'I've already started an investigation into her past, and her state of health. You're aware of the connection between Lucy Liversedge and Padraic O'Leary; if Elsie Crompton is also suffering from a terminal illness, I'd say we may be onto a winner.'

'All right, but we can't leave it too long. If someone appears to have committed a criminal offence, we can't let it look like we're doing nothing.'

'That applies to the police as much as the CPS.'

'We'd better stay in close touch on this one, Marcus. What do you think? Regular meetings? Lunch? Dinner? Breakfast?'

'Lead us not into temptation.'

'But deliver us from evil! That's a bit harsh.'

He laughed. 'Your words, not mine.'

She fixed an encouraging smile firmly into position. 'It was nice having dinner with you. Maybe we could do it again sometime?'

'Sure, Sally… sometime.'

'Sometime soon?'

'If I didn't know you better, Mrs Mansfield, I'd say you're flirting with me.'

She refreshed her smile. 'What a brilliant piece of

detective work! I am, because of your reputation.'

'But I'm happily married, as you well know.'

'Precisely, and that's why I know you're not the type to become emotionally involved with another woman. Not even one as pretty as me.' She began fluttering her eyelashes rapidly.

'It feels like your assessment somehow undermines my masculinity. Should I be disappointed?'

She grinned. 'It doesn't and you shouldn't. It's nice playing at having a man like you in my life, but I can't be doing with it really; not with four kids to bring up.'

'I remember Helen quoting research that focused on two, five, ten and fifteen as being the difficult ages.'

She stood and picked up her copious black leather case. 'Whereas non-academics find the awkward years are everything from two to twenty-two… and then they get worse.'

'Does that mean you don't see yourself ever having a life of your own, beyond being a mother?'

'Maybe I will have, someday; but for now I have to make do with chocolates and wine. I'd certainly like to have a man who could take me to the occasional "do". Would you like to volunteer?'

'If it was a professional engagement with colleagues, I'm sure Helen wouldn't mind my escorting you.'

'Great! And then we could have hot sex afterwards, with no commitment on either side.'

'Now I know you're joking.' His voice had sounded certain, though he suspected she had meant it.

She walked to the door, turned, and performed a shy smile. 'I'll be in touch if something comes up.'

Left alone to reflect, he decided he would need to tread carefully. If he overtly rejected her advances, it could easily damage their close working relationship.

He pondered on Elsie Crompton's written statement, provided via her solicitor. It claimed she had met Sylvia Batter by chance when shopping in the market, and had been invited to visit her at home. Once there, Batter had asked her to open a new pack of cards and extract the Queen of Clubs. She had then admitted to having been a lifelong card cheat, and was now wishing to pay the ultimate price for her "wicked" behaviour.

According to Crompton, Mrs Batter had obtained from an unspecified source a device that would deliver a fatal dose of cyanide. In order to ensure Crompton herself would be unaffected by the chemical, Batter had explained how she should cover her mouth and nose when delivering it. Crompton had flatly refused to have anything to do with the plan, but Batter had begged her to help, claiming it was the biggest favour anyone could ever do for a fellow human being. When Crompton had continued to refuse to assist her, she had threatened to use the lethal device on her instead. Fearing for her life, Crompton had finally agreed to perform the act, and to place the playing card in Batter's mouth after her death, as demanded.

The statement ended, "Knowing the police would find it difficult to believe this strange sequence of events, I decided I should say nothing to anyone. It was only when I overheard someone in a bus queue saying there was a court case where someone else was accused of being behind it, that I realised it was my duty to come forward and state what had actually happened."

He watched the recording of the police interview. In view of her previously unblemished record, and with no witnesses to argue against her, he thought there was a good chance a jury would accept that this was a case of a gentle old lady who had been coerced.

Knowing he would have to disprove the widow's assertions with solid evidence, he scanned for any small weakness that might provide him with a point of attack. Disappointingly, he found only two possibilities.

The first related to the conversation that Crompton purportedly overheard in a bus queue. The police could broadcast an appeal via the press for anyone with any knowledge of said conversation to make contact. If no one responded, then the prosecution could argue it had never taken place. But then the defence could claim the people may not have heard the appeal, or had simply declined to come forward.

The second concerned the lack of forensics to link Crompton to the crime scene. If she had arrived with no knowledge of what was about to unfold, the expectation is that there would be evidence of her visit. It could therefore be argued that the dearth of forensic evidence was very telling. If she had taken great care not to leave any traces from the moment she had first entered the property, then that would indicate premeditation. But it would be difficult to refute the counterargument that the SOCOs had been negligent in failing to find the traces.

He decided the only way to break the case was to establish a reason why Elsie Crompton would have lied. If the conspiracy theory were to gain credence, he would need to show she had had a reason for killing Batter on behalf of someone else. Due to their similar ages, the connection might be assumed to be with Lucy Liversedge, but there was no evidence to suggest Lucy had been involved in arranging the murder. He would therefore need to find a connection to her son, Aden.

Recognising one key question was whether Elsie and Aden had ever been to the same support group session, he called Witty and Plummer to a meeting in his office to explain his thinking. When he asked Witty if he had obtained the group's attendance records, he could read the answer clearly expressed on his furrowed brow.

'Sorry, boss; they say they don't keep any records because it's meant to be very informal. They note down the first name of anyone who turns up, but only so they can introduce them to other people, and afterwards they shred the list to keep things confidential. That means the only known attendees are volunteers who work at the hospital and go along to answer questions.'

Plummer commented in a subdued tone, 'It may be too late now to find out if our suspects ever met there; but if it's that informal, perhaps I should go along to the next meeting without letting on who I am, and see what I can find out. I could ask about getting support for my uncle, who has a terminal blood disorder from the time he used to clear blue asbestos out of boilers.'

Witty had turned to Lin and seen the concern etched on her face. 'I'm ever so sorry to hear about that, Lin; I didn't even know you had an uncle. Are the two of you very close?'

She grinned. 'I don't know; I'm still inventing him.'

Priestley smiled at her. 'You're such an actress! But I don't want you to go there and risk being abducted.'

She appeared unfazed. 'Actually, I think it might be best if they did try to abduct me; otherwise, this case is going nowhere.'

He shook his head. 'It's too risky. Let's go away and have a think about what we might do to move things forward. We'll discuss it in the morning.'

That evening, Helen took a phone call in the kitchen. She checked the caller display and answered, 'Lin?'

Plummer responded anxiously, 'Hello Helen. Is my boss there?'

Interpreting the key word and its emphatic delivery, she asked, 'What's the problem?'

Plummer sighed. 'I've put my foot in it.'

Helen made herself sound upbeat. 'Don't worry, Lin; I'm sure he'll sort it out for you.' She pressed the mute button and quickly took the handset to Marcus in the living room. 'Lin says she's put her foot in it.'

He pressed the mute button on the satellite recorder remote control before unmuting the telephone handset. With Helen standing listening nearby, he responded, 'Hello, Lin. What can we do for you?'

Lin heard the "we" and interpreted it correctly. 'I've let something slip to a senior officer. Can you come and talk to me about it and tell me what to do?'

He turned to Helen, keeping the telephone unmuted and holding it close to his mouth. 'She's said something to a senior officer and wants to talk to me about it. She's asking if I can go over.'

Helen looked sympathetic. 'Yes, you get off.'

He responded soothingly to Lin, 'I'll come straight over. And don't worry; I'm sure it can't be that bad.'

He drove the short distance to Lin's flat, wondering whether it was a genuine request for advice or just an excuse to see him. After parking in her newly vacated bay in the underground garage, he walked up the stairs to her floor. As he approached her door, she opened it and put her head out, holding onto the jamb to lean further into the corridor. To avoid being overheard by neighbours, he entered in silence. Once the door was closed behind them, he asked, 'Am I here for a proper meeting?'

She nodded. 'I'd better tell you what's happened, before we go to bed.'

Having not been together for more than a week, he was unsurprised by her casual invitation. 'It isn't like you to say the wrong thing; tell me all about it.'

She sat on the settee as he settled into an armchair. 'You know the "Women Higher in Policing" initiative that Deputy Chief Constable Dorothea Forbes-Smythe organises?'

'Yes, her response to the Masons.'

'No it isn't! It's just regular networking meetings where women get together to see what they can do to help each other achieve their full potential.'

'...thereby improving the promotion prospects of said women, to the disadvantage of men. If you reverse the genders, it certainly sounds like the Masons.'

'I'm not debating this with you. The thing is, she asked about the Crompton case, and I mentioned how I'd volunteered to infiltrate the next support group meeting, but you'd said it was too high-risk. She's going to be hauling you over the coals tomorrow for being sexist.'

'How was I being sexist?'

'What if the idea had been for *you* to infiltrate the meeting? Would you have said, "No, I'm not going because it's too dangerous?" Well?'

'That's unfair, Lin; it's different for me.'

'Are you saying it's different for men and women?'

'No, I'm not. I'm saying it's different for someone with my army background and physical strength...'

'But men always tend to be physically stronger. Doesn't that mean they have an unfair advantage?'

'It isn't an *unfair* advantage; it's a fact of life. Are we having an argument? It certainly sounds like it.'

'I'm sorry, but she says she's going to insist I be allowed to prove myself. I realise I've put you in an awkward position. What can I do to make it up to you?'

'Let's see if I can put you in an awkward position.'

She laughed dirtily. 'Come on then.'

Afterwards, driving home, he prepared his response to Helen's inevitable interrogation. It would have had to have been a lengthy discussion with Lin, to fit the time he had been away. Past training informed him never to offer any information beyond that which is specifically requested, and even then to limit it to the bare minimum that would be sufficient to pacify the interrogator. But with Helen asking the questions, she would recognise any sign of his reluctance to be forthcoming. He would therefore have to adopt a different tack: appearing to wish to tell her everything, while making it so boring that she would lose interest and ask him to stop.

Marcus found Helen in the living room. 'Lin hasn't really put her foot in it after all. She's just concerned that someone, whose name I won't mention, will have interpreted something she said, that I really shouldn't mention, in a way that might make them think she had mentioned something she shouldn't have.'

Her eyes glazed over. 'In that case, you shouldn't mention it to me; otherwise, I might interpret it that you shouldn't have mentioned that Lin had mentioned mentioning something to you that she'd previously mentioned to someone you won't mention. Obviously!'

CHAPTER 33

The following morning, Priestley arrived at the station and went to his office. There was no message waiting for him from DCC Dorothea Forbes-Smythe, neither on paper nor via his inbox. He looked out of the window and wondered how soon she would be in touch. The telephone rang shortly after. He checked the caller display, which identified the DCC. Mentally, he stood to attention. 'DCI Priestley.'

She responded, 'Marcus, there's something we need to discuss; an issue for us to work through together.'

He replied smartly, '*Vis Unita Fortior*.'

She hesitated, before asking in a puzzled tone, 'What are you on about?'

'Strength United is Greater. We're stronger when we work together. It's what was put on our coat of arms.'

'Are you trying to distract me, as per usual?'

'It's only the *quid pro quo*?'

'Are you saying I distract *you*?'

'Don't you think you're always distracting the men who work here?'

She gave a horsey laugh. 'I know you're trying to charm me, but it won't work today. Come and see me right away.'

He rushed up the stairs so he could justify arriving panting at her door. 'I came as fast as I could, ma'am; I wouldn't like to keep you waiting.'

She whinnied. 'Why can you never be serious with me? You know what this is about, don't you, Marcus.'

'Should I guess, Dotty?'

She reflected for a moment on whether she had been entirely wise to have previously insisted he address her in that familiar way in one-to-ones. Believing it might prove awkward if she now demanded formality, she allowed his use of her nickname to stand unchallenged. 'If I know my girl as well as I think I do, she'll already have had a quiet little word with you to put you in the picture.'

'Your girl being…?'

'Detective Constable Linda Plummer. Or were you thinking she was your girl?'

'Not especially.'

'Then why are you holding onto her?'

'I wasn't aware I was holding onto her. Any physical contact would be entirely inappropriate.'

She laughed again. 'You know I'm not talking about physical contact. I'm asking why you've been holding onto her when she should have been moved onward and upward. Are you a sexist under all that charm?'

'It certainly isn't sexism that makes me wish to keep her on my squad; it's because she's such an asset. Not only is she a great team player, but she's also a natural at adapting to new situations… like a chameleon.'

'There are more specialist rôles for people who can merge into the background, and I have a responsibility for ensuring women are not being held back. Make the most of her while she's still here, because I'm going to look into other options for her to allow her to spread her wings. She tells me she had an idea about going to a hospital support group that may be implicated in a murder conspiracy, but you turned it down. I say, give her the opportunity to prove herself.'

'But she doesn't need to prove herself; she's already done that, plenty of times.'

'Then give her the go-ahead.'

'But they may be the same people who have already attempted to abduct DI Baker and myself. It's just too dangerous for her.'

'Does she think it's too dangerous?'

'I'm not convinced she understands all the risks.'

'I recognise you're trying to protect her, but we both know she's highly capable, so you should allow her to try and infiltrate the group. In view of your concerns, I'm making it your responsibility to ensure her safety.'

'If she attends on her own, how can I keep her safe?'

'Is it feasible for you to go with her?'

'No, it isn't. If they are involved in the conspiracy, they'll know who I am; and if they aren't involved, then it's a waste of time.'

'In that case, you need to come up with a suitable plan to keep her out of danger, and then run it by me.'

He accepted the gestured instruction to leave. At the door, he turned and began again. 'DC Plummer and I have developed a working relationship that enables us to slot confidently into any situation. She's played the part of my wife, my girlfriend, my secretary…'

She interrupted him abruptly. 'Then you'll just have to develop the right rapport with a new DC. And in the meantime, let me remind you I previously offered to go undercover with you, but you still haven't taken me up on that, despite my years of experience.'

'But Lin's…' He was about to refer to the women's age difference, only he knew Dotty remained reluctant to admit she was well past her prime, so he seamlessly contrived a change of direction. '…not expressed any wish to move onward and upward, to use your words.'

'Then perhaps you don't know her as well as you think you do. She seems quite ambitious to me when we chat together at the WHIP meetings.'

'The what?'

'WHIP, Women Higher in Policing. It's my flagship crusade to get women into higher positions.'

He wondered if a flagship could also be a crusader. Thoughts about women in various positions suddenly entered his mind, which he did his best to suppress.

'And don't you look at me that way; I haven't said anything improper.'

He quickly wiped the smirk off his face. 'Did *you* make up that acronym?'

'Yes. How did you guess?'

'Male intuition.'

She stared at him. 'Are you making fun of me?'

He smiled. 'As if I would, Dotty.'

She shook her head. 'I should never have allowed you to become so familiar with me.'

'Just because I'm familiar with you, ma'am, that doesn't mean I don't still respect you in the morning.'

She read his grin. 'Get out of my sight, you wicked man. And come back with a foolproof plan.'

He found Lin and ordered her back to his office for a meeting. She put on an anxious look as she closed the door behind her. He motioned her to sit. She waited silently for him to speak first. He looked closely at her, putting on a heavy frown for effect. She concluded he was only playing at being annoyed, so decided to hold out the longer. He stared at her right eye, which seemed to become larger and an even brighter blue. She stared back at his green eyes and imagined him as a cat. He finally admitted defeat. 'I've just been to a meeting with your mentor. She instructed me to back your plan for infiltrating the hospital support group.'

Lin hid her self-satisfaction. 'But do you still think I shouldn't? I can tell her I've changed my mind, if you really don't want me to go.'

'That might act against your ambitions, which I am informed are lofty. But you told me you were happy to remain in your current position. So, where do you see yourself being in ten years' time?'

'Still in your bed, if that's what's worrying you.'

'Lin, I'm serious about this. Where do you see your career going? Where do you want it to go?'

'I don't want us to drift apart. If that means staying where I am, then that's what I want to do.'

'If we could still see each other often enough, what would you really like to do, workwise?'

'I had a taste of another world when we were on that case in Stockholm. My ideal would be to work with you in lots of exotic places, but I know you can't leave here, with your family ties.'

'That isn't entirely answering my question.'

'I'd rather stay close to you than pursue a career without you.'

'But that sounds like a recipe for a lifetime of regret. The DCC sees in you a highly capable young woman who could go to the very top in policing, and she's fully prepared to support you. I've also recognised just how good you are, but I've done nothing to move you up. You should have been assessed straight after passing your exam, and been assigned to work that's at a level which would justify your promotion. You really should be annoyed with me for holding you back.'

Trying to read his face, she found mixed messages. 'Don't ever say that. You've helped me to develop in so many different ways, I'll always be grateful to you.'

'That sounds like a line from a farewell speech.'

'Well, it isn't. I won't ever move from here on my own unless you promise me we'll always stay as close as we are now.'

'If I could unpick that, I'm sure I'd find a certain lack of logic.' He held his hands in front of him as though holding a singing score, seeing them as a proxy for his whole being. After reading his palms, he raised his gaze to her eyes. 'Just look at the two of us. Take a good hard look at me and then look at yourself, and you'll understand what I'm talking about. I feel I'm taking advantage of you.'

'If I remember rightly, Marcus, it was me who took advantage of you.'

He remembered with perfect clarity the first time they had made love. She had insisted and he had tried to refuse, but only with words. 'Or did I subconsciously allow a situation to arise where the outcome would be inevitable?'

She raised her voice and jabbed a finger toward him. 'You can stop all this soul-searching right now. Do you promise we'll always be together, even if we're apart? And don't quibble about logic; you know exactly what I mean.'

He glimpsed a flash of anger in her deep blue eyes. 'I do, so long as it's what *you* want.'

'Then I'll only consider career opportunities that keep us within seeing distance. And you know what I mean by that, as well.' She stood to leave.

'Hang on a minute, Lin. This meeting was supposed

to be about putting together a plan for you to infiltrate that support group. I'm tasked with guaranteeing your safety, so we need to think things through carefully.'

She sat down again. 'What do you suggest?'

'Gadgets and eyes.'

'Boys' toys and watchers? What exactly?'

'Multiple GPS trackers so I know where you are at all times, even if some of them become non-operational for one reason or another. Plus, hidden communication devices to ensure I can always hear what's happening. Then there's micro-cameras pointing in all directions so I can observe any threats to you and rush to the rescue if necessary. We'll need GPS-enabled transmitters to monitor your vital signs so I can read the telemetry and know if you're under some sort of stress. Lightweight body armour; no, make that full ballistic body armour. Three protection squads working independently, every member committed to taking a bullet for you if the need arises. Six snipers strategically placed to pick off any overt threats. You'll be transported by bullet-proof limo capable of withstanding high-velocity rounds, with a second vehicle so no one knows which one you're in.'

Her growing smile finally gave way to unrestrained laughter. 'Isn't that just a teensy-weensy bit OTT? I'd have thought Kevlar underwear and you hiding in the shadows would be enough to keep me safe.'

'We'll negotiate an intermediate solution.'

An unheralded feeling of sadness washed over her. 'I can't ever imagine enjoying working with anyone else the way I do with you.'

He tried to smile away her gloom. 'If you do leave for the brighter lights of distant shores, I'm sure you'll discover other enjoyable relationships.'

She felt entirely unconvinced. 'I'm sure I won't.'

He took out a pad of A4 paper and picked up a pen. 'We need to focus on the job in hand. I'll write things down as we agree them. Kevlar knickers: tick. Kevlar bra: tick. Man hiding in shadows: tick.'

She smiled wistfully. 'There'll never be anyone else quite like you.'

The next hospital support group meeting was due to take place two days hence in the morning. Information on the web page indicated that days and times rotated to minimise the accidental exclusion of potential attendees who had regular commitments. They discussed whether any conspirators may be untypically absent from the meeting, being on a Sunday. The subsequent one would be eight days later, a Monday afternoon; they agreed she may need to attend that one also.

Once the plan had been fleshed out, he insisted she should be the one to deliver it to the DCC. Recognising it may prove a significant opportunity for her to show off her presentational skills, he patiently allowed her to give an uninterrupted trial run. Following suggestions for improvement, she tried again. This time, he threw in a variety of questions, which she did her best to handle.

They agreed the third rehearsal was an unqualified success. When she thanked him formally for his help as though he were merely her boss and not her lover, he felt the separation was already beginning.

The DCC accepted the plan in its entirety, despite remarking how heavy it was on human resources.

Priestley invited Plummer to sit in his office while he made the arrangements by telephone. A disc-shaped GPS tracking device, about the size of a pound coin, would be provided just prior to use; as it ran off a tiny battery, its guaranteed lifespan was just ten days. An ostensibly Victorian ornate silver brooch containing a miniature camera would be delivered ahead of time, enabling Lin to choose suitably matching clothing. No equipment would be provided for picking up sounds or monitoring vital signs, as neither function was classed as essential. The wearing of body armour was deemed nonviable, as even a lightweight vest would be easily detectable. An armed unit would be on standby.

At the end of the day, alone in his office, Priestley reviewed the plan one more time. Having checked their preparedness to handle every conceivable threat, he turned to the inconceivable. He was fully aware such dangers could not be specifically identified in advance, but the types of threat could be classified and the ways they would react would be agreed. Beyond these, he knew the backstop must be their mental preparedness to respond to the unexpected.

Allowing his thoughts to wander in the hope of some new potential risks filtering through to his conscious mind, he found he was focusing on Lin herself rather than the possible dangers of her infiltrating the network he believed existed.

The telephone rang and broke his train of thought. 'DCI Prie…' The caller interrupted him.

'Marcus, it's me. I'm coming back next Friday.'

'Penny! That's great news.' Calculating the time in Australia, he added, 'You must be up late.'

She rattled out her correction. 'No, I'm up early. I heard about the confession.'

'You mean the Batter case?'

'Yes. Why didn't you let me know?'

'We're still assessing its believability. Anyway, the

risk factors that led to you leaving are still in play. But how did you hear about it?'

'Something like that spreads like bush fire.'

'Bush fires don't cross oceans! What arrangements have been made to keep you safe, back in England?'

'I've told them I won't need any protection. I'll be staying at my flat.'

'Penny, you're a mad bugger!'

She laughed delightedly. 'You must come and see me next weekend. I want to be put back on the case, and if I don't have a thorough briefing I won't be able to hit the ground running on the Monday.'

He assumed her justification was for the benefit of any listeners. 'I might not be available.'

Her tone became insistent. 'It will take a long time to review the case fully. You have to come on Saturday and stay 'til Monday.'

'That may not be possible.'

'Then make it possible. We have things to discuss.'

'But…'

'What's the expression? I know where the bodies are buried.'

He assumed she was making an oblique reference to their joint enterprise with the blackmail ruse. 'I could manage Saturday and maybe some of Sunday.'

She waited, hoping for a better offer. Eventually, she responded, 'Come early Saturday morning and stay 'til Sunday evening. You can use the same sleeping bag as last time.'

He knew this was to mislead any listeners. 'All right; it would certainly make sense to get you up to speed over the weekend.'

'Good. And by the way, I've a surprise for you.'

'What is it?'

'If I told you, it wouldn't be a surprise.'

'Well, I look forward to receiving it, whatever it is.'

'And I look forward to a comprehensive debriefing.'

Feeling she had pushed the use of hidden meanings too far, he abruptly terminated their conversation. 'I'll make sure I have all my notes up-to-date. See you at ten, if that's not too early.'

'Ten o'clock will be fine, sir.'

As he replaced the receiver, he wondered what she might be bringing him from Australia. His first guess was a boomerang or some other aboriginal artefact. He recalled hearing a white woman raging at the term "aboriginal", claiming it was deeply racist, even though it merely reflected how the indigenous population were regarded as having been resident in Australia since the beginning of time. He would have to ask Penny what the Antipodeans thought of Political Correctness.

Certain he would be staying overnight, he knew it would be impossible to decline the signalled invitation to have sex with her; they had become conspirators as well as bedfellows, so now she had a significant hold over him. Nevertheless, he felt determined to end their affair as soon as possible, with that Sunday perhaps marking the final day.

CHAPTER 34

Marcus drove home and sat in his parked car. Lin had asked him to stay with her the next night, arguing it would ensure she was fully prepared for the Sunday morning visit to the hospital. Penny was determined he should stay with her the following Saturday night. The idea of a weekend spent with his wife and children seemed increasingly appealing.

When he gave his excuses to Helen for the planned absences, she responded neutrally, 'Weekends away are a classic sign of someone having an affair.'

He sighed. 'For me, it would have to be two affairs: different people, different places.'

She smiled. 'Don't look so glum. But I do think you need to examine your work-life balance.'

He nodded, slowly. 'If anyone asks me to work the weekend after that, I'm going to refuse.'

She reflected for a moment. 'Yes, unless there's a crisis. Organisationally, no one should be allowed to become indispensable, so there must be other people who could fill in for you, mustn't there?'

'Absolutely,' he replied emphatically, while thinking the exact opposite as far as the next two Saturday nights were concerned.

'If you have to be up that early on Sunday morning, you'll be going to bed very early on Saturday night, I assume. Maybe you should start to adjust your body-clock a day in advance by getting up early tomorrow.'

'I wouldn't wish to disturb your sleep.'

'You wouldn't have to. You could set your alarm for four a.m. on minimum volume and then get up quietly without waking me.'

He knew it was too late to backtrack on his story about an operation taking place at the crack of dawn. 'I'll set it for five o'clock; that should be early enough to start adjusting.'

At five a.m. he was in a deep sleep when he heard the tiniest sound from the clock radio. A quick fumble for the top left button rendered it silent. He slipped out of bed and dressed without waking her.

As he crept downstairs he remembered to avoid the creaky step. When he went into the kitchen to lay the table for breakfast he found everything already in place. Wondering if this was her normal practice, or whether it was for his benefit, he realised how long it had been since he had last taken on that duty. Rather than eating alone, he found a woollen overcoat and a Harris Tweed jacket, and lay down on a sofa in the living room. The overcoat made for a warm blanket. He covered his head with the jacket to block out the light, and drifted off to sleep.

Helen slowly peeled back the jacket from his head. 'Breakfast is served.'

He blinked himself awake. 'I must have nodded off.'

She picked up the coats and took them away.

After breakfast and shopping, the family discussed what they would like to do later. It was agreed they would go to the park after lunch, to play cricket rather than football because it was more inclusive.

In the afternoon, as the children raced up and down, scoring freely from his underarm bowling, he wished such days would never end.

In the evening, Marcus picked up his bag and kissed Helen goodbye. She looked anxiously at him. 'You won't be doing anything stupid, will you?'

He smiled. 'Of course I won't; you know me.'

She remained troubled. 'I do know you, and that's the problem.'

He kissed her again, more affectionately. 'Don't you worry, love; I'll keep myself safe and sound.'

In Lin's flat, as he slid the sleeping bag out of its cylindrical sack, he commented, 'I'll just make sure I can open it up; it wouldn't do to claim I'd slept in it if there were any fasteners still holding the whole thing together.' He unzipped it entirely and spread it wide. Discovering a facemask tucked away at the bottom, he commented wryly, 'I'll be sure to thank Helen for her thoughtfulness.'

Lin took it from him and dropped it into the sack. 'Do you think she suspects you were lying to her?'

He shook his head. 'No, I don't; but it's in her nature to test any hypothesis.'

On the Sunday morning, Marcus woke to the sound of church bells. As he listened, his trained ear detected limitations to their sonority, which indicated to him it was only a recording.

Recalling how Lin had previously insisted he give her a final briefing in the morning, to ensure she was fully prepared for the encounter with the hospital's support group, he thought through every detail of the plan. The way she was snuggling closer informed him she was now awake. He turned and propped himself up on one elbow. 'Do you think you're as prepared as possible for this morning's big event?'

She took his hand and began leading it down her

body. 'I'm not at all prepared; that's your job.'

He stayed his hand. 'I meant for the op.'

She forced it lower. 'Sorry; my mistake. But now we've started…'

Afterwards, she took a shower. He waited until she was out and dressed before having one himself.

She made breakfast of cereal, fruit, toast and black coffee. He finished his muesli and held out his bowl. 'Please, miss: I want some more.'

She retrieved the bag from the cupboard. 'Here you go, Oliver.' As he poured it, she ruffled his hair, which he found so endearing.

On schedule, they put the plan into action, with the exception of the Victorian brooch camera. First, she claimed it was hideous and refused to wear it. Then, she argued it would stand out too much against her clothes and might be spotted for what it was. Finally, she stated it was unnecessary, as no one paid attention anymore to people using their mobile phones, so she could use hers to take photographs if required.

He drove her to the place where she was to wait in his car until a suitable bus was coming. When one hove into view, she hopped out and walked the short distance to the stop. A minute or so later, she caught it without a backward glance.

He overtook the bus and drove to the hospital. On most mornings the car park would be full, but Sunday was the exception. After paying for two hours' parking, he walked to the canteen, which was fairly close to the meeting room. As he sat with his untouched beaker of coffee, his mobile phone vibrated to inform him of an incoming call. He answered simply, 'Hello?'

A woman's voice stated, 'She's just arrived.'

He responded, 'It's nice to hear from you. I'm at the hospital right now, but I'll see you this afternoon.'

The voice replied, 'I'll call you when she leaves.'

Forty minutes later, the voice contacted him again. 'She's now leaving the building.'

He asked, 'She's out of theatre? I'll pop along and see how she's doing.' As he looked around, he doubted any of the patients, their relations, or the weary-looking members of staff, had any suspicions about him.

After driving to the agreed location around a corner from the main road, he sat watching the buses pass by. Lin appeared and walked to the car. When she climbed in, he asked, 'All right?'

She replied, 'All right.'

He started the car and headed for her flat. She began explaining what had happened. 'When I walked in, a sixtyish bloke came up and spoke to me. He introduced himself as Roger, and asked if I was there as an unwell person or on behalf of someone else.'

'An unwell person? That hardly seems to fit the idea of terminal illness.'

'They have their own language. He seemed genuine enough. I explained that my uncle has mesothelioma and I'm seeing him wasting away, and was wondering if there was anything I could do for him. He asked me for my given name and I said "Lynette". He checked the spelling and wrote it on a list, which gave me time to scan down the other first names. There weren't any surnames. Roger was first, then Graham, Jean, Philippa, Mick, Stevie, Mike and Carol. After we'd had a little chat, he introduced me to Jean. I told her something about Neville, my uncle, and she talked about her husband, Robbie, who has lung cancer. Other people came and chatted; they were all very sympathetic. The common theme was that I'm not alone, and that there are various coping strategies to help me deal with the anguish I'm suffering from my imminent loss.'

'Did they all seem genuine?'

'One hundred per cent. Then, a Dr Irena, again no surname, came in and gave a short talk. She said she was the group's new medical contact, as Dr Theresa had now returned to her home country due to a family crisis. She said her predecessor was not expected to return to Sheffield in the foreseeable future.'

'Did you ask about the previous doctor?'

'Of course I did, when I had the chance. Dr Irena described Dr Theresa as very tall, five nine, maybe five ten, and therefore not the small lady of that name I said I'd previously met in radiography one time. She may well be the one who drugged you and Penny; not many women are that tall.'

'Apart from in detective novels, where they're all six footers. We'll kick off some discreet enquiries, but not until tomorrow, so no one connects them with you.'

'Right, that's our work done then. So, home, James, and don't spare the horses.'

'There's no point in rushing. We'll have to think of something else to do now, so we aren't bored.'

'Don't worry about that; I'll make sure you're fully occupied for the rest of the day.'

In the late evening, when he returned home looking thoroughly worn out, Helen considerately invited him to sit quietly in front of the television, without asking for a blow-by-blow account of his activities.

CHAPTER 35

On the Monday morning, Priestley and Plummer gave a joint debriefing. Witty was assigned to establishing the identity and background of Dr Theresa.

When Witty called into the hospital's HR section and enquired about all non-British doctors, he was met with a predictable refusal to disclose information.

After a harridan had lectured him on the rights and wrongs of immigration control and how it was not the responsibility of hospitals to implement government policy, he dropped a subtle hint that the query stemmed from a whistle-blower having expressed grave concern regarding the hospital's procedures for checking the *bona fides* of overseas doctors. While maintaining the principle that information on current employees would remain entirely confidential, she insisted on disproving the allegation by disclosing documentary evidence relating to the credentials of former members of staff.

The fourth example was a Dr Tereza. Witty hoped this was the woman he was looking for. The virago had refused him permission to note down any details of the past employees, so he committed to memory as much information about the doctor as he could.

In order to avoid highlighting his real interest, he pressed her for more examples. After the seventh had been examined and their background proven to have been thoroughly checked out, she refused to continue to the eighth without his obtaining a warrant. He thanked her for her co-operation and assured her he had found no evidence to support the allegation.

In his car, he wrote down as many of the details as he could recall. Dr Tereza Nadya Hoxha had graduated from the Tirana University of Medicine in Albania five years earlier. They had confirmed her credentials and supplied a photograph to ensure no one was attempting to impersonate her; they had even stated her height, 176 centimetres.

Tirana hospital had provided documentary evidence of the four years she had spent with them, including her progression through a specialism, chemical pathology.

Sheffield had recruited her ten months back. She had left abruptly for a reason he was not permitted to know. The HR termagant had insisted her work had been entirely satisfactory, as she had with all the others.

Witty returned to the station and relayed his findings to Priestley and Plummer. Priestley asked, 'Would you be able to recreate her appearance on E-FIT?'

He stared down at the desk for a moment, trying to recall her image. 'No, sorry, I only had a quick glance; but she did have short dark hair, like the woman you saw at Penny's. I've just remembered something else: the word Roma was on one of the forms.'

Priestley asked, 'As in Italian for Rome? Or maybe she's a gypsy.'

Plummer quipped, 'You can't say that, can you?'

Priestley stared at her. 'I just did. Besides, it isn't a racial slur if used in the correct context.'

Unsure if Plummer had overstepped the mark, Witty aimed to defuse any awkwardness by returning quickly to the subject under discussion. 'We could always get a copy of that old photo of her from Albania.'

Priestley replied, 'Only if we don't mind showing

our hand. We should leave her on the back burner for now, as we don't have any forensic evidence that could link her to the attempted abduction... unlike the man; we have a sample of his blood.'

Lin commented, 'You described him as completely bald, with a scalp showing no signs of weathering.'

Priestley anticipated her likely interpretation. 'And you're thinking chemotherapy.'

'It has to be a possibility. I'll be keeping a lookout at future meetings for anyone who's a match.' Receiving a questioning glance from Witty, she added, 'Always assuming I'm to keep going.'

Priestley responded, 'We only have approval for the next one. If nothing comes of it, I expect the support unit will be stood down.'

Witty asked, 'So what do we do now?'

Priestley replied, 'Keep things ticking over. If there are any developments, let me know straight away.'

Plummer and Witty headed off. Priestley called out, 'Lin, just stay a minute will you please; I'd like a word with you. And close the door.'

Witty assumed it related to her disrespect. He gave her a surreptitious glance, pulled a face and covertly pointed to Priestley, to suggest she may be in trouble.

Marcus waved her back to her chair. 'Take a seat, Lin; we need to have a chat.' Unsure of the reason, she sat in silence. 'Your other mentor has been very busy on your behalf. She has asked me to relay certain things to you, so that I'm not being bypassed.' He watched her raise her eyebrows questioningly, and thought it made her deep blue irises look even lovelier. 'Your mission, should you choose to accept it, Lin, is to go to London for some tests and job interviews.'

'To join the Met?'

'That's one of the three contenders. The other two are MI5 and SIS.'

'Jesus!'

'She thinks you're cut out for undercover work.'

'Yes, but... there's a hell of a difference between going to a hospital support group meeting, and doing... whatever it is they do.'

'She's been contemplating the matter of your future ever since the Swedish case... or so she says.'

'I did put in quite a performance in Stockholm.'

'Indeed you did. So, are you game?'

'Only if I still have your promise.'

'You know you do.'

'It probably won't come to anything, anyway.'

'I'm confident they'll all want you, but I do wonder if you're entirely cut out for some of the work they do. For a start, you're much too attractive.' He realised he had just broken their rule against speaking intimately in a work environment. Seeing her cheeks redden and start to glow, he added, 'Also, you blush far too easily.'

In fun, she covered her face with her hands and peered over them. 'But why should my looks matter?'

He waited until she had returned her hands to her lap and was looking intently at him. 'Just imagine being a surveillance officer in MI5 and trailing someone. You would need to merge into the background, not stand out like a girl who turns heads.'

'I could dress down, or something.'

'I'm sure I'm not the only one who would always notice you, even in a crowd. Then there's SIS. If you were working abroad as an intelligence officer, I'm certain you'd be good at gaining the trust of potential agents; and with your people skills, you'd be great at managing them. But you may find yourself put in a position where every choice is in some sense against your moral code. Having to choose between the lesser of two evils is still choosing something evil, and that could well erode your inner sense of, well, innocence. Perhaps the old Special Branch would be your best choice; I mean Counter Terrorism Command, SO15. Maybe there would be an opening for you somewhere in the network that's not too far from Sheffield.'

She opened her eyes wider. 'You don't want me to go away, do you. You're in love with me, aren't you.'

He shook his head. 'You mustn't talk like that; you know it's against our rules.'

She looked out of the window with unseeing eyes, trying to marshal her thoughts. Finally, she turned back and smiled. 'We both know the situation, even if we can't talk about it. I'm going to go for the interviews, and if I'm recruited we'll see if it makes or breaks us.'

Unsure how to respond, he handed over a buff file. 'The details are in here. Let me know how you do.'

She accepted the manila folder without opening it. 'I love you, Marcus. There; I've said it.'

He watched as she walked away, absorbed by the familiar gentle sway of her hips.

She stopped and turned at the door, certain he would be watching her keenly, and gave him a sweet smile and a gentle wave. As she headed away, arguing with herself that her parting gestures had little significance, she wondered why she felt like crying.

A few minutes later, Priestley realised he was still staring at the piece of fluff on the floor he had first noticed when Lin had walked out. Sensing someone was watching him, he looked up. Seeing Witty standing at the open doorway, he set a neutral face and gestured him to enter. 'Come in, Neil. What is it?'

Witty closed the door and took a single pace inside. 'Permission to speak freely, sir?'

Thinking this must be one his jokes, he responded lightly, 'Of course.'

Witty took a few moments to draw on his courage. 'I know she's sometimes a bit cheeky with you, but you shouldn't have given her a bollocking.'

Taken aback, he responded, 'Who are you talking about, Neil?'

'Lin, of course.'

'But I haven't given her a bollocking.'

'Then why is she in tears?'

Realising Witty may jump to the correct conclusion about the two of them, he instantly decided to disclose the information he knew he would discover anyway in due course. 'I think she's probably just anxious about some important interviews I told her she'll be having.'

'What are they for?'

'I could tell you, but then I'd have to kill you.'

'Oh, I see… I think. Well, that's a relief, in a way. I'm sorry for doubting you, boss.'

'That's all right, but could you ask her to come back in, once she's settled herself. Oh, and don't mention this to anyone else. I mean *really* don't mention it. If she gets a job with the security services, only those with a need to know should know about it. And if she doesn't get offered a job, she wouldn't want it known she'd been turned down.'

'Understood; and sorry again, sir.'

'Apology accepted.'

Lin returned to his office, succeeding in appearing entirely composed. 'You asked to see me, boss?'

He stood up. 'Close the door.' They faced each other across his desk. 'Even if you were to pass the selection process with any of them, you should still think long and hard about whether you're really cut out for the type of work they'd want you for. I'm very concerned you may not be; I've never known you cry, before.'

She smiled coyly. 'Yes you have, Marcus.'

He held his frown. 'In the office, I mean. If you let your emotions give you away, in some situations that could be a matter of life and death.'

'Don't worry about me; I won't let it happen again.'

'But I do worry about you.' He took a deep breath, as though about to dive into a river in spate. 'One final thing: I love you, too. And saying that is something else that won't happen again.'

She smiled brightly. 'It's a good thing there's a desk between us.' Searching his face for further meaning, she found it had become frozen as though shocked by his own words. She continued breezily, 'I'll be catching the early train tomorrow. Make sure you come and stay with me tonight, so you can wave me off at the station in the morning.'

He finally managed a hesitant response. 'I'll have to ask Helen's permission for staying out again.'

She raised her eyebrows. 'Seriously?'

'Sort of.' As she left, he wondered if the torment he was feeling was due to the imminent end of their affair.

In the evening, Marcus dined at home with Helen. He held back any mention of being out overnight until after they had cleared the table. 'I hope you don't mind, love, but I promised Lin I'd stay at her place tonight.'

He firmly believed honesty on this occasion was the best policy.

For once, her response was not a questioning silence. 'Really? Has she room to put you up?'

'I'll take a sleeping bag and use the sofa.'

Her response was intended to suggest she had only a limited interest in the arrangement, but as she delivered it she knew a concerned edge had crept into her voice. 'I hope this isn't going to become a regular thing.'

He felt her scanning his mind. 'Quite the opposite; it may be just about the last time I ever see her.'

With competing emotions, she asked quickly, 'Why? What's happened?'

'She's going for some interviews in London. If she's offered a job, she'll be off.'

'So, your little protégé may be flying the nest.'

'Indeed. And Lo! The bird is on the wing.'

She saw how troubled he was behind his mask, so tried to lighten his mood. 'Anatomically, I think you'll find the wing is on the bird.'

He gave a thin smile. 'I hate to admit it, but I hope she isn't offered anything.'

'Because you'd miss her?'

'I certainly would miss her; there's no doubt about that. We've worked together really well in some very difficult situations, and I've come to rely on her. But that's not the reason.'

'Well, what is the reason?'

'It's absolutely confidential, this: she's applying to join the security services. I don't know exactly what she'd be doing, but whatever it is, I'm concerned it'll change her from the lovely lass she is, into something mean and bitter and twisted. I fear she would suffer from the invasive corrupting influence of evil.'

'You certainly sound philosophical this evening. So, why are you staying at her flat?'

'I think she simply wants me there to talk to, in case she has last minute concerns. She'll be taking the early train, so at least I can drop her off at the station.'

'If any of your other officers asked you, would you do the same for them?'

'Yes, of course, though I don't think any of them ever would.'

'The fact that she's anxious suggests she isn't ideal material for clandestine work. Perhaps *I* should stay with her instead, so we could talk things through, woman-to-woman.'

Calling her bluff, he responded enthusiastically, 'Would you? I'm sure she would really appreciate that.'

She maintained the mask that claimed her offer had been genuine. 'Yes, if you honestly think that would be best for her; though she knows you much better, of course.'

'That's true. Maybe it would be best if I went.'

'I think I agree. I'd probably end up giving her a detailed analysis of the psychology behind such work, when all she really wants is a bit of moral support.'

'I'm sure that *is* all she wants. When she comes back on Friday I'll go and ask her how she thinks she did with the first stages; her written tests and interviews are only the beginning.'

'In the past, I've consulted on various aptitude-based selection tests. They're not about passing or failing, but establishing whether someone's character makes them suitable for a particular type of work.'

'For instance?'

'Pathological liars may make ideal foreign office spokesmen; homicidal maniacs might enjoy wet work; nymphomaniacs could delight in baiting honey traps.' She grinned. 'I'm only joking. Well, maybe. Anyway, there must be lots of jobs a sweet, innocent, moral young woman would be suitable for, in the world of subterfuge.'

'When you put it like that, you make me think I should try to talk her out of going.'

'Just make sure you don't end up talking to her all night; if she wants to give it her best shot, she'll need plenty of sleep so she has a clear mind for the tests and interviews.'

He nodded. 'I'll make sure we're not up all night.' He shuddered inwardly as he realised what he had said.

Later, Marcus checked on the children and found them sleeping soundly. He went to his bedroom and collected together a few things in a small bag.

Downstairs, he kissed Helen and prepared to depart. She grabbed his arm and held him back. 'Don't go, yet; you're forgetting your sleeping bag. I'll go and fetch it for you.'

Having already received a kiss, she handed him the rolled bag in its cylindrical sack and held the door open for him to leave.

As he drove away, he asked himself why he was so unhappy about the possibility of Lin leaving. Though he found plenty of plausible reasons, he knew there were none that he could trust to be entirely honest.

CHAPTER 36

On the Friday evening, Helen intercepted the telephone call that Marcus had been anticipating all week. 'Hello, Lin. Marcus told me what you've been doing, but don't worry: I know how to keep a secret. Come over and tell us all about it. Have you eaten, yet? We were just about to get started, so we'll wait for you.'

Knowing Helen in gushing mode would not take no for an answer, she cast around for a suitable response. 'I'm too tired to be hungry, but I'll come straight over and have a tiny bite with you both.'

Helen relayed the message. 'Your secret agent is on her way. She'll have a bite to eat with us, so you'll just have to wait.'

A quarter of an hour later, Lin drew her car onto the driveway and parked hard against the wall. Marcus had positioned himself in the living room where he could watch for her arrival. He stood up at once, commenting, 'She's here. I'll let her in.'

Helen responded, 'I'll sort out the food.'

Lin had noticed the movement, so waited at the door without ringing the bell. When Marcus opened it, she scrutinised his face, hoping he would somehow express his feelings for her, if not with words then with signs.

He spoke quietly to her. 'Hello, Lin. I was intending to come over and see you, but…'

She smiled. 'I know.'

He welcomed her again, only this time more loudly. 'Come on in. We're dying to know what you've been up to, but don't tell us anything you shouldn't.'

She entered in silence and handed him her jacket.

He hung it up and directed her to the dining room. A finger to his lips warned her that Helen may be able to overhear. 'We're having lasagne. Are you hungry?'

She responded *mezzo forte*, 'I did tell Helen I'm not, but maybe I am after all.'

Helen arrived with two salad bowls and a jug of lime cordial. 'You start without me; I'll be through, soon.'

They picked at their salads as they waited, keeping the conversation inconsequential. Marcus fished the last of the lettuce from his bowl as Helen entered with three warmed plates. She returned with the lasagne, which she shared in three unequal portions, giving herself the least. Before starting on her food, she addressed Lin. 'I hope you haven't started telling Marcus what you've been up to; I want to know all about it as well.'

Marcus turned to Helen with a smile. 'Give her the chance to eat, first. Will we be having a pud?'

As the lasagne for two was being made to stretch for three, Helen had anticipated the need for an extra course. 'I've just put an apple strudel in the oven. It's cooking from frozen, so it'll be half an hour. We can have a cheeseboard while we're waiting; that would be the French way, if we were having wine.'

Lin had hoped to share her secrets only with Marcus. She glanced theatrically to one side and then the other. 'I'm not allowed to say much about my visits to River House and Thames House, but I can tell you a few things about my trip to GCHQ. The Bletchley Museum on the ground floor was quite interesting, though I was more impressed with the Operations Room; it makes ours look quite pathetic. There were masses of screens being monitored twenty-four seven. In the cyber-threat cell there was one screen that displayed a globe with Britain at its centre. All the current cyber-attacks from other parts of the world were shown on it as white, pink and red lines. The electronic brain behind everything is down in the basement. They have some amazing high-performance super-computers. I was allowed to take a look through a viewing-hatch; altogether, the computers cover about five acres.'

Marcus asked, 'What's that in football pitches?'

Helen answered for Lin, 'About three.' She proudly accepted their impressed stares. 'To be more precise, it's between less than two and nearly five, depending on the size of the pitch.'

'How on earth do you know that?'

'I once had to put together a visualisation exercise that related mountain slopes to recognisable flat areas. Anyway, let Lin tell her story.'

Lin responded to her, 'Well, there really isn't very much more I'm allowed to say.'

Helen looked questioningly, saying nothing.

Lin cast around for some non-confidential titbits. 'There's an Intelligence Officer's New Entry Course I'd have to complete successfully, if I wanted to go down that route.'

Marcus commented, 'With your background, I'm sure you'd pass with flying colours.'

She accepted his compliment with a worried smile. Knowing they were hoping for more information, she recalled a gobbet from a glossy brochure. 'By the way, did you know that in twenty fifteen MI5 became the highest-rated Gay-friendly employer in the country?'

Helen responded, 'Does that make them the most

appealing to you?'

Marcus thought about trying to field the question, knowing that Helen had previously been misled into believing Lin was a lesbian. Before he could intervene, Lin answered coolly, 'It doesn't really influence me.'

Helen asked immediately, 'Does that mean you no longer see yourself as a lesbian?'

Lin recalled exactly how Helen had been subject to a degree of misdirection. 'I really must put you straight on that: I've always been entirely celibate.'

Helen, for once, was taken by surprise. 'But...'

Lin chuckled as a prelude to glossing over the reason for the deception. 'I must just tell you about a couple of strange conversations I had. The woman at MI5 seemed really disappointed when I explained I'm not a lesbian, but the man at SIS seemed really, *really* disappointed when I told him I'm celibate and always will be. I said to him, I'm perfectly willing to lay down my life for my country... but not my body.'

Marcus had been laughing far too long by the time Helen stared him down to be quiet. 'That's the right attitude, Lin. Being willing to have sex to obtain secrets can leave people vulnerable, making them a security risk. Now, would we all like some cheese?'

Lin replied, 'Not for me, thanks.'

Marcus added, 'Nor me.'

Helen turned to Lin. 'We don't have any whipped cream for the apple strudel, but we do have custard, if you like. I keep cartons of ready-made for the children.'

Marcus interpleaded, '*Crème anglaise* would be nice if you fancied doing it properly.'

Helen acceded. 'Yes, it's much nicer when it's made fresh.' She retreated to the kitchen.

Having bought them some time, he looked earnestly at Lin. Quietly, he asked, 'How was it, honestly?'

She responded, 'It was all very exciting, but I don't really know why I was invited in the first place. I've done some clandestine work in the past, but not much, and certainly nothing to match their levels of operation, day-in, day-out. It wasn't me who applied to them.'

'I have a theory about that. Dotty is dotty about you, and wants you to pick up her career where she left off. It's almost a way of keeping herself young.'

'So you don't think I'm there on merit?'

'I didn't say that. Actually, I think you could be an exceptional operative in the right context. The problem with working in this country is that most of the terrorist activity is either being imported or derives from past immigration. You obviously don't have the right ethnic background to fit easily into direct contact with the key players, or even to move in their circles. That means you would need to operate as an outsider looking in, at least for some types of work.'

'Yes, that's true enough, but there are plenty of rôles that aren't culturally restrictive; for example, remote surveillance. I was impressed by the methods they use.'

'Well, if you were to become highly skilled in the latest techniques, you might return to the police force at a later date as an expert. As a career path it could have a lot of potential.'

'That certainly sounds better than working abroad for SIS. I mean, I don't have any proper knowledge of languages, so I've very little to offer them as I am.'

'Do you know if any of them will be inviting you to take it to the next stage?'

'Yes, they all will, though I don't know why.'

'It will be because they've looked beyond what you are right now and seen your potential.'

'It would be nice to think that.'

'Well, why shouldn't they?'

'I haven't exactly been recognised in the police force as a shining star; I'm only a constable.'

'But you said you weren't ambitious and wanted to stay where you are for now. You're only twenty-two, so it isn't as though you've been lagging behind.'

'But we both know there are other reasons that have a bearing on what I'd like…' Hearing Helen opening the door, she seamlessly changed tack. '…to do with my weekend off. It will be nice to have a rest; this week has been so intensive.'

Marcus continued as though Helen were not present, keeping his voice as low as before. 'Don't forget you have the support group meeting on Monday afternoon.'

'Should we get together this weekend to make sure we're completely prepared? In case you're too busy on Monday morning?'

'That won't be possible; I'm going to be away all weekend, closing off an old case I was involved in.' He felt ashamed to have referred to Penny as an old case, knowing she still held an intense passion for him.

They thanked Helen as she served the food. Lin took the merest taste and complimented her on the excellent custard. Marcus wholeheartedly supported her opinion.

After coffee, Helen suggested they adjourn to the living room. Lin stifled an almost genuine yawn. 'I'm going to get back now if you don't mind, before I fall asleep.' An authentic yawn materialised. 'Thanks for the meal; it was lovely, as always.'

At the door, Lin allowed Marcus to help her into her

jacket. She asked, 'Will I be seeing you tomorrow?'

He shook his head. 'No, I really will be away.'

'Well, I want an in-depth conversation with you.'

He read her meaning and whispered, 'Soon.'

His eyes followed her closely as she walked over to her car. As she set off, he stayed watching until she was out of sight. When he stepped back and closed the doors, he found Helen was standing behind him. 'Sorry, I didn't know you were there.'

Helen scrutinised his face as she asked, 'Do you think she's going to be leaving, then?'

He shrugged. 'It's a big step for anyone.'

She nodded. 'It is, but you shouldn't underestimate her. I know you like to try and protect her, but you need to accept she's an independent young woman who's perfectly capable of taking care of herself.'

'Even so, I still believe she isn't fully prepared for everything the big bad world could throw at her.'

Helen pondered on this as she walked away.

That night, Helen joined Marcus in bed and left her lamp switched on. 'I've been thinking.'

He turned and looked at her. 'I'd be more surprised if you said you hadn't been.'

She smiled. 'I've been thinking about Lin. It's very unusual for someone such as her to decide to remain celibate. I'm not entirely convinced she hasn't explored lesbianism; there were too many indications. But I think it's fairly obvious she's avoided any male contact so far. My main concern is that, being such an innocent, she may fall prey to the fake charms of an undesirable, such as an enemy agent. Perhaps what she needs, to prepare herself, is a proper love affair. And, of course, she ought to experience the related physical pleasure.'

He stared at her. 'Why are you telling *me* this? Are you expecting *me* to have an affair with her? I'm not just some piece of manhood that can be lent out like a timeshare apartment; I'm your husband.'

'Of course I didn't mean you.'

'Well, that's a relief. On the other hand, if it were to be me, at least it would be someone who likes her and isn't just taking advantage of her.'

'And you could even argue that you'd seduced her for her own benefit, as a way of protecting her from some future lothario who was only out to get what he could from her, such as state secrets.'

'So, if I did, you'd recognise I'd simply been acting in the best interests of our country?'

'Absolutely! I'd congratulate you on being a patriot, as I plunged a carving knife into your cheating heart.'

As he laughed, he searched her face for an indication that she had indeed invited him to have an illicit liaison with Lin, and that only her conventional morality was holding her back from being explicit.

She smiled knowingly. 'I can guess what's going through your mind right now. But if ever you ask, the answer will always be "no".'

He thought she may have just encouraged him to have an affair with Lin, subject only to the proviso that he must not ask for permission. On reflection, he knew his hormones could convince him of almost anything.

CHAPTER 37

The next morning, Marcus set off half an hour ahead of schedule for reaching Penny's flat by ten o'clock, to reinforce the lie that he had to attend a work meeting. He had predicted it would last all through Saturday and probably most of Sunday.

Penny remotely released the new electronic lock on the outer door and waited for him to come up to her flat. She stood barefoot in her doorway, wrapped in a bright red satin dressing gown. When he reached the top of the stairs, she stepped back. As soon as he had entered and closed the door, she glided toward him, breathing a few strained words as though in physical pain. 'God, I've missed you, Marcus.'

He tried to limit her to a simple hug, but she dragged his head down to her height and chased his retreating lips until she caught them. His attempt at a perfunctory kiss was thwarted by her insistent mouth. He conceded momentarily, before pushing her away and holding her firmly at arms' length. As he examined her elfin face, he commented, 'You haven't picked up much of a tan.'

A coquettish smile spread slowly over her lips. 'I'm sure I have; take a good long look.' She opened her gown to reveal her naked body.

He glanced down and observed three white triangles, contrasting with the light brown of her sun-touched skin. With the forced stiff neck of a man unexpectedly coming across his wife's best friend breastfeeding, he fixed his gaze at the crown of her head. 'Yes, you're right. Not bad, for their winter.'

She closed her gown. 'Let's go to bed straight away; I have a present for you.'

He stood his ground. 'Can't you give it to me here?'

She giggled. 'I could, but it will be better in there.'

As she headed for the bedroom, he detoured via the bathroom. Looking at himself in the mirror, he knew he would have to postpone his rehearsed speech on why the sexual side of their relationship must come to a halt.

He was taken by surprise as he entered her boudoir: bouquets of flowers decorated the usually bare room. As he looked closer, he recognised that only the red roses near to his side of the bed were in a proper vase. On her chest of drawers was a wine carafe, its narrow mouth crammed with alstroemeria. The items normally laid out on her dressing table had been piled together in the middle to make way for a jug at one end and a food mixing bowl at the other. The gerbera and zinnia sharing the pitcher created a collage of yellow, orange, red and pink petals. The stems of the blue cornflowers and red carnations sharing the mixing bowl would have floated to the surface, so a saucer had been placed in the centre to hold them down.

It seemed obvious to him that she had impulsively bought far more flowers than she could accommodate. An alternative interpretation scudded briefly through his mind, as he recalled *La Faute de l'Abbé Mouret*, where Zola's peasant girl dies from an excess of scents.

He looked at her as she lay on her back with her face and neck and bony shoulders visible above the plain, white cotton sheets. 'What lovely flowers!'

She asked anxiously, 'You aren't allergic, are you?'

'No, I'm not.' He closed his eyes and sniffed the air.

'They're so beautifully fragrant.'

When he opened them again, she gave him a long, sweet smile. 'I wanted today to be special.'

He dropped his clothes casually on a chair until he was down to his shorts, and then eased in beside her.

After a pull at his elasticated waistband, she released her hold. 'You take 'em off.'

He did as instructed, and then looked across to the place where her box of condoms had been usurped by the alstroemeria. 'Where are the, erm…?'

She smiled. 'I told you I have a present for you. We don't need them anymore; I'm on the pill.'

He drew away from her. 'But that isn't a hundred per cent reliable.'

She tugged him back. 'No worries. There are other options if something goes wrong.'

His concerns about accidental pregnancy and casual abortion had reduced his inclination. 'I'm not so sure about this.' She dived down the bed and began to kiss him intimately. Unable to resist her close attention, he quickly rose to the occasion. Embarrassed at having shown a degree of weakness, he set about proving he was still the man she had known before.

After some hurried foreplay, he mounted her, and took her intense reaction as an indication she had been waiting desperately for him, both today and throughout her time away.

When he rolled off her, she looked anxiously at him. 'But you didn't cum.'

'It isn't you; I'm just a bit worried about getting you pregnant.'

She climbed on top of him. 'We're going to have to do it again, and we'll keep doing it 'til it works!'

As she built up to a crescendo, he was impressed with her second coming. Unable to resist, he joined her in a shared burst of pleasure. Convinced she had had enough, he appreciated how she continued to move on him until quite certain he had exhausted his desires.

Anticipating her nestling up to him in her usual way, he was surprised to see her scamper to the bathroom. When he failed to hear the loud click of the electric shower being turned on, he guessed she was making do with a wash. As he lay back, waiting to take a shower, he closed his eyes and drifted off to sleep.

When she woke him, he asked the time. She smiled. 'Lunchtime. We're having steak, egg and chips.'

'Does that mean you've given up being a veggie?'

'I have for now, but maybe in some future year I'll go back to it.'

He took a quick shower while she prepared the food. When he had dressed, he headed into the kitchen, where beeps from the microwave announced the boxes of slim chips were ready. The fried egg was a little overcooked to his taste, but the fillet steak was perfect. Over lunch, she told him about her time in Australia, contrasting their officers' more relaxed attitude to life.

After the meal, he asked if she would like to go out for a drive and a walk, or whether she wished to be brought up-to-date on the investigations. She replied, 'Let's just stay in and watch television; I don't feel like exerting myself at the moment.'

They watched a DVD together. He was unsurprised to find it was all about a single woman falling in love. The inevitably happy ending had a kindly, henpecked man leaving his horrible, ambitious wife and driving off into the sunset with the heroine. Marcus decided to deal with the elephant in the room. 'If you chose that one because of how things worked out for them, you do know that isn't how it'll be for us.'

She smiled serenely. 'It's just a film, Marcus. And anyway, happy endings come in lots of different shapes and sizes.'

Rather than having to watch another film, he again invited her out. She accepted, agreeing they should take a walk somewhere remote to avoid meeting anyone who would recognise them.

In his car, he turned off the satnav and headed south, at each junction taking the road less travelled. When they parked up, he saw a path leading around an area of woodland, and stepping stones that headed toward it. He led the way across the river and into the trees.

Once they were hidden from sight, she stopped and turned to him, taking his hands in hers. 'You don't need to worry about me, Marcus; I'm not trying to steal you away from your wife.'

Relieved that she had broached the subject which had been uppermost in his mind, he indulged her with a flurry of kisses. Feeling comfortable with her at last, they meandered through the woods by the river.

Back at her flat, he sat on the settee and stretched out his legs. She beckoned him with a curling index finger. 'Take me to bed again.'

He shook his head. 'I'm not that young anymore.'

She stood in front of him. 'Well, I am, and I need to make up for lost time. Come on; don't be mean.'

Though he knew it was not the most gracious of invitations he had ever received, he recognised she had no intention of taking no for an answer. Her keenness encouraged him to rise to the occasion.

After a mutually pleasing session, she allowed him a short rest before pressing him to take the first shower. When he exited the bathroom, she handed him the television handset before taking her turn. Discovering a sports channel, he watched some cricket. Eventually, she emerged, and he noticed a pink bloom to her cheek, which he ascribed to the hot water. He found the modest blush effect enhanced her innocent charm.

After a mushroom pizza in front of the TV, he asked her whether she really wished to be brought back onto the investigation. She confirmed she did, and suggested he brief her on progress the following morning.

He was intending to watch the late evening news, but she climbed onto his lap and began kissing him. After a spirited show of resistance, he succumbed to her blandishments and took her to bed. Again, she ensured he was fully satisfied with her performance.

In the morning, he was aroused from a deep slumber when she began to caress him intimately. With no way of hiding his rising interest, he gave up the pretence of being asleep. He suggested they focus on her pleasure, but she insisted his own enjoyment mattered more to her. Barely conscious, he realised they were climaxing in harmony. After she got off him, he turned onto his side and went back to sleep.

In a dream, he was seamlessly transported to a hotel dining room, enticed by the smell of bacon. She gently shook him awake. 'I'm cooking breakfast.' He slipped out of bed and went to the bathroom.

By the time he had showered and dressed, she was already dishing out the fried tomato, bacon, sausage and egg. Her smile almost broke out into laughter. 'I need to make sure you keep your strength up.'

After breakfast, they sat together while he delivered a detailed review of the investigation's progress, or lack thereof. Once complete, she turned on the television set and satellite recorder and handed him the remote control box. 'You might be able to find some football.'

The league season being over, he spent time channel hopping as he made up an excuse for needing to return home. After a while, he put down the handset.

Recognising he was about to speak, she held up her hand to stop him. 'I've booked us in for a Sunday lunch at one o'clock. When we come back, there's a film I'd like to watch with you, on DVD. You could head off home around seven, maybe.'

At midday, she invited him to bed again. He refused on the grounds of exhaustion. She coaxed him with honeyed words, praising his physique and his abilities, until finally he acceded.

When he felt he was flagging, she covered his face with kisses until he reached the point of release.

With no time to sleep, he went into the shower and stayed there until he felt able to face the rest of the day.

Though she had assured him the restaurant was too distant from either home for them to be seen by anyone they knew, his enjoyment of the good food was marred by his preoccupation with being discovered.

Back at the flat, he found the chosen film portrayed a young American woman bringing up her children alone after her husband had died in the Second World War. The brave widow came through many trials and tribulations unscathed and without the need for a man in her life. He found the ending more befitting modern times than post-war America, and wondered whether the touching closeness the heroine had been displaying toward her similarly widowed female friends was to set up a sequel that included lesbian relationships. If so, he expected it would be even more anachronistic.

Assuming Penny intended to take full advantage of his presence, he asked if she would like to go bed one last time. She looked pleasantly surprised. 'My God, Marcus, you're insatiable.' Without hesitation, she led him away to her scented bedchamber.

Relieved to have proved himself capable of putting in one final good performance, he took a long shower as he considered whether it were feasible to raise the subject of their relationship becoming non-sexual. After so much intercourse, he accepted this was not the right occasion to bring it up for discussion.

He delayed his departure until a quarter past seven, to avoid the implication that he was desperate to leave as soon as permissible. Standing at the door, he asked, 'When shall we spend some time together again?' He wondered why she seemed unwilling to make eye contact with him; after all, having enjoyed his company so much, she was unlikely to be wishing to terminate their affair. When she finally looked him full in the face, he found he was unable to read her expression.

Before she spoke, she blinked rapidly several times. 'It's been really great having you here, but I know it isn't always easy for you to get away. Let's leave it for the next three weekends, but keep the fourth one free.'

He assumed she must have had enough satisfaction to last her a month.

CHAPTER 38

Priestley arrived at work early on the Monday morning, having made a decision to act in what he saw as Lin's best interests. Though she was entirely unaware of his intentions, he felt certain she would appreciate them in the fullness of time. The Chief Constable's parking space was empty, so he collected some papers from his office, to work on while sitting outside Coker's room.

Coker arrived soon after, at a brisk march. He threw out a quick 'Morning, Priestley,' before charging into his office and closing the door.

Priestley knocked three times, limiting the strength to suggest a suitable degree of deference. On hearing no response, he gave a louder double-knock and heard a shouted 'Come in.' He did as instructed and closed the door behind him. Coker asked, 'Is it urgent? I'm busy.'

He began, 'It could be urgent, depending on what else happens...'

Coker interrupted him. 'Make it snappy.'

'It's a personnel matter that I thought I should bring directly to your attention.'

'What sort? Be brief.'

'There's the possibility of a position in the security services...'

'Briefer.'

'It would mean a promotion...'

Coker finally gave him his undivided attention. 'So, that's what this is all about.'

'Yes sir. I believe it's long overdue and...'

'Hardly *long* overdue, but I understand where you're coming from. If you aren't moving ahead, then you're standing still, which means you're falling behind. You know you're earmarked for higher things, but I didn't expect you to be making your demands quite so soon. Well, I don't want to lose you, so I'll match anything you're offered out there. It might be more in the nature of a personal grade, but that's only to be expected, otherwise you'd be waiting for dead men's shoes. Are we talking superintendent or chief super?'

Priestley grinned. 'I'll take whatever you're offering, sir... but it's actually detective sergeant I was wanting, and not for me.'

Coker covered his mouth and lower jaw with his hand. 'Oh! In that case, forget everything I've just said. But why are you coming to me about a junior grade?'

'Deputy Chief Constable Dorothea Forbes-Smythe may have a different take on the matter.'

'Are you saying she might not approve? Well, if she doesn't think it's justified, you'll have to put together a very strong case.'

'It isn't that she wouldn't think the promotion was fully merited, but rather that she has other plans for the young woman in question. She arranged for her to have interviews with MI5, SIS and SO15, but I don't believe it's the correct next step for the DC in question.'

'Who are we talking about?'

'Linda Plummer, sir.'

'Very pretty girl, as I recall. So, what's your interest in her?'

'She's an excellent member of the team and has a great future in the police, but I fear she'll lose her way if she's thrown into the intelligence arena too soon.'

'And what does Linda think of your coming to me direct, to clear the way for her promotion? Has she been giving you some encouragement? Eh?'

'She doesn't know anything about it, sir. Sometimes, I believe it's appropriate for senior officers to take the initiative on behalf of junior officers when they may be unable to make the optimal choices for themselves. DC Plummer may not recognise all the possible pitfalls that might befall her if she were to...'

'Yes, yes, yes. Well, push it through as quickly as possible, but in the end it's her choice. She may be less inclined to move if she's promoted, but it isn't for any of us to make her decisions for her. Now, let me get on with my work. I have to prepare for a meeting with a bloody politician who knows nowt but reckons he can tell us how we should reorganise the entire force.'

'Best of luck with that, sir.' Seeing that Coker was already looking down at a letter on his desk, he quietly slipped out of the office.

Later that morning, Baker arrived and rapped hard on Priestley's open door. 'Good morning, sir.'

He looked up at her and immediately recalled their repeated intimacy over the weekend. 'Good morning, DI Baker. It's good to have you back on the team.'

'Thank you, sir.'

'Close the door.' She did as instructed. 'Try not to overdo it, Penny. I'm, still Marcus, remember.'

She smiled. 'Yes, Marcus.'

He smiled back. 'So, Penny, what are you wanting?'

'I'm leading the Batter investigation again, aren't I?' She settled herself onto a guest chair.

'Yes; I'm happy for you to run with it from now on.'

'In that case, should I personally deliver and collect

Lin Plummer this afternoon? You did the job of taking her to the hospital support group, before.'

He spent several seconds apparently considering the question, having already decided he would retain the duty. 'Leave that one with me, but make sure you keep yourself available. If Lin spots someone of interest, she'll call it in, and we'll have to decide what to do.'

'Our friends over the border had an armed unit on standby for us last time, but I see there hasn't been a repeat request.'

'That's right. It was discussed at the highest levels and agreed it wouldn't be needed in the future.'

'Do you mean someone cut the budget?'

'It did start out from that perspective, but the terms of engagement make it quite clear we should not be taking any precipitate action.'

'So it's identification only.'

'Correct.' He looked away for a few moments. As he turned back, his expression changed to a gentle smile. 'About the weekend: we should talk.'

She stood up. 'We need to avoid any mention of our relationship while we're at work; otherwise, someone might overhear.'

'Yes, that's very much what I was going to say.' He reluctantly accepted it would prove difficult to find any opportunity for raising the subject of ending their affair.

In the afternoon, Marcus was driving Lin to the same bus stop she had used before. When she saw a queue of people there, she ordered him, 'Don't slow down.'

He complied automatically. 'What's the problem? Have you seen someone you recognise?'

'No, but I wouldn't want anyone to connect the two of us.' She pointed into the distance. 'Take the second left after the bend and then drop me off. I'll walk to the bus stop just beyond. If I'm going to be working in surveillance, I'll need to think about things like this.'

'You're obviously a natural. Sometime soon we'll have a good long chat about your options.'

He let her out and then drove to the hospital, where he joined a lengthy queue of vehicles waiting to enter the car park. Once inside, he listened to the remainder of Puccini's *Che gelida manina*, the volume turned down low. When the track ended, he stepped outside and walked around with a worried frown, as though he shared the cares often found among the place's visitors.

Lin phoned him. 'There's a man with a walking stick who might be our suspect. His first name is Jerome. I'm sending a photo I took of him without him knowing. Should I follow him when he leaves?'

'We need more eyes for a surveillance operation. Do you think you could track him without being noticed?'

'Which takes precedence: tracking him; or not being noticed?'

'Not being noticed. We don't want you being added to any hit-list, if it is the guy I saw in Nottingham.'

Straight after terminating the call, he phoned Baker. 'Lin's seen a man with a walking stick who matches my description of your attacker. I'm sending a photo.'

'Are you putting a tail on him?'

'That's the plan. Drive over here and we'll work out what's best. You'll have to borrow a car in case it is him; yours might be recognised.'

He returned to his car. As he waited, a text message arrived from Plummer. "On 51 bus with Jerome going to Lodge Moor. I'll get off at Sandygate Road."

Priestley phoned Baker. 'Our man is on the fifty-one

bus heading for Lodge Moor. I'm going to follow it and look out for him getting off, but if it is our suspect then he'll probably know my car. Can you get here in time to take over from me and see where he goes?'

'Yes, sure. No worries.'

Priestley drove past Plummer, who was walking away from the bus stop where she had alighted. He gave a brief hand gesture to indicate he had seen her. She turned away from him as a covert indication she had noticed. Further along the road, to avoid tracking the bus too obviously, he pulled into the kerb and used his hands-free phone to update Baker. 'The bus is on Redmires Road. What's your ETA?'

'I'll be there in three minutes. No, make that two.'

'Keep your phone on and I'll update you.' He set off slowly, staying well back from the bus. A black VW shot past him. He heard a siren and saw in his rear-view mirror a distant police car with flashing lights speeding toward him. 'There's a police car chasing some nutter doing a ton. I hope they don't get in our way.'

After a short delay, she responded, 'I'm the nutter and it's ton-ten. Can you get them off my tail?'

He put on his hazards and parked the car sideways across the road, leaving enough space for the pursuers to pass either side if they chose to ignore his attempt to bring them to a halt. To emphasise his intentions, he jumped out of the car and ran toward the oncoming vehicle, holding out his warrant card so they would know he was trying to show them something, even though it would be too small for them to see it properly.

The police car driver looked with horror at the man running toward them, as he assessed which side of the parked car he might pass by. Seeing the man move to block him, he hit the brakes hard.

Priestley heard the tyres squeal and felt relieved they had chosen to stop. Seeing the passenger jump out and start sprinting toward him, his face burning with anger, Priestley held his warrant card in one hand and gestured to him with the other to come forward. The greeting from a fellow officer, albeit from a different force, was brief and direct. 'What the fuck?'

'Detective Chief Inspector Priestley.' He waved his warrant card and commanded him, 'Go and tell your mate to turn off the siren.'

Before he could obey, the driver jumped out of the car and rushed over, yelling, 'What the fuck?'

Priestley imagined they must have attended the same training course, which had evidently taught them non-standard procedures. He pointed to their car. 'Turn off the siren; otherwise you'll blow a covert operation.'

The driver hurriedly complied. When he returned, Priestley indicated the near side of the road. 'I'll park up and explain everything. And turn off your lights as soon as the road's clear.' To avoid further discussion, he climbed into his car and moved it to the roadside. After watching the liveried vehicle draw up directly behind him, he stepped out with his mobile and waited.

Both officers exited their vehicle. The driver asked, 'What's going on here, then?'

Priestley spoke into his phone. 'The pursuit has been halted. What's your status?'

She snapped, 'Busy!'

He turned to the officers and smiled disarmingly at them, first one, then the other. 'The driver you were pursuing is currently engaged in tracking down a suspect from a murder investigation. The aim is to establish where they live, but not to engage with them.'

The driver frowned. 'We'll have to report it all.'

Priestley pointed to their car. 'I'll get in the back, if you don't mind, and we'll get it sorted.'

The three were still engaged in a frank and forthright discussion as Baker slowly approached in her vehicle. Priestley spoke into his phone, asking her to park up. She acknowledged, before terminating the call.

As she joined Priestley in the back seat, she offered a breezy, 'Hello, gentlemen.'

The driver responded, 'Hello yourself, Little Miss Tearaway.'

She replied, pointedly, 'That's Detective Inspector Tearaway to you, thank you Constable.'

The driver glanced at his colleague, before politely requesting to see her warrant card.

When Priestley and Baker were finally allowed to leave, they decamped to his car. He asked, 'Did you manage to track him down?'

Her voice sounded triumphant. 'Yes, I was just in time.' She grinned. 'I'm glad I didn't have to hurry.'

His phone rang. Seeing the caller's identification, he answered, 'Yes, Lin?' before quickly adding, 'You're on speaker; I'm with DI Baker.'

Plummer asked, 'Am I supposed to catch the bus?'

He replied, 'I'll be right there. Are you where I saw you earlier?'

She responded, 'No; I'm walking in your direction.'

He thought he had detected a note of irritation in her voice. 'All right. I'll be setting off in a minute.'

Baker commented as she climbed out of the car, 'I still say she's far too familiar with you, Marcus.'

He smiled. 'Not like you, of course.'

Once back at the station, Baker organised a meeting of the investigation team. She began, 'The masked man who bled at my first abduction attempt may have been identified. DC Plummer took a photograph of a suspect and I tracked him down to an address in Sheffield. This is a tentative ID, as we don't yet have enough evidence to justify taking DNA from him to compare against the blood sample. Therefore, for now, what we need to do is to dig into his background and see if we can gain an idea of his character.'

Priestley added, 'May I say, what a brilliant piece of detective work. Well done, Lin and Penny.'

Baker replied, 'That's DC Plummer and DI Baker, sir.' She looked around at her colleagues. 'We wouldn't want the boss getting too familiar with us, would we?'

There was a ripple of laughter.

After the meeting, Priestley called Plummer into his office and closed the door behind her. 'I forgot to ask, by the way: how did you know the suspect was going to Lodge Moor?' He saw the disarming innocence in her big blue eyes, certain that their power was sufficient to convince any man of her honesty and sincerity.

'I heard him say so.'

'You were standing near enough to hear him?' She nodded. 'Because, of course, you do remember we did agree there should be no direct contact. Yes?'

'Yes, of course.'

'Yes of course what?'

She delivered a startled look. 'Yes of course, sir?'

'No, I mean, what exactly is it that you're saying "Yes, of course," to? When he saw how she smiled at him, he suspected she was hiding something. 'Did you make contact with him?'

'I'm saying, of course I remember you said that not being noticed takes precedence over tracking him.'

He was now fully convinced she was obfuscating. 'Tell me, have you deliberately allowed yourself to be noticed? Or were your covert surveillance abilities found wanting?'

She put on a hurt look. 'I also remember you said the reason was to avoid my name being added to a hit-list, if it was the guy from the first abduction. So I took an executive decision, to get close to the guy in such a way as to be in no danger of being added to any list.'

'And how did you do that?'

'I got on the bus straight after him and heard where he was going. As I know the route, I bought a ticket for a stop on Sandygate Road, and then sat next to him. We had a little chat about his condition, and my uncle's. If he'd asked where I was going, I would have said: to visit my uncle who lives on Sandygate Road. But he didn't ask, so I didn't volunteer the information.'

'Did you consider getting a ticket for Lodge Moor?'

'That would have been too obvious. By getting off earlier, he wouldn't suspect I'd targeted him. Also, if I'd had to use the cover story about visiting my uncle, he might well have asked for the address if it was in his area, so he could call in on him in a neighbourly way.'

'I agree with your rationale. You were quite right not to have offered any additional information, though I suggest in future you take care not to over-elaborate any cover story you invent. However, I must also point out that you disobeyed a direct order.'

'My understanding was that we had a discussion and reached a conclusion based on a number of underlying assumptions which could be revised, and indeed were.

Anyway, I was confident I could handle the situation without risk of disclosing my true identity.'

'You certainly display confidence, DC Plummer, but you did disobey a direct order from a superior officer.'

She grinned. 'So, do I get a smacked bottom?'

He remained stone-faced. 'No, you get a promotion.'

'For disobeying an order?'

'In spite of. I'd already put the wheels in motion.'

'Well, why now?'

'There are two reasons. One: you've earned it many times over. By rights, I should have put you forward earlier. Two: I believe your career would be at risk if you were to take on counter-terrorism work before you're ready, so I'm hoping the promotion gives you an incentive to stay, for your sake. And three: I don't want to lose you, as a fellow officer.'

'You said two.'

He threw off her correction with a shake of the head. 'And four: I don't want to lose you.'

'That sounds like number three.'

'Number four isn't anything like number three.'

She looked down for a few moments, giving her time to think. 'You may well be right about intelligence work; when I'm not playing a rôle, I'm generally an honest person, which could prove to be a weakness.'

He shook his head vehemently. 'I'm not saying you have a weakness; I'm simply saying you could have a successful career in policing, rather than moving to a higher-risk environment.'

'But what if I like the risk? And before you answer, let me just point out that everyone knows you seem to enjoy putting yourself at risk. I heard about your latest stunt, blocking the main road with your car.'

'That's different.'

'Because you're a man? That's sexist.'

'It isn't because I'm a man, *per se*. It's because I'm happy to take risks if by so doing I can reduce other people's level of danger.'

'But that's exactly what the security services do.'

'But... Oh, you're too clever for me. I'm simply saying that I'm not happy with you putting yourself in dangerous situations. And especially if you're only doing it to prove you're as good as any man.'

'Well, I appreciate your concern, but in the end I have to find my own way.'

'So what you said previously about wanting to stay close to me is all forgotten.'

'No, it isn't. I need to develop my professional life as I see fit, though of course I'll often seek your advice. But my private life stays with you.'

'In that case, just do me one favour.'

'Yes, of course.'

'Always keep yourself safe.'

She laughed for a moment. 'That isn't a favour, is it; but thanks for the thought.' She stood to leave. At the door, she turned and asked, 'Any chance of you coming over tonight? I'd like you to do *me* a favour.'

He shook his head. 'Sorry, but I've promised another young lady I'll be taking *her* out.' Having expected Lin to snap back at his humour with some biting riposte, he guiltily read her look of genuine concern. With a warm smile, he explained, 'It's Alice's birthday. She's seven.'

Lin quickly recovered. 'When it comes to your affections, I know that's one young lady I could never compete with.'

CHAPTER 39

The Friday morning team meeting was led by DI Baker. First on the agenda was the discouraging background information collected on the man with the walking stick, Jerome Wilberforce, OBE. He had qualified as an engineer, and had devoted many years to a charity that dug wells for the provision of pure water to villages in remote parts of Africa. Nothing had been discovered to suggest he was the type of person who would ever become involved in abduction. Without a legal basis for obtaining a DNA sample, Baker proposed they remain focused on the other key players. Priestley reluctantly allowed her recommendation to go unchallenged.

Elsie Crompton was found to have a similarly clean background. For many years prior to retirement she had worked as a clerk at a food processing factory, having previously been employed at a steel production plant. She had recently been widowed after a marriage that had lasted more than forty years. They had a son and a daughter. The daughter had had a child, Britney, who had died in her teens from a heroin overdose. Britney had been living with Timothy Walton, a man known to the police as a drug dealer. Since her death, Elsie had campaigned locally for Naloxone to be made available to drug addicts and their associates, arguing that it could have been used to reverse the effects of the heroin and thereby save her granddaughter's life. Beyond this, her public profile was non-existent.

Priestley recommended the team undertake further

research into Timothy Walton, being the only player with criminal connections. Baker assigned two officers to the task.

Plummer asked if she should attend the next hospital support group meeting, which would be on the Tuesday evening. Baker declared it would be a waste of time, as Wilberforce had already been identified as a suspect. Priestley suggested other new leads could be generated from that source. Baker dismissed the idea. He decided it would not be politic to disagree in public.

At the end of the day, Priestley invited Baker to his office to give him an update on progress. She expressed disappointment at the lack of any breakthrough, as she detailed the team's findings.

In order to make their working relationship appear normal, he asked her if she would like to go for a drink at the pub, and was surprised when she declined. Rather than attempting to fathom the reason for the rejection, he accepted it without comment.

As he passed through the office, he made a similar invitation to Witty, who apologised for needing to go straight home. Plummer chirped up, 'I'll go, if you need a drinking partner, boss.'

He looked disparagingly at her, holding the mask until certain Witty had noticed. 'Oh, come on then; I'll have to make do with you.'

Witty grinned at her. 'Tell me, how does it feel to know you're so unwanted?'

She responded, 'I'm sure he doesn't mean it.' She turned to Priestley, trying to appear anxious. 'Do you?'

He smiled serenely at her. 'No, no, of course not. And don't feel bad about being third choice.'

In the pub, she sat with him in a corner, watching as

he held up his pint of bitter to the light. She raised her half and peered through it. 'Good shine, nice colour.'

He stared at her. 'Are you an expert, now?'

She smiled. 'I'm just repeating what I've heard you say. So, I'm third choice, am I? Who was first?'

'Penny. She turned me down flat. I must be losing my charm.'

'I thought she was sweet on you for a while.'

'Yes, so did I, but thankfully it didn't last. Maybe she met an Aussie.'

'It's possible. Anyway, are you free this evening?'

'I was thinking of taking a look at Walton's place on the A625. It has to be quite a step up from the dump on Attercliffe Common where he was living with that girl.'

'Yes; there must be good money to be made out of the drugs business.'

'You mean bad money of course, Lin.'

'Yeah. So, what are you hoping to achieve by casing the joint?'

He frowned at her. 'Did I hear you correctly?' She grinned. 'I just want to take a look, in case we need to go calling.'

'But it's outside our jurisdiction; and anyway, even if it wasn't, wouldn't the National Crime Agency be taking the lead?'

'Yes, you're right; I don't really have a good reason to go "casing the joint".'

'In that case, let's do it anyway.'

'That's illogical; it doesn't make any sense.'

'Why should it? I'm a woman.'

He tutted. 'That is definitely sexist.'

They agreed that the simplest arrangement would be to take a small detour to Lin's flat so she could park up, and then he would drive them both to a side road close to Walton's property.

Half an hour later, as per the plan, he parked around the corner from the target's house. Before they reached the main road, she linked arms with him.

He turned and looked at her. 'Someone might see.'

She responded quietly, 'It's cover.'

He shook her off. 'Like I keep saying, I'm too old for you. As far as cover goes, it wouldn't look right.'

She left a gap between them. 'Well, what about this? Two people who aren't talking to each other?'

'No, that's even worse.' He took hold of her hand. 'Let's keep up a conversation while we go past.'

As they were passing a high stone wall topped off with railings, approaching the pair of towering wrought iron gates at the end of the property's driveway, a dog suddenly began to bark at them just above their heads. He felt Lin jump involuntarily, the twitch of her body relayed down her arm to the hand that now grasped his more tightly. They turned to see an Alsatian between the bushes that lined the earthen bank above the wall. 'It's all right; it's securely fenced in... I hope.'

When they were directly outside the gates, a second Alsatian appeared and began to snarl at them. They strolled along until out of sight of the property, then crossed the road and returned the way they had come. When they were again opposite the gates, she stopped him, ostensibly for a kiss. The dogs remained silent. As they walked away, she commented, 'They must be trained to ignore anyone on the other side of the road.'

He responded, 'They've gone for belt and braces. Did you see the CCTV?'

She replied, 'Yes, four cameras.'

He slowed his pace a little. 'I only saw three.'

She giggled. 'So did I; just checking.'

Having reconnoitred the place, he drove her back to her flat, where he accepted the usual invitation.

After they had showered and dressed, she offered him instant coffee. He checked his watch. 'Yes, thanks, but I'll have to be going soon.'

She gave a wry smile. 'But not too soon, I trust; that wouldn't be polite.' She made the coffee and placed his mug on a small table beside his chair, before sitting on the settee with her feet drawn up to one side.

He asked, 'Have you made any decision about what you want to do with your life?'

She raised her mug and stared at the black liquid. 'There are pros and cons to whatever I do. Let me ask you a question.'

'Sure; fire away.'

'If I were living in London, how often would you be able to come and see me?'

He flinched. 'That's a tricky one.'

She gazed at him. 'How often could you stay for a weekend? One in three? One in four?'

'I doubt we could make it that definite. There are times when I have to be working over a weekend, and I'm sure the same would apply to you. That's without even considering my family life, which you know isn't going to change.'

'So I wouldn't see you anywhere near as often as I do now.'

'That's for certain... but you know that.'

'But what about when I did see you? Would we be able to do more things together in public? Even simple things like walking along, holding hands, like we were earlier. I know we only have a part-time relationship, but I want it to feel full-time during those parts.'

'The further we are from my home, the more relaxed we could be. Around here when I'm with you, I always feel like I'm being watched. Like this evening when we were walking along together, and I don't just mean the CCTV. Did you notice anything suspicious?'

'You're talking about the builder's van, aren't you.'

'Yes, I am. It was all locked up, but it didn't look like it would have belonged to anyone living in that area. There was no sign of any activity in the vicinity, so where had the workmen gone at that time of day?'

'Maybe we should go back and see if it's still there.'

'Maybe we should check it on the database.'

'You mean you know the registration?'

'Yes; I made a mental not of it.'

'And I thought you were totally lost in the moment, walking along, holding the hand of the girl you love.'

He smiled as he shook his head. 'We were working, don't forget.'

'Well, let's check it now.'

He took out his work mobile and phoned it in. When he terminated the call, he saw her looking expectantly at him, so teasingly kept her waiting.

She asked, 'What is it? Something interesting?'

He shrugged. 'Yes, but I can't say how interesting; the information is blocked.'

'...which, of course, is interesting in itself. Should we start making backdoor enquiries?'

'No, let's leave it for now. Whenever I've made an enquiry on a restricted vehicle registration in the past, I've always found someone contacts me if I wait long enough. I wonder if it'll be any of your new friends.'

'Isn't it more likely to be connected with ordinary criminal activity?'

'Yes, I expect so. As to which criminal, it could be a coincidence that it was parked near our target's house.'

'But you don't believe that.'

'It isn't that I don't believe in coincidences *per se*; it's rather that my expectation of an actual coincidence diminishes as a probability becomes vanishingly small.'

'You mean, the less likely something is to happen, the less you believe it could happen, which is obvious.'

'Do you mind not stripping away my jargon, Lin? In senior team meetings, a few choice words such as those can transform the blindingly obvious into something that's perceived as a brilliant insight.'

'So, that's how you've earned your reputation for being smart, is it?'

'Absolutely. Behind this façade I'm just a man of straw.' He checked his watch and took his leave.

The next afternoon, Marcus was at home playing cards with his children, when his work mobile rang. He answered it formally. A man's voice asked, 'Are you the bloke we filmed yesterday evening walking past a drug dealer's house and holding hands with a young woman? Not to mention snogging.'

He responded, 'And you are?'

'Superintendent Marsden, NCA. You did an enquiry on our surveillance van. Why was that?'

Having yet to establish the caller's *bona fides*, he asked, 'Is this a conversation we need to conduct right now over the phone?'

The man replied, 'Just tell me, if you don't mind: is she your wife or girlfriend?'

Understanding the reason for the question, he stated

starchily, 'My DS, actually; well, acting DS.'

'So it wasn't a chance thing, then. In that case, just make sure you don't go anywhere near the place until we've had the opportunity to talk.'

'I didn't have any plans to.'

'Glad to hear it. Monday morning all right?'

'Certainly; I look forward to hearing from you.'

Helen entered the room. 'I heard you on the phone. You don't have to go in, do you? Food's nearly ready.'

He gave her a warm smile. 'No, I'm all yours for the weekend.'

Edwin jumped to his feet. 'What about me?'

He gave him a tender smile. 'And yours, of course.' So that Alice would not feel left out, he turned his smile on her. 'And yours too, sweetheart.'

CHAPTER 40

Priestley checked for messages as soon as he arrived at his office on the Monday morning. There was one from Superintendent John Marsden, explaining that the NCA currently had Timothy Walton under surveillance in connection with drug trafficking. Priestley phoned him. After extended pleasantries, Marsden provided further background as to their operation and team structure. Priestley commented, 'I hope we didn't give the game away by walking past the place, John.'

Marsden responded gruffly, 'I'm sure you didn't.' He gave a chuckle. 'The two of you looked so genuine together, especially when she kissed you that way, I'm certain nobody would have suspected anything.'

Priestley laughed too loudly, masking his unease at being caught on camera. 'Yes, she's a great actress.'

'Well, I'm relieved my DS doesn't try to kiss me like that.'

'She isn't as attractive as mine, then?'

'No, he isn't! Six foot four with a big bushy beard.'

Priestley laughed again, pleased to have developed a rapport.

Marsden changed the tone of his voice to suggest the serious side of the conversation was beginning. 'We had a tipoff, so we've set up an operation. You need to read me in on your investigation, to make sure we don't bugger things up between us.'

'Of course, John; and I'll instruct my team to liaise fully with yours at all levels.'

'I'm pleased to hear that, Marcus, but it may not be the most appropriate way of taking things forward; we're all geared up for a major drugs bust.'

'Which is tremendously important, of course; but we're investigating multiple murders.'

'And our man's involved?'

'We haven't yet made a direct connection, but it's only a matter of time before we tie the strands together. Could I suggest that I, and one of my key officers, be co-opted into your operation?'

'I appreciate your willingness to help, but my team are used to dealing with major villains. I'm happy to read you in, but direct involvement is another matter entirely. We can expect them to be tooled up if there's a serious confrontation.'

'I'm always up for a bit of action, but don't take my word for it; let me leave you to conduct a background check so you can decide if you'd like me involved. If not, I'll just pass everything we have over to you.'

'That's a very generous attitude, Marcus; I'll give you a call later this morning.'

Priestley hoped his track record would gain him full admission to the drugs team before he had to explain he was coming empty-handed, his own team having nothing new on Walton. He felt certain their operation would generate more excitement than his current case, where the likeliest suspects were the unlikeliest people. At least their bad guys would be easy to identify, in stark contrast to the nice folk he was investigating.

Within the hour, Priestley received a phone call from Marsden. 'Welcome aboard, Marcus.'

'Thank you, John. And could I bring my sidekick?'

'Certainly; I think we'd all like to work closely with

your actress.' Discovering a pun, he continued quickly, 'Your *acting* sergeant. What's her name, by the way?'

'Lin Plummer; but I was actually meaning Penny Baker, the DI who's handling our investigation.'

'Well, we'll have both of them, then. I'm assuming you'll all run off your budget, won't you?'

'I'm sure that will be acceptable to everyone here. When can we all get together for sharing of information and cross-fertilisation of ideas?'

'"Cross-fertilisation?" You can't use big words like that with my team; they won't understand.'

Hearing Marsden chuckle, Priestley responded, 'I shall attempt to expurgate every element of polysyllabic communication from my lexicon.'

'Yes, do that as well. How about four o'clock? We'll come to you; there'll be six of us.'

'I'll make sure we're fully prepared.'

Priestley called Baker and Plummer to his office. He began by explaining the background to the drugs case, before giving them the chance to opt out.

Baker responded immediately, 'Count me in; I like being at the sharp end.'

Plummer took a few moments to consider the matter. 'Same here, but I'm not an obvious candidate for this, so why have you chosen to include me?'

He shrugged. 'Why not? So, see you at ten to four.'

Baker headed out. Plummer began to follow, but turned back. She asked quietly, 'Are you trying to give me lots of interesting work to persuade me to stay?'

He responded even more quietly, 'They filmed us snogging, and now they're queuing up to work with you.'

She blushed. 'They don't know, then?'

'They probably think you're the type who'll cosy up to any of them in the line of duty.'

'Well, you need to put them straight on that; I'll only do that sort of undercover work with you.'

He watched her face for signs of emotional leakage as he asked, 'Does that suggest you're not really cut out for SIS? You know you'd never be expected to have sex with a contact; for one thing, they forbid it because it can be a security risk. But there could be less extreme situations where you might have to appear especially friendly. Remember Stockholm?'

'Ah, so that's what this is really all about: you don't want me to try for SIS.'

'All right, Lin; I'll put my cards on the table. I don't, because I'm worried about what might happen to you.'

'I appreciate your concern. Anyway, there are two other possibilities, and in the meantime, I've a bit of excitement to look forward to here; or do you intend to keep me well away from any dangerous situations?'

'I'll be keeping all of us out of harm's way, to the best of my ability…'

'…but me more than others. You need to allow me to play a full part in any action that's going.'

'Of course, Lin; of course.'

The four o'clock combined briefing proved to be an anticlimax. The drugs team had heard a whisper that Walton had been invited to step up to the big league, with a top player venturing north from London to seal the contract. In return, Priestley could only explain the speculative nature of their connection with Walton.

Marsden gave Priestley a hard stare. 'What you're telling us is that Walton may be the subject of a murder attempt because he allowed a junkie to overdose. So, is your plan to protect him, then? Will you be working with us or against us?'

Priestley answered quickly, 'We'll be working with you one hundred per cent. If we can solve our case at the same time, that'll be an added bonus.'

Marsden pressed his pencil too hard to his notebook, breaking off the point. 'I might be feeling like I'd just been conned, if it wasn't for the fact that I'm borrowing three officers at someone else's expense.'

Priestley responded, 'Me and two *top* officers, John. And I promise you, we won't let you down.'

Marsden gave a brief glance of acknowledgement to the two women, as he asked, 'If this isn't an impolite question, why do you rate them so highly?'

Plummer drew admiring glances for daring to speak out of turn. 'DI Baker is in demand internationally, and I was smart enough to spot your surveillance van.'

Marsden softened his voice as he asked her, 'How did you do that, by the way? We thought the equipment was disguised perfectly.'

She smiled at him. 'And so it was, sir, but the setup didn't ring true. No one owning a house in that area would be likely to work out of a van as a builder, so it had to belong to someone from outside. The van itself was closed up, yet there was no evidence of anyone working nearby. And then there's the fact that it was a Friday, the day our local builders traditionally celebrate POETS evening.'

One giant of an officer responded incredulously, 'Builders are into poetry around here?'

Another officer intervened before Plummer could reply. 'Piss Off Early, Tomorrow's Saturday. POETS. Geddit?'

Marsden gave a roar of laughter, despite having heard the expression many times before. All traces of his earlier dissatisfaction finally erased from his face, he terminated the meeting and departed with his team.

Priestley held back Baker and Plummer for a confab. He began, 'Why do we think we're getting involved in this drugs case?'

Baker responded, 'It's an ideal opportunity for a bit of excitement.'

A smile played on his lips. 'I thought you'd had plenty of excitement, recently.' Seeing how Baker had glanced anxiously at Plummer, he thought she may have misinterpreted. 'That was a *very* high speed chase. Incidentally, I've spoken to them on your behalf, but they're still not happy about it. As you were driving at speed without lights or a siren, they're taking the view that you represented a danger to the public. Have you heard anything directly from them?'

She shrugged dismissively. 'I've received a formal notification that they're investigating it, but I'm sure they'll come round to our way of thinking, eventually.'

He turned to Plummer. 'And why do *you* think we're getting involved?'

She thought of several alternative reasons and chose her preferred one. 'The best chance of solving our own case is by questioning anyone who makes an attempt on Walton's life. If they're part of a broader conspiracy, it could lead us to a whole network. To identify someone, we need to get close to Walton, and the drugs operation provides us with an ideal opportunity.'

He nodded. 'In which case, we need to give them our full support if we're to remain on their team.'

When he stood to signal the end of the meeting, Lin

caught his eye to suggest she wished to talk with him in private. Unaware of this, Penny began speaking. 'Could I have a few words with you, boss?'

He responded quickly, 'Yes of course. Lin, just close the door as you leave.'

Once they were alone, Penny began, 'I know I said I'd like you to come over every fourth weekend, but what about some weekdays as well?'

He guiltily masked his immediate reaction, which was to recall how much pleasure he had felt when she had been discovering her uninhibited sexual liberation. Smiling as he looked her in the eye, he steeled himself to give her a hard answer. 'That would be great, Pen; but now we've the extra workload, I don't think there's any chance of it happening this week or next.'

Her attempted smile died on her lips. 'Well, at least make sure you keep that fourth weekend free.'

'It's right at the front of my mental diary.'

When he returned to his office, Lin was hovering nearby. She followed him in and closed the door. 'What were the two of you talking about?'

He raised an eyebrow at her. 'My conversation with Detective Inspector Baker is none of your business, Acting Sergeant Plummer. Now, what did you want to see me for?'

'I need guidance on allocating my time between the two cases. For a start, should I be going to the hospital support group tomorrow evening? Or do I need to keep myself free for any sudden activity on the drugs case?'

'Good question. If Marsden hears Walton's drugs meeting is about to happen, we'll drop whatever we're doing. But until then, we carry on as normal.'

'And what exactly is normal? If you remember, I'm

not supposed to be going to the hospital in future.'

'Yes, I do remember; but let's go anyway.'

'Same routine? I have to catch the bus?'

'Oh, you'd rather I take you all the way.'

'Yes, I would. You can pick me up from home. Will you come early?'

'I'll try not to.' He gave her a wicked grin.

She laughed, before responding on the same theme. 'Will you be coming this evening, as well?'

'I'm trying to wean myself off you, Lin; preparing myself for when we can't see each other very often.'

'I think that's all back-to-front, Marcus. We should be seeing as much of each other as possible while we still have the chance.'

He squinted and pointed an index finger up into the air between them. 'Ah, so you are intending to leave.'

She imitated his gesture. 'Or perhaps I'm just using any excuse to get you to spend more time with me.'

CHAPTER 41

On the Tuesday evening, Marcus arrived just in time to pick up Lin for her trip to the support group.

The hospital car park was only half-full, so he chose a space near the exit. He waited until she had been gone a few minutes before making his way to the canteen.

Staring at his white plastic beaker of water, he felt a mobile phone vibrate in his pocket. He read the text message from Lin that instructed him to see her at once near the main entrance. Outside, he looked around and saw her hurrying toward him. 'Elsie Crompton is here; she's an unwell person.'

'That doesn't surprise me in the least.'

'What should I do?'

Seeing Crompton leaving the building and heading casually in their direction, he whispered, 'Don't turn around; she's coming over.'

Crompton hailed them from a distance, 'Hello again, Lynette. Is Mr Priestley your boyfriend?'

Plummer spun around as though taken by surprise. 'We're just good friends.' She winked at Elsie. 'Don't tell anybody, will you; it's a bit awkward, you see.'

'Ah, I understand; he's a married man, is he? Well, don't worry, love; my lips are sealed.'

Lin looked relieved as she replied, 'Thanks, Else.'

Crompton turned to Priestley. 'Have you been telling her the usual pack of lies? Saying you'll leave your wife for her, but not yet? I just don't know what the world's coming to, when you can't trust a policeman.'

Priestley opened his mouth to respond, but could find no suitable rebuttal. He watched as she turned on her heel and walked off to join a bus queue.

In the car, Marcus and Lin sat looking at each other in silence. Finally, Lin spoke. 'Have we blown it?'

He pressed his fingers to his temple, his thumbs hard against his cheekbones. 'Probably; but blown what? As far as the case goes, you did a great job of covering up. But what about us? I know what she said, but will she still start a rumour? It's easy enough for us to deny it, of course, because we're working; only, if *she* found out that we were working, she'd know you're a police officer, which would lead her to suspect she's under surveillance. But she didn't react like she was taken by surprise, so either she completely accepts your story, or she already knew who you were. There again, maybe she's a great actress too, and just reacted cleverly to the situation.' He took a deep breath and released it slowly.

She gazed out of the side window, and then the front windscreen, before looking directly at him. 'Well, she was definitely wrong about one thing: you've never said you'd leave Helen for me.'

A niggling feeling blocked him from responding. He felt something was not quite right about that interaction with Elsie Crompton; something intangible, undefined, insubstantial, unrevealed. Sensing Lin was preparing to speak again, he held up a hand. 'Let me think a bit.'

Lin wracked her brains, trying to second-guess what he was contemplating. After dismissing the idea that he was now considering saying to her what he had never said before, she decided he was focusing on the effect of Crompton's newfound knowledge in relation to the case against her, always assuming it was newfound.

Eventually, he gave a hesitant assessment. 'There was something wrong with that scene we just played out with Elsie Crompton, but I can't quite put my finger on it.'

She responded, 'I feel the same. It was as though she already knew exactly what she going to say, and once she'd delivered her lines she simply walked off.'

He assumed she had found the explanation that had evaded him. 'But that would mean she knew who you were, which would in turn suggest she knew what you were doing here.'

'So it would seem.'

Suddenly, he smacked the heel of his hand to his forehead. 'Got it! I feel like I know her because I've watched her being interviewed on video, but I wasn't there myself. So how does she know who I am?'

Subdued, they drove in silence back to her flat, each trying to imagine every feasible sequence of events that could have resulted in her discovering his identity.

He accepted her invitation inside, where they sat and discussed the case. An hour later, as he left for home, he realised it had been something of a first: they had tacitly declined an opportunity for intimacy.

For once, he was pleased to find the children were already in bed and sound asleep, as he wished to talk to Helen about the recent events before their freshness began to fade. He replayed the latest events while she listened in silence, ending with, 'What do you think?'

Casting around for an insightful reply, she found only vague supposition and uncertain conjecture, so settled for a simple statement. 'If there is a conspiracy, you'll need to identify everyone who is involved in it, if you're to have any hope of understanding not only what has happened in the past, but also what might happen in the future.'

He sat in deep contemplation, knowing Helen would not impose a limit to his thinking time. A few minutes later he responded, 'Everyone who attends the hospital support group is a contender, but I think the extreme nature of the various actions must indicate the presence of a distinct subset within that group.'

She spent a minute considering her response. 'You need to identify those with a strong moral compass, always bearing in mind how different people can hold sincere beliefs that are polar opposites when it comes to perceptions of morality.'

'Like with immigration? There are some who argue it's completely immoral to bar anyone from entering the country, and others who see it as a cardinal sin to allow anyone else in.'

'That's a valid example, but do try to keep yourself focused on the specifics of the case, rather than letting your mind wander off into other spheres.'

He considered every possible conspirator known to him, and eventually offered his assessments. 'Tell me what you think of this. If my theory is correct about a conspiracy, then Elsie Crompton has to be a member. The late Padraic O'Leary was at least a friend of a conspirator. By extension, Barry Blackstone is a friend of a friend of a conspirator, but may well be one in his own right. If Dr Tereza was a conspirator, she may well have left the cabal. The man with the walking stick in Nottingham, who may or may not have been Jerome Wilberforce, must surely be a conspirator. My attackers may have been full members, but more likely they were just outsiders who were helping out their mates.'

She nodded. 'It's right to make a distinction between the brains and the brawn; some of them may have no idea what's behind it all.'

'Speaking of brains, Aden Liversedge appears to be a bright bloke, and there's no evidence to suggest he's terminally ill, so he could be a permanent member.'

'I think you mean longer term, Marcus. Life itself is a terminal condition; no matter how young or healthy someone is, no one's permanent in the end.'

'True, though I'm starting to wonder how permanent the group itself is. What if it only comes into existence as the need arises, and then blinks out, like a distant star in a constellation?'

'You're drifting off course again, aren't you; but you have made a valid point. What if the number of actors is tied to the events that the nebulous organisation has in play at any one time? If the number of events drops to zero, then there is no current conspiracy, and so there are no current actors.'

'I take your point, but I wouldn't want to have to limit my work to investigating past cases; I'd really like to be able to head off future events before they occur.'

'You do have one possible event in play, of course. The drug dealer, Timothy Walton, is linked to the probable conspirator, Elsie Crompton, which means the group may well have him in their sights. Your best chance of breaking the chain is to catch someone in the act of committing an offence, which is what you're looking to do by working with the drugs team. But if you do arrest someone, you'll still have the same problem as you have with Crompton; that is, persuading them to spill the beans about a conspiracy.'

'Well, I can but try. One thing that worries me is that

the drug dealer and his associates are believed to have firearms. Lin is keen to be kept close to any action, but I can't bear the thought of something happening to her.'

She responded, seemingly casually, 'You're rather fond of her, aren't you.'

He knew anything other than a strong confirmation would leave him under a cloud of suspicion. 'I suppose I am, really. She's such a sweet girl, but she has this determined streak that might lead her into trouble…'

'…whereas you go looking for trouble, half the time. It might be possible for you to keep her safe and sound while ever she's in the police force, but if she goes elsewhere you'll be powerless to act as her guardian. Maybe you need to prepare yourself for such times by letting her take a few carefully considered risks.'

'You're quite right, of course; but I'd worry about her venturing into really serious danger.'

'Yes, I know you would. But then, you fret about all the officers, don't you; that is to say, all of them except yourself. It must be high time I gave you another deep psychological evaluation, to try to get to the bottom of your martyr complex.'

He quipped, 'But you gave me one recently.'

She pretended to be serious. 'Oh, come on, that was nearly a week ago.'

They looked into each other's eyes and smiled.

CHAPTER 42

There had been no significant progress by the time the next support group meeting came around a week later, so early on the Wednesday morning Marcus collected Lin from home and drove her to the hospital. He went to the canteen, reflecting on how waiting around for her was not the best use of his time. Twenty minutes later, as he was staring at his coffee, he felt a touch on the shoulder. Seeing Lin, he held up his phone. 'Sorry, I didn't get your message.'

She leaned close to his ear. 'That's because I didn't send you one. Come on, let's go; I've a lot to tell you.'

He poured away the dregs and binned the beaker. 'There's no point in hiding from Mrs C, so we might as well walk out the front door together.'

She ushered him toward a side exit. 'It isn't her I don't want seeing us; it's Mr W.'

In the car, she insisted he set off for her flat before she would disclose any information.

He demanded to know, 'Is this just an excuse to get your hands on my body?'

She gave him a steely glare. 'Not this time.'

Once they were on the road, she launched into an explanation. 'Jerome Wilberforce has shown his hand. He says he's intending to visit someone and he needs a witness. He doesn't drive anymore, so he asked me if I'd take him.'

'Where to?'

'I don't know. Not very far, but he wouldn't say.'

'Does that mean he knows you have your own car, even though you've never driven to the hospital? If so, it suggests he knows more than he's saying.'

'He asked me as though he didn't know either way. I told him I often catch the bus because of the problem with parking.'

'What else did he say about his proposed visit?'

'Just that it's to see a man he believes ought to be in prison. His idea is to get him to admit to something on a hidden audio recorder.'

'Did you explain about contemporaneous notes and the Police and Criminal Evidence Act?'

'Of course not; I'd have given the game away.'

'So he doesn't know you're a police officer?'

'Apparently not. He hasn't suggested any connection with you, either.'

'Does that mean…'

She interrupted him. 'This will work better if you just drive and listen.' She watched as he drew an index finger across his lips as though zipping them shut. 'His plan is simply to confront a criminal and to get him to admit to something. He wants me there so I can confirm that the recording is authentic and hasn't been doctored. Then, we'd go to a police station and he'd hand it over. After that, the bloke gets prosecuted and everyone else lives happily ever after.' She waited, to check he would remain silent until she had given him permission to speak. 'Now you can say something.'

'That's completely crazy. He can't be serious about that plan, so there must be something else he has in mind. Top of my list is he intends to abduct you.'

'It's obviously a trap of some sort, but I don't think I'm the intended victim. I said I'd go along with it.'

Priestley felt his eyes bulging in disbelief. 'You said *what*? You can't be serious.'

'Come on, Marcus; we can put everything in place to make sure we stay on top of the situation.'

'Don't you go calling me "Marcus", young lady; you can address me as "sir" from now on.'

Seeing the intensity of his stare, she suppressed her laughter. 'Yes sir. Whatever you say, sir.'

His face finally creased with a wry smile. 'When are you meant to be picking him up?'

'You mean it's OK to go ahead with it? I was sure you'd say it's too risky.'

'You do seem determined to put yourself in harm's way. If you swan off to London, I won't be around to look after you, so it's high time you started making your own risk assessments. Do you not believe it's too dangerous, going off with someone who's a suspect in an abduction attempt?'

'When you put it like that you make it sound so negative. Don't forget I'll be the one doing the driving, and we can have officers close by at all times.'

'On your head be it. We'll have a full team meeting and put together a detailed plan.'

'That'll be rather difficult, sir; I'm supposed to pick him up in half an hour.'

'Jesus wept! Don't you call me "sir" as though I'm the one taking responsibility for this plan; if it all goes wrong, you'll be left to pick up the pieces, because it's based on your risk assessment.'

'Fine. We'll stay in communication at all times, and you can track me by GPS. I'd like three cars on my tail, changing places. Not yours or Penny's, though; I'm assuming he would recognise them both.'

'So you *are* thinking he's the man in Nottingham.'

'Just like you, I don't believe in coincidences.'

She used her zapper to open the metal gates into the garaging under her block of flats. As the place was almost empty, he was able to choose a bay near her car. When he had turned off the engine, she began again. 'Obviously I can't use normal codes without blowing my cover, always assuming I still have any cover, so I'll have to use a distress word. I'll tell you what, if you hear me say, "That's a bummer," come and rescue me. "Turned out nice again," and I'm saying the situation is all under control.'

'And that's it? That's everything?'

'That's all we have time for; I need to get going. Here's the address.' She handed him a slip of paper.

'I'll arrange support, but be prepared to bail out at any time. Yes?'

'Yes.'

'Promise?'

'I promise, Marcus. Now, stop looking so worried; this'll be a walk in the park.' She quickly climbed out.

When she drove away, he followed close behind. Believing the eventual destination may be Walton's house, he phoned Marsden so he would be ready for action if necessary. Then, he called Baker to brief her and to request three unmarked cars.

Approaching Lodge Moor, Baker advised him as to their level of preparedness. He relayed the information. 'Lin, your escort hasn't arrived yet, so there's only me, though you are being tracked by GPS. Marsden's team will be ready if you're heading for the drug dealer's place. If you're directed to go anywhere else, be ready to make a quick exit.'

'OK. I'm setting your volume down to zero, now. Don't forget to listen out for my distress words.'

'Will do.' He checked he had been muted. 'Are you feeling calm?' There was no response.

He parked near the pickup point. Over his hands-free phone he heard the slam of a car door followed by a man's voice spelling out the destination, including the house number and a description of the property. Using his other phone he asked Baker to cancel the escort and to inform Marsden they were heading his way.

GPS tracking indicated Plummer was taking a direct route to the advised address, so Priestley sped there in anticipation. Approaching the property, he slowed as he passed the side road where Marsden's team was tucked away out of sight, before continuing past the house and parking around a corner.

Soon after, Baker roared up in her borrowed VW and parked behind Priestley's car. She climbed out and tapped on his roof. He lowered the electric window. Looking out, he was amazed to see her wearing full body armour and carrying a SIG SG-552 assault rifle. As she unfolded the skeletonised stock, he asked, 'Just what are you expecting? World War Three?'

She slotted a thirty-round magazine into place. 'It always pays to be prepared.'

He put a finger to his lips to request silence. They heard Wilberforce say, 'Just in case there's any trouble, I don't want you coming into the house. You park up nearby and I'll walk the last few yards on my own.'

Plummer's response was heard clearly. 'If I do that, I won't be able to confirm your recording is kosher.'

They caught his quieter reply. 'It's more important that I don't put you in peril.'

Even as Priestley felt relief on hearing Plummer was to stay out of harm's way, he realised the man evidently understood the danger he himself would be facing.

Shortly after, they heard Plummer's voice. 'Are you there? He's just gone into the house. He had to wait while someone moved the dogs.'

Priestley responded, 'Can you hear me now?'

She replied, 'Yes, loud and clear.'

'I'm parked up with a one-woman commando team. She's armed and extremely dangerous.'

Baker leaned inside. 'It's me he's talking about. I thought I'd get kitted out to remind myself how it feels. It's ages since I last…' She stopped dead as the sound of a gunshot was heard, first over the phone and then as an echo through the air.

Priestley called out to Plummer, stress resonating in his voice, 'Are you all right?'

She replied, 'Yes. It came from the house.'

Seeing Baker sprinting off, he made the briefest of calls to Marsden as he set out in pursuit. When Baker was passing Plummer's car, he saw the driver's door open. He reached the vehicle and bundled Plummer back inside, yelling at her, 'Stay there and don't move!' Before she could argue, he slammed the door on her.

Baker turned the rifle's setting from Safety to Single Round and aimed it at the gates' lock. After a second shot, it disintegrated. She pushed one gate open and dashed for the front door. Before she could reach it, two Alsatian dogs came racing toward her down the long driveway. She set the selector to Full Automatic and sprayed them with a hail of bullets, leaving a mass of blood, bone and hairy flesh strewn across the concrete.

Turning the selector to the Three Rounds position,

she shattered the front door's lock with one quick burst. Priestley caught up with her as she prepared to enter. She blocked his powerful frame with her frail body. 'You aren't wearing armour; get back out of the way.' After pushing the door wide open, she ran inside.

He chased after her and grabbed her shoulder. 'Wait for backup; the drugs team will be here in a minute.'

She shrugged off his hand. 'Stay there while I check the rooms.' She eased the first door open and looked inside. Finding it empty, she called out to him, 'Clear.'

Knowing she had had no intention of waiting, he had simultaneously been checking the second room. More quietly, he announced its status. 'Clear.'

They reached the third and final door together. She elbowed him aside, determined to be first in, as she was the one wearing protective gear. Hearing a voice, she burst into the room. Seeing two men holding pistols, she yelled, 'Armed police; drop your weapons.'

When she stepped further into the room, Priestley followed behind and saw Wilberforce lying dead on the floor, his head in a pool of blood and brawn that had escaped from a gaping wound to the back of his skull. He noticed there was also a thin red trickle from the bullet hole neatly drilled through his forehead.

The man they recognised as Walton swung his gun toward Baker; without hesitation she fired a three-round burst into his chest. The other man raised his arms, before gingerly lowering the hand that was holding an automatic pistol. After carefully placing the weapon on a table to one side, he moved away from it and lay face down on the floor without waiting to be instructed.

Baker pulled off her helmet and turned to Priestley with a warm smile. 'It's really hot with all this gear on.'

A single shot rang out and she crumpled to the ground, an eye socket smashed by a bullet.

The gunman had slipped in at the rear door and was now wildly waving his pistol around. He screamed out, 'She shot my fucking dogs.' Priestley snatched Baker's SIG from her dead fingers and gave the moving target a three-round burst that tore through his neck. Blood spurted out in a wide arc as he spiralled to the ground.

The man lying prone on the floor, finding himself sprayed with blood, feared he would be the next target. He scrambled to his feet to retrieve his pistol from the table.

Priestley, with a flash of foresight, waited until the man had picked up his weapon, before hitting him with three well-aimed bullets to the heart. Knowing he was now the only living soul in the room, he automatically set the rifle to Safety and put it to one side.

Marcus knelt low beside Penny's body and cradled her head in his arm, before peeling off one of her gloves so he could take a tender hold of her hand. He looked at her face and tried to make it whole again, imagining the undamaged side reflecting unblemished as a mirror image. Oblivious to everything going on around him, he remained focused on turning the self-deception into some sort of a reality, and was taken unawares when two pairs of powerful arms began to lift him to his feet, as another pair claimed her head and body from him.

A familiar female voice emanating from some far-away place spoke softly by his ear. 'Marcus. Marcus. You need to let go of her.'

CHAPTER 43

Priestley studied the coffee and biscuits as he sat in the sun-drenched office of Philippa Hatchette, the Head of HR. He anticipated she would begin with a minute of inconsequential chat before getting down to the serious business in hand.

She picked up a biscuit. 'I've always liked bourbons, two chocolaty flavours in one. Sometimes I even dunk them in my coffee when no one's looking, and then I suck them dry. Well, it isn't really *dry*, but you know what I mean.'

He reached for a bourbon biscuit and dipped it into his coffee, holding it in place not quite long enough for it to disintegrate and flop into the black liquid. Lifting it vertically to keep the edges attached, he bit off the wet half. That should show her I'm paying attention, he thought, as his mind wandered off.

'…You do see that, don't you Marcus. Marcus?'

'Sorry, Pippa; run that by me again.'

'We need to know how you're coping. You've come straight back into work as though nothing has happened to you… or anyone else, for that matter.'

'I had duties to perform.'

'Yes, and I'm sure we all appreciate your dedication to your work; but sometimes you have to take time out to smell the roses.'

He wondered if that was an emotional trigger she was attempting to employ. Did she know he had placed red roses on her desk, before her meagre possessions could be cleared away and her space reallocated?

'In one sense, it's good that you are so resilient. But it's normal, nowadays, to feel a need for resetting your perceptions of the world, when you lose a colleague.'

'I'm sure that's very true.'

'There's a need for personal readjustment, to rebuild the world without her in it any longer. Tell me, Marcus, do you miss her?'

'Of course I miss her, just like everyone does.'

'Yes, but you were there, which must make it so much more painful for you.'

He understood he was not exhibiting enough pain for her liking. 'Logically, that shouldn't make a difference. The fact is, she died, and that should affect everyone to the same extent they would always have been affected, whether or not they were present.'

'Logic, Marcus, rarely has any part to play in such a situation as this.'

'I'm sure that's true, in some sense.'

'I'm glad to hear you're willing to accept that logic isn't everything, and to allow that there may be other forces in play. On an entirely personal level, did you like Penny?'

She had spoken her name out loud, whereas he was still avoiding doing so. 'I do my very best to like every one of my colleagues, though that's not always easy.'

'Did you find Penny was easy to like?'

'She had some likeable qualities; yes.'

'And you worked closely together?'

'Yes.'

'Did you like working with her?'

'We developed a certain rapport.'

'Now that she's gone, do you feel like there's a hole

left where she once stood?'

'I don't know what you mean by that, Pippa.'

'Do you feel a personal sense of loss?'

He gave her a little of what he knew she wanted to hear. 'I feel a deep sense of loss; it's the senselessness of it all.'

'Does that senselessness make it worse for you?'

'A waste of a life always seems senseless.'

She waited in case he would offer more. Seeing him dunk a second biscuit, she accepted it was again her turn to speak. 'There were four other lives wasted, too, weren't there. Does their loss seem just as senseless to you?'

'I don't believe it would be right to group them all together. Three of them were clearly criminals, whereas the fourth may have acted from higher motives.'

'Then let's look at them separately. Or at least let's look at the two men who died by your hand. Does the taking of their lives weigh heavily on you?'

'It should never be a small matter, to take a human life.'

'And you took two, whereas you're still alive.'

'I'm not sure what *that* has to do with anything.'

'Does it pain you to know you took those two lives?'

'I find it regrettable. I would rather they were alive to face justice.'

'And could that sense of regret be called pain?'

'Yes, I suppose that would be one way of expressing how I feel.'

'Would you say such pain makes you weaker or stronger?' Receiving only an uncertain shake of the head, she tried again. 'Given the choice, would you rather not feel that pain?'

'It's normal not to wish to feel pain.'

'But you're not feeling *much* pain for them, are you. Does that mean you don't see all lives as equal?'

He wondered how to express his belief that the life of a drug dealer was less consequential than his own, without appearing callous by the liberal standards of the modern era. 'Under the circumstances, I would say that their actions indicated they saw their own lives as being more valuable than those of others, such as mine; so an equitable view might reasonably lead me to display the same attitude, only with our rôles reversed.'

She scrutinised his face, hoping to discover the true feelings hiding behind his carefully controlled speech. 'So you didn't simply shoot them because you saw an opportunity to rid the world of two criminals.'

He realised this, for her, was the heart of the matter: that, without witnesses, she was wondering whether he had executed them. 'As they were both holding guns and preparing to shoot me, I felt entirely justified in shooting them first. I wasn't suffering from adjustment disorder, if that's what you're thinking.'

'No, of course you weren't. So, let's turn back to the question of how you feel about Penny's death. You killed the man who shot her. Does that make you feel better or worse about her death?'

'I see the two deaths in quite separate terms. She was a brave officer who was murdered by a criminal. He in turn was a murderer who had just taken a life.'

'You have no real regrets about killing him, then?'

'None beyond what I said before.'

'Hmm. Do you still insist you don't need time off to grieve for your colleague? I understand, at the scene, you were, shall we say, reluctant to let go of her.'

'I believe the human mind can continue to function for a little while, even after the body has suffered a fatal blow, so I wished to make sure any final moments she had were in the knowledge that I was there with her.'

'That's all very logical, Marcus. Well, I can't insist you take time off, but I must ask you to have a medical check-up. Not to do so would be a dereliction of duty.'

'I'll arrange an appointment right away.'

'Good. Now, if you have a sudden change of heart, you know I'll be more than pleased to accommodate any request you make for time off.'

'That's very kind of you, Pippa, but I don't believe it will be necessary.'

'Well, you know where to find me.'

Once the meeting was over, Hatchette went to see the Chief Constable. 'I've had a chat with Marcus.'

'And how is he taking it?'

'He's very resilient; he seems virtually unaffected by what's happened.'

'Ah, good; he's a stout fellow. I've been considering how to help further his career. Do you have something to offer on that subject?'

She prepared herself for a disagreement that should not appear like a conflict. 'That sort of resilience is no doubt ideal for the army.' Coker sensed a "but" coming. 'And yet, there are facets of police work that require a substantially greater degree of emotional intelligence than might reasonably be expected in the military.'

'Are you saying he lacks intelligence? I don't think you'll find much support for that assessment, Pippa.'

'It's his emotional side that I fear may be weaker than would be appropriate for someone who might be expected to operate proficiently at the highest levels.'

'You're saying that if he were weaker in some sense, you'd find him a stronger candidate for promotion?'

'It isn't just me who looks at things this way now, Charles. Soft skills are seen as essential in a society where an objective of gender equality is a driving force behind repositioning all staff toward more feminine attitudes.'

'So, even if he's the best detective we've ever had when it comes to solving cases, he wouldn't receive your seal of approval for promotion if he doesn't get upset when bad things happen.'

'I wouldn't put it quite that way.'

'But essentially, what I said is what you meant.'

'I wouldn't wish to quibble about your wording.'

'If I were to put him forward for promotion, are you saying you'd argue against it?'

'I think it's fair to say I'd need some persuasion.'

'Well, I can't say I'm not disappointed; I've always thought he was destined for the highest office.'

'Perhaps I'm mistaken; I'll keep an open mind.'

'All right, Pippa; but I'll need a better reason than you've given for holding him back. In my experience, most tough men aren't naturally emotional, so it seems to me quite unfair they should be discriminated against simply because their attitudes aren't more feminine.'

Seeing how irritated he looked, she tried an amusing exit line. 'But without loading the dice, how else are we women going to take over the world?'

He frowned. 'If government, security services and the police are anything to go by, I believe that's already happened.' Fearing she may interpret his response as misogyny, he hurriedly added, 'And a good thing, too.'

CHAPTER 44

Priestley returned to his office and stood at the window, looking out at the bright sunshine playing on the rocks. He allowed his mind to wander, so it might more easily find the answer to a conundrum: had Hatchette been concerned *for* him or concerned *about* him? And was she expecting him to be more demonstrably upset about Penny? All the pain he was feeling lay hidden deep within him, and he intended to keep it that way. He also wondered if she thought he should be visibly agonising over his right to take two lives. Well, they were not the first men he had ever killed, and may not be the last, but they were probably the most deserving.

Hearing his telephone begin to ring, he went to sit at his desk. The call was from the pathologist, Dr Patel. 'What can I do for you, Paal?'

'You knew Penny Baker, didn't you?'

He wondered what was coming next, but answered neutrally, 'Yes, of course.'

'I did some quick tests on her blood and discovered something I wasn't expecting.'

'Let me guess: you found contraceptive medication? Well, just because she was a single woman, that doesn't mean she couldn't have a sex life, does it?'

'You're wrong on the first count: she wasn't taking contraceptives. But you're very probably right on the second... she was pregnant.'

Marcus felt an almost physical blow to the chest. 'Do you know how far along she was?'

'Tests nowadays are accurate to a matter of days, which puts conception around the time she returned from Australia. You don't know if she's been sexually active back in England, do you?'

'Well, she was only a work colleague, so obviously I wouldn't know personally; but I'm sure she was far too busy with casework when she first came back.'

'Yes, that's only to be expected, but it does leave me with something of a problem. What if she and her guy in Oz were intending to settle down and make a future together? If I include the finding in the post-mortem report, someone here would have to try and locate him, to let him know he was going to be a father. Is that something you'd be willing to do?'

Though his head was swimming, he knew he must try to appear calm. 'Yes, of course Paal… if you think that's the right thing to do.' He waited.

Patel took the bait. 'Do you think it might not be?'

'Well, yes and no. I mean, it might just have been a holiday romance, so it wouldn't exactly serve much of a purpose to find out who the father was, even if we were able to.'

'That's true. I can certainly imagine how it could have happened that way; going to the other side of the world must have been very exciting for her.'

'I definitely agree that's the most likely explanation; after all, for a permanent relationship, one of them would have had to move to the other side of the world, which would be a massive step for anyone to take. But there again, what if there really were someone she was hoping to see in the future? The first question would be: were they just as keen to keep seeing her? If so, they'll be devastated to hear the news of her death, and how much worse will it feel for them when they find out she was pregnant. I can't imagine anything more terrible than losing a child, even if it's one you didn't know you were going to have.'

'You're right, of course. When you put it that way, it's obviously better not to inform her bloke. I could just mention the result in my report, but not officially draw it to anyone's attention.'

'Yes, you could do that. Of course, someone will probably notice it, and then the story will spread, until everyone knows. Call me old-fashioned if you will, but I don't think it would do anything for her reputation, for everyone to know she was pregnant but no one to know who the father was.'

'Yes, I can see that. I suppose I'd already realised I shouldn't be mentioning it in the report, but I needed someone else to say it for me. After all, it doesn't have any relevance to the cause of death.'

'Well, obviously you need to make up your own mind on the matter, but I know what I'd do if I were in your shoes.'

'It does mean I'll have to delete the test results, but it's clearly the right thing to do. Thanks for talking it through with me, Marcus.'

'Anytime, Paal.'

He looked out of the window again, at the path down the valley where he had walked with her. She had lived a lonely existence, and then he had come along and given her some pleasure. Well, he could hardly blame himself for having made her happy, could he?

And neither was he to blame for her death. That is, not unless her high-risk behaviour had been entirely for his benefit, designed to impress him, to make him see her as an all-action woman. First, she had deliberately crashed a van. Then, she had put her foot to the boards in a high-powered car. And finally, she had bravely charged into a house to face one or more gunmen alone. He had found no evidence to suggest she had ever behaved in such ways in the past, despite her claiming to have been a regular rule-breaker. So, perhaps he was in some way responsible, though clearly not culpable.

As he continued to argue his defence, a few of his words came back to him with an overwhelming force. "She was only a work colleague." Something broke inside him. Here was an accusation that could not be readily dismissed. She had certainly seen him as more than a work colleague, so why did he lack the common decency to admit she had also been special?

As his sudden sadness began to take hold, a warm glow grew out of nowhere. Knowing that his endocrine system was soothing him by releasing endorphins, he did nothing to stop the tears running down his nose and dripping onto the carpet.

He felt someone's fingers touching his hand. For a fleeting moment he imagined it was Penny, until he saw that Lin was the one looking up at him. He accepted a paper handkerchief from her before turning back to the window, not wishing anyone passing by in the corridor to notice his display of unmanly weakness.

She spoke in a voice as soft as silk. 'I was going to ask you how it went with HR, before I have my turn. You'd better come with me. Come on, let's go.'

He allowed her to lead the way, knowing she would naturally deflect any casual glances from colleagues.

Rather than risk him being observed while waiting outside HR, she knocked and entered as one action.

Taking several uninvited steps inside, she instructed the nearest clerk to deliver them directly to Hatchette.

Philippa closed her office door behind them and looked at them both. 'What seems to be the problem?'

Lin took hold of Marcus's arm as though he were a schoolboy reluctant to tell the teacher about bullying. 'DCI Priestley is clearly upset, and it wouldn't do for other officers to see him like this.'

Hatchette indicated her comfy chairs with a sweep of her arm. 'Come and sit down, Marcus. Would you like Lin to leave, while we have a chat about things?'

He sighed deeply. 'No, I'd rather she stayed.'

When they were seated, Hatchette asked, 'Were you bottling it up, earlier?'

He sighed again. 'I suppose I was.'

'Well, it's good to let it all out. Now, we can talk for as long as you wish.'

'I think it would be better if I just went home.'

'Yes, that may be best. Are you all right to drive?'

'Of course I am; I'm just a bit upset.'

'Still being brave, aren't we. You should take the rest of the week off, and all next week as well.'

'I'll do that; I think I need to get away from it all.'

'I do believe counselling would be appropriate, but I'd rather not use one of ours. Would it be best if Helen were to provide professional support?'

'Yes; I know I can rely on her to sort me out.'

'All right, Marcus. I'll have my chat with Lin, now. Would you like to stay in my other room until you're feeling a bit better?'

'Yes; I'll wait until you're finished.'

Lin laid her hand on his arm as he prepared to stand. 'I'd like him to stay, if that's all right; he's the only person who can really understand what it was like.'

Hatchette visually checked with him for agreement, before turning back to Plummer. 'You were the first to arrive on the scene after it had all happened, weren't you, Lin. It must have been awful for you.'

Plummer took several rapid gulps of air as though on the point of tears. 'Yes, it was.'

'I'll arrange counselling for you.'

'I'd rather just talk to Helen Priestley; I know her very well.'

'And you'll take some time off, won't you.'

'I'd like to; it would give me the chance to get my head straight. It was all so horrible.'

'I can barely imagine. How long do you think you might need?'

'Well, perhaps the rest of this week and the whole of next week, and then we'll see how I feel.'

'Yes, that's sensible. Now, don't worry about work; someone else will do it if you're not here, so just go and get yourself sorted.'

'Thank you. I'll go straight away, if that's all right.' She turned to Marcus. 'Come on, sir. If we leave the office together it'll look like we're working and no one will think there's anything wrong.'

Once Hatchette was alone, she telephoned Coker. 'Charles, you remember we were talking about Marcus, earlier? Well, I was mistaken. His emotional response had simply been held back by his strength of character. I'll happily give my support for any future promotion.'

CHAPTER 45

At home, Marcus sat next to Lin and briefly described what had taken place at the drug dealer's house. Helen listened in silence with a rapidly escalating feeling of alarm. To deflect from the day's events, he concluded, 'If there are still people in the hospital self-help group who are willing to take action on behalf of others, we may have more cases to investigate in the future, as well as the ones in the past. Shall I tell you how I think things are connected?'

Helen replied, 'Explain everything chronologically, if it makes sense to do it that way.'

'I know the dates of certain events, and I can guess what else may have happened, but not when. I'll start with the first definite incident, though there could have been others further back in time. Anthea Blackstone was killed in an RTC near Colchester. The Serious Collision Investigation Unit determined that the other driver, Yasser Khan, was responsible. When Khan was found not guilty in court, her widower, Barry, enlisted the help of two army mates to kill him. One of them was the late Padraic O'Leary, who must have confided in someone at the hospital's self-help group. Either a secret network already existed, or this was the seminal moment that spawned it.' He suddenly lost the thread.

Lin prompted him to repeat his theory on structure that he had expounded in his parked car at the station, where she had stayed with him until confident he was settled enough to drive home safely. 'How might such a network be organised? Would members have to do certain things to make it work?'

He felt grateful to Lin for giving him an opportunity to speak dispassionately on a subject that seemed far removed from the day's events. 'An infinite sequence of actions could be generated if someone, let's call them person zero, acts altruistically on behalf of person one, thereby placing an obligation on person one to act on behalf of person two, who in turn must then act on behalf of person three, and so on and so forth.' Having observed Helen flick her hand upward at the wrist, a familiar gesture he recognised as indicating she would like to interrupt him when convenient, he gave her an almost imperceptible nod to invite her to speak.

She observed, 'Though person zero may have acted in the perceived interests of person one, it may be misleading to use the word *altruistically*, as it could be interpreted as an indication that such altruism relates to the actor rather than the play. Clearly, any such altruism does not extend to the set of victims generated by the sequence of actions. The word does not sit comfortably in the context of criminality.'

Marcus sighed. 'I stand corrected, as always; but can you not let anything go? Not even today?'

Aware she should have shown more empathy, Helen felt the criticism deeply, exacerbated by the presence of a witness. 'I'm sorry, Marcus; just pretend I didn't say anything.'

His lips briefly formed a smile, grateful that she had made an apology despite being correct. 'No, you were quite right to make the point.'

Lin, wishing to smooth over the awkwardness, asked another question to which she already knew the answer.

'How do you see the actual network operating?'

Bringing the conversation back to the events of the real world rendered him less at ease. He responded, 'I suspect their rules are nowhere near as prescriptive as in the theoretical model. I imagine people volunteer to help, or they could perhaps be asked to assist, without this necessarily being tied back to their own requests for action; more of a self-help group approach, which is of course how it all began.'

After a lengthy pause, Helen prompted him, 'What about the other incidents?'

He needed several seconds to collect his thoughts. 'The next one was the killing of Sylvia Batter by Elsie Crompton. I'm confident this must have been at the instigation of Aden Liversedge, acting on behalf of Lucy Liversedge but without her knowledge. Or should I have said *initiation*?'

Helen shook her head. 'There is a value judgement implicit in your use of the word *instigation*, but I think it's appropriate under the circumstances.' Seeing Lin looking perplexed, she offered her an apologetic frown. 'Our interchanges are not always so abstruse.'

Marcus flashed Lin a smile. 'Whatever that means.' She mirrored it back. He continued, 'Elsie Crompton wanted Walton, the drug dealer, to be subject to some measure of justice for the death of her granddaughter, which I should have mentioned earlier, as it happened some time ago. Jerome Wilberforce altruistically...' he paused, certain this time he would remain uncorrected, '...sacrificed himself, so that Walton would be charged with killing him. Judging by the recording, I think he may have tricked Walton into believing he was about to take a gun out of his briefcase.'

As Marcus appeared to have finished, Lin added, 'I really think Jerome never intended me to risk going into the house with him; he will only have said it in the first place to justify my needing to be there.'

Marcus responded, 'I'm sure you're right; he would never have put you in such danger. He knew exactly who you were, so would have expected you to arrange backup. Just to make sure, he'd even provided false information to the drugs team about some supposed supply deal, to encourage them to be on hand as well.'

Helen asked, 'What actually happened at Walton's house? You haven't really explained.'

He listed the shootings in sequence, suppressing the more unpleasant details as much for his own sake as for theirs, and emphasising the necessity for his actions.

Finally, as he haltingly described kneeling beside his fallen colleague, his voice choked.

Helen considered what she could do to help him, willing to try anything possible for the man she loved. After a respectful silence, she asked him, soothingly, 'What do you think you should do to begin putting all this behind you?'

He countered, 'What do *you* think I should do?'

As she gave her analysis, she occasionally looked at Lin to keep her from feeling like an eavesdropper. 'We don't want to see the return of PTSD symptoms, but we do need to keep a lookout for them. In the past, you learned about various psychological considerations and developed a mindset that allowed you to overcome the problems using your willpower. There are now some ground-breaking treatments available that encourage the brain to function normally again. Let me check a few things with you. First of all, would you say you're in a state of hyper-awareness?'

He shook his head. 'Not really.'

'Do you feel agitated or anxious?'

'I suppose I do, but that's hardly surprising.'

'Have you had any flashbacks?'

'I keep seeing what happened, but in a normal sort of way, like anyone might.'

'Are you finding you're too distracted to concentrate on things at work, such as reading reports?'

'No more than usual, not that I've been doing much reading this afternoon; I spent ages making a statement. Anyway, my mind tends to wander at the best of times.'

'I think you're being unfair on yourself, Marcus; you simply explore far more connections than most people, which is really a measure of your intellect.'

Lin looked intently at Helen to check if she might speak. Having received her tacit approval, she turned to Marcus. 'Everyone thinks your powers of concentration are phenomenal, so I don't believe anyone would ever imagine you're not entirely focused whenever you need to be. I wish I had a mind like yours.'

He smiled weakly. 'Thanks, Lin, but I really don't need my ego massaging. Perhaps it should be the other way around, and my ego should be held more in check, so I don't always imagine everything will go my way.'

Helen responded, 'Maybe you don't have a martyr complex, after all; perhaps you're simply convinced you're invulnerable. A learning point for you: you're only mortal, so stop putting yourself in danger.'

'When it's just me to consider, I tend not to think about any danger until afterwards.'

'Then maybe you need to keep someone close by who can point out risks in advance.' She indicated Lin with a quick flick of her eyes.

'I do recognise risks in advance, but only in relation to other people. I wouldn't allow Lin to follow...' baulking at saying "Penny", he revised the sentence, '...anyone into a place where firearms may be present if she wasn't wearing full body armour.'

Helen interpreted Lin's fleeting glance toward her as an indication she also had understood his hesitation. 'Then why don't you imagine yourself as Lin if you're facing a dangerous situation?'

He gave a slight shake of the head. 'You're asking me to change who I am.'

She responded vehemently, 'No, I'm asking you to steer clear of danger, and not just because of PTSD.'

Hearing her stressed voice betraying the extent of her suffering from his latest gung-ho exploit, he stared at the ground, ashamed to meet her eyes. Feeling her gaze burning into him, he finally looked up. 'Sure, Helen. And if I were to suffer from PTSD again, you could always sort me out, anyway.'

'If it started up again, despite you knowing how you might suppress it, we'd have to consider other options. Neuromodulation is a highly promising line of research. PTSD sufferers are treated with magnetic or electrical stimulation, targeted at areas of the brain that have been affected by psychological trauma. Some success has been recorded with transcranial magnetic stimulation, and trigeminal nerve stimulation as well. In the future, it may prove possible to delete bad memories by using surgery to remove engrams; that's neural networks of cells. Neuroscientists hypothesise that hippocampus-dependent memory may be partially mediated by... I'm sorry, I'm losing you.'

He confirmed as much with a nod. 'It sounds like there may be other methods in the future, but what's the best way of stopping symptoms returning right now?'

Agonising inwardly, she dispassionately dispensed her painfully reasoned advice. 'Different methods work for different people. Some might want to keep working, as though everything is normal. Others want to spend as much time as possible with their loved ones. Then there are those who prefer to take themselves off into the wilderness; that could be a desolate location, or simply a place where they're not known. For you, the best thing might be to go off into the wilds with an old army pal, but you may find none of them are available at short notice. Out of your current colleagues, first choice may have been Neil, except he has Lily to take care of, especially now she's pregnant.'

He reflected, 'I'd really like to be at home with you, but I certainly wouldn't want the children to see me all upset. I mean, what would they think of me?'

'I'm confident they would understand, but I accept you wouldn't want them to see you that way.'

'I guess forty days in the wilderness is best for me.'

'It's Edwin's birthday a week on Monday, so I think you should make sure you're back home by then.'

'Yes, I was only meaning...' His voice died away.

Helen turned to Lin. 'You witnessed the aftermath, which would be deeply traumatising for anyone. What do you think would work best for you?'

Lin looked down as though in deep contemplation, unaware it was Helen's plan that had already taken root in her mind. 'Going off into the wilds on my own might have been the best option, except right now I wouldn't want to be *entirely* alone.'

Helen glanced repeatedly from one to the other as she tried to keep her voice from betraying her feelings. 'In that case, the solution's obvious: the two of you should go away together, somewhere remote, where you can start to come to terms with what's happened. It's nice in Snowdonia at this time of year, I believe.'

Lin brightened visibly. 'That sounds to me like the ideal treatment; I've always wanted to go hiking in the Welsh mountains.'

Helen directed her response to Marcus, fighting to control her emotions. 'You should organise everything today, and then set off early in the morning.'

He looked questioningly at her. 'Are you sure it's all right for the two of us to go away together? I mean, erm, it's rather, err…' His voice cracked and died.

'Having shared that traumatic experience, spending time together recuperating is probably the best possible therapy…' She aimed to appear dispassionate as she looked directly at Lin, but flinched at the intensity of her bright blue eyes. Her voice quavered, revealing her true feelings. '…for the both of you.'

Lin tried to emphasise her earnestness with a frown. 'I'll make sure I take good care of him.'

Marcus maintained a stunned silence.

Believing the outcome would be inevitable, Helen bravely smiled away her heart-wrenching sacrifice.

SEND OFF SIR

The seminal Detective Marcus Priestley novel

A games master is red-carded at the annual school v. staff football match. His body is discovered shortly afterwards in the changing room, blood seeping from a wound to the back of the head.

The police set out to establish the underlying cause. A senior investigating officer has an ulterior motive when he assigns a particular policewoman to lead the investigation, which flounders due to her inexperience.

When a second teacher is found dead, the series' principal detective returns from secondment and takes over the two cases. In resolving the investigation he is forced to choose between a successful prosecution and a morally satisfactory outcome.

Send Off Sir was originally published in 2014 under the pen-name *Marc de Caen*. Copies are available in the UK from Colley Books Ltd while stocks last. Future reprints will be under the author name Mark Basford.

BIRDS IN THE GRAVES

Sequel to Send Off Sir

DCI Marcus Priestley is feeling bored with mundane police work. The presumed suicide of an artist is re-evaluated when a toxicology report suggests foul play. Priestley takes the case and sets about understanding art and artists, in order to apply his psychological approach to finding the perpetrator.

He has dinner with beautiful art expert Anna, where she explains her unconventional views on modern art. She shows a personal interest in him, but Priestley is happily married and fully intends to remain so; nevertheless, he cannot avoid being attracted to her. Being an essentially moral man, he strives to remain faithful to his wife in the face of mounting pressure.

SANTA'S SPECIAL

The third Marcus Priestley novel

On Christmas Eve, DCI Marcus Priestley is aboard a Santa's Special at a heritage railway, with his wife Helen and their two children. The steam train is halted and a signalman is found dead. Helen, a doctor and psychiatrist, examines him and concludes he was murdered.

Derbyshire police have the case taken off them by the Met, who rig a post-mortem to conclude he died accidentally. Helen insists Marcus should conduct his own unofficial investigation. He meets with the British Secret Intelligence Service and the CIA. When the suspect's mobile phone is traced to Stockholm, he flies out with Lin Plummer, a DC. Ginny Long from the CIA meets them at the airport, and together the three set about tracking down the assassin, aided by the Swedish Security Service.